ACCLAIM FOR LAUREN K. DENTON

"A poignant and heartfelt tale of sisterhood, motherhood, and marriage, *Hurricane Season* deftly examines the role that coming to terms with the past plays in creating a hopeful future. Readers will devour this story of the hurricanes—both literal and figurative—that shape our lives."

—KRISTY WOODSON HARVEY, NATIONAL BESTSELLING AUTHOR OF *SLIGHTLY SOUTH OF SIMPLE*

"Any reader who values the comfort of family, the possibility of second chances and the simple truths of love and sisterhood will devour Denton's novel. In many ways, *Hurricane Season* feels like the calm before a storm that changes everything—for the better."

—BOOKPAGE

"Denton (*The Hideaway*) crafts a beautiful story with well-drawn, complex characters about the bonds of family, the trials of parenting, and the power of love to soothe the difficulties of daily life. Suggest for readers of Jane Green."

—LIBRARY JOURNAL FOR *HURRICANE SEASON*

"Refined language and dialogue along with beautifully descriptive scenes will draw readers right into Denton's latest novel. Well-developed, genuine characters and a well-crafted plot that embodies the tenuous ties between family are the highlights of this story . . . With a Southern backdrop, this poignant tale about sisters navigating through their emotion-laden relationship as each deals with individual struggles will resonate with readers. A truly remarkable read."

—RT BOOK REVIEWS, 4 STARS, FOR *HURRICANE SEASON*

"Overall, the emotional conflict is gentle, as is the touch of faith that drives everyone, especially Ty. Perfect for readers looking for low-drama women's fiction."

—BOOKLIST FOR *HURRICANE SEASON*

"Denton has created a heartwarming, character-driven story that will appeal to fans of Southern fiction."

—PUBLISHERS WEEKLY FOR *HURRICANE SEASON*

"Inspiring and heartwarming fiction that will please many a heart. Lauren Denton has done it again. In *Hurricane Season*, Denton delivers emotional depth while examining the many types of 'storms' that cause havoc in our lives. After making us love her characters and feel every ache of their journey, she brings us full circle through a beautiful story, reminding us all that *this too shall pass*."

—JULIE CANTRELL, *NEW YORK TIMES* AND *USA TODAY* BESTSELLING AUTHOR OF *PERENNIALS*

"It's true what they say. There's no place like home. And reading a Lauren Denton book feels like coming home. With characters you'll want as friends, a setting you can step into, and a poignant story of sisters and family ties and all the messiness of a wonderful life, Denton has penned another tale that will settle in deep and stay awhile, long after the last page is turned."

—CATHERINE WEST, AUTHOR OF *THE MEMORY OF YOU*, FOR *HURRICANE SEASON*

"An engaging, lyrical story of sisterly love. *Hurricane Season* is sure to add to Denton's growing fan base."

—RACHEL HAUCK, *NEW YORK TIMES* BESTSELLING AUTHOR

"Denton's *Hurricane Season* feels like home. Through sisters Jenna and Betsy you will recognize which sister you are, the sister you could be, and the sister you yearn to become—the woman you hope to become. It's an absolutely lovely story of love, loss, and the hope of new beginnings."

—KATHERINE REAY, AUTHOR OF
DEAR MR. KNIGHTLEY AND *THE AUSTEN ESCAPE*

"Denton's delicious debut [*The Hideaway*] is a treat for the senses and the heart. Her exquisitely lyrical writing and character-driven story is a must-read."

—*LIBRARY JOURNAL*, STARRED REVIEW
AND DEBUT OF THE MONTH

"*The Hideaway* is the heartwarmingly southern story about the families we are given—and the families we choose. Two endearing heroines and their poignant storylines of love lost and found make this the perfect book for an afternoon on the back porch with a glass of sweet tea."

—KAREN WHITE, *NEW YORK TIMES* BESTSELLING AUTHOR

"This debut novel is the kind of book you want to curl up with on a rainy day or stick in your beach bag for your next vacation. It is poetic and compelling, emotional and full of life. Its haunting beauty will linger long with readers."

—*RT BOOK REVIEWS*, 4$\frac{1}{2}$ STARS, TOP
PICK! FOR *THE HIDEAWAY*

"In this fine debut, Denton crafts a beautiful, heartbreaking story of true love that never dies. This book will please inspirational, contemporary, and historical fans alike."

—*PUBLISHERS WEEKLY*, STARRED REVIEW OF *THE HIDEAWAY*

"Denton's first novel charms readers with her idyllic settings and wonderful cast of characters . . . *The Hideaway* is a deeply satisfying exploration of family, friendship, and the meaning of home."

—BOOKLIST

"From the opening of *The Hideaway*, the reader is captured by the voice of a woman who has for too long kept a story that must be told, one the reader wants to hear. Denton has crafted a story both powerful and enchanting: a don't-miss novel in the greatest southern traditions of storytelling."

—PATTI CALLAHAN HENRY, *NEW YORK TIMES* BESTSELLING AUTHOR

"*The Hideaway* is a delightful tale of secrets, past regrets, and second chances. You will fall in love with these characters, and their intriguing stories will keep you reading long into the night! A lovely debut novel!"

—CATHERINE WEST, AUTHOR OF *WHERE HOPE BEGINS*

Hurricane Season

Also by Lauren K. Denton

The Hideaway

Glory Road (available March 2019)

HURRICANE SEASON

Lauren K. Denton

THOMAS NELSON
Since 1798

Hurricane Season

Published in Nashville, Tennessee, by Thomas Nelson. Thomas Nelson is a
registered trademark of HarperCollins Christian Publishing, Inc.

Thomas Nelson titles may be purchased in bulk for educational, business,
fund-raising, or sales promotional use. For information, please e-mail
SpecialMarkets@ThomasNelson.com.

Publisher's Note: This novel is a work of fiction. Names, characters, places,
and incidents are either products of the author's imagination or used
fictitiously. All characters are fictional, and any similarity to people living
or dead is purely coincidental.

ISBN: 978-0-7852-2458-7 (mass market)

Library of Congress Cataloging-in-Publication Data

Names: Denton, Lauren K., author.
Title: Hurricane season / Lauren K. Denton.
Description: Nashville : Thomas Nelson, [2018] | "A Southern novel of two
sisters and the storms they must weather."
Identifiers: LCCN 2017039715 | ISBN 9780718084257 (softcover)
Subjects: LCSH: Self-realization--Fiction. | Motherhood--Fiction. |
 Sisters--Fiction. | Domestic fiction. | GSAFD: Christian fiction.
Classification: LCC PS3604.E5956 H87 2018 | DDC 813/.6--dc23 LC record
available at https://lccn.loc.gov/2017039715

Printed in the United States of America

19 20 21 22 23 QG 5 4 3 2 1

For Kate and Sela
and for Matt

ONE

BETSY

She usually stayed in bed until at least six, but this morning she was restless, like animals get when the barometric pressure drops before a storm. It wasn't the cows, or the approaching hurricane season, or even the milk prices, which had dipped lately. It was something else, something she couldn't quite name. She felt like she needed to both run a mile and go back to sleep for the next three hours. It was energy and lethargy, anticipation and dread. Anna Beth would likely diagnose it in a heartbeat, but Betsy had always been good at pretending everything was just fine.

She kicked her legs out from under the sheet, her feet searching for a cool spot in the bed Ty had just vacated. Even with the windows closed and the AC pumping, heat still seeped in, filling the cracks and crevices of her old house with thick Alabama heat. The meteorologists on the news last night had been in a frenzy as they pointed out heat waves radiating across the country. It was only mid-June, but two tropical waves had already rolled off the shores of Africa. Thankfully, they'd fizzled out before reaching land.

"We likely won't be so lucky later in the summer," the forecasters thundered, striking terror into the hearts of all those living near the coast, including those in Betsy's small town of Elinore, fifteen miles north of the Gulf of Mexico. "The most active hurricane forecast in two decades," NOAA predicted with eager excitement.

El Niño this, La Niña that, everyone had a handy explanation for the coming tide of heat and storms that promised to pummel south Alabama and surrounding coastal areas, but Betsy had her own ideas. This summer she'd turn thirty. Not as big a milestone as forty, but it was a milestone nonetheless. The idea of thirty had always felt maternal, heavy with maturity and substance. While everyone else was talking about the fanfare of an active season—every word punctuated by an exclamation point!—all she felt was a slow hiss of air. It leaked gradually, lazily, not so quickly that anyone else would notice, but she felt it. Like a slow but steady lightening.

Downstairs, the toe of Ty's boot beat out a rhythm on the kitchen floor as he waited for the coffee to finish dripping. She heard his jumbo-size metal coffee mug scrape across the shelf and thunk down on the counter. The coffee pouring into the mug, the carafe sliding back into place on the hot pad. She imagined Ty's face, prickly with the night's passage. His hands, big and warm, knuckles sticking out from his long, sturdy fingers. His brushed-silver wedding ring.

When the screen door thudded closed, she swung her legs over the side of the bed. She grabbed a clip from her nightstand and twisted her long brown waves up into a bun, then pulled her light cotton robe around her shoulders and padded into the kitchen. At the window over the sink, she brushed aside the curtain to peek into the backyard. Ty made his way across the dewy grass to the barn. Only the curves of his shoulders were visible in the moonlight.

The coffee was good and hot, scorching her throat on the way down. After pulling her breakfast casserole out of the fridge and popping it in the oven, she opened the back door. Damp morning air met her face with a whisper. On the porch Etta was curled up in a tight ball in her favorite spot on the couch. Betsy couldn't stand the layer of fur Etta always left behind, but the cat was too cuddly to stay mad at for long.

She reached down and scratched Etta's chin and behind her ears. When she pushed open the screen door, Etta jumped down from the couch and slid between Betsy's feet. By the time Betsy reached the bottom of the porch steps, the cat was already halfway to the barn to check for spilled milk.

Crossing the yard, she inhaled the aroma of damp grass, earthy hay, and fresh sawdust coming from the henhouse. It was the same henhouse generations of Ty's family had used on this property. She and Ty had repaired as necessary and added extra space a few times to accommodate more hens, but the house was basically the same. Not a typical box made of wood and screen. It had a shingled roof, weathered wood siding, even a screened porch. A trumpet vine covered in long red flowers climbed one corner post, and a gravel walkway snaked around the side. Some mornings, when dewy fog hung heavy over the farm and everything was blurry and half erased, Betsy imagined the henhouse as a home for fairies or hobbits.

The hens got anxious if she robbed them of their eggs too early in the morning, so she crept in quietly, eased the door closed behind her, and locked it to keep the determined hens from making a quick escape. The interior was full of quiet clucking. The hens were mostly content, but Betsy knew from experience that exasperation at her intrusion wasn't far off.

"Good morning, little mamas," she murmured as she pulled out eight brown eggs, lightly speckled, two yellow, and one as blue as a robin's egg. "Worked hard this morning, didn't you?"

She placed the eggs in the basket hanging by the door, then scattered a few scoops of feed across the ground. The hens fluttered down from their perches to dine, all indignities forgiven.

With the henhouse door locked tight behind her, she paused before turning back to the house. It often stopped her, the beauty—almost perfection—of their little space on this earth. Franklin Dairy Farm, the land Ty had worked and shaped and brought to life. The sky was now streaked with bold purples and blues, bright pinks and yellows. Oaks and hickories—tall, thick, and majestic—dotted their five hundred acres. She could hear the steady *whoosh whoosh* of the milking machines even out here in the yard. Faint strains of Chris Stapleton's "Tennessee Whiskey" floated out of the speakers Ty and Walker had jiggered up in the nooks and crannies of the barn.

Through the steadily increasing light, she could just make out Ty's outline as he stooped over a cow hooked up to a machine. Ty was thick but not overweight. Just solid, as if he could carry the weight of the world on his shoulders and not buckle or even protest. She'd liked that about him when they first started dating, and it hadn't changed.

She thought about going out to the barn and kissing him good morning. It would surprise him, delight him. She closed her eyes and could feel his lips, warm and soft, faint prickles at the edges. He'd still smell like sleep, but also like oats, grass, and good outside air.

She opened her eyes, lips tingling, and grabbed the basket of eggs off its hook. The eggs clattered against each other but didn't break.

Instead of turning toward the barn, she retraced her steps back to the house, keeping her head down to avoid the two ant beds that always magically reappeared, always in the same place, the morning after she'd poured vinegar and boiling water over them. It was amazing—they had the most industrious animals, even insects, on their property. Ants that did nothing but work, just as they were supposed to. Cows overflowing with maternal milk. Hens that offered eggs each morning without fail, their bodies giving forth life as they should. Even Etta had once offered them a litter of kittens, much to their surprise. It seemed every *body* on the farm consistently obeyed God's natural order of things, producing and giving life, working and contributing as they should.

Betsy sidestepped the ant mounds, and when she looked up, the first thing she saw was the swing, moving slowly in the breeze. The swing hung from the lowest branch of the sweeping oak tree in the backyard. The tree was like something from Grimms' fairy tales—it sat in the middle of an otherwise treeless yard, its limbs extending twenty, thirty feet from the trunk, arms of Spanish moss swaying in the breeze, fingers of ivy trailing up and across the limbs. The shade underneath was thick and dark, always at least fifteen degrees cooler than the heat-saturated yard.

It was the kind of tree Betsy and her sister, Jenna, would've loved to have had in their backyard growing up—a backdrop to their adventures, even if most of their adventures were only in their minds.

Under the swing was a dirt patch where broods of kids—including Ty—had swung, their feet trailing in the dirt and stomping out the grass. That swing was the first thing Ty had showed Betsy when he brought her to the farm their senior year of college. They'd been together for about a year, but it wasn't until she saw this place that she understood who he really was and what a life with him would look like. When he had pointed out the swing, she was confused at first.

"The swing?" she asked him. "You want to take over your grandfather's farm because of a wooden swing?"

"No, not the swing. The farm will be profitable. I can make a few changes and get this place running smoother than lake water. It's gonna be great." Then he put his hands on her shoulders and turned her so she faced the swing directly. "Tell me what you see there."

"Wood. Dirt. A tree."

"I see children," he said. "I hear laughter. I see a childhood spent outside in the heat and air and light. I see our future."

Staring at that swing now, Betsy took a deep breath and squeezed her eyes closed, then opened them again. The swing swayed back and forth on an invisible breeze. With her free hand, she brushed back a lock of hair that had escaped her clip and started for the house. On her way past the swing, she raised her leg and gave it a swift, hard kick.

TWO

JENNA

The babysitter was late, Addie and Walsh were flying around the house in superhero capes yelling the Batman theme song—"Da-na-na-na-na-na-na-na Batman!"—and Jenna had just poured a mug of coffee when Walsh bumped into her from behind, spilling hot liquid down the front of her black Full Cup Coffee T-shirt.

"Walsh, please!" She set the coffee mug down and pulled her damp shirt away from her skin.

"Sorry, Mommy." Walsh's brown eyes were wide. She crept backward, then turned to run but stopped to grab a dish towel off the kitchen table first. "Here." She dabbed at Jenna's shirt with the towel, itself too damp to do the job.

Jenna took the towel from Walsh and kissed her cheek. "Thank you," she whispered. Walsh grinned and took off, her cape flying behind her.

After wiping her shirt as well as she could—she'd be wearing an apron over it anyway—Jenna leaned against the counter and took a long swallow. She still didn't understand how she could make coffee all day long, then drink the stuff at home. But at least she believed in what she was selling. Full Cup did make a good cup of coffee.

She sighed. Where was Kendal? Her head hurt and she had ten minutes to get to the coffee shop, a drive that usually took twenty with traffic. She thanked her lucky stars she wasn't opening today—as manager, she had the ability to pencil someone else into those early-morning slots—but it meant getting home later.

As Addie and Walsh zoomed through the kitchen and wound around her legs like cats, part of her wanted to call in sick and stay home with the girls all day, but another part of her wanted to get in the car and drive away. Maybe not come back for a while.

She squeezed her eyes closed and raked her hands through her hair. Then the doorbell rang and there was Kendal, her stand-in babysitter for the next two weeks until summer daycare began for the girls. With red, puffy eyes and a trembling voice, Kendal explained that she and her boyfriend had broken up the night before.

"But don't worry, Miss Sawyer, I'm fine. I brought my craft box for the girls. We'll have a blast." With one more messy sniff and a swipe at her eyes, she dropped her bag in the foyer and attempted a smile.

Jenna sighed and pushed the door closed. With her long blonde hair and killer legs, Kendal was Jenna a decade ago, except Jenna never would have allowed herself to wallow in misery over a boy. If anything, it had been the boys miserable over her. Back then, she always left before they did.

But no sense thinking about those old days—Kendal was here and she was a mess. Jenna wasn't super comfortable leaving Addie and Walsh with her, but what else could she do? She'd already been late to work this week—car troubles, a lost stuffed hippo, long story—and she couldn't afford to lose this job. It paid for the girls' school, offered surprisingly good insurance, and on good days, it made her feel like she was contributing something to the world, even if it was only a perfect heart in milk foam. Not quite the artistic contribution she'd had in mind all those years ago, but it was something, and it was all she had.

"Addie? Walsh?" she called. "I'm heading out."

Small feet pounded on the hardwood floors, then two tornados of early-morning energy slammed into Jenna's legs, their arms squeezing her tight.

She knelt in front of them. Addie's blonde curls were a tangled mess, but her blue eyes were bright and her mouth curved into a smile. Walsh's still-pudgy wrists were covered in every plastic bracelet in their dress-up box and a few of Jenna's. Walsh reached up for a hug, her breath soft and sweet in Jenna's ear. "Bye, Mommy," she whispered.

Jenna smiled. Thoughts of running evaporated like steam over a cup of French roast. She pulled the girls close and kissed their foreheads. "Listen to Kendal, okay? I think she brought some fun things for you to do today. I'll be home after work, and we'll have something yummy for dinner."

"Breakfast! Can it be breakfast for dinner?"

As both girls chanted, "Pan-cakes! Pan-cakes!" Jenna kissed their cheeks one more time and slid out the door.

In her car she exhaled a rush of air. Through the front window of her tiny two-bedroom East Nashville house—once crisp white but now faded to a light gray begging for a new coat of paint—she could see the girls still bouncing, the sparkles from their princess pajamas visible from the driveway.

Kendal pushed her hair back from her face, offered a bright smile, and led the girls into the den, out of Jenna's sight. Only then did Jenna remember her almost-full coffee mug sitting on the kitchen counter.

. . .

Traffic was lighter than usual and she skidded into the small side parking lot with a minute to spare. Just enough time to shove her purse into a locker in the back, grab her apron, and put on her best smile.

She checked the time. Eight fifteen. She switched her phone to silent and slid it in her apron pocket. She was setting out a stack of CDs a local songwriter had dropped off when a customer burst through the door. Jenna looked up to see Lisa Rich, CEO of Trust Partners, a well-known accounting firm with an office down the block. Purse dangling from her elbow, Bluetooth in place on her ear. Obnoxiously complicated drink order. Notoriously bad tipper.

Jenna slipped behind the counter and tapped the barista on the shoulder—the new girl, Melissa, already bracing herself for Lisa's deluge. "I got this," Jenna whispered.

"Thanks," Melissa whispered back before cowering behind Jenna.

"Hi, Miss Rich," Jenna said, despite the obvious fact that Lisa was talking to someone on her Bluetooth.

"It's *Mrs.* and I'm in a hurry."

"I'm so sorry," Jenna said, discreetly pulling a Post-it off the underside of the counter by the register. "We'll have your order out to you in a moment."

Lisa reached up and pushed a button on the contraption stuck to her ear. "Wait—I haven't given you my order."

"Would you like your regular?" Jenna's voice was innocent.

The woman's right eyebrow rose just a millimeter. Probably all the Botox would allow. "Yes. My regular."

"We'll have that right out." Jenna turned and handed the slip of paper to Melissa.

Melissa eyed it with suspicion, then looked back up at Jenna. "You're a genius."

"I know."

Melissa grinned and reached for the fat-free milk. "Does this even taste good?" she whispered.

"I have no idea and no desire to find out."

As Melissa worked on the grande double shot, four pumps sugar-free peppermint, nonfat, extra-hot, no foam, light whip, stirred white mocha, Jenna walked the counter and checked the three other baristas working hard to fill drink orders. She was able to get a pack of napkins for Mario and open a sleeve of cardboard cup sleeves for Jensen before Melissa had the drink ready.

"I'll let you do the honors." Melissa handed the drink to Jenna like it was gold plated. "Think it'll do the trick?"

"Nah," Jenna muttered. "Probably nothing will. Mrs. Rich?"

Mrs. Rich pressed the button again on her Bluetooth and clicked her heels across the tile floor. She stared at Jenna before taking the cup. "The peppermint's sugar-free?"

"Yes, ma'am."

"Extra hot?"

"Extra hot."

"Stirred wh—"

"It's just like you like it. If not, it's on me."

The woman hesitated, then put her mouth to the edge of the cup and took a dainty sip. Jenna could almost feel Melissa's nervousness buzzing behind her. But Mrs. Rich just swallowed and gave a slight nod, her bright-red lipstick smudged onto the lip of the cup. After swiping her credit card and signing, she shouldered her massive Louis Vuitton bag and turned without a word. When she pulled open the glass door, a breeze of warm air floated in, and she clicked up the street to begin her day.

Jenna turned to Melissa and rolled her eyes. Melissa bit her lip to hold in her laughter.

A few minutes after nine, Mario poked her in the side. "Your date is here." He grinned.

"Shut up. He's not my anything, and it's not a date."

"It happens every morning. It's a date."

"Not every morning," Jenna said, working to make a latte "extra foamy" for a woman in white Nikes and a wide-brimmed straw hat about to set out on a downtown walking tour. "He skips Fridays because he meets a buddy to run in Riverfront Park."

"See, you even know his schedule."

Jenna rolled her eyes. "It's not a date."

"Whatever it is, he's waiting for you. And looking extra cute today, I might add."

Jenna looked over her shoulder. Sam always looked cute. Cute wasn't his problem.

After handing the woman her extra-foamy latte, she ducked out from behind the counter. "Be back in ten," she said to no one in particular. Other than Melissa, who was still training, the baristas on shift this morning were the A-team. She could be gone an hour and come back to smooth sailing, but ten minutes was all Sam would get.

She slid into the chair across from him and smoothed a loose curl away from her face. He smiled and nudged her coffee toward her. Black, double shot, and not a drop of syrup. "Thanks," she said. Then she smiled too.

"You're welcome. It's nice to see you." He started every conversation with her the same way. He'd been doing it for the two months they'd been having this almost-daily nondate. From anyone else, it would be annoying, but coming from this guy, it was close to endearing.

"You always say it like it's a surprise. All you have to do is open those doors any morning, Monday through

Friday, sometimes Saturday, and you'll see my smiling face."

"I know. That's why I come here. You know, I tried the Starbucks around the corner before I settled on this place."

"Oh yeah? What made you switch?"

"The manager didn't like me." He leaned back in his chair and stretched his long legs out to the side of the table. "I thought I was charming, but she never gave me anything for free."

"I never give you anything for free."

"Except the ten best minutes of my day."

"I think I know why that manager didn't like you. She saw right through your whole charming act."

"Nah, not possible."

She laughed.

"Did you see *Mrs.* Rich this morning?" he asked.

Jenna nodded, sipping her coffee.

"That woman is . . . Well, let's just say she makes me think of opening my own accounting firm every day. Many times a day."

"Why don't you do it?"

"Open my own firm? Let's see, money, office space, clients . . ." He counted each barrier off on his fingers. "It could happen one day. But I'm not there yet."

She nodded again, watched him over the rim of her cup. The first day Sam Oliver walked into Full Cup, he was just another guy in a button-down and khakis with a cell phone pressed to his ear. But then he hung up when he got to the front of the line where a barista was waiting to take his order. He ordered a large coffee, no frills. Then he smiled at the girl and added a tip onto his receipt.

Jenna had been wiping down tables and fielding requests from customers scattered among the tables. When he sat down to wait for his coffee, she couldn't resist. "You may be the only person this morning who's ordered a plain coffee. Maybe the only person this week."

"My coffeemaker decided to quit on me this week. I haven't had a chance to get out and buy another one, so I'm just trying to get a shot of caffeine to my brain." He smiled. He had a nice smile. "Plain coffee is all I need."

"So you make coffee at home and you drink it straight up? You sure aren't our typical coffee shop customer." She swiped the towel across a just-vacated table, then turned back for the counter.

"What's your favorite coffee then?"

"Kind of a personal question. I only just met you."

He smiled, slow and amused. "If you don't tell me, I'll just come back tomorrow and ask again."

She looked at the clock above the counter. "See you then." She took her place behind the counter and resisted the urge to look back at him.

That first quick conversation was nearly two months ago, and he'd yet to buy a new coffeemaker. They'd progressed from exchanging a few words while he waited for his coffee to spending her ten-minute break at a table in the back. Every day except Friday.

"How are Addie and Walsh?" he asked now.

"They're fine. Addie is learning to write her name, and Walsh spends most of her time upside down in one form or another."

"My sister did gymnastics her whole childhood. Always flipping around, turning cartwheels, and whatnot. Maybe Walsh is destined to be a gymnast."

Jenna smiled. "I wouldn't be surprised."

"And Addie will be something studious. A teacher maybe."

"Or a therapist. A psychiatrist maybe."

"You think?"

Jenna shrugged. It was tempting to think Addie, at almost six years old, was too young to understand a lot of things. But lately, it seemed every time Jenna assumed something would go over her older daughter's head, it instead went right in her ears and came back later in the form of a pointed, intelligent question.

She fiddled with the cardboard sleeve on her cup. Sam watched her for a moment before speaking. "Are you ever going to let me take you on a real date? Somewhere you don't have to wear an apron, where we can talk for longer than ten minutes?"

Jenna bit her bottom lip, glanced at the clock over the counter.

"Don't do it," he said, hanging his head. "You just sat down."

"It's a busy morning. Melissa's new. I need to get back up there."

He sighed. "I'm just going to keep asking. I'm like a bulldog when I put my mind to something."

"So what does that make me? Your chew toy?" She smiled as she stood, retying her apron strings into a tidy bow.

"No. You're the girl I can't stop thinking about every time I leave this place."

She paused behind her chair. This had gone on long enough. "Sam . . ." He waited, ever patient. "Look, I'm not right for you. My life is . . . complicated."

He shrugged. "People are complicated. Our lives are too."

She glanced around before continuing. "I work all the time because I have to. I have to make money to pay for daycare, for insurance, for rent. Any free time I get I spend it with Addie and Walsh." She swiped her thumb over a drop of coffee on the table. "You could have any girl you want. I'm not the one you need to be chasing. Trust me." She could have given him a hundred more reasons, but she figured this would be enough.

"The only thing I know I want right now is a chance. With you." He leaned forward on his elbows. "That's not going to change unless you tell me to get lost. I may be persistent, but I can take that kind of hint."

She smiled in spite of herself. "Guess I'll see you tomorrow then."

. . .

Though Full Cup was one of the busiest coffee shops in the city, lulls occurred during the day. Midmorning and midafternoon were for the college students, white earbuds snaking up to their ears, laptops open, concentration intense. They could be demanding—too much caffeine made them impatient and snappy—but this afternoon the line at the counter was short, giving

Jenna a chance to work on the shift schedule. Alexandra had just planned an impromptu surprise party—in the Bahamas, no less—for her sister and needed five days off at the end of the month. As the "cool" manager, the one people actually wanted to work for, Jenna had no choice but to rework the schedule.

She wedged herself, the store laptop, and the big scheduling binder into a booth in the back where she could see most of the store but was out of the way enough that she might be left alone for a few minutes if she was lucky. The back of the store was known as the gallery. A few times a year they asked artists in town to submit art to hang on the walls. Any type of art was accepted, even a few pieces she knew Addie—or for that matter Walsh—could do better.

As she opened the laptop and waited for it to power up, she focused on the fishing line–clock face–teddy bear conglomeration suspended from the ceiling. If it was art, she was Superwoman. Back in the day, she would have been willing to call most anything art, as long as it made the viewer *feel* something. Today, all that teddy bear nightmare made her feel was annoyed. But then again, that was something.

She slid her eyes left to an eight-by-ten photo hanging on the wall. Black and white, Ilford Galerie paper, skinny black frame, white mat. Simple, understated, nothing to draw the eye except the face in the photo. The old woman had her eyes closed, her lips curving upward, her head tilted back to catch the last rays of the sun as it dipped below the mountains in the west. Of course, you couldn't see the mountains in the photo, but Jenna remembered the smell of the crisp air, the sting of the cold on her cheeks as she clicked the shutter, the way the wind funneled through the mountain pass. The photo was eight years old. Could Rickie, the woman Jenna had befriended out west, still be alive?

Finally, the laptop chugged to life and she dove into the job of figuring out how to get her best, most popular barista to the Bahamas for a week and balance the remaining baristas' school schedules, family obligations, and need for shifts in her absence.

Between helping customers, cleaning up the mess from a flushed diaper in the bathroom—seriously? Who does that?—and searching for a missing bottle of raspberry-peppermint syrup, she finally finished the schedule. As she closed the laptop and stood, her phone buzzed with a text. She pulled it out and saw she'd missed several texts, all from Max.

I have news. Call me.

Then: I know you keep your phone on you at work. I need to talk to you.

The last one said: Now's not the time to ignore me.

Before she could punch the button to call him, the phone buzzed again, this time with a call.

"I'm not ignoring you," she said before he could unload on her. "I'm at work. What's going on?"

"You got in."

"Got in where?" She gestured to a waving Mario that she'd be just a minute.

"Halcyon."

Jenna sat back down in the booth and leaned her head against the wall behind her. Mario held his hands up in frustration.

"How?" She ignored Mario's well-practiced drama.

"A spot opened up and you got it. I may have pulled some strings, but I didn't have to pull many. They loved what you sent."

"But they were just shots of the girls . . . and trees . . ."

"Doesn't matter. It got you in."

"What about the money? I felt like an idiot even applying, knowing I couldn't afford it."

"All you have to do is get yourself here. Everything else is paid for."

"How in—?"

"Believe it or not, there are wealthy art patrons who love to pay for people like you to go on retreats like this. Don't ask too many questions. Just get yourself here by Friday. And don't forget your camera."

THREE

JENNA

Two hours later, Jenna was on her way home, the scent of roasted coffee beans and vanilla syrup saturating her clothes and skin. She propped her elbow on the edge of the open window and dug her fingers into her hair. Max was nothing if not abrupt. To the point. It was one of the things she loved about him. Well, loved or hated, depending on the situation.

Max was the head of the photography department at Belmont University and the only person who really knew her passion for photography. She'd met him at the Botanical Gardens in Nashville a couple years back. She noticed him watching her as she stooped over a pile of leaves, craning to catch the edge of a ray of sunlight.

"Can I help you?" she asked without looking up.

"Just wondering who taught you to get low like that. Under the light, I mean. It's not how most people would do it."

Jenna pulled her face away from the camera and shrugged. "I'm just playing around."

"Not what it looks like to me."

Since then, they met every month or so at the gardens and other places around town to take photos together and discuss her "creative future," as he called it. They always went somewhere the kids could come, which limited their excursions to an hour, tops. They'd met at the downtown library a few times. At the top of the atrium stairs, they used Addie and Walsh as their models, capturing the flood of light from the windows on their faces. Old enough to be her father, Max had become her friend, and their excursions were her sole creative outlet.

Three months ago, he'd blown in the door of Full Cup, marched to the counter, and slapped a flyer down in front of her as she counted money in the register. He stared at her until she looked up.

"You made me lose count," she told him.

"This is more important." He jabbed the flyer with his finger. "You need to do this."

She stuck the money back in the register, closed the drawer, and glanced down at the piece of paper.

HALCYON ARTIST RETREAT IS A CALM REFUGE
HIDDEN IN THE PRISTINE AND PROTECTED
SINGER CREEK NATURE PRESERVE NEAR THE
GULF COAST OF FLORIDA. WE OFFER THE GIFT
OF TIME, SPACE, AND BEAUTY TO PURSUE
THE ART THAT MAKES YOU FEEL ALIVE.

"You're kidding, right?"

"Do I look like I'm kidding?" He arched a thick gray eyebrow, his mouth set in a straight line.

"I'd never get in."

"Lucky for you, I'm on the advisory committee. But you won't need my help—your work will speak for itself." She held up her hand but he continued. "Before you ask, they offer scholarships, and being on the committee means I have input regarding who gets them." He tapped his finger on the flyer. "This is a great opportunity for you."

She glanced back down at the flyer. The bold print at the bottom said artists could stay as long as they wished—as briefly as two weeks all the way up to the full eight weeks. Eight weeks of solitude? Too heavenly—too terrifying—to even consider. Not to mention impossible.

"You've been looking for a way to get back into your photography, and this is a solid chunk of time of nothing but that. Plus you'd have a photography mentor there. I know him. He's good. Little rough around the edges, but that might not bother you."

"This sounds amazing, but if you remember, I have two small people to take care of. What would I do with them for even one week?"

"Details." He waved his hand in the air. "We can work all that out. Look, just go to the website, read what people say about Halcyon. It doesn't get better than this. And you have to drive through Alabama to get there—isn't that where your sister lives?"

Jenna nodded absentmindedly. One photo on the flyer showed a lake at dusk, cabins in the distance, a ring of people sitting around a small campfire. Sparks like fireflies shooting up in the air. Dark trees reaching toward the sky. Another showed a woman standing before a huge canvas set against a backdrop of thick oaks dripping with Spanish moss. It all reminded her of another life. But that was a lifetime ago.

"I don't think so." She pushed the piece of paper back across the counter.

He stared at her without taking it. "Jenna, you have the best, most natural untaught talent I've ever seen, and I've seen a lot. It's time to get back to it. Drawing hearts in milk foam doesn't count as art."

A loud horn from behind jolted her from her thoughts. In her rearview mirror, she caught the rude gesture from the driver behind her and held her hand up in apology. Her speedometer told her she was going thirty in a fifty, annoying everyone around her. She sped up and shook her head to clear away Max and his insane ideas. Just before turning onto her street, she heard a *ding*, her car's polite way of telling her she was low on gas.

"You've got to be kidding me," she murmured.

She'd had to pay for the girls' summer extended-day programs this pay period and her next paycheck wasn't until Friday. She dragged her free hand through her hair. She felt like one of those hamsters on a spinning wheel, going faster and faster but never actually going anywhere. No fancy art retreat would fix that.

At home Jenna opened the front door expecting Walsh's thirty pounds to careen around the corner and into her arms as she did every day, but today it was quiet. Kendal sat on the couch, wiping her nose, her eyes still red and puffy as pillows, her cell pressed to her ear. *Pull yourself together*, she wanted to tell the poor girl.

"Kendal?"

Kendal jumped up. "Oh, Miss Sawyer, I didn't hear you." To her boyfriend, she said, "I gotta go. I guess I'll just see you around." Ex-boyfriend, apparently.

As Kendal gathered her things, Jenna dropped her purse on the table and found Addie on the floor in her bedroom surrounded by a pile of pink and purple Legos.

"Mommy! Will you help me put this castle together?"

"In a minute. Where's your sister?"

Addie shrugged. "She was in here but she left to find more Legos."

Jenna's heartbeat picked up as she went room to room looking for Walsh. She pulled back the shower curtain and peeked behind the couch, checking all the normal hiding places. In her tiny house, it only took a few seconds to realize Walsh wasn't inside.

"Kendal, where's Walsh?"

"I— She's not with Addie?"

"No. When's the last time you saw her?" Jenna tried to keep her voice from rising.

"I don't know," Kendal said, panic creeping into her own voice. "It's been a little while. I thought they were both in Addie's room."

"I've told you, you have to know where Walsh is all the time."

"Mommy, what's wrong?" Addie stood in the doorway to the kitchen, her brow scrunched in worry, a familiar sight on her older daughter's sweet, sensitive face.

Jenna crossed the room and threw open the front

door, calling Walsh's name. Again. Again. She checked the bushes around the side of the house where Walsh liked to look for ladybugs and the tree next door that she liked to pretend she could climb. After a few minutes, she was walking up and down the sidewalk yelling Walsh's name. Finally, she heard Walsh's voice.

"Mommy!"

Jenna whirled around to see Walsh running toward her. Delores was walking with her, trying to keep up as well as she could with her bad hip. Walsh ran straight into Jenna's legs.

Jenna knelt so she was eye to eye with her youngest. "Where have you been?"

"Playing with the puppy," she said, as if it were the most normal thing in the world.

Jenna's pulse thudded in her ears. Delores held up her hand and jogged toward them, out of breath. "I'm so sorry, Jenna. I was making my dinner when I saw her out on my patio playing with Greta. I was going to call, but I figured I'd just bring her back over before you started to worry."

Jenna swiped at a tear at the corner of her eye.

"Oh dear," Delores said. "I suppose I'm a little too late."

Jenna held Walsh to her chest and tried to slow her breathing.

There were times when she wished Addie and Walsh had been lucky enough to be born to someone else, someone with a more solid, together life—a happy, All-American, dog-in-the-backyard, cookies-in-the-oven family. Sometimes she longed for that life for herself, missed it as though it was something she'd once had and let slip through her fingers.

Other times she wished she was still Jenna Sawyer, girl on the run. An old boyfriend had called her that once. Never sticking around too long, always chasing the next bright, shiny possibility. Things were different now, though there were times—like this one—when she wished she could still run. Leave before it started to hurt.

But the reality of Jenna's world, in all its terror and beauty, stared back at her on the sidewalk. She brushed Walsh's hair back from her face and kissed her forehead.

. . .

That night, after a dinner of pancakes and scrambled eggs, a serious talk with Walsh about not leaving the house by herself, and four bedtime stories, the girls were finally asleep. Jenna stood by the stove finishing the cold eggs. She was exhausted and still rattled from the afternoon. Even though Kendal should have been more responsible, Jenna felt the weight of it on her own shoulders.

She pulled a bottle of red off the counter and poured a few inches in two wineglasses, then settled down on the couch to wait. A few minutes after eight, Delores gave her customary three soft knocks and let herself in. "Hey there." She closed the door behind her. "Girls to sleep okay?"

"Yes, ma'am. Haven't even heard a peep from Walsh."

Delores laughed as she sat on the other end of the couch. "That little girl's gonna run you ragged. Good thing she's so cute."

"It's always something. The daycare hours change, the babysitter has boyfriend problems, customers think their skinny latte is the most important thing in my life. Then Walsh goes missing."

Delores patted Jenna's knee. "She wasn't missing. She was just at my house. It's a familiar place for her. She probably didn't realize she was doing anything wrong."

"I know. You're right. But not knowing where she was? It was terrifying. All I could think about was some guy in a wife-beater cruising the street in a van with dark windows." Jenna rubbed her eyes.

"Well, you can't let yourself go there. Walsh is fine, safe and sound in bed, and all is well. It was just a little hiccup." Delores reached for the wineglass on the coffee table. "Don't mind if I do. Doctor says a little bit is good for my heart."

Jenna smiled. Delores said the same thing every night.

"Did that cute boy come to see you today?"

"As always."

"It tells me something that he comes to see you every morning on his way to work."

"Tells me something too. He has too much time on his hands."

Delores shook her head. "That's not it and you know it. Why won't you let him—?"

"It won't work."

"And why not?"

"Because . . . he's just not my type."

Delores narrowed her eyes over the top of her wine-glass. "And what does that mean?"

"He's too . . . innocent. And he's smart—he's probably never made a bad decision in his life."

"Honey, everyone makes bad decisions and he's no different. Plus, you're too young and too smart to shut down all romantic interests before they even get off the ground."

Jenna shifted on the couch and settled deeper into the soft pillows behind her back. As she did she glanced at her friend. Delores had been "popping over for a quick visit" almost every night now for months. She usually stayed just long enough to have a glass of wine. And long enough, Jenna suspected, to ward off some of the loneliness that crept in at night.

Her husband, Willard, died a year ago, a day after their fiftieth wedding anniversary. Jenna's love life was always a hot topic of conversation when Delores visited. But they talked about other things too—the best way to make a perfect cup of coffee, Delores's dismal attempts to fit in with the "Silver Sneakers" crowd at the local gym, Jenna's once-promising photography dreams.

As if reading her mind, Delores nodded toward the wall across from the couch. "I love those photos, you know."

Jenna nodded. "Me too. But I was such a mess then."

"All new mothers are."

She'd taken the series of photos soon after Walsh was born. Jenna had been a postpartum wreck—trying to keep a two-year-old alive on her own while nursing an infant who wanted to nurse round the clock, breasts like hot rocks in her chest, her brain a sleepless blur. In her fog, she'd pulled her camera from the back of the closet, popped in some film, and started shooting.

Walsh, with her olive skin and head full of dark hair, was asleep, temporarily paused in her constant quest for more milk, her eyelashes hints of color on her pale cheeks. Addie sat on the floor with a basket of wooden blocks, her blonde hair hanging in perfect round ringlets. Jenna took photo after photo, not knowing how they would turn out, but not really caring either. What mattered was that her fingers had found freedom, her hands and legs moving in familiar motions as she twisted to focus, kneeling to capture the light on Walsh's cheek, bending to catch the whirl of hair at the back of Addie's perfect head.

Even now she could still remember how the fog had lifted, the cobwebs cleared. Her fatigue—an almost tangible beast in the room with her at all times—crept off into a corner and gave her a few minutes of peace and clarity. Behind the camera, she hid herself from reality and escaped to a place where at the click of a shutter, she could make everything perfect.

When she met Max, their monthly excursions were a breath of fresh air, but not the same as diving full into that creative river and letting it flow without thought or care, trusting the current would take her to just the right shots.

"Do you remember that artist retreat I mentioned a

while back?" Jenna turned to Delores. "The one Max wanted me to attend?"

Delores nodded. "You told me you didn't think you were going to apply."

"I didn't plan to, but then I did, even though I knew there was no way I could afford it, much less take time for the trip. It was mostly to get Max to stop hounding me."

"And?"

"I found out today I got in. And it's paid for."

Delores sat up. "So you're going?"

"I don't know." As she said the words, she knew what she wanted the answer to be. But even if she was able to take time away from work, kids, the house, laundry, babysitters, all the things that kept her away from that creative river inside her—which was more like a trickle these days—would it all come back?

"What do you mean, you don't know? Seems like it was just handed to you. You tell them yes."

"What would I do with the girls?"

Delores tapped her fingernail against the edge of her glass. "Well, you know they love coming to my house." She smiled.

"Delores, I can't leave my rowdy kids with you for a week. They'd wear you out."

"I can handle kids, my dear. I have four of them."

"But they're grown adults. When's the last time you bathed a squirming three-year-old or made dinner for a picky five-year-old?"

"True. What about family?" Delores already knew about Jenna's parents. Her mom had died six years ago, and her dad, never all that involved in the child-raising aspect of parenthood, became even less so after his wife's death. He was still in Birmingham, intent on working until he was too old to hold his arms up before his orchestra, poised and ready for action. "Your sister?"

Jenna shrugged, but the truth was, she'd already thought about Betsy. The idea made her nervous though. It had been a little while since they talked—really talked—and telling Betsy she wanted to go off and do nothing but take photos for two weeks would come out of left field.

"They live on a farm, right? Do they have kids?"

"Nope. Little sister gets the kids. Big sister gets the perfect husband."

"That man is not perfect, I guarantee it. The question is, would your sister and her imperfect husband be willing to keep the girls while you go?"

Jenna drained the rest of the wine in her glass, then set the glass back on the table. "I don't know. Maybe? But seriously, how could I do this? Even if she did keep them, I can't take time off from my life and go do something like this. It's too much."

Even as she spoke, she thought of the savings account she'd set up after Walsh was born. She'd been tucking money into it each month with the intention of planning a surprise vacation for the three of them. Maybe a couple of weeks at the farm could be like a vacation for the girls. It wasn't Disney or riding horses on the beach in Georgia, but she wouldn't have been able to afford something like that anyway.

Delores shifted in her seat so she faced Jenna. "You know about the oxygen masks on airplanes, right?"

Jenna stifled a smile. "Yes, I've heard of them."

"They always tell passengers if the masks come down, put the mask on yourself before you try to put it on anyone else. It's the same with kids, honey. You have to take care of yourself so you can go and take care of your kids. I see how you are over here. I know it's hard."

"They're good kids. I can't just—"

"Of course they're good." Delores put her hand on Jenna's knee. "They're good because of you." Jenna shook her head but Delores continued. "You need to be good to yourself too. Look, I wasn't a single parent like you, but with Willard's work schedule, I was on my own a lot. More than I thought I would be. I loved those kids, still do, but there were times I wanted to turn left instead of right into our neighborhood. Just drive off into the sunset—not forever, just for a little while. Just to breathe without four other little people taking all my air. Maybe this would be a chance for you to breathe for a little while. On your own."

Delores glanced at her watch and rose from the couch amid a chorus of protests from her ankle and knee joints. "It's almost my bedtime. I'll keep an eye on my back patio tomorrow in case Walsh comes over for more playtime." At the door she paused. "You need to do this, Jenna. Call your friend and say yes."

After Delores left, Jenna remained on the couch, her mind running through possible scenarios. The logistics made her head hurt, but part of her wanted to jump in the car and be free of it all. To pretend, just for a little while, that she was like she used to be—on her own, untethered. That she wasn't living with two beautiful, innocent consequences of a failed relationship and mistakes. That at twenty-eight, she wasn't a woman who had put her own desires and goals on the back burner to be drop-kicked into single, working motherhood.

Her eyes were growing heavy, but she pulled her old laptop out of the drawer in the coffee table and turned it on. On her bank's website, she entered her password to be directed to her accounts. Her checking account was perilously low—that was to be expected this close to payday—but the total in her savings account filled her with a delicate hope. It wasn't a gold mine, but it could cover bills and rent for a short time.

The AC clicked on and she pulled a blanket off the back of the couch. She shivered, whether from the cold or anticipation, she wasn't sure. She thought of Betsy and Ty's farm, basically a five-hundred-acre playground for kids, with an assortment of animals added in for good measure. The girls would have a blast—like summer camp. Betsy and Ty would probably love the entertainment.

Before she could change her mind, she grabbed her phone and scrolled until she found Betsy's number.

"She won't mind," she whispered.

But she put the phone down without calling and rested her head against the back of the couch. She pulled the blanket up to her chin and closed her eyes. Mornings were a better time for favors. New mercies and all that.

FOUR

TY

Ty Franklin's mornings began hours before everyone else's. Every night before bed, he set his alarm for 4:30 a.m., an hour he once thought was only for late-night bar hoppers and graveyard-shift workers. When he became a dairy man, he saw that the darkest hour before the sun rose was actually one of the most beautiful in the entire twenty-four-hour masterpiece. He now considered himself a lucky man, awake to the day's first sighs and stretches.

With coffee in hand he pushed open the barn door. It stuck a little, as it always did. He muttered to himself, annoyed that he'd forgotten to buy another can of WD-40. It was the hinge, just the hinge, but it made sliding the door open louder than necessary. He liked to disturb the girls as little as possible before they shuffled to their places in the milking line.

Walker was already in the barn, attaching tubes and lines. The kid tried hard, but he was just so young. He wanted to be a dairy farmer too, and his daddy, the owner of a neighboring farm, insisted that he get a job in another barn to learn the ropes. A little arrogant, Ty thought, but he didn't have a teenage son so he couldn't judge another man's parenting choices. He just tried to teach the boy all he could while keeping him from overturning milk buckets and scaring the cows.

"Morning, Mr. Franklin."

Ty nodded. He leaned over Walker's shoulder. "Rework that line. See that kink there? It'll keep the milk from flowing. The cow will kick at it and hurt herself."

"Yes, sir." Walker fumbled to untwist the cap and straighten the line.

Every morning.

Ty took his cap off, rubbed his forehead, and jammed it back on his head. He made his way through the barn to his small office on the side. Every day he carefully wrote out the details from each milking. The dusty file cabinet in the corner held a stack of yellow legal pads, the pages covered in his tiny, neat script. He knew what Excel was and he knew punching in numbers on a spreadsheet could take the place of him hunching over legal pads every morning. But he liked the security, the familiarity of paper. He'd rather not entrust his life's work to an invisible cloud.

At five o'clock he and Walker swung open the gate and stood back. The girls shuffled out of one side of the barn into the other. They knew exactly where to go, so all the men had to do was stay out of the way. As number 013 passed by, she paused and swung her head toward Ty. He reached out and rubbed the top of her soft, black-spotted nose. The cows could be as affectionate as a dog—a Labrador even. Nothing quite compared to a fifteen-hundred-pound Holstein sidling up to you, cud breath and all. It made you feel a certain something inside.

Especially if this cow, and two hundred like it, were your ticket to a glorious retirement, as they were for Ty. He wouldn't be purchasing any thirty-foot fishing boats or houses on Ono Island, but he wouldn't have wanted that anyway. He imagined himself kicked back on the porch in a rocker with Betsy next to him. Iced tea at their elbows, a bucket of snap beans, or maybe pecans, at their feet.

That was all he'd ever hoped for, ever since he first laid eyes on her their junior year at Auburn. It was as if he skipped all the in-between life and his mind went straight to the end—the two of them in rockers, hands together, enjoying life. At one point, he assumed a few towheaded kids would be there frolicking in the front yard, but the way he saw it, he had 218 cows in his barn and a handful of rowdy farmhands to corral. He had just about as much mischief as he could handle.

• • •

Once the girls were all hooked up, happily munching oats while their milk flowed, Ty walked to the barn door to dump out a bucket of water. While shaking it to get the last drips out, he saw his wife up by the henhouse. He usually kissed her good-bye when he wrenched himself out of bed, but this morning he hadn't. He wasn't even sure why. She'd been curled up on her side, facing away from him, the outline of her body visible through the thin sheet. Her knees were pulled up, her hands together in front of her face like she was fending off the world.

He traced a light finger down her spine. When her defenses were down—when she was asleep or lost in a fog of thought—that's when he could tell the shadows were still there, tangled in her hair, grasping at her elbows, yanking on her heart.

Sometimes he wondered if maybe Betsy would've been better off marrying one of those fraternity boys at Auburn. She could have had anyone, and she picked Ty. He still didn't understand it. He told her when they started dating that he'd do anything for her. He meant it then, when they'd known each other for all of five minutes, and he still meant it now. But what if the one thing he longed to give her, he couldn't? It went against the core of who he was—this *not* being able to give her what she wanted.

Instead of disturbing her that morning, he'd just let her sleep, praying she was in the middle of a good dream—something soft and warm and easy. But seeing her up by the henhouse, staring at the swing he used to play on when he was a kid, he wished he'd taken the two seconds to kiss her. To remind her that he loved her, that they'd be okay.

She talked so breezily about how she was looking forward to the summer, making day trips to Orange Beach, maybe booking them a night somewhere nice. But her armor wasn't strong enough to fool him. Sometimes he wondered if his was strong enough to fool her.

FIVE

BETSY

When the rush of the morning milking was over, the men came to the house and ate her breakfast and drank her coffee like it was the last oasis before a cross-desert journey.

Betsy pulled up a kitchen chair and sat with her knees tucked under her chin, her arms around her legs. She loved to hear Ty in the midst of friends, joking and poking fun as only a group of men-boys could.

"Mrs. Franklin, have you heard anything from Quincy's?" Walker asked.

"Still working on it. I talked to the owner's wife again yesterday. She says they're getting close to a decision."

Quincy's was a market up in Dadeville that had been hemming and hawing for months over whether they wanted to stock Franklin milk. As the one responsible for all the marketing and publicity for the farm, Betsy had long been working on the deal. Quincy's had spread from Dadeville to six different towns, all in areas without major chain grocery stores.

"It'd be a big step, getting Franklin milk on those shelves," Ty said.

"If you need me to, I can make the drive up there one afternoon," Carlos said. "See if I can't convince them in person."

"And how would you do that?" Ty asked. "Nothing but your charm?"

"Hey, I'm great with little old ladies."

On the counter by the coffeepot, Betsy's cell phone dinged, alerting her to a new e-mail from Bankston Detention Facility. The director said the group of twenty boys, aged twelve to sixteen, would arrive at ten for their tour of the milking barn.

Another e-mail had slipped in unnoticed. This one was from Valerie, the head of the children's program at Elinore Methodist. For years, Betsy had been a regular face on the rotating schedule of nursery volunteers, but last fall she quietly took her name off the list.

Betsy typed out a quick reply to Valerie's request for more help. "Sorry I can't be there this Sunday." With any luck Valerie would take the hint and stop asking.

When the guys finished eating, they lined up at the sink to rinse off their plates and place them in the dishwasher like dutiful schoolchildren. Betsy stood to help, but Ty put a hand on her shoulder.

"Let them do it." Betsy smiled and sat back down. He stood next to her and wrapped his arm around her shoulders.

"Oh, I'm meeting Anna Beth for lunch today," she said. "Leftovers from dinner last night are in the fridge if you want them for lunch."

"What's all this?" Carlos asked. "Grown man and your wife has to make your lunch?"

"No, I'm a man who's lucky enough that his wife thinks of him and leaves lunch for him. Not that you'd know about that."

Betsy shushed Ty, but Carlos laughed. "*Ay, mi hombre*. You just wait. Gloria will come around. Latino women don't like their men to get soft." He jabbed Ty's stomach.

Ty laughed and slapped his hand away. "I'm not soft, man. You ready to go?"

Carlos hopped off the stool. "Ready, Boss."

The phone rang before the guys made it out the door. Ty backpedaled and picked up the receiver from the kitchen wall. After a moment, his face changed and he looked over at her. He held out the phone. *Your sister,* he mouthed.

She took the phone. "Jenna?"

"Hey, Bets. How are you?"

"I'm good. Everything okay there?"

"Yeah, everything's great."

After a last glance over his shoulder, Ty followed the men toward the barn. Betsy sat back down. "Really?" she asked. Jenna's voice was a notch too chipper, a glaring sign that something might not actually be that great.

"Really. Things are good."

"Addie and Walsh?"

"They're into everything, driving me crazy half the time." Jenna laughed. "But they're fine."

It had been almost a year since Betsy had seen Jenna's

daughters. Addie would turn six in December and Walsh, the baby, was three. Betsy had only seen Walsh a few times in her short life, the most recent being last summer when Betsy drove to Nashville—seven hours in Ty's truck with a busted AC—for a visit. What she'd hoped would be a bonding weekend with her sister had turned into an unexpected babysitting gig while Jenna took on extra shifts at the coffee shop.

"I actually . . . ," Jenna began. "I need a favor. Do you have a minute?"

Twenty minutes later, Betsy replaced the phone in its cradle. Two weeks with Addie and Walsh. She should have checked with Ty first, but when it came down to it, Betsy could never say no to Jenna. She thought of long-ago days, lying under the bed with her little sister, eating pudding with plastic spoons and trying to keep her from crying. She'd do anything for Jenna—then and now.

A sigh ached to escape her lips, but she bit it back. Who was she to judge Jenna's life choices? From what she knew of Addie and Walsh, they were happy kids, and that spoke to Jenna's abilities as a mother. Good thing, because if Betsy had to give her any wisdom about how to be a good mother—much less try to be one herself—she wouldn't even know where to begin.

· · ·

At ten on the nose, the battered gray school bus from Bankston Detention pulled up out front, and twenty teenage boys shuffled off, hormones and pent-up energy swirling around them like almost visible steam. Whether it was a group like this, a well-behaved home-school co-op, or a YMCA camp group, Betsy knew from experience that the educational part of the field trip had to be as exciting and hands-on as possible. If she dared to talk about farming practices and environmental threats—vital concerns in the lives of dairy farmers but boring to anyone not making a living from farming—she risked mutiny.

Betsy had started the farm's educational program a couple of years ago. It had been an expensive endeavor, renovating the barn to accommodate touring facilities, but thankfully, it took off quickly. During the school year they hosted field trips from schools all across Mobile and Baldwin Counties. In the summer most were from day camps and playgroups around the area. Bankston came every week.

As soon as the teachers had gathered the group outside the barn, Betsy positioned herself front and center and held her hand up. After a few outbursts, the boys quieted down. With that raised hand she pointed out three children who she knew needed the most attention. The first, a tall kid with linebacker shoulders and a cocky smile, sauntered to the front of the group. The other kids laughed and slapped him on the back. Catcalls echoed off the barn walls.

"What's your name?" Betsy asked him.

"Whatever you want it to be," he said with a smirk.

Gigi, one of the Bankston staff members whom Betsy had learned not to get on the wrong side of, clapped her hands once, hard. "Jerome!"

"Sorry, sorry. Yeah, it's Jerome, but my boys call me the Juice."

"Farmer Juice." Betsy put her hands on her hips. "I like it."

The other kids laughed and Jerome did a little jig, spinning around in a circle and bowing, much to the delight of the group. Gigi clapped her hands again.

"Welcome to Franklin Dairy," Betsy said. "I have a lot to show you. Most of the cows have already finished their first milking of the day, but there's plenty more work to do and I'm going to need your help with something special."

She put her hand on Jerome's shoulder and led him into one of the pens, then motioned for the rest of the group to follow. Jerome's friend punched him on the shoulder. "Boy, get ready! You gonna be pulling on some . . ." He cut his eyes to Betsy. A sly grin crossed his face.

Betsy willed herself not to smile. "Teats. They're called teats."

"No, sir, I'm not." Jerome turned to Betsy. "I'm not putting my hands on those . . . things." He peered into the barn where a pregnant Holstein was undergoing a routine checkup. "That's just dirty. And wrong."

"They're not dirty. That's how the milk comes out. You like cold milk with your cookies?"

Jerome and his friend nodded.

"Cheese?"

Nodded again.

"Yogurt? Ice cream? Cake? None of that can be made without milk. Or if it is, it's not very good." She lowered her voice to a whisper. "But don't tell the anti-milk crusaders I said that."

The kids looked confused, but it squeezed a laugh out of Gigi.

"But no, Farmer Juice, that's not what I need your help with. I need help with this."

In the side pen was a calf, only six weeks old and cute as a puppy.

"I need you to feed her." Betsy handed Jerome a bottle Ty had already prepared. It looked like a regular baby bottle, only bigger.

Bankston often sent the hardest-to-crack kids to the farm because of the bottle feeding. In some mysterious way, the gentle, nurturing act did something to the kids. Sure, they walked through the viewing room and learned how dairy farming contributed to their daily life, but it was the bottle feeding they loved. Anytime Ty had a new calf on the farm, Bankston was the first group Betsy called. They always scheduled a trip and brought the roughest and toughest of their kids.

These kids—Jerome, his friend, and the others—passed the bottle back and forth between them, wiping the calf's chin when milk bubbled out and smoothing the hair on her back and head. It seemed the act of taking care of another small life calmed them, soothed their agitation and restlessness. By the time they piled on the bus an hour later, all the kids high-fived her, and a few gave her hugs.

"Can we come see her again?" Jerome asked, one hand on the bus door. "Maybe when she's a little bigger. Or if another baby cow comes along."

"I'm sure there will be more calves, but you know what? I hope the next time I call Bankston, they tell me Farmer Juice has moved out and is living his life, working hard at school, and doing well."

Jerome smiled and pulled himself up the steps of the bus. Gigi was the last to step onto the bus. "You have kids?" she asked.

Betsy raised her eyebrows and shook her head no. They'd never talked about anything more personal than what percentage of fat they liked in their milk— Gigi skim, Betsy 2 percent.

"You planning on it?"

Betsy let out a laugh, awkward and too loud. "That's getting a little personal, don't you think?"

"All I'm sayin' is, you should. Women like you are who we need raising kids in this world. Raise them up to be respectful and hardworking." The woman nodded. "Farm kids are what you need."

Betsy knocked on the glass door and waved at the driver. "I do have farm kids, Gigi, a bunch of them. You bring them to me every Friday morning."

Gigi grunted and heaved herself up onto the bus. The engine roared to life, and the bus pulled out of the small grass parking lot, arms sticking out of windows on both sides of the bus, waving to her.

She waved until the bus disappeared around the curve in the driveway. The sounds of children's laughter and conversation died away as quiet fell on the farm again.

SIX

BETSY

"Anna Beth?" Betsy checked the clock on the oven and cringed: 11:58. She was supposed to meet her friend for lunch at noon.

"Girl, where are you?" Through the phone, Betsy heard the murmur of lunchtime conversation. "I'm halfway through my first mimosa, and before you ask, yes, I did say 'first.'"

"I didn't say anything. Although it is a tad early, even for you."

"School is out, the little monsters are gone, and I have a three-week break before I have to woman the front office. I'm enjoying my time off. Now, where are you?"

Betsy grabbed a damp rag from the sink. She squeezed the water out and wiped breakfast crumbs from the counter as she spoke. "I'm so sorry, but I'm going to have to miss lunch. My sister called this morning. She's driving down tomorrow and dropping the kids off with us for a little while."

"What?" Anna Beth screeched. "How long's a little while?"

Betsy squeezed one eye closed. "Two weeks?"

"Girl, you are crazy. And very nice."

"Anyway, I thought I'd be able to swing lunch, but I just finished up with Bankston, I'm dirty, and I have a million things to do before they get here."

"Well, I'm not having lunch by myself. Lucy and Jackson are squared away at friends' houses, so I have the afternoon. Tell you what. Why don't I bring lunch to you? I can help you with your million things."

"Oh, you don't need to—"

"Hush. I'll get some chicken salad to go and I'll be there in twenty."

Betsy exhaled and tossed the rag in the sink. "Thanks."

"No problem. And let's see . . ." Anna Beth's acrylic nails tapped the tabletop.

"What is it?"

"This is Jenna you're talking about, right? Wild child, boyfriends, the whole bit?"

That described Jenna's younger days to a T, but now? Betsy shook her head. "She's not like that anymore. She can't be—she has Addie and Walsh."

"But she's all of a sudden leaving them with you for two weeks?"

"Well . . . yeah. I'm fine though."

"Mm-hmm. I'll stop at the Pig on the way. I'm bringing you a bottle of wine. Sounds like you may need it."

Betsy took a quick survey of the house: The casserole dish from this morning's farmer breakfast still in the kitchen sink. Two baskets of laundry on the couch waiting to be folded and put away. The back porch coffee table covered with printouts of Excel files, results of Ty's and her last financial "state of the union" meeting. She glanced out the back window just in time to see Ty climb onto the seat of the tractor and crank it up. Carlos stood by directing him between the fence posts into the back field.

She should go out and tell him about Jenna's imminent arrival with the kids—especially since she hadn't asked him first. In this case though, it seemed asking for forgiveness might be easier than asking for permission.

Upstairs, the guest room was already made up with crisp sheets and an empty water carafe on the bedside table, ready for Ty's parents in case they decided to come for an overnight visit. Uninterested in having any part in the family farm, they rarely did. Down the hall, she poked her head into the empty room. It had remained bare all these years except for a double bed with a sky-blue iron headboard salvaged from an estate sale, an old white dresser with glass knobs and an attached mirror, and a white rocking chair from Betsy's grandmother. Addie and Walsh would need more than this.

She rummaged through the hall linen closet and pulled out a set of sheets with tiny roses set against a white background. Roses always reminded her of Jenna. As sullen as she had been as a teenager, Jenna had helped their father tend his rose garden in the backyard with scientific precision.

She also found the cream-colored cable-knit blanket her grandmother knitted for her before she was born. Betsy had draped that blanket across every bed she'd ever slept in, from her childhood home to Auburn then to Elinore. She couldn't remember when or why she'd folded it and put it away. She held it in her hands now, thick stitches of cotton as soft as the fingers that made it.

Her grandmother spent decades knitting, her nimble fingers purling and plaiting in ways Betsy never had a desire or inclination for. Spending weeks at her house during summer breaks with Jenna when their parents worked long hours, Betsy grew familiar with the vocabulary and shape of stitches, even if she didn't pick up the knitting needles herself. As the older, calmer granddaughter, the one more concerned with making others happy, she was the one who sat and kept their grandmother company while she knitted. Jenna ran free on their grandparents' four acres, laughing with kids from neighboring houses, sneaking kisses and cigarettes.

Even if she never purled on her own, Betsy knew the significance of a dropped stitch. It would start with a little puff of air from her grandmother's nose, a slight shake of her head, then her fingers quickly working backward to recover that disobedient stitch. She'd go back to just before things fell apart and make the necessary change to prevent the same thing from happening again.

Betsy unfolded the blanket on the double bed and held it by the ends, gently flapping it to settle it across the sheets. Her grandmother's stitches had held tight all these years, not a dropped stitch in sight. She smoothed her hands across the blanket, straightened the corners, and imagined the room holding two little girls after holding nothing but dreams and damaged furniture. She sat on the corner of the bed, across from the antique dresser, then reached over and ran her thumb across the crack in the top drawer.

"Hey, girl," came Anna Beth's voice from downstairs, then a slam of the back door. "I ate some of this chicken salad on the way over here. Hope you don't mind." Her feet thudded up the staircase. "I was starving since you left me high and dry for lunch."

Her friend appeared in the doorway to the empty room, fanning her damp face. "It's hot as two cats in a wool sock out there. And you wouldn't believe the line at the Pig. They've got their chicken legs on sale ninety-nine cents a pound, and it's brought out all the bargain shoppers. You know there's nothing I hate more than bargain shoppers with their coupon binders. Now, how are you?"

Betsy smiled. Anna Beth was always in a frenzy about something—the blazing heat that blanketed their part of Alabama for at least eight months out of the year, beachgoers invading Elinore for its "charming" dining and shopping, or how parents in their district always disregarded the deadlines for signing kids up at the elementary school. She was the school registrar and had to deal with the latecomers who insisted their child be registered, even after class lists had been posted. Talking to Anna Beth, you'd think those parents were late for tea with the queen.

"I'm fine," Betsy said. "Thanks for bringing lunch."

"Mm-hmm." Anna Beth glanced through the bedroom. "Your nieces'll sleep in here?"

Betsy nodded. "It's not much. I need to pick up some coloring books or something for them."

"I'll bring a few things over. I have some toys up in the attic, and we still have a ton of books."

"Thanks, but I'm sure Jenna will pack some of their toys."

Anna Beth snorted. "From what you've said, Jenna might not come prepared. You'll need something if it rains. Kids go stir-crazy when it rains. At thirteen and fifteen, mine still go crazy when they're stuck inside all day, despite a whole world of electronic doodads all over the house."

Anna Beth turned toward the stairs. "You ready to eat? I got the chicken salad you like—the kind with all the grapes and nuts in it."

"That sounds great. I just need to grab one more thing."

She opened the top dresser drawer and pulled out *Henderson's Book of Fanciful Flowers*. Written by Albert Henderson in 1918, the back cover was held on by threads and the corners were jammed and bent, but the pages inside were still crisp and flat. She'd bought the book years ago at a used bookstore, the first and only time she'd let herself buy something to decorate the room she hoped would one day be her nursery. Back then, she was in her garden every day weeding, pruning, and fighting off aphids. She used to love it— getting her hands dirty, seeing her hard work result in color and life popping up from the soil—but it had been a while since she'd visited. The garden was mostly full of dandelions and crabgrass now.

The *Book of Fanciful Flowers* may not have been a true children's book, but the dreamy watercolor loops and swirls, depicting everything from sunflowers and roses to peonies and forget-me-nots, seemed whimsical and childlike. Along the edges of each page, Mr. Henderson had written, in careful ink, descriptions of each flower.

A peony bush full of flowers brings good luck, but if the flowers fade or fall off, prepare for disaster.

While known to signify everlasting union, dahlias can also symbolize betrayal and dishonesty. Use caution when gifting dahlias to a beloved.

Her plan had been to cut out the pages and frame them, but the pages remained between the covers, and the book had been shut up inside that dresser drawer since the day she threw it in there and slammed the drawer closed with enough force to splinter the wood. She ran her hand across the fragile cover, like reintroducing herself to an old friend, and propped it against the mirror.

Anna Beth leaned forward and peered at the cracked drawer. "Gorilla Glue will take care of that. That's what I love about antiques like this. You never know what troubles they've been through." She patted the top of the dresser. "But it makes 'em tough."

Downstairs, they spread their lunch out on the table. While Betsy dragged one of the two laundry baskets from the couch over to her kitchen chair, Anna Beth retrieved two wineglasses from the cabinet and poured cold pinot grigio.

"I don't know, AB," Betsy said, already bringing the glass to her lips. "It's a little early for happy hour."

"Psshhh," Anna Beth muttered. "Cheers." She clinked her glass to Betsy's. "Oh, this reminds me. I'm having a little get-together at my house on Wednesday for some new neighbors. I'd ask you and Ty to come, but we're having margaritas and tapas from El Gato. Not exactly kid-friendly."

"What about Lucy and Jackson?"

"They'll spend the night with Tom's parents in Elberta. They'll eat a pound of Cheetos, drink a gallon of sweet tea, and come home with three kinds of stomachache, but it'll be worth it for a night off." She took a sip of her wine and looked pointedly at Betsy. "So what's up with Jenna? Does she always make plans at the drop of a hat like this?"

Betsy smiled. She was used to Anna Beth's express train of thoughts, swerving and veering all over the place. "She's spontaneous—or at least she used to be—but she just found out yesterday she was accepted at the retreat. I think she told me as soon as she could."

Anna Beth narrowed one eye. "How close are y'all, really?"

Betsy hesitated, tapped her fingernails on her wineglass. "I don't know. We were close once, but it was a long time ago. When I left for Auburn, she still had two years at home with our parents, which didn't go over very well. They never appreciated her free spirit. Always wanted her to calm down, behave, sit still."

Betsy picked a pair of Ty's socks out of the basket and folded them together. She passed them back and forth between her hands before tossing them back in the basket. "It was probably hard for her to be there without me. When I was home, I was sort of the mediator between her and my parents. Without me there . . . well, Jenna's not naturally submissive."

"Who is?" Anna Beth asked around a bite of food. "Give me that." She leaned over and pulled the laundry basket to her. "I already ate half a basket of bread at the restaurant waiting on you. You eat, I'll fold."

"Yes, ma'am." Betsy popped a grape in her mouth. "Anyway, Jenna moved around a lot after her stint in college, had some boyfriends here and there. We just have different lives. But she does have those two sweet girls."

"How'd she let that happen? Seems she wouldn't want to be tied down by kids."

"Oh, I don't think having kids was her intention. She just . . . got lucky. Or unlucky depending on how you look at it."

"Humph." Anna Beth folded a pair of blue jeans, then sat back in her chair, her eyes on Betsy.

"What?"

Anna Beth pursed her lips, then shook her head. She reached forward and grabbed a T-shirt.

Betsy looked down and pushed the chicken salad around the plate with her fork. It had always been easy for others to dismiss Jenna because of her wildness, her disregard for rules, but Betsy never could. Jenna was her sister, after all. No one else had been through their particular childhood. Not that it was especially bad—in fact, it should have been pretty close to perfect.

Their parents, Drs. David and Marilyn Sawyer, were models of professionalism in their respective fields—David as conductor of the Birmingham Symphony Orchestra and Marilyn as the head of the UAB Cancer Research Center. Having had children much later in life, they were dedicated to their work with a single-minded passion and focus. They threw themselves into civic causes and charity work, were devoted to organizations that helped better the world, and generally tried to be good stewards of their money and influence. All good, noble things, but models of how to be an attentive, involved parent? How to cherish and encourage? Not exactly.

With their parents always focused on their careers, it had been Betsy and Jenna against the world. Huddled together under Betsy's bed. Hunched over rocks in the backyard looking for cicada shells and long, wiggly worms. Lying in bed together at night listening to their father's concertos on the stereo downstairs, Betsy whispering fairy tales to Jenna into the wee hours. Betsy never asked to be pushed into the mother role, but it was a role she learned early to play.

It had been a long time since Betsy had had a need—or a desire—to mother Jenna, but even so, she always felt the deep-down urge to defend her sister.

"Jenna loves her daughters. I think she's just still trying to figure out her place in the world."

"If you ask me, at twenty-eight and two kids, you're

long past the time of figuring things out," Anna Beth said. "Best get your butt in gear."

Betsy shifted her chair to move out of a sharp ray of sun and caught sight of Ty standing just outside the barn doors, laughing at something she couldn't see. It was always a treat to see him laughing and carefree. He was often so reserved, so focused on the task at hand, but when he laughed—cheeks stretched wide, blue eyes squinted, shoulders shaking—it was a gift.

Anna Beth followed her gaze out the back window. "You two are such lovebirds. Big house, great farm, tons of room for kids. Life already figured out."

"We don't have everything figured out." She finished her last bite of chicken salad and reached for a shirt to fold. "Who does?"

"Tom does. And Ty does too. Tell me your husband isn't doing exactly what he wanted to do with his life. No farmer gets caught up in a life of farming, whether it's cows or crops. You're only in it if you chose it. Maybe you and I got caught up in it, but we did it willfully when we married these boys. They have it figured out."

Betsy glanced back at Ty again. He pulled off his cap, revealing his blond hair damp with midday heat, and threw it at Carlos. Carlos picked it up and dropped it in a bucket, causing Ty to shout. He pulled his cap from the bucket and wrung water out of it.

"You're probably right," Betsy said. "I think he does have things pretty much figured out."

"Of course I'm right. That's why you love me."

SEVEN

TY

At 8 a.m. EDT, a tropical storm warning has been issued for the south and southeast edges of Puerto Rico in the Caribbean Sea. Interests elsewhere in the central and eastern Caribbean should closely monitor the progress of this system.

Ty sat in his office, his grandfather's old black radio tuned to the AM station that sent out a constant flow of crop stats, animal prices, and weather reports. That crackly radio usually made him feel like a real farmer, but today the steady stream of numbers and words annoyed him. He fiddled with the dial, turned it all the way to the right hoping for even a hint of real music—country, rock, something—but all he got was static.

He turned it back to the left, slowly. Maybe he'd find that same music his grandfather used to play in the barn—wordless melodies, a river of gospel, bluegrass, folk. But even at the lowest end of the dial, there was nothing but politicians and rural Baptist preachers.

He was about to turn the thing off when a computerized weather report crackled through. "Tropical Storm Bernard has taken a northwesterly turn," said the robotic voice. "It is expected to continue to the north . . ."

Ty swiped at the Off button, leaned forward, and rubbed his temples with his thumbs. The radio wasn't the problem, and neither was Bernard. A tropical storm this early in the season wasn't anything to get worked up about, especially one that would no doubt curve back out into the Atlantic. He'd been tracking storms long enough to know when to worry. But the alarming predictions about this year's hurricane season—not to mention its similarities to another season years ago— had him on edge.

The summer he turned fifteen was predicted to bring an especially severe hurricane season. Ty had spent every summer since he was nine working on the farm with his grandfather—along with any weekends he wasn't busy playing baseball—and this one was no different. By August, his grandfather's old radio had sent out so many alarms and beeps, cautions and warnings that it had become background noise. So far, none of the storms had affected the farm directly—just fallen limbs and debris and a few short power outages. As a result, Ty paid little attention to the reports about Hurricane Louis that came through the radio, and even brushed off his grandfather's concerns and extra efforts to secure the farm.

Louis roared through Baldwin County a few days later, damaging everything in its path and chastening Ty for having the nerve to doubt his grandfather's ability to sense coming danger. Ty had always known his grandfather was a good man, but waiting up with Granddaddy as the storm blew through, seeing how worried he was about the farm, the land, and the house, changed his view of him forever.

"Hurricanes have come and gone every season since my father built this place," Granddaddy said by candlelight after the power had blinked off. Wind rushed and moaned outside, and lightning forked through the eerie gray-green sky. His grandfather was on edge, waiting for the winds to die down so he could get outside and survey his property. "Lord willing, the farm will be here for many seasons to come. And one day it can be yours. It's a big responsibility. Are you up for it?"

Ty nodded. "Yes, sir. It's what I want."

"I know you do, son. Your daddy didn't want the farming life, but I see it in you. So be it. Franklin Dairy will pass on to you."

Later, after the worst of the storm had passed, Granddaddy pulled on his boots and opened the back door. He turned to Ty. "You comin'?"

Together, they stepped through the debris in the yard and dodged tree branches still swaying in the wind. Everything looked okay until they passed the barn.

"Oh no. No, no." Granddaddy took off running to the fence that was supposed to have kept the cows safe in the field during the storm. Instead, one large section had fallen, the old wooden boards snarled and splintered at the ends. Thirty-two of Granddaddy's 150 cows had escaped through the gash in the fence. Even at his young age, Ty knew the rules of the game: a loss of cows meant a loss of milk, which meant a loss of money. It was a hard hit for the farm.

Ty might have started the summer still a boy, but he took an important step toward manhood the night of that storm. Now, more than fifteen years later, he still remembered what it felt like to know Franklin Dairy would one day be his. It was an intimidating but welcome weight of responsibility. A weight that had only increased over the years.

He heard a knock at the door and glanced up. Carlos leaned against the doorframe, beating dust from his blue jeans with his faded Crimson Tide ball cap.

"What's up, man?" Carlos asked, not really looking for an answer, just someone to shoot the breeze with for a minute.

Ty leaned back in his chair, springs and metal squeaking. "Checking numbers. The usual." He nodded to the hat in Carlos's hand. "I'll help you with the stalls if you leave that cap off."

"Nuh-uh." Carlos set it firmly back on his head. "Hat stays with me."

While the men forked fresh bedding into each of the cow stalls, Ty relished the peace that came with doing a job well and quietly. With the herd in the fields and the music off, the only sound came from industrial fans on either end of the barn and the swishing of their pitchforks into bags of sawdust. Ty's mind was free to roam, although today, his mind wasn't going anywhere easy.

It shifted from memories of his grandfather to the broken pump he and Carlos would have to fix later to the phone call that came this morning.

Jenna. He didn't even have to see her to feel the thorn digging into his flesh.

Carlos could only stand to work in silence for so long, and after a few minutes, he broke it. "Something under your skin? You're shoving that pitchfork mighty hard there. Remind me not to get in the way."

"I'm good. Just . . . distracted."

"What did Dr. Evans say about 186?"

They'd lost a cow yesterday, a female soon to have a baby. Ty hadn't been sure what it was, but the thought of infection—something that could spread to the rest of the herd—had worried him.

"Undetected heart condition, no infection. He couldn't say specifically what it was, but he offered to do an autopsy to be sure." Ty patted down the last layer of sawdust and moved the bag down to the next stall.

"For a pretty penny, I bet."

"Bingo."

"Good there's no infection. Nothing that'll affect the rest of them," Carlos said. "So if it's not the cow, what is it? Tell me to mind my own business if you want, but I'll just ask you again later." He grinned.

Ty shoved a fork-load into the stall. Patted it down. Lather, rinse, repeat.

"It's nothing, man. Just heard a weather report earlier is all. Tropical storm down in the Caribbean."

"Yeah, I heard it too. Staying out in open water, don't you think?"

"Probably. Can't let our guard down though. That's the same as begging the thing to come and unleash destruction. We have some boards left over from last summer. I'll see about getting more. May have time later today to make a run to the Feed and Equipment."

"You like to be prepared for everything, don'tcha, Boss?"

"I can't prepare for everything. But this farm's been here a heck of a lot longer than I have. It's not going to be blown to bits on my watch."

Ty paused and ran his free hand over his head, then picked the fork back up again. Maybe he was being too hard on Jenna. Betsy tried to take care of her. He should probably try to do the same. But her calling meant she needed something, and Ty wasn't sure Betsy had anything to give. Not money, not energy, certainly not another chunk of her heart. Last summer was the last time, as far as Ty was concerned.

Betsy had been so confident that first procedure would work. He'd hoped it would too, of course, but he knew it was usually better to expect the worst. Not as hard of a fall that way. Betsy, on the other hand, had expected the best, even planned for it—she'd use the weekend in Nashville to give the good news to Jenna. It didn't pan out that way though.

After they got the call that the test was negative, Ty had expected Betsy to bail on the trip, but she didn't. Putting five hundred miles between her and the double glass doors of South Alabama Fertility Specialists would feel good, she'd said. Give her something else to focus on. And anyway, Jenna had asked her to come, and Betsy would do whatever she could for her sister.

He still kicked himself for letting Betsy go, but at the time, he didn't have the heart to say no. When she pulled up the driveway at the end of the weekend, both she and the truck were on their last legs. She hadn't gotten the rest and peace she'd gone to Nashville to seek. Jenna had been a sour taste in his mouth ever since.

So the phone call? It was the same as the leaves swirling in the wind, the animals all jittery in their pens, the weathermen loosening their top buttons and rolling up their shirtsleeves. Everyone knew something was coming.

EIGHT

BETSY

It was a long day, as Ty had predicted. Betsy didn't see him before the afternoon milking, which took him through the early evening. He blew in the back door as lightning bugs floated around the backyard and cicadas in the trees chirped out their scratchy melodies. He wolfed down a bowl of spaghetti, then ducked back out the door.

"Sorry, babe," he said. "Broken pump. Carlos and I have to fix it before tomorrow."

It was well after ten before she heard the back door open and his footsteps, heavy with fatigue, on the stairs. She was propped up in bed reading.

"Everything okay?" she asked when he trudged into their bedroom.

He shrugged, unbuckling his blue jeans and stepping out of them. He pointed to the bathroom. "Shower."

Ten minutes later, he entered the bedroom, smelling of musky soap. She'd planned to tell him about Jenna and the girls as soon as he came out of the steamy bathroom, but then he collapsed onto the bed next to her, flung his arm over his eyes, and groaned.

"That bad?"

"It's working again, but I don't know how long it'll hold up. It's the second time we've had to rig it. Wish I could have called Chuck."

For years Ty had used Chuck Panter anytime a piece of equipment broke or malfunctioned, but with the closing of several dairy farms in south Alabama, there wasn't enough broken machinery to keep him in business. At one time there had been twelve dairy farms in his territory. Now there were three, and Franklin Dairy was the biggest by far.

After a moment, Betsy reached over and turned off the lamp. In the semidarkness she had the nerve to ask, "What about us? How are we doing?" She knew the numbers, but numbers only told half the story. Many times their numbers had been down but Ty said not to worry, that the next season would bring them well into the black, and it always happened.

But he didn't immediately dismiss her concerns, which made her concerns feel that much more real.

"I was thinking about calling the principal at the elementary school," she said. "See if he'd be interested in setting up some more field trips for next school year. And I talked to the head of the summer program at the Y. They're adding us into their weekly camp schedule this summer."

"That's great, Bets."

She turned her face toward him. He stared up at the ceiling, one arm behind his head.

"The field trips help," he finally said. "They really do. The renovation set us back, but it'll pay off. We'll be okay." He reached over and pulled her toward him. She scooted close enough to feel the heat radiating off his body, slid one leg between his, and nestled her head under his chin.

He sighed. "We always make it work, don't we? When something doesn't go our way, we try something else."

"What are we trying this time?"

"We'll be creative, how about that?" He pulled his head back and smiled at her. His face, weathered from spending hours of every day of the year outside in the elements—heat, cold, rain, wind—bore straight white lines between his eyes and temples. He said he couldn't be outside in the sunshine without his sunglasses on or his light-blue eyes would scald right off his face. She reached up and traced the line to his ear.

"Maybe it's time for that vacation you've been talking about," he said. "A long weekend. What about Destin? Or New Orleans? You could take me to that antique shop you like on Magazine Street. Walker and Carlos could keep an eye on things here for a few days."

"How can we do that when we can't pay to fix a broken pump?"

"We *can* pay to fix it; I'm just choosing to fix it for free."

"Hmm." She pressed her cheek into his chest. His heartbeat was as steady and insistent as the metronome that used to sit on top of her parents' Steinway. "That would be nice." A vacation would be good for them. Help them reconnect, away from the responsibilities of the farm, from the distraction of the milking schedules. The veterinarian visits and field trips.

He rolled onto his back again, keeping one arm tight around her. "So what's up with Jenna?"

"Things are good. She's getting ready to go on a two-week art retreat. It's a big deal, I think. Something she didn't want to turn down. It's in Florida."

"Two weeks at the beach? Sounds right up her alley."

"It's . . . I don't think it's actually on the beach. And maybe it'll be good for her. She's wanting to get back into her photography, and this will give her a chance to get away and focus on it. She used to be really good."

"What about Addie and Walsh?"

Betsy paused a moment too long. Ty turned to her with wide eyes. "Betsy?"

"I told her I'd run it by you, but I said I thought we might be able to keep them here."

"And when is this retreat?"

She took a deep breath and bit her lip. "It starts tomorrow."

Ty lifted his shoulders and peered down at her. "Tomorrow? As in twelve hours, tomorrow?"

Betsy nodded.

He sat up and leaned his elbows on his knees. "You've got to be kidding me."

"It's two weeks. Nothing at all. It'll be mostly me taking care of them anyway. I know you'll be busy. And I should have asked you earlier."

He laughed, almost a grunt. "You think?"

She put a hand on his back. "I'm sorry. Really. I just . . ." How could she explain the deep-down kernel of need inside her—the need to protect, defend, shelter her sister? Even when Jenna made rash, spur-of-the-moment decisions, even when she infuriated Betsy like no one else could.

Betsy closed her eyes. Jenna had once begged her parents to let her attend some kind of photography program the summer after her freshman year at Alabama. Betsy made it clear she thought her parents should let Jenna go, but they said no. They hadn't even considered it.

"Jenna was always happiest when she was behind a camera. If this is her shot at trying photography again, I want to give it to her. And I can't shake the feeling that something else is going on with her too, but I don't know what it is."

Ty turned and looked at her over his shoulder. "I don't know if you believe all that or if you're just saying it to make things sound better." He sighed and lay back against the pillows. "I love you for taking care of your sister. I don't love the situation, but it'll . . . It's fine. You're right though—I won't have much time for visiting. Or helping you with the girls."

"It's okay. I don't expect you to change anything. I'll take care of it all."

Ty exhaled through pursed lips and rubbed the top of his head. "I wish she'd given us a little more of a heads-up before we become babysitters."

"I know." Betsy's chest squeezed at the thought of little feet pounding up and down the stairs of the old farmhouse. Laughter in the hallways. She hoped she hadn't made a big mistake in saying yes.

Outside, the faint sound of lowing cows, content in the barn, crossed the expanse of grass and yard and crept inside the house. The sound was strangely comforting.

Ty's arm around her tightened. "You looking forward to seeing Addie and Walsh?"

She nodded. "Yeah, I am. It's been over a year. Walsh was still a baby last summer."

"I remember last summer."

Betsy squeezed her eyes closed, shutting out the memory. She swallowed. "Things are different now, you know that. We've moved on. It'll be easier."

Ty was quiet. After a moment, Betsy propped herself up on one elbow to peer down at him. "I'm fine."

"Good. Because I'd rather them not come at all if it's going to be hard for you."

Betsy leaned down and kissed him on the lips. "Thank you for worrying about me. But I'm a big girl. I can handle it."

He pulled her to him again, his arm tight around her back. He nuzzled her cheek with his nose and kissed her, soft but pressing, urgent. She gave in for a moment, the familiar and pleasant ache rising in her belly, but when his hand slipped down to the waistband of her thin cotton pajama bottoms, she inhaled and pulled her lips away, just a fraction of an inch, so small she almost hoped he hadn't noticed.

But he dropped his head back against his pillow. She put her hand on his chest and lay her head on the pillow next to his, her forehead pressed into his cheek. "Another night?" she whispered.

She felt him nod. In minutes he was asleep.

. . .

Long after Ty nodded off, Betsy lay awake. The half-full moon shining through a hazy film of cloud made a soft glow on the bedroom walls. The clock on her night-stand glowed red numbers—1:24.

Nashville last summer had been hard. At first she'd expected it to be a chance to celebrate good news of a positive pregnancy with her sister. Then after the nurse had called with the results, she hoped it'd be a chance to rest, lick her wounds, and get her feet back underneath her. It wasn't until she dropped her bags in Jenna's cozy little house that she learned Jenna had been offered the chance to pick up extra shifts at Full Cup and would be working for much of the weekend, starting with the late shift that night.

All Betsy had said to Jenna about the doctor visits was that she was "having some tests done," making sure things were running normally. Nothing to indi-cate any real problem. Still, Betsy had hoped that Jenna would have somehow read between the lines. Used some sisterly wavelength and instinctively known Betsy needed her. Not walk out the door the minute Betsy arrived.

"You don't mind hanging with the girls, do you? I know they'd love to spend some time with Aunt Betsy without boring old Mom around," Jenna said.

"I don't know, Jenna, I kind of thought . . ."

"Please? This is good money for me. And I'll be in and out. I'll have a break between shifts around lunch tomorrow, then you and I can catch up on Sunday."

"I have to leave Sunday. I have a field trip lined up for Monday morning."

"Oh. Well . . ."

Betsy exhaled. Thoughts of bonding, reconnecting, evaporated. "It's fine." What else could she do? "The girls and I will have a great time." She imagined a protective layer, like bubble wrap, creeping up the walls of her heart.

Betsy spent the weekend building sheet tents in the cramped living room, making pizzas with the meager offerings in Jenna's kitchen, and making up fairy tales about mermaids and seahorse princes. When Jenna arrived home after her Sunday-morning shift, Betsy pulled her suitcase, now stuffed with crayon drawings and a pink feather boa Addie insisted Betsy take with her, out to the truck. She turned to say good-bye to the girls.

"I wish you could stay longer." Tears slid down Addie's cheeks.

Betsy's heart filled with a potent mixture of longing and anger she'd never felt. She bent down so she could talk to Addie at her eye level. "How about this?" she whispered. "What if we make plans to see each other again real soon? Maybe you can even come to the farm and get to know the cows."

"Can I ride one?" Addie asked, her bottom lip still trembling.

Betsy laughed. "We don't usually ride the cows, but I don't think Uncle Ty will mind. He'll pick out the perfect one for you to ride."

That perked Addie up enough for Betsy to leave

without dissolving into tears herself. Before she climbed into the truck, she cupped Walsh's plump cheek in her hand, then turned to Jenna.

"Thank you." Jenna's arms were tight around Betsy's neck. "This has been a huge help. And I'm sorry we didn't really get a chance to catch up."

It was now mid-June and that bright July morning last summer was the last time Betsy had seen Jenna or the girls. She FaceTimed with Addie and Walsh often, but whenever Jenna got on the phone, she kept the conversation light and easy—what the girls were learning, funny things they'd said recently. Anytime Betsy asked about anything more personal—whether Jenna was satisfied with her job, if she'd met anyone nice, if she was happy living in Nashville—Jenna would change the subject.

Maybe the act of keeping the girls here for a little while would somehow bring her and Jenna closer. There were so many conversations Betsy wanted to have with Jenna, about so many things, but there always seemed to be some sort of dividing wall between them. Betsy didn't even know how it got there. Things used to be so different with them.

She wished Jenna could stay even just one night at the farm. She imagined the two of them sitting up late on the porch, talking and laughing as they did when they were much younger, before real-world problems invaded their make-believe universe.

NINE

BETSY

Betsy was waiting on the front porch when a car turned off Highway 35 onto the gravel driveway. It was a moment before Jenna's small blue Honda appeared from the tunnel of trees that lined the drive. Betsy smiled when the driver's side door opened and Jenna's blonde curls popped out.

"Hey there," Betsy called on her way down the steps. "Welcome to the farm." She enveloped her sister in her arms and squeezed, breathing in the strawberry scent of her shampoo. After a moment, she pulled back, her hands still on Jenna's shoulders. "Your hair is shorter."

Jenna put her hand to her head. "It's easier this way. I still can't control it, but at least it's out of my face."

"It looks great." Whenever she thought of Jenna, it was usually as the wild, defiant teenager she once was. But here she was, an adult. A mother. The reality always caught her off guard. "It's really good to see you. I wish you could stay."

"I know. I have to be there tonight though. They do this big welcome thing, I don't know." She looked past Betsy to the house. "This place is gorgeous, as always. Addie's been talking about the cows since we crossed into Alabama. Did you tell her she could ride one?"

Betsy was about to explain when a knocking came from the backseat, loud and insistent. They both turned to see Addie's face pressed up against the glass.

"Let me get them out," Jenna said with a laugh. She ducked her head into the backseat. Addie had already unbuckled her seat belt and clamored around Jenna to hop out of the car. Jenna pulled a sleeping Walsh from her seat, then stood.

Addie took a few cautious steps toward Betsy, then stopped and turned back to Jenna.

"It's okay." Jenna ran her hand down Addie's hair.

Addie moved toward Betsy, then ran the last few steps, knocking into her knees and burying her face in her legs. "Aunt Betsy!" she said, her voice muffled by Betsy's shorts.

Betsy closed her eyes for the briefest moment, then smiled big. "Well, hello to you." She pulled Addie's face up so she could look at her. "You've grown about a foot since I saw you last. And your hair—it's so long!" Addie's blonde curls reminded Betsy of Jenna as a child, her curls almost taking on a life of their own, especially in the summer.

"And here's my baby." Jenna switched Walsh to her other hip. Betsy knew mothers often called their youngest child their "baby," but there was nothing baby about Walsh. Not anymore. Her dark hair hung to her shoulders in gentle waves, her small upturned nose was flecked with tiny freckles, and her rosebud lips were a deep magenta.

Betsy's heart ached as if Walsh were her own child and she'd missed her growing up. She reached over to Walsh clinging to Jenna's shoulder. Walsh tucked her chin and hid her face in Jenna's neck. Betsy tickled Walsh's cheek with the tip her fingernail, just enough to see the girl's cheeks stretch into a grin.

"There it is," Betsy said. "I knew a smile was in there somewhere." Walsh giggled and Betsy turned to Jenna. "Y'all come on in."

Addie ran ahead of them into the house. Inside, her eyes darted here and there to take it all in. "Wow," she breathed.

Addie's reaction was similar to how Betsy felt when Ty brought her to the farm when they were dating. The house wasn't grand or huge, but it was comfortable. Broken in. Even with his grandmother's collection of ancient weaver's looms standing in the corners and orange-and-yellow afghans covering every piece of furniture, it had felt like a place of welcome.

Now, deep slipcovered couches had replaced the looms, and fabrics in a mix of ticking stripes and faded flowers had replaced the afghans, but it still felt like a haven, a place for rest.

Walsh squirmed and Jenna set her down. "Be careful." Jenna ruffled Walsh's hair. "Don't mess anything up."

"Don't worry about it," Betsy said. "We don't have anything they can mess up. If they could, Ty would have already dropped something on it or broken it."

The girls scrambled into the window seat and stared out at the fields and the faded red barn in the distance.

Jenna breathed in deep. "It's so peaceful." She stretched her fingers out, then squeezed them closed. Was Jenna itching for her camera? There'd been a time—years ago in high school—when Jenna rarely went anywhere without it. She'd had a talent, somehow always able to capture just the right angle or shadow to make the viewer see her subject—whether a child at play or a leafless tree in winter—in a different light. She'd even carried that talent for artistry to Wyoming where she took photos and served as a yoga instructor at a remote artists' colony. Thankfully, that was before Addie and Walsh.

Betsy took two glasses from the cupboard and filled them with ice. "I'm excited about your retreat." It wasn't a lie, exactly. Just an extension of the truth.

Jenna sat on a stool at the kitchen counter. "Thanks. I am too. I think."

"What do you mean?" Betsy poured iced tea into the glasses and passed one to Jenna.

"I don't know. It was all so quick. Two days ago, I was making the schedule for work, penciling myself in for a full week, and now I'm leaving the girls with you and headed to who-knows-what."

Betsy nodded. Two days ago, she was planning a month of field trips, some marketing for the farm, and a meeting with a farmer's market in Foley. Now she was wondering what she'd do with two young kids for half a month.

"But impulsive decisions are my trademark, right?" Jenna smiled, but it was halfhearted.

Betsy tightened her hands around her glass. "Do you think if you'd taken more time to think about it, you would've decided not to go?"

Jenna shrugged. "I probably would've talked myself out of it, but . . ."

"But what?"

Jenna kept her eyes down and swirled her tea in her glass. "Things like this don't come my way very often. Or ever. If I'd said no, who knows when I'd have a chance to get away and do something like this again?"

Etta zipped through the kitchen then, the girls following just behind her.

Betsy finished her tea, then set the glass in the sink. "Hey, you two," she called. "How about those cows? Want to go see them?" She looked at Jenna. "Is that okay?"

"Of course. They'll love it. As long as Ty's okay with it." She bent down to help the girls with their shoes.

"He's in the middle of the second milking, but we can see the cows already out in the pasture." She turned to Addie and Walsh. "Maybe later on he'll let you try milking one of them."

Addie's eyes widened. "Does it hurt them?"

Betsy laughed. "You don't have to do it if you don't want to, but no, it doesn't hurt them. It'll hurt them if we don't milk them." She ushered them out onto the back porch and down the steps. The openness of the yard was too much to contain Walsh's excitement. She wriggled out of Jenna's arms and burst into a run. Addie ran a couple of steps, then stopped and looked back at Jenna.

"I'll stay with you, Mommy."

"It's okay, baby. Go ahead and run."

Addie waited another second, then took off. "Walsh," she hollered. When they reached the wooden fence, they peered through the slats and pointed at the cows in the distance.

"That's some love," Betsy said as she and Jenna picked their way across the prickly grass that had grown inches since Ty last cut it.

"Sometimes I don't even know how it happened. I look at them and think, Where did you little girls come from? I know that sounds crazy."

"Not too crazy. But they seem happy. Look at them."

Addie held Walsh around the middle from behind, Walsh's legs kicking and reaching for the bottom rung of the fence. As soon as her feet connected with the rung, she grabbed onto the top of the fence to get a better view of the cows beyond. Addie supported her little sister from behind.

"You must be doing something right," Betsy said.

Jenna shrugged. "I think they're just glad to be away from our house for a bit. This will be good for them."

Addie and Walsh's chatter grew quiet, and Betsy turned to see Ty walking toward them from the barn.

"Hey there," she called to Ty. "They're here."

"I see that." He unlocked the fence and pushed it open wide, then knelt in front of the girls. "Hello," he said formally.

"Hi," Addie said. "I like your cows."

"Thank you. I like them too." He tousled Walsh's hair, then stood up. "Hey, Jenna. It's good to see you."

"You too, Ty." Her voice was hesitant, but she relaxed when Ty held out an arm and gave her a quick hug.

"Sorry to run, but I need to get back out there." He rubbed the creases on his forehead. "I just wanted to say hey. I'll be back up as soon as I can." He looked at Betsy and she nodded, then he was gone, headed toward the barn. His mind, Betsy knew, was wrapped around pumps, quotas, and the two weeks ahead.

Jenna raised her eyebrows. "Is he okay?"

"He's fine. Just busy."

Back inside, Betsy pulled out crackers and strawberries for Addie and Walsh, then cut two thick slices of buttery pound cake. "Milk, right?"

"Of course," Jenna said.

Betsy placed the slices of cake on blue-and-white transferware plates and handed one to Jenna.

"Are these Nana's plates?"

Betsy nodded, her mouth full of pound cake.

"I wish I'd had the sense to say I wanted some of her things when she died. I was too wrapped up in my own teenage dramas to care." She ran her thumb along the edge of the plate. "The girls would love to eat off their great-grandmother's china."

"I have twelve of these," Betsy said. "I can wrap up half of them and send them home with you."

"No, I wasn't . . . I didn't mean that. I just . . . You've had your head on straight for a long time. I wish I was more like that."

While the two women ate, the girls took a couple bites, then darted off to one part of the house or another, exploring and chasing the cat. Betsy pulled out a pad of paper and a pen to jot down the girls' schedules, but Jenna laughed.

"I just want to make sure I know what to do. Remember, I have no experience with this."

"If I figured it out, you can too, and probably better than me. That reminds me . . ." She fished an envelope from her purse and held it out to Betsy.

"What's this?"

"Just a little money. I wanted you to have some extra on hand to cover the girls' food and incidentals while I'm gone."

"You know you don't have to do this. We can take care of it."

"I know, but it'll make me feel better. Just take it."

Betsy hesitated, then took the envelope from Jenna's hand.

When they finished going over everything about the girls' routines and particular challenges, Betsy cleaned up the kitchen, wiping spills and dribbles that didn't usually appear in her kitchen. Jenna walked through the house, picking up framed photos, books, and other knickknacks, then absently placing them down again. She was so lost in thought, Betsy just let her roam. When Jenna's phone rang in her bag, she checked the screen, then moved toward the back porch.

"I need to take this, but I'll just be a minute." She opened the door as wind blew against the house, pulling the screen door on the porch wide open, then slamming it shut.

Betsy peered out the window above the kitchen sink. Dark purple spread across the sunlit sky. "Guess that storm decided to come on in." Thunder cracked and a bolt of lightning skittered across the sky. A flock of doves took flight from the side pasture and zipped to the east. *I'll check on the girls for you,* she mouthed to Jenna.

She found Addie and Walsh in the empty room, lying on their backs, staring at the ceiling and talking. Betsy stopped in the doorway and knocked on the jamb. "Mind if I come in?"

"Sure." Addie sat up. Walsh rolled over onto her stomach.

"What are you girls chatting about? Still playing a game?"

"We're looking for clues."

"Oh yeah? What kind of clues?"

"Just clues about the house. What kind of place it is."

Betsy raised her eyebrows. "Well, what did you find out?"

Addie looked around her. "We like the house. A lot. And the cows. And Uncle Ty. I think we could stay here for a while. Maybeeee . . . about four years."

Betsy laughed. "Four years, huh? That's a long time. I think you'd miss your own home by then."

"Yeah," Addie said. "Probably." She pulled down Walsh's pant leg where it had stuck up above her knee. "But this house just feels good. And we packed my favorite princess dress and Walsh's blanket, so we can stay as long as we want!"

She jumped off the bed and ran to their small pile of bags in the corner. She reached her hand into an old University of Alabama duffel bag, then tossed a well-loved blanket to Walsh and laid out the dress for Betsy to see.

"Very pretty," Betsy said.

Walsh pulled the blanket over her face and folded her knees up under her belly. "Find me!" she yelled to Addie.

Addie giggled. "I can still see you, silly."

As the girls began a game of hide-and-seek, Betsy stepped out. Rain was falling hard now, splattering the windows and turning the world outside steamy and blurred.

Jenna stood in the kitchen, leaning against the counter with her phone to her ear. She was smiling and chewing on her bottom lip. "Okay. Max told me it was a single cabin. It's just me, so that's fine." She glanced at the clock on the microwave. "Yes, I can make it by then, but don't worry about saving any dinner for me. I'll grab something on the way."

Betsy tiptoed back up the stairs. Jenna called her just as she reached the empty room. She sat on the bed and tried to look like she hadn't been eavesdropping. Addie and Walsh stood by the window peering at a honey bee buzzing on the other side of the glass.

Jenna tapped on the door. "Hey, you two."

"Mommy, there's a huge bee in the window. Come see," Addie said. Walsh's face was pressed to the glass.

"Hmm, wow." She leaned down and looked over their shoulders. "That's a big one. Come sit with me a minute." She pulled the girls to her.

As Jenna talked to them, giving them a list of dos

and don'ts while staying at the farm, Betsy stepped out of the room to give them privacy. In the hallway she leaned back against the wall. Photos of the farm, left over from Ty's grandparents, clattered behind her.

"It sounds like you've already made up your mind," Betsy had said to Jenna on the phone the day before.

"No, it's not like that. I'm asking you before I tell them anything. But I have to give them an answer soon. Like . . . today. This is . . . Oh, Betsy, please say yes."

Betsy walked out into the backyard and breathed in the warm morning air as the two weeks swirled in her mind.

"Look, I understand if it's not going to work," Jenna said. "I'm sure I can figure something else out."

Betsy exhaled. "Of course they can stay here. That's not the problem. I'm just . . . I'm trying to understand you. It's a quick decision, dropping the girls off with barely a heads-up. Have you thought this through—your job, money, bills while you're gone? What about—?"

"Betsy, I've thought about it from every angle. Trust me. You don't have to worry about me. Or the girls. I know I used to be . . . irresponsible, but I'm not now. I can't afford to be—not with two kids who are stuck with me as their mom."

"They're not *stuck* with you."

"You know what I mean. They only have me. I have to do things right. And that's part of the reason why I want to do this retreat. To let them see me pursuing something that matters to me. To see me working toward a goal. I appreciate your concern, but this is something I need to do on my own. Can you let me do that? You're my sister, my friend. We're partners, right? Isn't that what we always said?"

Betsy nodded. "Yeah. We did."

"It's not like I'm leaving them with strangers. And as far as kids go, they're a breeze. They sleep late in the morning, they love Curious George, and they can drink their weight in apple juice."

Betsy smiled, in spite of her frustration.

"Oh, and Addie has to sleep with her stuffed elephant or she stays awake all night. Don't forget that."

Betsy gave a small laugh. "I think we can handle it."

"It'll be great. They'll probably want to stay forever."

• • •

Twenty minutes later, Betsy stood by Jenna's car, already cranked with the AC blasting. The storm had pushed through quickly, leaving behind a blanket of thick humidity. Kneeling, Jenna hugged the girls tight. "Listen to Aunt Betsy, okay? I want her to tell me how well you're behaving when I check in later."

"Will you miss us?" Addie asked.

"Oh yes," Jenna said. "I will miss you tons. But I'll take some pretty pictures and when I get back, I'll need you to tell me if they're any good. I'll need your help too." She poked Walsh gently in the stomach.

Jenna stood and wrapped her arms around Betsy. "Thank you," she whispered. "And sorry again for the late notice. I'll make it up to you."

"Just be safe. Let us know when you get there."

"I will." She climbed into the car. "Love you girls," she called as she ducked her head.

Betsy thought she saw tears in Jenna's eyes, and her arms ached to hold her little sister one more time. She stepped closer to the car, but when Jenna rolled down her window and turned her face to them, her eyes were dry. A little red, but no tears.

Wet gravel crunched under the tires as Jenna pulled away. Betsy and the girls waved until the car disappeared around the curve of the driveway. Then she put her hands on their backs and guided them up the steps. The afternoon sun was just beginning to peek out from behind the dark clouds.

. . .

One afternoon when she was fifteen, Betsy visited her mother's office and stood in the dim light of the quiet lab, all the other techs gone for the day. Her dad had picked her up from school and dropped her at her mom's office on his way to the Alys Stephens Center for a symphony performance. She and her mom would pick up Jenna at school in half an hour. Jenna had detention. Again.

Betsy stared at the wall. Faces stared back at her from photographs. Mostly young people, children, babies even. Some were photographed in light moments— laughter, a smile, or at least a hint of one. Playing, working, cooking, living life. But a few were taken toward the end—faces barely suppressing the pain that raged inside them. Eyes full of the knowledge of the truth about their lives.

She scratched the back of her leg with the laces of her tennis shoe, then reached out and touched one of the photos. A teenager wearing a backward ball cap grinned loosely, as if all was right with the world. His arm was flung around the shoulders of a tall girl whose eyes were closed in laughter. "Mom, tell me about him."

Her mom crossed the room. Her lab took up most of the eleventh floor of the UAB Cancer Research Center. It smelled musty—like damp newspaper or old dirt—with a hard edge of Lysol mixed in. This lab was where really smart people—scientists, doctors, technicians—made groundbreaking discoveries in the field of brain cancer research, and Betsy's mom was the head of it all. Her black orthopedic shoes padded across the floor, her rumpled white lab coat billowing behind her.

She grazed her fingers across the teenager's face. "Brian McLaurin," she said, her voice low and reverent. "He was only seventeen. Bone cancer that spread to his brain. He was a stand-out basketball star on his high school team before the pain started." She moved to her right and nodded toward the next photo on her "inspiration wall," as she called it. "Cynthia Graves. Left a young family behind. Juanita Powers, the lead in her middle school play."

She kept going, calling out the names of each face on her wall. Her mother hadn't always focused on cancer of the brain, but it was always something horrible and tragic. Betsy was only fifteen, the same age as some of the people on the wall, and she couldn't imagine someone choosing to devote her life to something so depressing, even if it did save lives.

She tuned out her mom's words but kept watching her. The way she touched each photo, a gentle smile on her face, a little laugh when she noted something funny about the person in his or her precancer life. She knew every detail about them—their hobbies, families, jobs. Where they went to school, what sport they played, what their dreams and hopes had been. Somehow that careful attention didn't extend to remembering that Betsy didn't like green beans. That at the age of twelve, Jenna still wanted the nightlight on in the hallway outside her bedroom. That the two girls in her own house needed a mother who paid attention to the small things.

Her mom wiped a tear away and sniffed, then strode back to her desk on the other side of the room. Betsy followed her. Her mom's desk was empty of any personal items—no photos of her or Jenna, no calendars with puppies or exotic islands. "Why do you keep those photos up on the wall if they make you so sad?"

"They remind me why I'm doing all this." She waved her arm around at the lab. "They inspire me to pour all I have into finding cures. Not for them—it's too late for them—but for their families, friends, children. The ones they left behind." She gazed back up at the wall. "They're why I do everything."

Her mom said plenty, but it was the unsaid words that cut the deepest. They left an empty pocket, a vacuum that sucked a hole in the center of Betsy's chest. It was the first time she realized with utter clarity that her mom actually wished those kids had been hers. Maybe even instead of Betsy and Jenna. It was the way her constant tension slipped away for a moment, the way her smile became real, not forced and tight. She was a better mom to these poor dead kids than she was to her own fully alive children.

Betsy looked at her watch—a yellow-and-green Swatch her favorite babysitter had given her two years before. "Mom, we've got to go. It's almost five."

"Mmm?" Her mom kept her gaze on the paperwork on her desk.

"Jenna. Detention. It's over in five minutes."

Her mom looked up, her eyes hazy, faraway. "Detention," she said, as if it were a foreign language. Which it kind of was. If it wasn't related to cancer or her lab or grant money, it was an unknown concept. She straightened the papers on her desk and clipped them with a black binder clip, then gave Betsy a sad smile. "What would we do without you?"

TEN

JENNA

Google told her the drive from Elinore would take six and a half hours, but she figured if she pushed it, she could make it in less than six. Singer Creek Nature Preserve. Halcyon Artist Retreat. Two weeks of solitude, a chance to stretch creative muscles that had once been brimming with promise.

It wasn't the first time she'd tried to get away to chase her dreams. Sometimes she wondered what would have happened if her parents had said yes to the artist's residency the summer after her freshman year of college. If they'd believed in her art, trusted that she had something to say through her camera, something she couldn't find a way to say with words, or even a paintbrush or pencil. Could attending that summer program in Seattle have changed her whole life? Set her on a straight path toward creative fulfillment? Toward good decisions, respectable boyfriends, satisfying jobs? Maybe not. But maybe.

Instead, that spring night when she had driven back home to Birmingham from Tuscaloosa to talk to her parents about it, they'd glanced at each other and shared one of those quick looks that meant, "What in the world are we going to do about Jenna?" Part of her thought they might be happy she'd not only found something she was good at but was pursuing it. Pushing for it, asking for it.

"I think it's great," Betsy, who was home from Auburn for the weekend, had said when Jenna explained that the opportunity was offered to only a handful of students in her photography class and she was one of them. It was expensive, but it would offer her a furnished apartment for the summer, daily workshops with professional photographers, and priceless instruction from the famed but elusive Theodore Griffs.

"Photography as a hobby is great—something to do with your extra time." Her mom set her fork down next to her plate. "But it's just not something you can pursue as a regular, dependable job. It's not something that will make you any money."

"Who's talking about money? Maybe she just wants to have fun with it," Betsy said.

"Fun? Fun is taking photography as an elective. Using it as a creative outlet outside your regular classes. Maybe you could even set up a side business taking photos at birthday parties or events. That'd be fun. Going clear across the country to work with a man who looks like a serial killer is not my idea of fun."

Nothing is your idea of fun, Jenna thought. And she regretted her decision to pull up the photographer on Google earlier to show her parents that he was a real, well-known—if a little scary-looking—photographer.

"So you're going to let this guy's looks scare you off? He's a big deal—did you read what it said about him? Spending a summer learning from him could be huge for Jenna. Why can't she go?" Betsy always stuck up for Jenna—it was part of the unspoken code of their sisterhood, as ingrained as their hair or eye color.

"Betsy, it's fine." Jenna wiped her mouth with her napkin and pushed back from the table. "You don't have to—"

"No, wait a minute. Y'all let me go clear across the globe for my semester in England two years ago. This isn't half as far or nearly as expensive. I don't get it."

"That was different. It was—"

"Girls." Their father was known for his silence and calm demeanor, so when he spoke, and with force as he did this time, they listened. "That's enough. Your mother has given her answer." He turned to Jenna. "If you want to pursue your photography on your own, that's fine. Anything in the arts is a worthy endeavor, as far as I'm concerned. But you spending a summer across the country with no supervision is out of the question."

Jenna's cheeks flamed. His voice had been steady, but she heard the emphasis on *you* anyway. It was as clear to her as the roof over her head or the hard chair she sat on—if it had been the other sister asking, the answer would have been different. But she was Jenna, ever dependable if solely as the disappointment. She'd proven that with lackluster grades, unsuitable boyfriends, and questionable after-school activities. Disappearing behind the camera was the only thing she was good at.

She left the dining room but paused unseen in the kitchen when she heard their conversation pick back up.

"I get that I don't have any sway here," Betsy said. "I just think you could give her a shot. She never asks to do anything and this one thing, you won't let her do."

"Jenna asks to do plenty, it's just not often for very smart reasons. We're thinking of her future, Betsy," her dad said. "She needs to concentrate on her grades, not some summer getaway with a bunch of friends in Seattle."

"Dad, I think it's more—"

"Her grades are already hanging by a thin thread," her mom broke in, "and that's without the distraction of this summer fling. She needs to focus, maybe even take some summer classes—*on* campus, *real* courses— and think about what she wants to do with her life." Jenna peeked around the edge of the door just in time to see her mom smooth her hair and brush imaginary crumbs off the front of her blouse. "Anyway, no telling what kind of trouble she'd get into in Seattle, of all places. Isn't that where those grunge people are? She'd probably end up on drugs. Or pregnant."

Jenna pulled back to avoid being seen, her stomach clenched as if her mother's words had been a physical blow.

"Jenna's a little wild, but she's not like that." Jenna heard the exasperation in Betsy's voice. "Why can't this be a way for her to figure out what she wants to do in the future? You let me do it, and it's not even like someone would hire me just because I worked at a marketing firm in England for a semester."

"Maybe not, but it shows that you challenged yourself, that you're determined to succeed, that you value hard work and dedication."

"Really? I think it shows I found the one semester-abroad program that let me combine my major with quaint English pubs and British guys with cute accents."

Dad scoffed. "That's not why you went and you know it."

"Why do you always think it's Jenna who does things for the wrong reason? Why do you automatically expect me to do the right thing? The good thing?"

"That's just the way you are, Betsy." Their mother's voice was maddeningly calm. "It's what you do. Jenna, on the other hand . . ." She cleared her throat.

I what? Jenna screamed in her mind. *What am I?*

Betsy stood, her chair scraping against the floor. "I think you're making a big mistake by not letting her go."

Alone now in her car, driving toward a mysterious destination that promised similar space and time to pursue her art and sharpen her skills, Jenna wondered at the prophetic nature of Betsy's comment. It was sort of true, wasn't it? Her parents' refusal to allow her to go to Seattle almost ten years ago had been the beginning of a downward spiral that dumped her out with two kids, a job filling recycled cardboard cups with fancy coffee, and a handful of abandoned dreams. Part of her wanted to blame it all on her parents, but she was old enough to know that was a weak excuse. She'd made her own choices.

• • •

Instead of the interstate, she stayed on small highways and two-lanes. Signs with happy names like Seaside, Rosemary Beach, and Sunnyside slid past her windows. Panama City, Port St. Joe, and Apalachicola, then national forests and wildlife management areas. Everything green and lush, full of life. As she drove she twisted the bracelet on her wrist until her skin grew sore. The bracelet—purple-and-blue pipe cleaners twisted together—was a gift from Addie the night before.

"Here, Mommy," Addie had said. "You can wear this on your trip."

Jenna slipped it over her hand and onto her wrist. "I'll keep it on the whole time."

"To remind you of me?"

"I don't need something like this to make me think of you. You're in here." She tapped her chest, over her heart.

Addie beamed, then frowned. "Wait. How am I in there if I'm right here?"

Jenna rolled down the windows and inhaled the warm, salty air. When she felt the magnitude of what she was attempting—going fourteen days without seeing her kids, resurrecting a long-dormant passion—she pushed the anxiety back and focused on the road. In her little blue car hurtling east, then south, she smiled as the air through the windows whipped her curls. She rolled up the window and cranked the AC. Freedom, light and elusive, won out over the panic and set her fingers tapping on the steering wheel.

The woman Jenna had spoken to on the phone warned her not to use GPS to get to Halcyon. Those instructions would send her to Chopper's Alligator Farm, the owner of which would not be amused by another misguided artist showing up at his front gate and asking for directions. So when Jenna saw the first sign for Singer Creek Nature Preserve, she took the woman's advice and ignored the blue dot, trusting that the signs would point her to her destination.

She didn't know much more about Halcyon than what she saw on the flyer Max had shoved across the varnished coffee shop counter three months ago. She'd been too afraid to read much about it, to hear about artists who'd left there full of new ideas, determination, purpose. The way she saw it, it was better not to get her hopes up. But now it was happening. The space that had opened up for her felt too good to be real. More than she deserved.

All art begins as a passion, an idea set deep inside the soul of a person, the flyer had read. *Often, all that person needs is space to bring the idea to fruition. Halcyon is this space. It is a refuge to pursue the art that makes you feel alive.*

Not until now did Jenna have a spark of memory about "halcyon." She was probably thirteen or fourteen and had walked into her father's office on the second floor of their house without knocking. He was hunched over his desk, scratching out music notes and drawing new ones on a score. Treble clefs, bass clefs, 3/4 counts.

"What are you working on?" she'd asked.

He glanced over his shoulder, then turned back to

the sheet music before him. "I'm writing a new piece for my summer concert series. It's called 'Halcyon Days.' It's going to be beautiful if I can just figure out this coda . . ." And with that, he retreated again to the space in his mind where no one could reach him. Later, he explained to her the story behind "Halcyon Days." The beautiful widow. The kingfisher. The unusual calm.

When she pulled off the highway at the sign for Singer Creek, her hurriedly scrawled directions told her to drive ten miles south on a thin two-lane road, then turn off onto another road for a few miles. Her directions didn't mention that this road was white sand instead of asphalt and just wide enough for her car. Leafy tendrils and vines encroached along the edges and tall trees lined the road, meeting above to form a canopy that blocked out the last of the daylight.

This must be wrong, she thought. But as she inched forward, just past a sprawling oak with Spanish moss drooping down to brush the top of her car, a driveway opened up. Not even a driveway really, just a blip of space carved out between trees. She pulled in. Down the path, her headlights illuminated a sign hung on a tree, suspended from a scrolled arm of iron and squeaking back and forth in the breeze. *Welcome to Halcyon*.

• • •

"Don't worry," a voice behind her said. "You're in the right place."

It was full dark now, and constellations of stars popped out bright against the heavy sky. Jenna had just climbed the steps to the screened porch on the front of the dining hall where the schedule—if it could even be called that, loose at it was—had told them to meet.

The woman who spoke to her was bent over at the edge of the porch in a triangle pose, legs in a V, one arm reaching down to her blue yoga mat, the other stretched up high. Despite her obvious confidence, her body was at the wrong angle over her lead knee. Jenna was tempted to tell her she needed to realign her torso to get the most benefit from the stretch, but she kept her secret to herself.

"Were you expecting a classroom?" The woman straightened up, stretching her arms over her head.

"No, I . . . Well, I don't know what I expected. Definitely not a campground."

On the walk from her cabin—small, clean, comfortable—to the porch of the dining hall, Jenna had passed a lake ringed by other cabins like hers, each with its own small deck extending over the water. A fire pit was situated at the edge of the lake, and before darkness fell, she spied a couple of small buildings – studios, she presumed—up the hill past the dining hall. Halcyon was like its own little world in the middle of the wild jungle of the nature preserve.

"Good guess," the woman said. "That's exactly what this is. Or was. It used to be a summer camp for children whose parents wanted them to be future environmentalists or something. A group of philanthropists bought it back in the nineties, dumped a bunch of money into it, and invited artists to come play. I'm Casey, by the way." She extended her hand and Jenna took it. "You're

Jenna Sawyer from Nashville, right? Former photographer, now coffee extraordinaire?"

Jenna stared at her, unsure if she was the butt of a joke she wasn't aware of. "How'd you know that?"

"We're selective about who gets in. We have to be. Hundreds apply for each session. We only take ten. And anyway"—she gestured to the camera hanging around Jenna's neck—"you're the only photographer we have this session. I figured you'd be pretty easy to pick out."

Jenna fidgeted with the camera strap that suddenly felt like it was biting into the skin of her neck. "Calling me a photographer is probably a stretch."

"You are. Otherwise you wouldn't be here. The whole point of Halcyon is to reconnect, right? Dive back in. Like I said, you're in the right place, like it or not. Now, if you'll excuse me for a minute . . ." She grinned, then greeted someone else approaching the porch.

"Hundreds apply for each session." Must have been some mighty big strings Max had pulled to get Jenna in. She already felt way out of her league.

Quiet conversation and laughter floated all around her on the porch where a handful of lamps lit the space in a comforting glow. Palm branches pressed against the outside of the screened walls. A ceiling fan whirled above, disrupting cigarette smoke rings and rustling pages of open sketchbooks. A handful of artists had scattered around the room, some seated on deep couches, some on the floor leaning against the porch rails.

Artists all had a certain look, Jenna had always

thought. It didn't matter if they were painters, photographers, writers, whatever. It was something "other"—a little different, a little off-kilter, often out of step with the world around them. She'd had that look at one time, but she figured it'd been swallowed up by life and spit out in some vague, bland form.

She'd just settled on a metal glider when Casey walked to the center of the porch and cleared her throat, halting the hushed talk.

"I hate to break up the camaraderie, but I wanted to go over a few things before everyone goes their separate ways. I'm Casey Malone, one of the mentors here this summer. My drug of choice—that is, my art of choice—is the physical arts: yoga, Pilates, Barre." She put one hand up around her mouth. "And for my own personal plug—I do yoga three times a day—a five-thirty sunrise session, eleven o'clock before lunch, and a six o'clock evening session. Anyone is welcome to join me, but I won't be offended if no one does. End of plug." Everyone laughed and she took a small bow.

"Now, your other mentors are Lane Michaels, oil and acrylic painting. Denise Trimm, creative writing. Yannick Bello, charcoal and pencil drawing." As she said each name, the mentors raised their hands and smiled. "And our last mentor is Gregory Galloway." She looked around, eyebrows raised. "It seems our resident photographer is missing. Big surprise." Nervous laughter rose in the room. "If he shows up, I'll just let him introduce himself." Casey was smiling, but the undercurrent of annoyance wasn't buried deep.

"You may have already figured this out as you've

been chatting, but all of you are here for varying lengths of time, something that sets this retreat apart from others like it. Halcyon exists for eight weeks every summer. Some of you are here for just a couple of weeks and a few of you are staying the entire two months as a sabbatical. Regardless of the length of your own personal retreat, I know I speak for all the mentors when I say we're excited to have you here.

"Unlike most of your real lives, there's not much of a schedule at Halcyon. You're free to do your thing however and whenever you want. The preserve is magnificent and you may find all the inspiration you need right here. However, we're only a few miles from the coast, so if you need more, don't be afraid to venture out.

"We do encourage you to come here to the porch every evening at seven. It's where we discuss our work, what we did or didn't accomplish during the day, or any problems we're having. It's a workshop atmosphere where everyone is respectful and encouraging. We're here to support and offer constructive feedback, and most people find this is the most helpful part of the retreat."

Then she asked everyone to tell their names and what they hoped to get out of the week. Jenna always hated icebreakers like this. They reminded her of the week in college when she lost her mind and thought she might actually want to join a sorority. Five grueling days of prim parties, saccharine conversation, and ridiculous icebreakers where one by one, girls explained through tears how their future happiness depended on having a certain arrangement of Greek letters tied to their name. All except for Jenna, of course. After the second day, she called her mom and told her she'd have to accept having just one daughter follow her footsteps into sorority life. And it wasn't going to be her.

There were no tears in this group, but even still, everyone had a good answer. Most of them had a specific goal for their time at Halcyon—work on a novel, learn how to use a new medium, finish an MFA thesis. As each of the other artists spoke, Jenna thought about Addie and Walsh and what they thought of her. What they'd think of her when they were teenagers, then grown women. How she'd measure up. She thought of how sometimes she wished she'd made different decisions, decisions that had taken her to other places, other lives.

"Jenna?" Casey prompted.

Jenna looked up. It was her turn. She opened her mouth to say something—anything—but then she noticed a man standing at the top of the stairs, just on the other side of the screened door. He hadn't been there a moment ago, and judging by the rest of the faces turned in her direction, she was the only one who saw him.

"Anything?" Casey asked.

"Yeah, I, uh . . ." She glanced back at the door where he still stood. His gaze sliced through her protective layers like a scalpel and made her forget everything. "I'm not sure why I'm here," she finally said.

While a few people in the room smiled, some looked at her with scrunched eyebrows, concern crossing their faces.

"We appreciate the honesty," Casey said. "And I have to say, figuring out *why* you're at Halcyon might be the whole point to your time here." She turned to the rest of the group. "I want each of you to remember, not everyone gets a chance like this. You're the lucky ones, so soak up all you can. The time goes fast."

As she spoke, the man pulled open the screened door and climbed the last step onto the porch. Wearing black jeans, a white T-shirt, and a black leather jacket despite the heat, he looked as out of place as Jenna felt. At the top of the steps, he crossed his arms and leaned against the porch railing.

"Gregory Galloway, everyone," Casey said.

He nodded, arms still crossed. The dull roar outside from cicadas and tree frogs seemed even louder for how quiet the porch was. A single sheet of paper blew off a table and coasted to the floor. No one moved to pick it up.

"So we just wrapped up introductions." Casey spoke into the awkward silence. "Sorry we didn't wait for you, but I'm sure you can catch up with folks later on and get to know everyone."

He nodded again. "I heard what I needed to."

"Care to add anything?"

He took a deep breath. "Actually, I do have one more thing. I didn't hear anyone talk about why we call this place Halcyon. If you don't mind . . ."

Casey held out her hands. "Be my guest." She stepped out of the center of the group and sat on the floor.

Gregory stayed where he was, leaning against the rail with ease. "The name *halcyon* comes from the ancient Greeks. It was their name for a small, brightly colored bird called a kingfisher. Legend tells us that these birds built floating nests on the sea. There on the water, their nests tossed around by winds and waves, the females realized they needed calmer waters for their eggs to have any hope of hatching."

His words were slow and deliberate, as if to make sure everything soaked in. Jenna was lulled by his voice, his presence. The glow from the lamps caught the strong edge of his jawline, making him appear chiseled out of something hard. But his eyes were bright as he looked around the room. Even though she knew the story from her father, she hung on every word.

"So these tiny birds"—he held his thumb and forefinger up a few inches apart—"they charmed the god of the winds, who allowed a period of temporary calm while the babies in the eggs grew and developed. This physical peace and calm, which we now call halcyon, surrounded the nests until the eggs hatched and the babies flew away, able to live and thrive on their own.

"Here at Halcyon, our gift to you is this calm— separation from your life and its chaos and responsibilities—so you can grow and develop as an artist. Your gift to the world is who you become while you're here."

He paused a moment, looked around at the faces peering at him, then crossed the room and pulled open the door into the darkened dining hall.

"That's it, folks," Casey said. "You're on your own. Breakfast is at seven in the morning."

The artists stood and stretched, resuming conversations from earlier and collecting their belongings.

Along with their mentors, they all left the porch, several smiling in Jenna's direction as they passed, but most absorbed in conversation about the work they'd begin tomorrow. Already she felt herself removed from the group, set apart. But she wasn't concerned. She kind of liked it that way.

Alone on the porch, she pushed back with her foot, sending the glider into gentle movement. The cry of a bird, the sound foreign and strange, echoed above the other nighttime noises. She twisted the pipe-cleaner bracelet around her wrist again in soothing circles, the fuzz tickling the delicate skin on the inside of her wrist. Off in the distance, thunder rumbled.

She'd called Betsy earlier before coming to the dining hall. With no reception on her cell, she'd placed a long-distance call on the landline in her cabin.

"They're having a blast," Betsy said when Jenna asked about the girls, partly expecting Betsy to tell her to get in the car and drive back to Elinore. "They spent the day exploring every corner of the house and yard. Maybe tomorrow we can get them into the barn."

"Are you sure y'all are going to be okay?" She hated to think that she'd shoved her kids off on her sister just so she could be alone with her camera. "Maybe if I—"

"Jenna," Betsy broke in. "We're fine. Really. Try to enjoy yourself."

Before they got off the phone, Jenna gave Betsy the address of the retreat and the official phone number. There was a front desk with a landline in the main studio. Surely someone would be around to answer the phone in case of an emergency.

She dug her hand into the pocket of her rain jacket and pulled out her cell to check the time. Eight thirty. With any luck Betsy would already have the girls in bed. Jenna could check in quickly to make sure the evening had gone well. She didn't want to call so much that Betsy would think Jenna didn't trust her, but she was dying to hear whether the girls missed her, whether they'd been scared going to sleep. If Betsy had remembered Addie's stuffed elephant.

But when she swiped her thumb across the screen and scrolled to find Betsy's name, she noticed her phone still wasn't getting any service. She held it up a little higher in the air— the very thing she always made fun of other people for doing—keeping an eye on the screen to see when things kicked back into gear. Nothing.

"Great," she muttered.

Behind her, the door from the dining hall creaked, humidity making it stick as someone on the other side tried to open it. When it finally released, Gregory walked through the doorway, a small bowl of something dark in his hand, and pulled the door closed behind him. He didn't see her.

"Hey," she said.

He turned, his fork halfway to his mouth. "I thought everyone was gone," he said, his face hard.

"I was just trying to make a phone call."

"Don't bother. This metal roof is like a force field. Nothing gets through." He pointed to the ceiling with his fork.

Jenna glanced up. "Is it any better outside?"

He shook his head as he took a bite. "Service is terrible everywhere around here. You can try, but we usually have to drive outside the preserve if we need to make any important calls. For some reason, texts seem to work better. Sometimes."

Jenna watched as he took another bite.

"It's chocolate bread pudding. The good stuff comes out late." He raised his fork in a small wave and headed for the porch door. She smelled cigarette smoke and rich chocolate as he passed her. She surprised herself by speaking, not wanting him to walk out into the night just yet, leaving her alone.

"You left out part of your story earlier."

"Oh yeah?" He stopped with his hand on the door. "What'd I miss?"

"Alkyon," she said, her voice surer than she felt. "The widow who threw herself into the sea when she found out her husband had died in a shipwreck."

He paused a beat before speaking. "Where'd you learn that?"

"The gods turned her into a kingfisher and renamed the bird after her. Somewhere along the line Alkyon was changed to Halcyon."

He watched her for a moment in silence, making her stomach churn. He was older than her—midforties maybe—with bits of gray sprinkled into his dark hair. With a scruffy beard, tan skin, and crow's-feet, he looked like someone who'd lived a good life outside, in sunshine and warm breezes.

"Do you always tell that story to the new people?" she asked.

"Yep. And you're the first to correct me. Or to have any prior knowledge about the legend."

Jenna shrugged. "Just thought you might want to know the rest of the story." Rain began to fall, the drops hitting the metal porch roof like pebbles. He pulled his gaze away from her and peered out into the damp night.

She stood and tugged on her raincoat.

"You going out in this?" he asked.

"It's just water. It won't hurt anything."

He grinned. It was so fast, she'd have missed it if she hadn't been looking. The quick smile cracked the hard edges of his face, softening it and deepening the creases at the edges of his eyes. Then it was gone. He pushed the screened door and held it open. "After you."

At the door, she zipped her raincoat up over her camera and started down the steps. At the bottom she inhaled deeply. The scent of rain mixed with salty air, Spanish moss, and sandy dirt was almost intoxicating.

"*Petrichor*," Gregory said behind her. The rain hitting his jacket made a soft *pat-pat-pat*.

"Excuse me?"

"It's the name of what you're smelling. That scent when rain first starts to fall. It's Greek. The smell of the fluid that flows in the veins of Greek gods."

"You sure do know a lot about Greek mythology." Jenna pulled her hood closer around her face.

"I like figuring people out. Even better if they're not around to tell me I'm wrong." He kept his gaze on her, making her shuffle her feet and readjust her camera strap.

"So I guess you're my mentor."

"It would appear so."

"I'm not so hard to figure out. Not much to analyze."

He cocked his head. "We'll see." He regarded her a moment longer, then shoved his hands in his pockets. "You know where you're going?" He tipped his head to the dark expanse in front of her.

She looked toward the general direction of the cabins. At least she thought it was the right direction. She was turned around now that everything was inky dark except for the porch above. Everyone else had disappeared. "No idea."

He took a few steps and stood next to her. "The cabins are down there." He pointed through the trees to a faint glow. "Follow this path, two hundred yards that way. And watch out for deer. They like to come out when it rains." He turned and headed up the path away from the porch in the opposite direction. "I'm sure I'll see you around."

"Thanks," Jenna called.

He didn't answer.

She started down the sandy trail. The rain was still light, making a chorus of drips and drops on the branches around her. She reached up and pushed her hood back, letting the warm rain hit her face and hair, and followed the glow through the trees.

ELEVEN

BETSY

Betsy was in the kitchen cleaning up from the girls' dinner when Ty came in that evening, a little earlier than usual. The girls were upstairs in the empty room playing with My Little Ponys. He kicked his boots off on the porch, then crossed the kitchen to kiss her cheek. "How'd the afternoon go?" He reached into the fridge for the pitcher of tea.

"Good, I think." She wiped the last of the spaghetti sauce from the table. "They explored the house, I took them to see the hens, then Anna Beth brought by some toys, thank goodness. They brought a couple things with them, but I don't have much here for them to play with."

"They don't need much, right? We live on a farm. There's plenty for them to do outside."

"I guess so. That's what I'm hoping anyway."

Ty drained his glass and nodded. "They'll be fine. The hens and cows should keep them occupied. Just make sure to keep them out of the way during milkings. Don't want anyone to be trampled." He set his glass in the kitchen sink. "I need a shower."

"I'll walk up with you. I closed the other doors upstairs, but Walsh seems to be pretty industrious. I found her standing on the counter in the bathroom earlier, eating toothpaste."

Ty laughed and rubbed his hand over his face. "This is going to be interesting."

Upstairs, he poked his head in the girls' room. Addie was still busy with the ponies, making them "talk" to each other. Something about a parade and wearing crowns and high heels. Walsh was lying across both pillows at the top of the bed, already fast asleep, her dark hair covering half her face.

"The little one's wiped out," Ty whispered. He backed away from the door and headed for their bedroom.

"You don't want to say good night to Addie?" Betsy whispered.

He shook his head. "I'll catch her tomorrow." He crossed into their room and closed the door behind him.

Part of her wanted to follow him in there, protected behind the closed door, but she turned back to the girls. "Let's get you kiddos ready for bed."

"Can I sleep with the ponies?" Addie asked quietly.

"Sure. We can tuck them in right next to you and Walsh."

"Are we both sleeping in this?" She gestured to the double bed.

Betsy nodded. "Is that okay? I don't have two beds for you."

Addie scratched her chin and looked at Walsh. "I think that's a good idea."

Betsy picked up a limp Walsh and carried her into the bathroom with Addie close on her heels. Addie showed Betsy where she'd lined up their toothbrushes on the bathroom counter, then reminded her that they both had to use the potty before bed. Betsy brushed Walsh's teeth as well as she could, then helped her sit on the toilet. The child barely woke up, her head drooping to one side, her thumb lodged in her mouth.

Back in the bedroom, Betsy folded down the blanket and laid Walsh on one side of the bed. Addie climbed up into the other. She nestled down in the bed and pulled the blanket up to her shoulders, her stuffed elephant under her chin.

"Are you going to be okay in here?" Betsy asked. At this point, she was fairly certain a hurricane wouldn't wake Walsh, but Addie seemed almost too calm. "It must feel strange not to be in your own bed. If you need me, I'll be right downstairs."

"Where do you sleep?" Addie asked.

"In that room right across the hall." She pointed to her closed bedroom door.

Addie nodded and turned onto her side, facing Walsh. When she closed her eyes, Betsy stood, not sure of the right thing to do. She turned off the lamp next to the bed.

"Don't worry," Addie said in the dark. "I'll take care of Walsh."

Betsy stood in the doorway a moment before she pulled the door closed behind her. Then she opened it back up a couple of inches. Wouldn't hurt to let in a little light.

. . .

Betsy and Ty waited until they were in bed before they talked about the day. It was always like that—they might spend two hours together downstairs, looking for something to watch on TV or sitting on the back porch, but if they had something important to discuss, their unwritten rule was to wait until they were in bed before bringing it up. It was as if the darkness softened the hard edges, blurring any anger, frustration, or annoyance until it was easier to manage, easier to pull out into the open.

Betsy slipped between the cool sheets while Ty was still in the bathroom. The lights were off, but the moon was bright, and it filtered through the windows, the curtains casting thin shadows across the floor and bed.

"So, we're parents for the next two weeks," Ty said as he climbed into bed. "I always thought we'd be here, but not like this." He stretched and yawned. "How are we supposed to know what to do? What if one of them gets sick? Or baths—how does that work?"

"We'll figure it out. I do know a little bit about kids." She smiled. "And you probably know more than you think."

"I doubt that. My only experience with kids was the one time I babysat a neighbor's nephew while she went to work. The kid jumped out his bedroom window and ran to a friend's house four streets away while he was supposed to be napping."

"You never told me that story."

"Why would I? Doesn't sound too good, having a kid escape on my watch."

Shadows darted and danced across the ceiling as the fan swirled. Ty shifted his leg so it pressed against Betsy's. She could feel his gaze on her cheek, but she didn't turn her head.

"Maybe this is our chance to see if we have what it takes to be parents." She gave a little laugh, but her throat felt funny. Too tight.

Ty rolled up onto his elbow, his face above hers. "I have no doubt—not even a hint of a doubt—that we have what it takes to be parents. We have buckets of it. Acres of it." He kissed her, then lay back again. "Anyway, the thing about having kids is that they usually start out as babies. It'll be a different ball game practicing with two kids raised by a single mother who works all the time. No telling what life is like for those three."

Betsy rolled to her side and punched her pillow into shape beneath her cheek. She thought of Addie and her fierce protection of her little sister. "The girls are fine."

. . .

Sometime during the night, Betsy awoke to an unfamiliar sniffling, then a small moan. It was quiet, muffled, but it was enough to bring her out of a dead sleep. She sat up in bed, flung the sheets away, and patted the bed until she found Ty's arm.

"Ty? Ty! Someone's—"

Then she remembered. They weren't alone in the house.

"Which one is it?" he mumbled.

"Go back to sleep. I'll check."

She tiptoed across the hall, her eyes adjusting to the darkness. Walsh's side of the bed was still and quiet, but as Betsy stood watching, unsure of what to do, another sniffle came from Addie's side. She knelt next to the bed and patted the small lump under the covers until she reached Addie's face, her damp cheeks. "Addie? What's wrong, honey?"

"I had a bad dream. A scary one."

"There's nothing to be scared of," she said, cringing as the words left her mouth. She had terrible night terrors as a child—much later than most kids had them. She still had them at nine, ten years old, old enough to remember the sheer terror and fear that accompanied those awful nights. Her parents always told her there was nothing to be scared of and that she should just go back to sleep, the worst words they could have said.

She tried again. "Tell me what scared you."

"It was Mommy. She was leaving. She was driving away in a big school bus."

"That must have been sad. But you know what? Your mommy isn't in a big school bus, and she's coming back very soon."

"And she'll bring me a treat?"

"That's what she said, isn't it? I bet she'll find you something wonderful."

Addie nodded, sniffled again. "Could you sleep with me? Just for a little bit?"

"I don't know if I—"

"Please? I'll be quiet and I won't move a muscle."

Betsy smiled in spite of herself. "Okay. But just for a little bit."

Addie scooted toward Walsh, leaving a space of about eight inches for Betsy to squeeze into. Betsy scooped the parade of My Little Ponys onto the floor, then stretched her legs out and pulled her grandmother's blanket up over herself. When she settled, the girls' scents filled her senses. Was it possible to get light-headed over the smell of sleeping children? She inhaled. It was sleep, a little sweat, lingering cinnamon from the snickerdoodles she'd given the girls after dinner, and something else she couldn't quite name.

Addie had been still a couple of minutes, not moving a muscle, just like she said, when Walsh grunted in her sleep and flopped over, one arm flinging against Addie. Addie giggled, then stopped. "Sorry."

"It's okay," Betsy whispered. "Did that hurt?"

"No. She does it all the time," Addie whispered back.

"Do you and Walsh sleep together at home?" Betsy remembered the girls being in separate bedrooms last summer.

"Sometimes. When Mommy has to work late, Walsh usually comes into my room after the babysitter puts her to bed."

"You take good care of Walsh, don't you?"

"I do."

She couldn't see Addie's face, but she could almost hear the smile.

• • •

Betsy woke to Ty standing over her next to the bed. "Are you okay in here?" he whispered.

She tried to sit up, but Addie's arm had pinned her in place. In her sleep Addie had curled up next to Betsy's side. Walsh lay partially on top of Addie, her plump arm draped across her sister and onto Betsy's right shoulder. All three of them filled half of the double bed; the other half was empty.

"You're like a magnet," Ty whispered, grinning. "Look at them. They can't get close enough to you."

In the midst of that tangle of warm skin and sleepy breaths, dreams she'd packed away into a tiny space in her heart flooded back. She lifted Addie's arm and slithered out from underneath it inch by inch.

"You don't have to get up," Ty whispered as Betsy tried to free herself without disturbing the girls' sleep. "I just got up to go to the bathroom and saw you weren't in bed."

"It's okay. I can't . . ."

Addie whimpered as Betsy pulled herself free. "Aunt Betsy, please don't go."

"It's okay," Betsy whispered. "Uncle Ty is going to lie down with you for a few minutes." She turned to Ty. "Please stay with her."

She was already out in the hallway when Ty caught up to her. "Wait, where are you going?"

"Addie had a bad dream and needs someone to lie with her. Just please do it for me."

She closed her bedroom door and leaned against it, relishing the stillness of the air, the empty bed, the familiar, unchildlike scents of her space. She stretched out in bed—her side cool, Ty's side still warm—and put a hand over her thumping heart.

It's just two weeks.

Then guilt, like a heavy tide of truth, washed over her, soaking her spirit and her soul. It didn't tell her anything original. It just confirmed what she already knew: she'd make a terrible mother. Her own mother had been distant and distracted—how could Betsy possibly hope to make a good one?

The truth that had come to her inch by inch over the last two years now blazed with certainty. If Betsy had kids, she'd mess them up in a million small ways, and if God had a hand in it, and she figured He probably did, then He was doing the only natural thing a father would do—protect those kids. Protect them from her. It was the only thing that made sense.

TWELVE

Ty

Ty's internal alarm clock buzzed at four thirty as usual, even though he was still in Addie and Walsh's bed, nudged to the very edge by Addie's poky backbone. He pushed himself up on his elbow. Walsh was curled up next to her sister, both their faces relaxed in easy slumber.

He was used to sharing a bed, but not like this. Betsy and Ty often lay in bed together, legs and arms entwined, but when the light went out, they pulled apart, no skin touching. It had always been like that—no offense meant or taken, just two people who wanted to sleep free and undisturbed. These two girls knew nothing about that. For hours, they'd either slept on top of him, hung arms over his head, kneed him in the stomach, or dug toes into his legs. They were completely and blissfully unaware.

He crept into his bedroom, brushed his teeth in the dark, and pulled on blue jeans and a clean shirt. He grabbed socks and his belt and tiptoed to the door, the taste of coffee already on his tongue.

"Babe?" Betsy's whisper floated to him from the bed.

He turned and crept back to the bed. "Sorry. I tried to be quiet." She shifted and he sat on the edge of the mattress. Her sleepy warmth curled around him, poured into his bones. "You okay?"

"I'm good." She yawned. "Have you heard anything from the girls yet?"

"Not a peep. I just left their room and they didn't even move when I got up."

"You stayed the rest of the night?"

He nodded. "They had me in a vise grip."

She smiled and let out a small laugh, just a puff of air, really. But it was something.

"Were you okay last night? With the girls?"

"Yeah," she said with a shrug. "I was fine. Why?"

"You just seemed a little edgy."

"It was nothing," she said, as he knew she would. But then she inhaled and paused, as if thinking of the right words. She bit her bottom lip.

"What is it?" *Steady, Ty.*

She shook her head. "I think I'll make pancakes for breakfast. Think they'd like that?"

He hesitated, watched her face for . . . for what? It wasn't like she was depressed. Or angry. Or volatile. She was his Betsy. His sensitive, funny, private, and beautiful wife. What would he even be looking for?

He smiled. "They'll love it."

. . .

When Ty pulled open the barn gate, he was sixteen minutes late to the morning milking. The first round of forty were already in place in line, their udders plugged into the machines, the soft *whoosh* of milk filling the pumps and flowing into metal tanks. Such a beautiful sound, the sound of milk and money.

He walked through the line, checking tubes and attachments, pleased to find Walker had done a better job than usual. Maybe he was finally learning something.

"Wild night, Mr. Franklin?" Walker pushed the wide broom near Ty's feet.

"Watch yourself, kid." Carlos straightened up from underneath number 039. "That's your boss you're talking to."

"Right, I'm sorry. I didn't mean anything by it," Walker sputtered, his cheeks pink and awkward. He backed away and took the broom to the other side of the barn.

"But seriously," Carlos said. "You're never late. How wild was it?"

"As if I'd tell you anyway."

"Come on, man! Throw a boy a bone here."

Ty shook his head. "You need to take that up with Gloria." He reached over and adjusted a milk line, then ran his hand down the bristly back of lucky number 040.

"I'm in the doghouse." Carlos sat on a stool and pulled off his boot. Dumped it upside down and two pebbles fell out. He kicked them to the door of the barn. "I missed our anniversary a few days ago. She let me get all the way until ten o'clock that night before saying anything about it. Just kept her anger pent up all day. It's a wonder that woman doesn't implode with all the things she doesn't tell me."

Ty patted 040 once more, then strode to the back office to make a note to call the vet about a possible bruise on her hoof. He kicked at Carlos's foot as he passed by. "You need to take care of that, my friend. I heard Ollie's Meat-and-Three is having a buy-one-get-one-free night. Maybe you should take Gloria out for an apology dinner."

Carlos was still laughing when Ty reached the privacy of his office. He grabbed a notebook and pencil off the desk and sat on the couch, but he didn't open the notebook. Carlos's words had cut a little close. "Woman troubles," is what Carlos would call it, which was why Ty rarely confided anything real to him. His marriage, his life with Betsy, seemed too private, too covered in nerve endings to even talk about. But the idea of imploding under the pressure of things left unsaid—that touched something raw in him.

He'd had a girlfriend named Summer his first year at Auburn. It was the perfect name for her. She was perky and pink, with a light splatter of freckles across her nose. Always happy. If he did something nice for her—brought her a bunch of daisies he'd bought at Toomer's Drugs or waited for her after one of her classes in the Haley Center—she'd grin bigger than the moon, wrap her arms around him, and kiss him, front and center, unafraid of anything or anyone watching. If something got under her skin, she'd talk to him about it, work out the issue, then leave it behind. She wasn't the type to say, "Fine," when she meant anything but.

In the end they broke up but remained friendly, because things with her could never be anything but friendly, and he'd breathed a sigh of relief. It wasn't that he wanted someone dark or angry or hard to read, but something about Summer's open-faced honesty and the easy way she talked about her feelings and desires made him feel less like a man than he was comfortable with.

Ty heard the clang of number 026 kicking at the machine. She always got antsy at the end of her milking, ready to be released to the field.

"Time's up, Boss," Carlos called. Ty scratched out the note to call the vet and tossed the notebook back on his desk.

Out in the barn Carlos was halfway through unhooking the cows from the machines. Ty started at the far end of the line, releasing udders and dabbing on a thin coat of Bag Balm to prevent irritation.

When they finished the line, the cows shuffled into the field to graze for their breakfast. Walker opened the gate to allow the next forty into the milking parlor, then he, Carlos, and Ty went through the line, dipping the udders into antiseptic, hooking them into the milking machines, and checking each cow for potential problems.

While they waited the few minutes it took to milk the group, Carlos poured a cup from the Mr. Coffee sitting on top of a plastic barrel and leaned against the wall next to Ty. "So, Ollie's. Think that'd work?"

Ty glanced sideways at Carlos, judging his seriousness. "Man, no. Don't take her there. I was kidding."

"Why? They have a great catfish plate."

"Sure they do. But do you really want to take Gloria to a backwoods diner for an anniversary dinner? When you're already trying to climb out of a hole?" Ty shook his head.

"Well, what do you suggest, Mr. Romance? There's not much else around here."

"We're twenty miles from beachside dining at sunset. Start there."

Carlos gulped his coffee and grunted. "This stuff is terrible." He tossed the half-empty cup into the trash barrel, but it bounced and sent coffee up the wall. He muttered a string of obscenities under his breath and grabbed a rag to wipe down the wall. "You been married, what, ten years?"

"Eight." Ty leaned over and felt number 080's udder. Just another minute or so to go.

"I've been married fif—sixteen years. How'd you get so smart about women?"

"Good luck, I guess."

"Nah. You probably just give Betsy whatever she wants." When Ty didn't correct him, Carlos chuckled. "So, what Betsy wants, she gets. I see who wears the pants around here."

Ty looked at his friend. "You're an idiot." He grabbed the damp rag and wiped some coffee Carlos had missed.

When the second group of forty was done, they began the process over again and Ty took a knee next to number 096. Smack in the middle of the line. He knew it'd get Carlos all messed up—he liked to go through the line in order—but Ty didn't care. Number 096 was Rosie, and Rosie was special.

As he cleaned her and hooked her up, he thought back to his junior year at Auburn when he first saw Betsy. She jogged by the ag field every day in her little running shorts and tank tops, her hair bouncing. Even from the barn, he could hear her friend's constant chatter, but Betsy was usually quiet, her eyes glued to him. He could feel her gaze without even turning his head. It sank into his shoulders, the back of his neck.

When they started to see each other officially—no longer separated by a wood and metal cattle fence—he discovered that different was good. While she wasn't the exact opposite of his old girlfriend Summer—she wasn't gloomy or irritable or depressed—she wasn't a spoonful of sugar either. When she'd get worked up about something, she'd occasionally vent to him about it. She'd rant and rave and he'd watch, pleased to see a real woman let herself feel her anger. But most times she'd clam up, and he had to use superhuman powers to decipher her mood.

That generous dose of mystery, the unknown depths, made him feel like a man. Like it was his job to spend his days plumbing those depths, deciphering her particular brand of hieroglyphics.

He'd still choose her now. Of course he would. Even if he suspected that, as with Carlos's wife, there were volumes of words Betsy was leaving unsaid.

THIRTEEN

JENNA

Though Halcyon focused on freedom and a lack of structure, Jenna slipped into a routine in her first couple of days. Breakfast, camera, woods. No yoga. Then the same thing after lunch. And she did it all alone. Some of the other artists teamed up and worked together—painting, drawing, building—but the thought of forced politeness, of awkward camaraderie, of other people asking her opinion and waiting for her deep, philosophical answers made her squirm with discomfort. No thanks.

She did, however, wish she had a little more mentor input. Other artists meandered around the preserve with their mentors deep in conversation or with their heads together, looking over the day's work. With her mentor mostly MIA, she couldn't help feeling left out.

It was late afternoon on the third day. She'd called Betsy that morning from the cabin so she wouldn't have to worry about the call dropping. When she'd again apologized for the retreat, for the kids, for her and Ty's messed-up plans, Betsy had come close to scolding her.

"Jenna, you're there. You made the decision and you need to stick with it. It'll all be wasted if you don't actually *do* something while you're there." Funny that she echoed the exact words running through Jenna's mind. "Let it go. We are fine. The girls are completely fine. Don't worry about us. Just . . . go do your thing. We'll all be here when you finish up."

Jenna had exhaled, long and deep. Betsy was right. She'd made the decision, and she needed to trust her sister—and her own choices. Right or wrong, she needed to stick by them. She thought of Delores's words about airplane oxygen masks the night she found out she'd gotten into Halcyon: *"Sometimes you have to take care of yourself so you can take care of your kids."*

Buck up. Do what you came to do.

With the reassurance that her children were well taken care of, she longed to sink back into her creativity, to find it waiting for her, ready for her eye and fingers and steady breathing, but every single photo she'd managed to take was worthless. She couldn't put her finger on it, but something was off in all of them. There was no focus, no purpose.

Before kids, her photography focus had usually been people. Bodies at rest, bodies in motion. When she picked up her camera after having Addie and Walsh—on her excursions with Max to the Botanical Gardens or Centennial Park, or just playing with the kids in the front yard—she tried to broaden her focus into the natural world, but her favorite subjects were always people and their expressions. Desires and fears splashed across their faces.

At Halcyon, alone for the first time in she didn't know how long, she had no idea where to start. Trees, moss, sand. Murky ponds, skittery birds, strange animals—was that what she was supposed to be capturing? That's all there was out in this "pristine and protected" nature preserve, as the flyer had said. That and heat.

Her phone, tucked into her camera bag, had buzzed with a text message earlier in the day. She'd brought it with her in case of an emergency—either hers or Betsy's—but the service on it had been next to nothing every time she checked it. The buzz—the first non-nature sound she'd heard since leaving the dining hall after breakfast—startled her. She unzipped the bag and checked her phone, thinking of everyone it might be— Betsy, Max, maybe even Delores checking in on her. But she didn't recognize the number.

> Missed you this morning. The guy behind the counter— the really chatty one—told me you'd skipped off to the beach. Lucky girl. He gave me your cell number. Hope it's okay I used it. Also hope you're having fun and relaxing. You deserve it. Sam

She thought of Sam arriving that morning at Full Cup, searching the line for her as he always did. The tall black coffee he probably ordered for her before Mario gave him the news that she wouldn't be joining him for their nondate.

It wasn't like she'd had any way to let him know she hadn't just "skipped off to the beach," as Mario put it. They hadn't exchanged phone numbers, their only contact being the ten minutes a day when she could partially let her guard down. Even with Sam though, she never could let it down all the way. She hadn't wanted to hurry his inevitable realization that she was too much, too risky, too . . . something.

She tried to send a text back—Thanks for checking in. Not having too much fun yet, but better than making drinks for Mrs. Rich.—but service had dropped back to zilch. It was probably part of the master plan of Halcyon: get a bunch of artists out in the middle of nowhere, cut off their lines to the outside world, and see what happened. So far for Jenna, what had happened was a whole lot of nothing.

Occasionally, she held her camera out and scrolled through the images. Halcyon provided a large-format Epson printer, and she had the option to print any images she wanted and discuss them with the group during the evening workshop. So far she'd avoided that, not ready for complete strangers to talk about her work like they could better explain what she was trying to say with it. And what was it with everyone here going on and on about what they were trying to *say* with their work?

Why do I care? She knelt to the ground, one knee pressing into wet dirt and soaking her jeans. *It's their art. Who am I to do anything but appreciate it?* At least they were making progress. She, on the other hand, was at least half a mile away from the retreat center, alone except for two hawks circling above and huge fox squirrels rustling in the trees. The beauty around her was so new, so savage and raw, but she couldn't capture it in a way that felt real. She was spinning her wheels, missing her girls, and waiting for inspiration to strike. And sweating.

Enough. She zipped her camera into its bag and headed back for dinner.

. . .

The dining hall was abuzz with chatter when she entered. Artists and mentors mixed together at tables in the long room and the screened porch at the front. By now she was used to not having her own mentor at her elbow like the others. It was fine. Everyone already had food on trays, so Jenna hurried to the buffet tables at the back and picked up a tray, filling a plate with grilled shrimp, wild rice, roasted asparagus, and salad. At the end of the line was a platter of brownies. It wasn't chocolate bread pudding, but it would work.

Standing alone with a tray of food and a glass of iced tea in her hand, she felt like she was in high school all over again. All the cool kids were already seated at tables, talking, smiles on their faces. She found an empty spot at the end of a table and set down her tray. Before she could even sit, Casey appeared before her. Clad in different but equally as strappy and trendy yoga gear, she sat on the bench across from Jenna. "How are things going for you?"

"Good, they're good." Jenna arranged her food and drink and sat. "I mean, I'm still trying to find my footing, I guess." She took a sip of tea.

Casey nodded. "I totally get it. It can take a little while to get used to the quiet and lack of distractions.

We're so wired for noise and activity that when life does slow down, we can feel a bit . . . disoriented. Does that sound about right?"

Jenna had paused with her glass in her hand. "Sure. Yeah. That's it."

"Mm-hmm," Casey murmured, her chin in her hand, then sat up a little straighter. "I've noticed you haven't said much in the workshops at night. We'd love to hear how you're feeling, what you've learned so far. You may think it's nothing, but even small steps are forward progress, you know?" She squinted and nodded, a perfect combination of pretension and encouragement on her face. Jenna wondered if she practiced that look in the mirror.

Just over Casey's right shoulder, Jenna saw Gregory at a table with Yannick, the mentor she had seen hunched over a large sketch pad and a box of charcoals in various parts of the preserve. They were deep in conversation, but as Jenna watched, Gregory glanced her way. He paused for a brief moment, then turned his attention back to Yannick.

"Right, I know." Jenna fiddled with her napkin. "I may. It's just . . . Sometimes things make more sense in my head without me trying to mess it all up with words. Does that make sense?"

"Sure, absolutely. Just remember, we're all in the same boat here. We're all trying to connect to the passion, to that internal drive." She stood and adjusted her slim black tank. "I look forward to hearing your insights whenever you're ready."

Then she glided away, her footsteps quiet and

graceful. Jenna had met people like Casey before, back in Wyoming when she taught yoga at the colony, commune, whatever Betsy had called it. It was a place for creative, enlightened people to feel at home. They preached all the same things—connect to your passion, find your inner light, blah blah blah. While she'd loved being there—far from her family's disapproval and lack of understanding—she always felt like she was standing on the rim of something deep, peering over the edge but unable to jump in like everyone else. Even as she taught yoga and heard herself say the words that went along with it, she felt removed, set apart from the hive mind. She only jumped in deep when she was alone with her camera.

After dinner, everyone gathered on the porch with their work of the day. Canvases, notebooks, sketch books, and laptops filled the space not occupied by artists and their mugs of tea or glasses of wine. She found a seat close to the door, comforted by the nearby escape route. As everyone pulled out their work, Jenna stared down at her camera. She wanted to be assured by its presence, this little black box that served as her ticket to spend a couple weeks away with these people, these true artists, when she felt like a fake.

Max had said she had rare, untaught talent. Put the girl in the wild, he must have thought, and she'll blossom into the photographer, the artist, she's meant to be. But instead, the camera had done nothing but block her out. Fend off her attempts to create something worthy, as if her fingers on its buttons and dials were clumsy blocks of wood.

They went around in a circle, each person speaking of his or her experience of the day, how it shaped the art they put before the group. As a woman a few feet away from her wiped away tears, explaining how she had broken through her month-long writer's block and cranked out fifty pages of her Great American Novel, Jenna stood and opened the screened door a few inches, just enough to squeeze through but not enough to make it creak. After closing it behind her, she exhaled and descended into the comforting dark.

The night air was thick, saturated with scents of pine needles and damp earth. By now Jenna could make her way through the dark to the cabins. She'd left the lamp on in her own cabin, and as she trudged down the path, the glow from her front window drew her like a magnet.

She'd said to Casey on the first night that Halcyon seemed like a campground, and she wasn't too far off in that initial estimation. Everything was built from logs and thick planks of wood, but the buildings were somehow sleek too, as if the place had been built for discerning adults as well as kids. The cabin—hers, at least—was small and tidy, outfitted in smooth, fragrant cypress and cedar. Downstairs was a mini-kitchen and bathroom, while the loft upstairs contained a twin bed, comfortable side chair, and small dresser. Just the basics, but all she really needed.

Inside, she set her camera on the tiny kitchen counter. What she wanted to do was take it outside and throw it into the lake. Instead, she climbed the ladder to the bedroom and lay down across the bed's patchwork quilt. Having just been here a handful of days, she was surprised by how at home she felt in the small space. She could stay here a while, holed up in the woods, leaving only for food and dips into the lake. But her camera, sitting alone on the counter downstairs, would beckon. It wouldn't leave her alone for long, that much she knew.

She exhaled and willed the tension to leak out of her shoulders and neck. She held her hand up and prodded the space between her thumb and forefinger where a sandspur had pricked her earlier in the day. It was still sore, the prick a tiny red dot on her skin.

She turned her hands this way and that in the dim light. Small palms, short fingers. She had her mother's hands. Even her fingernails were shaped the same— thin ovals with deep crescents. How she knew that, she wasn't sure. It wasn't like she and her mom had ever bonded over manicures. They hadn't bonded over anything.

Jenna pressed her fingertips to her forehead, remembering how the phone call six years ago had come so out of the blue. She'd only spoken to her mother a handful of times since she'd left Tuscaloosa and moved away, first to Wyoming, then to Asheville, North Carolina. Each time they spoke it was clear they didn't agree on what Jenna should be doing with her life. That morning though, it was Betsy on the phone, relaying bits of information in staccato bites. Their mom, the totaled car off the edge of Highway 31, the sheet of stationery on her desk at home with the meager beginnings of a letter. *Dear Jenna, I wish . . .*

Jenna pointed and flexed her toes, then pointed them again to stretch her legs as far as they'd go. She had the letter. Not with her now, but it lived in the bottom drawer of her bedside table at home. She hadn't looked at it again since the day her dad said she should keep it, but those four words were imprinted on her brain.

She pulled off her shoes and dropped them to the floor with a satisfying *plunk*. Sometimes she liked to imagine what the rest of the note from her mom would have said, had she taken the time to finish it before she left for work that day. Before she lost control of her car when another driver crossed the median into her lane.

Dear Jenna, I wish things between us had been different.

Dear Jenna, I wish I could tell you how much I love you.

Dear Jenna, I wish you knew how extraordinary you are.

But Jenna was a realist, not that kind of dreamer. More likely it was along the lines of *Dear Jenna, I wish you were more like your sister.*

FOURTEEN

BETSY

After that first day, when she ended the evening in bed, emotionally depleted and physically spent, Betsy roused her sea legs. Up before the girls in the mornings, she made breakfast, helped them get dressed, and took them outside. Inside the house, their sweet routines and innocent sleepy movements pulled at her loose threads, threatening to unravel all her determination. Outside was easier. Fresh air, space to breathe.

Walsh loved the hens and eggs the best, having overcome her initial fear of the shadowed henhouse, but Addie loved tending to the cows. With Ty's supervision she'd choose one and brush her with the stiff-bristled brushes he kept in a wooden box by the barn door. After a thorough brushing, Addie fed her as many apple cores, banana peels, and chunks of stale bread as she could before Ty caught on.

"Why can't I give them treats?" Addie asked one day after Ty gently pried the bag of bread from her hands.

"Treats make everyone happy, even cows. You should know that, Uncle Ty. You're a cow farmer."

Ty glanced up at Betsy and bit back a laugh. "Yes, I am. And you're right, they do like treats. But we can't spoil them. They'll get sick like kids who eat too much candy." He patted the cow on the rump and steered Addie out of the barn.

Both girls loved to run through the fields, darting between the silent cows chewing grass and clover. When they tired of running and dodging steaming patties, Carlos or one of the other guys would hoist them up onto a tractor and take them for a short ride. Addie laughed every time she caught sight of the honey wagon out in the fields. Ty had painted a huge bee on its side in white and black paint, leading Addie to think the long, tube-shaped container was full of honey.

Addie stopped laughing when she realized what it actually carried, even more so when she learned that what was inside the honey wagon went straight back into the fields, helping to grow the grass and grain that fed the cows. Ty tried to explain the importance of the cycle of nutrition, but she wrinkled her nose and gave the honey wagon a wide berth.

. . .

Jenna finally called again on Wednesday, just as Betsy was wiping the girls' faces with a damp washcloth and getting them into pajamas. Betsy gave the phone to Addie so she could say good night, but the call dropped just after Addie said hello.

"Mommy, I'm here, I'm here," Addie repeated, pressing the phone tighter to her ear and shouting.

Betsy pried the phone out of her hands and tried calling Jenna back. It went straight to voice mail. Addie stormed off and threw herself onto the bed, a rare flash of anger. Walsh's eyes grew big and her bottom lip trembled. Jenna texted later and said cell service was spotty and that she'd try again when she could. Betsy tried to explain about phone coverage and dropped calls, but both girls went to bed with tears in their eyes.

The next night Jenna called again, but it was after nine o'clock. The girls had been in bed for almost two hours.

"Sorry to call so late," Jenna said. "I've had no service bars on my phone all day. This is the first time the call has gone through."

"It's okay. I wish you'd been able to call earlier though. The girls are dying to talk to you. I'd get them up, but . . ."

"No, no, don't worry about it. I'll call again soon. They're doing okay?"

"They miss you, of course, but they seem to be pretty happy. What about you? Have you been able to take a lot of pictures?"

Jenna paused before speaking. "Yeah, I have. I'm out all day with my camera, and there's plenty of time for whatever I want to do. The schedule is super loose. And it's beautiful here. Palm trees, Spanish moss, ponds with tree frogs and geckos. Everything is lush and overgrown."

"That sounds beautiful." Betsy pulled back the quilt

on her bed and climbed in. Ty was still downstairs catching the last few minutes of a Braves game.

"Yeah . . . ," she began. Then she was quiet for a moment.

"Everything okay?"

"I've just been thinking about Mom a little. Do you remember when we used to drag our blankets under your bed and hide?"

Betsy smiled. "Sure. That's where we kept our stash of chocolate pudding cups."

"That's right. Mom never understood why they disappeared so fast. I guess she never noticed the empty containers in your garbage can. You used to tell me stories of what it would be like to be a grown-up, all the jobs we could have. Whatever we wanted to be. You were going to work at Prescott Branding. Do you remember that? All those summer internships practically guaranteed you a job there."

Betsy stretched her legs under the sheet. "Oh, I remember." Her onetime goal of being an account exec at Birmingham's top ad agency seemed like a lifetime ago. "You always wanted to be an actress and a vet and a photographer."

"And you told me I could do it if that's what I wanted."

"Yep. It's probably the same thing you tell Addie and Walsh. That they can be whatever they want to be."

"That's what we tell them, but . . . we can't just *be* anything, you know? Sometimes it just doesn't work out. I mean, look at you. You were supposed to be cranking out genius ad campaigns for big companies, but instead you married a farmer and live with a bunch of cows. No offense, it's just not what you planned way back when." Jenna took a breath. "All that time, we thought we really could just go and do and be and things would fall into place, but it doesn't always happen that way."

Betsy stilled her legs. She could have said a million things about what had and hadn't worked out in her own life, but she focused on her sister instead. "What's going on with you, Jenna?"

"Nothing. Just that . . . we can't always get what we want." She paused. "Sorry, that's stupid. And I've always hated that song."

"What do you want that you're not getting?" Even as she said the words, she imagined a long, winding list of things Jenna probably wanted. Or maybe Betsy was just thinking of her own list, the one that swirled around her head, out the window, and up into the still night air.

"I just . . . I wonder if maybe coming here was a bad idea. I've already given up my photography. Why try to force it to work again?" She paused, then her next words were soft. "What do you think Mom would say about me being here?"

Betsy closed her eyes and spoke carefully. "I think she would be glad you're pursuing something you feel passionate about."

"Really? That's what I was trying to do with Wyoming. And even before that with the program in Seattle. What makes you think she'd feel any different this time?" Jenna laughed, small and tired. "She said

I'd either end up on drugs or pregnant. She always did have such high hopes for me."

"Oh, Jenna, she didn't mean . . ." But she stopped. That had been one of the things about their mother that sometimes hurt the most—she always said exactly what she meant and she never minced words. And in Jenna's case, her words cut deep.

"No, it's okay. It's fine. I mean, one of her worst fears for me has already happened. I'm not planning on doing any drugs, so what else can go wrong?"

Betsy sat up and leaned forward, as if her sister were sitting right in front of her. "Look, what Mom would think about you going to Halcyon doesn't matter anymore. You're older now and . . . I don't think going there was a bad idea. Last weekend you were so excited about it. It's got to be hard to get yourself back into that . . . creative place, but it's in you. I know it is. Just give it time." What was she saying? Trying to convince her sister to try to be *more* artistic, *more* free-spirited? She was glad Ty wasn't there to overhear her.

"Mom definitely wouldn't want you to give up, regardless of what she thought about you going there in the first place."

Silence. "Maybe you're right." Jenna sighed. "I'm sorry. It's late. I'm probably keeping you and Ty from going to bed. Have the girls been waking up early?"

There she went again. When conversation got too personal or raw, Jenna always changed it to something easier. But then again, so did Betsy. It was better than focusing on the things that hurt. She sighed. "Not too early. Walsh usually wakes up first, then she wakes

Addie up with her singing. Then they both come downstairs."

Jenna chuckled. "Are you and Ty surviving?"

"We're fine. The girls will be happy to see you though when you get back."

Jenna inhaled, then exhaled into the phone. "I'll let you go then. I'll call again soon."

"You sure you're okay? If there's anything else bothering you . . . I'm here if you want to talk again." It used to be so normal, so natural—confiding in each other. At one time, they were the keepers of each other's secrets.

"I know. Thanks. I'm good."

Then she was gone. Betsy tossed her phone down and lay back against the pillows.

She had been ten when she spotted a lofty, regal bed in a magazine and asked her parents to prop her bed up on casters. When they said no, she begged. Finally, one Saturday afternoon before her dad had to be downtown to conduct his orchestra, he brought in a box of casters. Clothed in his tuxedo and gold cufflinks, he slithered under her bed and lifted each corner, one leg at a time, and slid the casters into place. When he finished, he was covered in a thin scrum of dust and her bed was six inches higher. She beamed; he searched for a lint roller.

From that afternoon on, the pocket of space under Betsy's bed became her and Jenna's refuge from the world. They colored, listened to the radio, ate their pudding, and told wild, far-fetched stories filled with mermaids, dragons, dark enemies, and handsome princes. Good always won, evil was always defeated, and dreams always came true.

Later, that private sanctuary was where Jenna first revealed her love of photography to Betsy. Betsy already knew Jenna was artistic—she could draw anything, painted with quick and sure brushstrokes, and sometimes stayed after school to help clean paintbrushes in the art room. But until then, Betsy hadn't known how much Jenna loved to take pictures.

One particular day in seventh grade, Jenna slid under the bed and told Betsy in angry whispers how she'd swiped their mom's Nikon—the one she used to take photos of cancer patients for her inspiration wall—and taken black-and-white photos of trees and leaves to use in a presentation about her favorite artist.

"That's awesome, Jenna," Betsy had said. "Mom will kill you when she finds out you used her camera, but I bet your pictures look great."

"They did, but it didn't matter. Mrs. Lipscomb gave me a D because I didn't use the right kind of poster board for the presentation. But it wasn't my fault! By the time I got Mom to take me to buy some, all they had left was plain yellow. Mrs. Lipscomb wanted white trifold."

"That's it? She gave you a D for yellow poster paper?"

Jenna sighed. "I was supposed to use a certain kind of tape on the photos. I used the Scotch tape from the kitchen drawer."

Betsy handed Jenna a plastic spoon and a cup of pudding. "I'm sorry." At fifteen, Betsy already knew chocolate could fix most problems. Or at least dull their sting.

Jenna peeled the lid off and licked the pudding from

the back of the shiny foil. "She also said Ansel Adams wasn't a real artist. Or at least not the kind we were supposed to focus on. She said if I wanted to study photography, I could wait until high school and take a photography class."

Betsy scraped her spoon around the edge of the cup to get the last bit. "Well, of course you'll do that. You'll probably be a better photographer than the teacher. You're good, Jenna. Just keep practicing. Maybe Mom will let you use her camera more."

Jenna shook her head. "I dropped it when Mr. Barton's dog barked behind me. Cracked the lens."

Betsy closed her eyes. That was always the way it was for Jenna. She had good intentions, but somehow she always screwed up the follow-through. So much for dreams coming true.

Now, lying in bed in her grown-up house far away from that secret shelter, Betsy wondered about all those stories she used to tell Jenna. Were they really just lies? Real life held plenty of good and evil, battles and rescues. And if you worked hard, you really could be anything you wanted to be. Right?

Maybe it was only partly true.

Some dreams were too far-fetched—the short kid who wanted to slam dunk, the chubby girl who had a crush on the prom king, the painfully shy kid who wanted the lead in the school play. Then there was the young girl who wanted to take pictures, but only heard that she hadn't chosen the right dream and that her methods of achieving her goal were wrong. Betsy's first and deepest instinct was to tell that young girl to keep pressing ahead, to fling aside doubts and naysayers, to pursue her desire with a single-minded focus.

But what about Betsy's dream? She'd pressed and prayed and pursued as much as she was able, but nothing had happened. At what point did pursuing the dream become futile? Was there a point at which the dreamer should just let it go? But what were you supposed to do when the dream felt fundamental to the fabric of your being, of your soul? What then?

FIFTEEN

BETSY

"Can we go see the cows?" Addie asked the next morning as Walsh darted out of her chair to follow Etta into the den. "Do you think they're awake yet?"

"They've been awake for hours." Betsy had just poured her second cup of coffee. "We can go see them when they have their breakfast, but I have an idea. Let's get dressed and go see the hens first. We can see how many eggs they have for us, then we'll check on the cows."

Addie's eyes grew wide, "Will there be any baby chicks?"

"Probably not today. But you can help me pull the eggs out of the nests."

Walsh ran around the backyard while Addie tiptoed into the henhouse. She was hesitant at first, but curiosity and the anticipation of speckled eggs got the best of her. Betsy showed her how to feel underneath the hens for the eggs and place them in the basket. Addie sprinkled a scoop of chicken feed on the ground, then darted out the gate to join Walsh on the swing. Betsy gave the hens one more scoop and locked the gate behind her.

By the time they made it to the barn, most of the cows had been turned out to pasture. A few, those with any hint of ailment or problem, were still in the side pen for a closer inspection. Ty looked up when they entered the barn. "Well, good morning," he said to the girls. He drew close to Betsy, snaked his arm around her waist. "And good morning to you," he whispered.

Addie pulled on Betsy's hand. "Aunt Betsy, did you know Uncle Ty snores?"

"Hey now." Ty squatted down and looked in her face. "That's supposed to be our secret."

Betsy laughed. "It's not a secret, Addie. I think the neighbors down the street know Uncle Ty snores. The cows know for sure."

Addie giggled.

"What's on tap for today?" he asked as Addie stepped away from him and Betsy to explore the barn. Walsh ran headlong into a bench, tumbled over it, then righted herself and knelt down to peer at something on the floor.

"You're looking at it. The girls wanted to see the cows. Addie keeps saying she wants to ride one."

Addie whipped her head back around to Ty when she heard that.

"Hmm," he said, scratching his chin. "I have to go see Roger about a part for the tractor, but Walker owes me, so I think he's your guy."

Walker's head popped up from the other side of a

cow lingering in the milking line. "What's that, Mr. Franklin?"

"I need someone to show these little ladies around the barn. Since you ditched me early last Saturday to visit your girlfriend, you can help out for a little while longer today, right?"

In addition to his weekday work, Walker also helped with the milking and cleaning on Saturday mornings. His daddy wanted him to work as much as possible while he was out of school for the summer.

"Oh, uh, sure," Walker said, his Adam's apple bobbing. "I mean, I'm supposed to meet Erin . . ." He caught the look in Ty's eye. "But yeah, I can help."

Ty clapped his hands together. "Great. Why don't you take Addie and Walsh to see Rosie?"

Betsy smiled. Rosie was her favorite out of all 218 cows. Her face was kinder than the rest, if that was possible. Breeding attempts had so far been unsuccessful with her. Ty suspected she was sterile, but Betsy had high hopes for her.

Addie and Walsh followed Walker to the side pen. She turned to follow them, but Ty caught her arm. "How do the girls seem to you?"

Betsy shrugged. "I think they're okay. Neither of them has mentioned Jenna today."

Ty nodded, bit the inside of his cheek. "Two weeks is a long time to leave your kids."

Betsy inhaled, watching as Walker led the girls into the pen where Rosie stood, munching grass.

"I bet she misses them," he said. "I hope she misses them. I mean, look at them."

Addie stood in front of Rosie's face, rubbing the top of the cow's nose. Then Walsh held her face against Rosie's huge fuzzy cheek. She closed her eyes and smiled. Rosie kept munching, unconcerned about the two small people petting her.

Betsy nodded. After all these years, she could still read her sister's face like fingers on Braille. And what she'd seen on Jenna's face when she left the previous week spanned the entire spectrum of emotion, from the delight of sudden freedom to the terror of someone letting go. Which of those faces came closest to the actual truth?

· · ·

"We can't eat these."

"You can't eat grapes?" Betsy had just set a lunch of grilled cheese and grapes in front of the girls on the back porch. "Why not?" Had Jenna forgotten to tell her the girls were allergic to grapes?

"Mommy always cuts our grapes in half. If we eat them like this, they could get stuck in our throats and make us choke."

Of course. Betsy got a knife from the kitchen counter and returned to the porch. "Note to self: cut grapes in half," she said as she cut. "Got it."

Addie pulled Walsh's hand back when she tried to grab a grape as Betsy sliced them. "Careful," she said.

After lunch—during which thankfully she hadn't made any other mistakes—she left Addie on the porch love seat with a stack of Anna Beth's books while she tucked an already half-asleep Walsh into bed upstairs. When she returned, Addie was asleep too, as Betsy suspected. The girls had played hard all morning with every animal they could find, be it cow, cat, barn mouse, or annoyed hen.

As she straightened the kitchen, gathering cups and shoes, Ty returned from Roger's place. Betsy thought of the meager amount of food he sometimes kept in the barn office for days when he couldn't make it up to the house to eat lunch. It was nothing more than a few bags of chips. Maybe an apple. She deposited the cups in the sink and the shoes by the back door. After a quick check on Walsh upstairs, she ducked out the back door, a Tervis cup of iced tea in one hand and a pimento-cheese sandwich in a brown paper bag.

She spotted him out by the back fence shielding his eyes from the bright sun. The tractor moved slowly out in the field, and three men stood close to it in a group, peering at the ground as if it were a crystal ball. As she drew closer, Ty turned and walked back into the barn from the other side, his stride purposeful and quick. She entered the doors and smiled. "Hi," she called. She crossed the floor and met him near his office.

He looked up and grinned. A sheen of sweat covered his top lip and brow. She reached up and brushed a few specks of grass out of his hair. His hair was still as thick and blond as it had been in college, except now he had patches of gray at his temples. She loved that gray as much as she loved the crease in his forehead.

"Whatcha got in that bag?" he asked.

She held it out to him. "I brought you a sandwich.

And tea." She passed the glass to him and he drank half of it in two gulps.

"You're an angel. Thanks." He took the bag from her hand. "Whatever this is, it's much better than what I would have been eating."

"What's going on with the tractor?"

"Belt's worn out. It made it through spring planting, but we have to fix it before harvest when we're dodging storms. Speaking of, Roger's bringing some extra plywood when he brings the spare part for the tractor. I want to cover some of the upper windows of the barn."

"Already? There's not a storm out there, is there?" Betsy usually paid close attention to the weather reports, but in the chaos of the last couple of days, she'd forgotten to check. She'd never admit it to Ty, because big storms meant a possible loss of milk, but she always felt a rush of excitement when tropical storms rolled in. Hurricanes, not so much. But it was possible for a tropical storm to bring nothing but strong breezes, cooling rain, and an excuse for Betsy to hole up with a book in the front window. She was almost embarrassed by how much she liked them.

He shook his head. "Doesn't hurt to go ahead and have everything in place though. Things could get ugly later in the summer. The Gulf waters are heating up early."

Betsy peered at him, trying to detect the level of his nerves. The hurricane he went through with his grandfather years ago was always in the back of his mind, pushing him to do all he could to keep the farm safe. "Warm water isn't a good sign."

"Nope." He rubbed the back of his neck, then took another swig of tea. "The girls in the house?"

"They're both asleep. The morning wore them out." He glanced back out the door of the barn.

"I'll let you get back to work then." She backed away, but he reached out and tugged her hand.

"Come here." He pulled her to him.

"What?" she asked, but she already knew. His eyes always gave him away.

"Seeing you out here earlier this morning, all I wanted to do was this, but we had those extra little eyes around." His lips met hers. A little salty, but warm and familiar. His hand went to the small of her back, pulling her hips toward his.

"Ty." She looked over his shoulder. Walker was just outside the barn, his fingers dancing across the screen of his iPhone. He was oblivious to anything except the message he was typing, but Carlos and the others could return any minute.

"Don't worry about them. They'll be out back until Roger gets here." He kissed her again, the prickles around his mouth bothering her, but only a little bit. "Right about now, I'm pretty glad we decided to put that couch in the office."

She pulled back and opened her eyes. "You aren't serious." One corner of his mouth pulled up. She thumped him on his chest. "You're crazy. No way."

"I'll be quick." His cheeks reddened when she smiled. "We can be fast. Discreet." He raised his eyebrows.

Betsy bit her lip. "I don't think so. I'd rather not shock the cows." She looked over his shoulder again. "Or Walker."

Ty kept his gaze on her, his mouth and eyes caught somewhere between hope and disappointment. Finally, he looked down at his boots, scuffed one on the ground. "Definitely wouldn't want to shock anyone. Maybe . . ." He took a breath.

"What?" She pulled close to him again, her stomach twisting into a tight ball of desire and embarrassment.

He shook his head, then kissed her cheek. "Nothing. I'll see you later."

Etta bounded into the barn and twined between Betsy's legs. Betsy reached down and scratched her head, then turned toward the door, Etta in step next to her.

"Betsy?" Ty called.

She turned to face him.

"Thanks for the lunch," he said after only the briefest hesitation.

. . .

Betsy had fallen in love with Ty's neck first. The back of it, to be specific. Then his forearms—thick, strong, blond hair fuzzing freckled skin. She didn't even know his name at first. He was just a guy—an ag student, she later learned—feeding cows in a field she jogged past. That was back when she jogged for exercise, and even then it was really just a chance to hang out with friends and hope they'd pass the football team on its way to practice.

Farmers weren't her thing—the only ones she knew of in Birmingham were at the Pepper Place Farmer's

Market on Saturday mornings—but then she saw him, his arm outstretched, feeding an enormous bull from the palm of his hand. The skin on the back of his neck was tan and soft-looking. As her friend babbled about her date the night before, Betsy had to fight the urge to hop the fence and lay her cheek against that soft skin.

They passed the field, but she turned around for one last look. His calm, confident stance, the way his hat sat on his blond hair, the way his jeans sat on his hips. She imagined a life with him before they'd even said hello. They married a year and a half later, the summer after they graduated, and spent the next two years working hard on the farm.

The days were long, sweaty, and demanding—getting the fields ready for their first full harvest in two years, organizing the cattle, meeting the farmhands who'd worked for his grandfather, and deciding who else they needed to bring on. Betsy put her marketing degree to work and got Franklin Dairy on social media, joined various dairy associations in the Southeast, and began talks with stores and markets across the area. She quickly fell in love with the farm and the ways they could contribute to the life of the community and the region as a whole.

But the physical work was unending—hammering, hoeing, seeding, herding, feeding. She worked as hard as Ty did and used muscles she didn't know she had. Occasionally she wondered what in the world she'd gotten herself into, but then he'd cross the barn to kiss her, his lips salty and sweet. He'd catch her eye from across the room and her legs would melt. He'd find her hand under the table at a dairy association meeting and she'd remember why she chose him and this life. *Their* life.

At the end of each day, they collapsed in bed, exhausted but happy. Happy with the farm, with each other, with the years that lay ahead and all the life that would fill those years. Back then, she wouldn't have been so shocked by what Ty had suggested in the barn. The thought of making love there, especially with the other guys so close at hand, made her cheeks burn now, but back then, she might have been the one to suggest it.

Betsy tiptoed up the back steps and eased open the door, but her stealth was unnecessary. Addie was sleeping hard, her mouth open slightly, her cheeks pink in the afternoon heat. Betsy reached up and pulled the chain to turn on the ceiling fan. When the breeze lifted strands of Addie's hair, Betsy slipped into the house, pressing the door almost closed behind her. Upstairs, Walsh was still asleep as well. Betsy had no idea how long they were supposed to nap. Just one of the many things she hadn't thought to ask Jenna before she left.

She entered the coolness of her own bedroom, the fan still spinning, the bed still unmade. Instead of tidying up as she normally would have, she kicked off her shoes and lay down on the bed, arms and legs starfished out to the sides. Then she reached up and pulled Ty's pillow to her, hugged it close.

Would things ever go back to how they used to be, back when she had no problem letting go? Ty would tighten his grip on her hips, his mouth an inch away from her own, and her legs would turn to water, bone and sinew dissolving to nothingness. The air between them crackled with anticipation and desire. It used to be so easy to let herself go—like drifting into the Gulf, the warm, languid water covering her skin and holding her tight.

But that was *before*—before the poking and prodding, before all that captivating mystery and spontaneity and optimism was reduced to circled numbers on a calendar and biweekly dates with a nurse practitioner in pink polka-dot scrubs. Back when things between them were fun and easy, fresh and new.

Somehow Ty had been able to move past it all, compartmentalizing the facets of his life into neat pockets with clearly defined boundaries. Betsy, however, was stuck somewhere in the in-between, twisted and twirled into a messy, tangled knot she didn't quite recognize. A close match, but not the real thing. And if this Betsy didn't work the way God and nature intended, how was she supposed to offer herself up for pure pleasure or even accept the offer? It seemed too bold. Too easy after such an upheaval.

Dr. Fields, however, seemed to think that part wouldn't, or shouldn't, be an issue.

"Spontaneous pregnancy can happen," he'd said. "So you two need to keep at it. Try to enjoy yourselves."

Those were his parting words, tossed out like a consolation prize as they stood to leave his office. Just before that, they had listened as he rattled off all the things that could be wrong since he'd yet to find a single thing that was definitely wrong. The usual course of action—intrauterine insemination, two words Ty could barely make his mouth say—hadn't worked for them, even though they'd tried the relatively easy process three times. The doctor had suggested four, but three negatives seemed like enough.

"So there's . . . is there anything else we can try?" Ty had asked.

Betsy lifted her eyes. Ty hadn't been eager about visiting the fertility specialist in the first place, so she was surprised he'd ask about more treatment.

"Oh, there's always something," the doctor said. "I think IVF would be an appropriate course of action for you."

"Would it work?"

The doctor paused. "There's always a chance."

It was the pause that did it for Betsy.

For Ty, it was the money.

The cows gave them a nice life, a fine life, but they wouldn't pay for something like IVF. The financial advisor at the clinic went over payment plans with them, ways they could finance the procedure and the drugs, not to mention the various tests, scans, and other related steps that went along with the deal. All told, they would be out of pocket way more than they could imagine spending. They had insurance, but it laughed in the face of voluntary fertility treatment.

Yes, it was an investment in their future children— as the advisor had repeated—but what kind of future would they have if they mortgaged their house, barn, and cows to give them life? What would they have left to raise those children with, other than their wits and love?

Ty had shaken his head, his mind made up. Betsy knew they'd talk about it that night in bed, the lights off, legs together. He'd hear her out, let her cry, maybe shed a tear of his own at the thought of saying good-bye to such a longing. But facts were facts. That kind of treatment was out of the question. Time to move on.

That's when the doctor had mentioned natural pregnancy. "You could also try praying," he'd said, a helpful afterthought.

That was five months ago, in early January, a particularly raw way to start the new year. The doctor's words echoed in her brain at all hours—*"anything is possible"*—but she just didn't see any way through that vast, gaping hole between what she wanted and their actual reality: unexplained infertility. Plain old infertility she could have dealt with—diagnose the problem, fix it. It was the unexplained part that was so hard to swallow. Nothing was actually wrong with them? All his parts worked and so did hers, but they weren't working together? How was that possible?

Weeks of going round and round like this in her head made her feel like a children's carousel she couldn't stop, so on a dreary day in March with spring just around the corner, she stuck her leg out and stopped the spinning. She wrapped her grandmother's yellow crocheted baby booties in tissue paper and hid them in her closet. Threw away the marked-up calendar from the previous year. Shoved her book of fanciful flowers to the back of the dresser drawer in the room that was to have been the nursery. Moving on was the only choice she had, so she did.

She always thought she'd be done having kids by the time she was thirty. She thought by now she'd be happily absorbed in the living and raising part. And here she was, approaching her thirtieth birthday with two little girls sleeping in her empty room—they just weren't hers.

SIXTEEN

JENNA

Jenna stood in the middle of a rickety bridge that stretched over a bayou ringed with needlerush, cattails, and huge, knobby cypress knees poking out of the water. A patch of lily pads covered one side of the water, and on one, a frog sat in the bright sunshine. With elbows perched on the railing, her eye fixed to the viewfinder, she tried to get a shot of him before he jumped away, but the harsh light washed everything out.

She'd been at Halcyon for seven days. Casey and Gregory had both explained that the solitude and quiet—and the lack of real structure—were meant to encourage deep focus and hard work. They were right. The lack of structure—not to mention the absence of the photography mentor—meant Jenna could go days without seeing anyone if she wanted. She ate meals in the dining hall, of course, but she'd managed to miss the nightly workshops with no repercussions.

However, the solitude also meant no one knew she'd

yet to produce anything of worth. She was surrounded by beauty she'd never seen before—murky swamps, bright-yellow croaking frogs, palm trees with lime-green fruit, towering pines, and scrubby oaks covered in Spanish moss—yet every time she tried to capture that beauty, it came out flat. Like she was trying too hard.

It was nice to have no one checking up on her, tapping her on the shoulder and asking to see her work, but somewhere around the middle of the week, she'd started to panic. For once, she'd had an incredible opportunity dropped in her lap and now it was sliding through her fingers. No way did she want to go home with nothing to show for her time here. She hadn't left her kids for that.

Behind her, something moved in the trees on the other side of the bridge. She peered into the shadows, but the glare made the shade appear deeper. It was all tree trunks and leaves until she noticed one trunk was moving toward her. Not a trunk. A man.

"Sorry. Didn't mean to startle you," he called. It was Gregory, this time without the leather jacket, which would have been ridiculous in this heat, but still in the beat-up jeans. Camera around his neck, tripod under his arm.

"I'm just glad you're not an alligator."

"An alligator?"

"Yeah." Jenna shaded her eyes as Gregory approached. "Don't they have those in Florida?"

"True, but you're more likely to see a fox or an armadillo. I've seen a couple of gators around here, but they don't seem to be too interested in humans."

"Good to know."

"How's it going?" Was that a smirk on his face? Yes. It was small but it was there.

"Awesome." She held up her camera. "I think these are going to be great."

He raised an eyebrow. "Good, that's good. Think you'll be ready for the workshop tonight?"

Jenna exhaled, blowing air out in a rush. Now he was doing his job? "I don't know. I'm not much for public displays of embarrassment."

"What's so embarrassing? We're all here to learn, right? To connect to our passion?"

She tried to hold it back but she couldn't. Her eyes rolled almost involuntarily.

Instead of the glare she expected, Gregory laughed. "I know what you mean. It can get a little repetitive. And annoying."

He stepped up to the railing and propped his elbows on the edge. A cloud floated in front of the sun, relieving the brightness of the light for a moment.

"So do you have other jobs going on other than here at Halcyon?" She leaned back against the railing and shot a glance at him. His eyes were on the water. "I assume you're not just hanging out at the beach all day." Heat crept up her cheeks and she closed her eyes for a second. Since the very first night at the dining hall, something about his swagger brought out a defense mechanism in her. She needed to be more careful. She didn't know this man well enough to be sarcastic.

"I'm not sunbathing, that's for sure. I'm a working photographer. Magazines, journals, some textbooks. I go where the job takes me. Which is why I've been a little absent these last few days." He cut his eyes to her. "I've been told I'm not always the most attentive mentor." If she expected an apology—which she halfway did—she didn't get it. "Anyway, right now I'm working on something I'm hoping *National Geographic* will pick up. It's on forgotten places in Florida. Unseen angles and views. This mentor gig at Halcyon is perfect because I needed to be down here anyway. Kill two birds, you know?"

"What kind of forgotten places? This preserve doesn't seem too forgotten to me. It's crawling with artists."

He nodded. "You're partly right. But the cool thing about places like this is that you can be in a populated area, but two or three hundred yards away is a little slice of swamp that's true wilderness. Untouched. In fact . . ." He pointed to their right, in the deeper woods behind the creek. "That's where I'm headed. I found something last week on the rare occasion I didn't have my camera on me. You can come with me, if you want. I'll show you what I'm talking about."

At the end of the bridge, they stepped off the wood onto a sand and dirt path just wide enough for one person. The shade deepened the farther they walked into the trees.

"This is like another world," Jenna said. Limbs stretched overhead, making a canopy that dimmed the light. All around them were sounds and stirrings of unseen animals and birds. "Not like the Deep South I know, that's for sure."

"Geographically, we're in the Deep South, but that's

about it. It almost feels prehistoric, doesn't it? Like maybe this was how it looked billions of years ago. Dark and wet. Strange noises. Creatures around every bend."

"Okay, you're creeping me out a little bit."

Gregory laughed. "Sorry. I get a little excited when I'm in places like this. That's why I love my job. The world is my office."

As they walked he pointed out various trees and plants. Black gum and coastal plain willows. Pond and bald cypresses. Leggy banyans. And the birds: egrets and night herons. White pelicans and roseate spoonbills. Even a mangrove cuckoo, which apparently was a rare find. He seemed to know a little about everything.

"This cypress here—judging by its size, it's at least a couple hundred years old. The forest has probably looked just like this for all those years. No real change other than everything getting bigger and fuller."

She thought of that proud cypress, growing year after year toward the sunlight, unconcerned with the pace of anything around it.

"Okay, we're close. Look here." He guided her off the trail to the left, into a dense thicket of tall grass and hanging vines.

From somewhere came the sound of running water. With the sun behind clouds and the thick trees overhead, everything was dim, blues and greens fading into each other, until the tangle of foliage opened into a hidden cove of clear water surrounded by boulders. Water trickled down the face of the rocks, creating a waterfall ten feet high that splashed into the pool below. A thin creek—narrow enough to step over—ran away from the pool, winding off through the trees.

"It's not Niagara, but it's a rare find in Florida." Gregory set his tripod and camera down on a bed of dry leaves. "Not much elevation change anywhere, but there's just enough here to create this little pocket of water."

"Where does it come from?" Jenna knelt and peered into the water. It was so clear, she could see straight to the bottom. It tapered from the shallow edges to deeper waters in the center. "Everything else around here is murky and still. I've yet to come across water that's moving. Nothing like this creek."

"Singer Creek, to be exact. Legend says an Indian woman who stayed behind when her people were run out would sit here and sing to her lost children. She was known as 'the singer.' I guess someone thought it had a nice ring to it, and they named the creek and the preserve after her."

Jenna dipped her fingers in the water. It was crisp and cold. Gregory leaned over and did the same thing.

"Some say this comes from an underground spring straight from the Appalachians," he said. "I have my doubts, of course. The closest Appalachian foothill is up in Alabama, a long way from the Florida marshes. But who knows? Maybe this water has traveled underground all that way. Just to spit out in these rocks."

He sat on a dry patch of rock and pushed a smattering of leaves away to make room for Jenna. With her camera still hanging around her neck—no way was she going to trust it sitting alone near all this water—she sat next to him. After pulling her shoes off, she dunked her feet in the cool water.

"Nice, huh?"

"Very." She leaned over and cupped her hand and poured water over her calves, up to her knees. Sweat on the back of her neck evaporated, leaving her with a chill.

They sat in silence a moment, the only sound the trickling water and movement all around them in the forest.

"Now your turn," Gregory said, his voice low, as if to leave the peace undisturbed. "Tell me about you. Have you figured out yet why you're here at Halcyon?"

"Not really. Maybe my epiphany is still coming."

"Okay. Well, tell me about your photography then, what you do with it at home."

She shook her head. "I don't do much with it at home. I don't have time."

"Sure you do."

"What? How do you know?"

"We make time for things that are important."

"But isn't that what this place is about? Time to connect to our art—time and space that's not in our regular lives? It's all I've heard about since I got here."

"Sure, sure, that's what we say." He reached down and flicked water into a school of minnows. "And it's true to an extent. But I stand by the idea that if something is important enough, you'll squeeze it in. In the margins. Here, the margins are stretched, but when you get back home, everything goes back to normal. The passion, the drive has to be there. You get it?"

She nodded. He didn't know anything about her life. Of course a man would think it was as easy as just picking up the camera. But it was never that simple.

Then he reached over and lifted her camera from around her neck. She grabbed on to the strap. "What are you doing?"

"May I?"

She let go and averted her eyes. She didn't want to see his expression as he scrolled through the images she'd captured over the last handful of days.

After a moment, with her eyes still on the water, she sensed rather than saw him shake his head. "These are crap," he murmured.

"Excuse me?"

"You're taking shots you think you need to take." He scrolled through her images. "Sun shining on the water, palm branches, a pretty little mound of wildflowers. This is amateur. I'm just guessing here, but I'd say there's more to you than this."

"And what makes you say that?" She forgot about trying to be careful. "You haven't been around long enough to find out anything about me. I've been floundering, trying to figure out what I'm doing here. I thought I was supposed to have a mentor to offer some guidance."

"Having a mentor, especially one like me, isn't going to help you find your muse, if that's what you're looking for."

She stood and took her camera back.

"Go ahead. Get mad. Use it. Put it in here." He reached up and tapped her camera.

She turned and crossed back over the rocks the way they'd come, trying not to slip and embarrass herself as she made her exit.

"You're gonna need thicker skin to work with me."

She stopped and spun around, almost losing her footing in the process. She reached out and grabbed a low-hanging limb for balance. "If you remember, I didn't ask to work with you. And since it sounds like you aren't that excited to be working with me, why are you here? Why didn't you just go the other way when you saw me back there on the bridge?"

"A couple reasons. One, I'm the photography mentor at Halcyon. Seeing as you're the only other photographer here, you are my job. Two, Max asked me to watch out for you."

"He did what? When?"

"He called me up and told me a friend of his was coming and asked me to . . . well, just to make sure you were okay."

Unable to wrap her head around Max and Gregory working together to keep tabs on her, Jenna just stared.

"Don't be mad at him. I could tell he cares a lot about you. I told him I'd keep my eye on you."

"That's just perfect." Still holding the limb, she stepped carefully down the rocks to the firm ground.

"You have to find your creative eye on your own," he called. She resisted the urge to turn and toss another barb his way. "If I had to guess, I'd say it's there already and you just need to uncover it. That's why you're here, right?"

SEVENTEEN

JENNA

On Monday of the second week at Halcyon, Jenna squatted low among broken, stripped pine trees and thin saplings struggling to push themselves through the thick underbrush of The Bottoms. She'd heard of the place that morning at breakfast. Another artist had mentioned it, an area of the retreat where, a couple of years before, a tornado had ripped through during a summer storm.

"Everything else around here is so lush and alive," Mark, a painter sitting at her table, had said. "I don't know why they don't just clean it up. Or clear-cut it to get rid of the broken tree trunks and let everything start over."

"They can't do that," a woman said. "It's a nature preserve. They have to let Mother Nature do her thing."

Over the woman's left shoulder, Jenna saw Gregory filling his coffee mug a few paces away. His back was to them, but Jenna sensed he was listening. Or maybe he was just taking way too long to fill up that mug.

"Yeah, well, nature hasn't done its thing yet. It's a wasteland."

Jenna rose and picked up her tray. Gregory said her images were amateur. Too pretty. A wasteland should be perfect.

Outside, she'd almost made it to the start of the path when he called to her. She turned slowly, unsure of what to say—or what he'd say—after how they parted at the waterfall a few days before.

"Do me a favor," he said in place of a greeting. He set his coffee down and pulled a camera from his bag. "Play around with this today."

She gasped. "Is that a Rollei?"

He nodded.

She took the camera from him, her fingers finding the familiar crevices and notches. A photographer out in Wyoming had let her use his Rollei and she'd fallen a little bit in love. "Why are you giving me this?"

"Just trying something different." He shrugged. "Have fun with it. See what you think."

She tried to hand it back to him. "I already have a camera. Anyway, I don't think changing cameras is going to fix my problems."

"You're right. It won't. But changing your focus will. Just try it." He shouldered his bag again and picked up his coffee. "See how it feels."

Now, squatting in the bright sunshine, she was determined to prove him wrong. It wasn't that she wanted to take bad shots—to squander her time, to waste her opportunity—but she kept hearing his words. *This is amateur. You're taking shots you think you need to take.*

She'd known those shots weren't great before he looked at them—and she hated that those were all she had to show him—but hearing the words out loud made something inside her deflate. And because of that, it made her angry. She'd come here to open herself up to creativity, not have someone squash it.

So she did what she always did when someone made her feel small and inadequate—she pushed in the opposite direction. Here she was in The Bottoms, searching for the muse Gregory said she wouldn't find. Broken trees? Check. Sun-parched grass? Check. A barren space ruined by a storm? Check.

But in what was supposed to be a wasteland, all she saw was life. Yes, much of the area was damaged, but she saw bright-green vines encircling twisted and broken tree trunks, golden wildflowers growing out of a hole in a tree lying on its side, a white-tailed deer bounding over a section of tangled fencing. It was exquisite, so different from the pretty scenes she'd tried to capture the week before.

Though she still wanted to be mad at Gregory, it seemed his harsh words had given her a necessary shove. She wasn't sure if this was the creative eye he wanted her to uncover, but it seemed her eye was better suited for finding the inferior, the unloved, the damaged, and The Bottoms provided an abundance of them all.

She worked for a while with her own camera, capturing the sharp colors and angles of light. When she switched to Gregory's Rollei, which produced square-format black-and-white photos, it was all about texture and shadows. The Rolleiflex TLR was what most people associated with old-time photos. The photographer held the camera at chest level and looked down into the finder instead of holding it to the face and looking straight ahead.

Shooting with a camera like this was a whole different experience than using a standard camera, and it took her a while to get used to it—holding it steady at the correct level, remembering that the mirror reversed the viewfinder image. It also forced her to slow down, to think about a shot before hitting the button. Once she got the hang of it though, she was able to focus on the trees above her, balancing on top of mounds of sand and dirt to get an angle right, taking her time, enjoying the peace.

She wondered about the film though—did Gregory develop it himself? Take it into town to get it developed? Other than the Epson printer that printed digital shots, she hadn't seen evidence of a photo lab or darkroom in any of Halcyon's studios. One thing was for sure—she was glad for the lack of an LCD screen on the camera. No need to waste time seeing how the pictures were coming out. She could continue shooting and just imagine she was capturing things the way she wanted.

When her growling stomach told her lunchtime had come and gone, she paused and ate a granola bar in the shade. As she rested she pulled her phone out of her bag. She didn't even check to see whether she had service, she just wanted to see the photo she used as her home screen, a recent shot of Addie and Walsh. They sat in the middle of their front yard, searching for the one four-leaf clover they were sure they'd find.

Jenna had taken the photo before the girls heard her approach. The late-afternoon light was perfect, almost creating a halo around them, and the girls filled the shot in a way that would have made Max proud. Maybe not Gregory—he'd probably find something wrong with it.

She'd shown the photo to Sam one morning as they drank their coffee together.

"They're beautiful, just like their mother." He set his coffee down and looked closer at the photo. "The blonde one looks like you."

"You just say that because of the hair."

He sat back in his chair and picked up his cup again. "Do they look like their father?"

Jenna's stomach did that uncomfortable clenching thing it did whenever anyone brought up the girls' father.

"Maybe a little." She blew a stray curl out of her eyes and felt his careful gaze on her.

"How long has it been? Since the divorce?"

Jenna stared at him a moment without speaking.

"I'm sorry, I . . ." He inhaled. "I just assumed you were divorced. Is he . . . ?" From his pained look, she knew she had to say something quick before he got the impression she was a widow.

"No, no, that's not it. It's fine. It's been, uh . . . I've been on my own for a few years now."

By the sweet and well-timed grace of God, Mario waved at her then, allowing her to sidestep any more questions she didn't want to answer.

A bird chirped nearby and brought her back to the present. She shifted her position against the rough bark of the tree and stretched her legs out in front of her. What she'd said to Sam was mostly true—as long as five, going on six, years was still considered "a few." It was just easier to gloss over the truth than spill it across the clean table in the back corner of Full Cup as Carrie Underwood blared on the speakers.

Her girls had had no choice in who their father was, even who their mother was. Whenever she wished she could pack up and head west again, or north, or anywhere but where she was, she thought of her girls, touched their skin, listened to their laugh, and reminded herself that they only had her. They depended on her for everything. So what she was doing now— these two weeks—it was all for them. She owed them at least that much.

. . .

That evening she stopped by her cabin to change into clothes that weren't damp with sweat and speckled with sandspurs. Outside, the air was alive with warmth and the scent of something sweet. Around the edge of the lake, canoes in various faded colors jostled against each other, tied by thick ropes to nearby trees as if someone had been afraid they'd drift away. One of them—it looked like it used to be painted red—had slipped from its rope and was trailing away from the others.

She looked around. After a moment, she slipped her shoes off and walked to the edge of the lake. The water was warm as bathwater. She lifted the hem of her skirt and took a couple more steps until she could grab the canoe to pull it up to the shore.

It wasn't until something rough bit into her fingers that she noticed the tattoo of jagged, rusty holes on the sides of the hull. The hole at the front where the rope had been tied was rusted out, leaving sharp edges and splotchy orange patches. The pads of her fingers were coated in the same orange rust, and a spot of blood seeped out of a shallow cut. She swished her hand in the water around her knees, but when she pulled it out and examined her finger, blood bloomed in a small dot.

So much for trying to do a good deed.

As she pressed her thumb and forefinger together, her gaze settled on the offending canoe. Maybe it had once held a load of laughing, frolicking kids, intent on pushing each other out. Or maybe they raced their canoe against others, seeing which team could skim across the lake the quickest. She imagined the little boat gleaming cherry red in the sun, tanned arms and legs tumbling from the sides, excited voices carrying over the water. Now it was nothing more than a mass of rust and danger.

But there was something about it. The mix of former glory and present decay. She tilted her head and caught a glimpse of the bright-green grass at the edge of the lake through a hole in the side of the canoe. Just a sliver of green against the orange rust and faded red metal. Life against death.

She tapped her fingers on her camera hanging around her neck, then pulled it up to her eye. She snapped and snapped again. After a moment, the light changed as a cloud skirted the sun. Shadows and glare, light and dark. Then, without bothering to check the outcome of her efforts on the LCD screen, she stepped out of the water, slid her feet back into her sandals, and continued to dinner.

• • •

On her way out of the dining hall, Casey called to her. Expecting to be urged to join the workshop, Jenna continued down the steps, just turning her head to speak. "I have a few things I wanted to wrap up from my work today. I'll try to make it tomorrow night."

"I was just going to let you know Gregory asked for you to meet him in the barn. And to bring his camera."

Jenna paused and looked back at Casey standing at the top of the steps. "Why?"

Casey shrugged. "I'm guessing he wants to discuss your work. He is your mentor, so that's his job."

"Yes, as I keep being reminded."

Casey raised an eyebrow.

"Sorry. Thanks for letting me know. I'll head that way."

The path down the hill toward the barn took her away from everything else, past the lake, to a part of the preserve she hadn't seen yet. After stopping at her cabin to retrieve Gregory's camera, she wound her way across a low bridge that spanned a muddy creek and through a tunnel of oaks and hanging vines. Palm branches pressed in from the sides of the dirt path, which opened to a clearing. A crisp white barn sat a couple hundred feet off the path, its upper casement windows open to catch the breeze.

There was no sign of life until she noticed Gregory sitting in an Adirondack chair to the side of the barn. His head was tipped back, his eyes closed, his boot-clad feet propped in another chair pulled up in front of him.

"You're not making me clean horse stalls, are you?" Jenna called as she approached.

He opened one eye. "Funny."

"Why are we meeting way out here?"

He dropped his feet to the ground and heaved himself out of the chair. "Come with me."

From the outside, the barn looked like most every other barn she'd seen in the hills of Tennessee: peaked roof, weather vane on top, vertical wood siding. Even a fenced horse corral to the side. But when Gregory grabbed the handles of the double doors and slid them open, any chance of this being a standard barn evaporated. Inside, it was around the same size as Ty's barn, but with the individual stalls taken out, the space seemed larger. No ropes hung on the wall. No straw on the floor. No animal smell.

Instead the area was sleek and modern, the faint scent of vinegar and chemicals both sharp and familiar. The floor was covered in clean, cool tiles that made Jenna want to take her shoes off and walk barefoot. The lights were low, but gallery spotlights shone on the art on the walls. A few paintings here and there—bold, impulsive jabs of color—but most were photographs. Some black and white, some color, all striking.

"Are these . . . ?" Before she could finish her thought, a particular photo caught her eye.

Gregory continued across the room toward a door at the back, but Jenna moved closer to the photo. It showed a woman and two children—obviously hers by the way she draped her arms around them. They sat on a defeated couch in a dingy room. Behind them, a wooden board covered most of a window. Black metal bars covered the rest. All three had smudges of dirt on their arms and faces. It was poverty—the kind that scared her and made her stomach hurt—but it was also joy. The children, a boy and a girl, were caught in a laugh, their faces open. The mom's eyes were tired, and the lines around them made her look older than she probably was, but her smile was soft. Their joy—even if just temporary—radiated outward, pushing back the bonds of their bleak life.

Jenna paused to make sure her voice wouldn't break before she spoke. "Did you take this?" She'd never seen any of his work, and yet she felt sure it was his. That he'd been the one to draw such life and light out of this family's impossible situation.

He joined her in front of the photo. "I did."

She pointed to a group of acrylics. "What about those?"

He shrugged. "I paint every now and then. It loosens me up. I'm not very good though."

She snorted. "Yes, you are. All of this is . . . Tell me about them." She gestured to the photo of the family.

"A few years ago *TIME* magazine did a story on fracking in the Appalachians. The woman's husband was killed in an accident on the job, leaving her with five kids and no income. These are the two youngest." He scratched his bearded chin. "They could barely keep the lights on, but she offered me tea and a home-made biscuit. The kids played marbles with me."

Painful things made beautiful.

She made a slow turn, taking in the array of photos. People, landscapes, old buildings, street scenes. "Are they all from *TIME*, or . . . ?"

"No, that one's *National Geographic*. That's *Travel + Leisure* . . ." He started to point to another photo but let his arm fall. "It's just a random assortment. They asked me to bring some to leave on display this summer while I'm mentoring."

"I didn't realize you were so . . . Are you famous?"

He laughed.

"I'm serious. Are you some famous photographer I should know about?"

"What difference does it make? I'm just a guy who takes pictures and gets paid for them. At least that's the goal."

"These are more than just 'pictures' though. They're incredible. Why are you wasting time at this little art retreat when you could be out winning a Pulitzer or something?"

"Now you're just embarrassing me." He stepped back from the wall. "I don't know. You've seen how well I fit in." He cut his eyes to her and she smiled, then remembered she was supposed to be mad at him. "For some reason, they keep asking me to come back and I keep saying yes. I guess one day maybe I won't, but it works for now. And Halcyon isn't just some 'little art retreat.' It's a big deal to a lot of people in the art world."

He turned toward a door at the back of the room and pulled his boots off. "None of this matters though. What I really wanted you to see is in here. Take your shoes off, if you don't mind. I like to keep it clean." She dropped her sandals next to his boots, then followed him as he opened the door and turned on the light. A counter along one wall held bins, trays, and bottles. A thin metal wire dotted with clips was strung across one wall.

"A darkroom? How come no one told me about this?"

"It's my job to let the photographers know about it." She stared at him.

"Well, I'm telling you now. And you haven't needed a darkroom until now."

He reached in front of her and flipped another switch on the wall. The main lights went out while another one clicked on, coating the room in a soft red glow. "Let's see what you got today."

She passed his camera to him. "I haven't developed film in a while."

"Don't worry. I'll walk you through it." His voice was low, as if excess noise would damage the film as much as light.

He pulled the film out of the camera and loaded it into the spiral developing reel.

"The reel goes into the processing tank here." He picked up a bottle of developer and poured the liquid into a clear beaker, along with water from a bucket on the counter. "It has to be the right temperature or it'll ruin the film. Hand me that thermometer, will you?" She gave it to him and he slid it into the beaker. "Perfect. Now, I want you to pour the developer into the tank and we'll start the timer."

The red light offered enough light to see shapes and forms, but not enough to see small details. When she had trouble finding the hole at the top of the tank to pour the developer, he reached over and moved her hands to the right place. "There. Pour it in, then hit the timer."

They inverted the tank to make sure the developer coated all the film inside, then repeated it twice more, waiting a minute or so between movements.

"Next is stop bath, fixer, and holding bath, in that order." He held a pair of tongs out to her. "Use these, never your fingers, although I'm sure you remember that. And don't forget to rinse them off before you move them to another solution." He turned the sink faucet on, and she rinsed the ends of the tongs before moving the photo paper to the next tray.

The manual process was fickle and each movement, no matter how insignificant it seemed, could have a huge effect on the outcome of the photos. She hardly knew this man—wasn't even sure if she liked him very much—but in the soft light of the darkroom, he was kind, helpful. A surprisingly gentle teacher.

As they waited for the final wash, he hopped up onto the edge of the metal counter behind her. "I owe you an apology."

"Oh?" She leaned against the table and faced him. "What for?"

He glanced down at his bare feet and leaned forward

onto his hands. "Calling you an amateur. Saying you weren't taking the right shots. It was too much."

Part of her wanted to make a joke out of it, to brush it off as nothing and move on to something easier, but instead she nodded. "It was hard to hear. You made me mad."

"I know and I'm sorry." He gave a small half grin. "People don't always like me very much. I'm sure you can see why."

She shrugged. "You won't win any etiquette contests, I'll give you that. But I get it. And your push helped me, I think."

"Then I'm glad I could help."

She smiled. "Don't take all the credit. Yes, I wanted to prove you wrong—and maybe prove myself wrong too. Prove that I really am supposed to be here. But I also just needed to find my footing. Something about The Bottoms— the ugliness, the desolation—it worked for me."

"Like I said, you didn't need to look far to find your creative eye. I knew it was in there. It just gets buried by life if you let it."

She sighed. "Tell me something I don't know."

"Okay, here's something you don't know." He sat up straighter and ran a hand through his hair, leaving bits sticking up in tufts. "I almost gave up photography five years ago."

Jenna raised her eyebrows. "Why?"

"Why else do men make bad decisions? For a woman."

"Ah. We do tend to mess things up."

"Granted, she wasn't trying to mess anything up—she just wanted me to stay."

"And you wanted to go."

He nodded. "I've been a photographer since my early twenties. I don't put down roots. I never stay long in one place. I have an apartment in Atlanta, but I'm usually only there to catch up on sleep and pack for my next gig. I love to travel, so the life fits me well. But it's hard on relationships, family and otherwise. Callie wanted me to stop traveling, to stay in Charleston with her." He rubbed his forehead. "She actually wanted me to work for her dad at his investment firm."

Jenna wrinkled her nose. "You don't seem like the investment firm type."

"Exactly. But I considered it. I figured Charleston had enough opportunities for photography and maybe I could travel some on the weekends."

"So what happened?" She turned to the tray behind her to check the progress of the photos.

"Be patient."

She faced him again.

"I was asked to mentor here for the summer. Then I was offered a freelance spot with *National Geographic Traveler*. I realized what I had going with work was too good to give up to sit in an office all day wearing a suit and drinking scotch with old men."

"But you had to give her up too."

He gave a slow nod, his gaze unfocused. "Haven't talked to her since the day I told her I was leaving. I tried to call her a few times after I left, but she never picked up." After a moment, he blinked and focused on Jenna.

"All this to say I understand the pull photography has. Any art, really. Anything that lets you capture the world as you see it and say things you can't say with words. Sometimes it's more important than anything else."

He hopped off the counter and peered into the trays where the photos floated in solution. The images were suspended somewhere between undefined blobs and what she hoped would turn out to be not terrible.

"Tell me something about you." He set the dripping tongs back onto the towel.

"What do you want to know?"

"Anything. I just bared my soul."

"I don't like talking about myself. I'm better if you ask questions." She leaned against the counter and crossed her arms.

"Okay. You're not married."

"That's not a question."

He smiled. "Okay. You're young, you're talented, you seem like a nice girl—why are you not married?"

"Why aren't you?"

"I just told you. I'm elusive. Hard to pin down. But this isn't about me anymore. And you told me to ask questions."

She took a deep breath. "It's kind of a long story."

He gestured to the trays behind her. "We have nothing but time."

She tilted her head side to side, stretching her tight neck muscles as if preparing for battle. "I'll give you the abbreviated version. I moved to Wyoming with some friends after my freshman year of college. Worked, played, took pictures. Fell in love."

Gregory shrugged. "It happens."

She closed her eyes, then opened them again. "Jeremy was a photographer too, and a musician. Probably a better photographer, but he decided to make music his thing."

When he packed up to join his band back home in Asheville, North Carolina, he'd asked Jenna to come too, and with nothing tying her to Wyoming, she went with him. Her camera continued to be good to her in the Blue Ridge Mountains. She sold her prints in galleries up and down the Blue Ridge Parkway and had a robust Etsy business, shipping her prints across the country, even some internationally.

"Etsy?" Gregory asked. "What's that?"

"Are you serious?" She peered at him through the dim light. "It's a website where people sell things."

"Like Amazon?"

"No, not like Amazon. Just . . . look it up."

"Okay. So you were in Asheville with your boyfriend and your thriving photography business. What happened?"

She held up her hands, then let them drop. "I got pregnant."

She discovered she was pregnant on a Tuesday morning via a Clearblue Easy in the restroom of the Asheville Folk Gallery where she worked. Jeremy's band had hired a publicist after a run of good shows, and the publicist had lined up a long string of gigs in the Northeast. Jenna waited until he returned from the tour before telling him. She was already three months pregnant by then, although still another month or so away from showing. He was a little excited but more hesitant. She saw it in his eyes right away: a baby didn't have quite as much pull as the road did.

After that, his band went on longer and more frequent tours—up the East Coast, as far west as Texas, and even up to Boston. She moved out of his apartment and into a house with some friends so she wouldn't be alone. Her roommates told her she was crazy for hanging on, but she thought being a few months away from holding an infant in her arms was a pretty good reason to hang on. Her only other choice was to do it alone, which was what ended up happening when Jeremy moved with the band to New York City.

"Did you ask him to stay?"

"I didn't want to have to ask. So no. He left and I watched him go." She hadn't meant to tell him the whole story, but once she started talking, the story flowed.

"What'd you do?"

"I called my sister in the middle of the night. I hadn't told her I was pregnant, so it was a bit of a shock. But Betsy just . . ." Jenna paused, remembering the silence on the phone when she blurted out the news to Betsy with no warning. "I know she wanted to say a lot, but she didn't. She just showed up at my door the next night with a car full of diapers and baby gear and stayed until a couple weeks after Addie was born."

"You have two kids though, right?"

She ran her hands across the smooth counter surface and nodded.

As luck would have it, she ran into Jeremy again soon after moving to Nashville. She hadn't talked to him in over a year so she didn't know he'd moved there to work with a new studio. He was happy to see her—and Addie—and Jenna desperately wanted her child to know her father.

"Deep down I knew he couldn't have changed much, but I ignored that instinct and we gave it a shot anyway. It was good at first—the three of us together. But then I let my guard down. In every way." She peered at Gregory to see if he understood. "Who would have thought I'd get pregnant a second time?"

She rubbed her eyes. "That pretty much ended things. He made himself scarce, and I just let him slide out of the picture again. It was easier that way. Well, it wasn't easy, but at least I wasn't trying to force something that obviously wasn't supposed to work."

It was quiet in the room. Too quiet. She wanted him to say something, but he was silent.

She laughed to cut the tension. "Clearly I have terrible taste in men and have no business trying to date anyone."

Gregory shook his head and rubbed his cheek. "Geez, kid. You're breaking my heart here."

She stood up straighter and brushed her hair back from her face. "That was a very long answer to your question, but that's why I'm not married. I might have said yes if he'd asked, but it's probably better for all of us that he didn't."

He nodded. "If he had, you might not be here."

"True," she said, then pushed off the counter and turned to the trays, cutting off more questions and any possible sympathy she didn't deserve. "Are they ready yet?"

It was a moment before he spoke. Finally, he stood next to her. "Pull them out and let's see what we have."

She gripped the edge of the first photo, holding it a moment to let the last of the water drip off, then clipped it to the wire. One by one, she lifted the photos and hung them up to dry. When she'd clipped all twelve photos, she stood back and studied them.

Not terrible, just like she'd hoped. New, vibrant life pushing against the barren and wasted. Promise seeping into the dark places. Not terrible at all.

"See what you did? You were patient. Rather than shooting the first scene you came to, you waited until you saw something of worth. And because of that, I see it too." He moved down the line. "Without color as a distraction, the contrast between light and dark is the focus. Look at the pattern here on the leaves." He pointed to the repeating stripes on a palm branch. "You angled the shot just right to draw our eye here. And this one—this one is different."

He paused in front of a shot Jenna took of one of the other artists, Terry, standing under a towering oak, his face tipped up and just catching the light. "Adding the human element here increases the emotional impact of the scene. It also gives us some perspective as to just how massive the tree is." He turned to her in the dim light. "How do you feel about these?"

She heard the smile in his voice, and she smiled too. "Good. I feel good."

"I think you've found your place, kid. *You* did all this. Own it. Enjoy it."

EIGHTEEN

Ty

Between an important South Alabama Dairy Farmers' Association meeting, working with Carlos to keep the pump from giving out again, and a weekend lightning storm that temporarily took out power to the milking barn, it was early the next week before Ty could take a breather.

Roger Daily had his grandchildren for a few days, and not knowing what to do with three kids underfoot, he brought them to Ty's place to play with Addie and Walsh. His wife, Linda, came too, the five of them piling out of Roger's ancient blue-and-white truck like clowns at a circus. Addie and Walsh were playing on the big swing when the Dailys arrived, and the grandkids ran straight for them.

Roger trudged over to where Ty stood next to the fence of the holding pen. He took off his cap and brushed his hands through his stiff white hair. "I can take 'em for a few hours, but all weekend?" He laughed a little. "Little ones just wear me out."

"I know what you mean," Ty said with a smile, although he didn't really know. Being so busy in the barn, the burden of keeping up with the girls had fallen mostly on Betsy's shoulders. Not that they were much of a burden. He'd liked having them around this week—their laughter, their excited faces peeking around the barn door, their loose and limber joy.

He was starting to think he'd miss them a little when they were gone.

"I know you heard the reports from the weather center." Roger slapped his cap back on his head and squinted into the sun. "There's already one storm out there. Only June and they're lining up like dominoes."

Ty laughed. "You always so gloom and doom, Roger? You and I both know those things come and go as they please. Active season doesn't always mean it'll be active around here."

"That's true. But we're nothing if not prepared, right?"

"You're right about that. I already got your plywood on my upper windows."

"Farmers help each other out. Your grandfather would have been the first to say that."

"Yes, sir."

"I think I'll go check out the placement of those boards, if you don't mind. I'd hate for water to seep in somewhere, ruin your hard work."

"I don't think I missed any holes, but you're welcome to check for me."

"I do it for your grandfather. He'd want me to keep an eye out for you."

Ty smiled. "I appreciate that." He didn't need the help, but Roger and Ty's grandfather had been close, and if the man wanted to take care of him, it was best to just let him.

Down in the yard, most of the kids were horsing around on the grass under the big tree, but Addie stood a few yards away, near the house. Hide-and-go-seek, maybe.

Betsy and Linda stood next to what used to be Betsy's garden. Now it was barely more than a briar patch. The soil was hard and untilled, and any vegetables still buried in the earth must have been hard rocks by now. It was a shame, really. Betsy had enjoyed that garden when they first moved to the farm. She worked it every day, coaxing everything from potatoes and carrots to marigolds and roses to grow just a little bit higher, a little bit fuller.

It had been a long time since he'd seen her out in the garden. A year, maybe two? She stood next to it now, one hand shading her eyes, her other hand on her hip. Linda tugged on a limp stalk that leaned sideways against a fence post. Betsy shrugged and Linda shook her head. When Linda pointed at something else in the garden, Betsy patted her on the arm and motioned for her to follow. Away from the garden, away from her forgotten mission.

Linda waved to Ty and followed her husband out to the barn. Together, they walked around its perimeter, pointing at who-knows-what and nodding like they knew exactly what Ty was doing wrong on his grandfather's farm, making a list of what he needed to do to fix it.

Betsy crossed the yard, dodging running children, and climbed up on the fence rail next to where Ty stood, hooking her toes under the board below her. She tilted her face up and closed her eyes. Late-afternoon sunshine filtered through the big oak and cast long shadows on the grass.

Ty reached up and propped his elbow on her knees. "What insightful wisdom did Linda share with you?"

"That I'm a miserable gardener."

Ty laughed. "Really?"

"Mm-hmm. No gardener worth her salt would start something like that and then just let it all go. She offered to come over and help me whip it back into shape."

"What'd you tell her?"

Betsy sighed and stretched her arms out in front of her. "I told her I'd let her know if I needed help."

Ty nodded. "Think you'll ever get back out there? It seemed like something you enjoyed."

"Oh, I did enjoy it. I just . . . It got out of hand, and the longer I stayed away, the worse it got. Maybe one day."

Down in the yard, Roger's grandkids—ages seven, nine, and eleven—had circled around Walsh, who was happy to be the center of attention. While the older kids watched, she performed trick after trick—sloppy headstands, rolls on the grass, jumps, leaps. The kids cheered and hugged her. Walsh beamed.

"Where's Addie?" Ty looked to the corner of the house where he'd last seen her.

Just then, the screen door to the back porch opened and Addie tiptoed down the steps. As Walsh's laughter rang out and her antics became even more animated,

Addie took careful steps toward the group in the grass. At the last minute she darted off toward the henhouse, where she paused in the shade along one side of it, her eyes still on the other kids.

"What is she doing?" Ty asked.

"I think she's nervous around the bigger kids. She wants to play, but she's scared to join in."

"Why? Look at Walsh out there. No fear."

"Come get me," Walsh called to the kids, and she darted off to the side of the yard. Addie took a few steps out of the shadows, but not enough to join in the game.

"Jenna was like that when we were little," Betsy said. "I was more like Addie. I used to be jealous of how Jenna was so brave and daring."

"Daring. Yep, I'd say that's a good description of Jenna."

"But it was more than just that. She'd jump in the middle of a group of kids and start playing with them like it was no big thing. I was always too scared. I'd wait until someone asked me to play. I was Addie, tiptoeing around the edge, wanting to be a part of things. Jenna never tiptoed."

Betsy shifted on the fence, straightened out her legs, then tucked them back under the rung. "I remember I had a slumber party once. I think it was for a birthday. My twelfth or thirteenth, I don't remember. It was the same thing. They were my friends, but Jenna was the center of attention. She had bought some nail polish with her allowance money. It must have been the one time she actually did enough chores to get her money for the week. She showed the polish to my friends and they were goners." She laughed. "I still remember what it looked like. Purple with glitter in it. Very Jenna."

"You didn't tell her to leave? Kick her out of your room or something?"

"I couldn't. Even though she made me mad, borrowed things without asking—and usually returned them broken or stained—she was . . . magnetic. I remember watching all my friends watch her, their eyes glued to her. I wanted to be mad, but really, I just wanted to be more like her."

Ty shook his head. "And now? Do you still wish you were like her?"

Betsy was quiet, studying her feet on the wooden board. She shrugged. "Parts of her, I guess. I'm not sure I'd want to spend two weeks in the Florida wilderness, but there's something appealing about having the courage to jump at opportunities as they come. To not think twice."

"I don't know, Bets. Maybe she should have thought twice about it. She has two good reasons to have thought long and hard before she booked this retreat on barely a moment's notice." He gestured toward the girls out on the grass.

"That's not exactly what happened. You know that. We had barely a moment's notice, but that's just because she didn't find out she got in until a few days before she was supposed to be there. She didn't just drop the kids off on a whim."

"Well—"

"She didn't. Or that's not what she meant to do. Anyway, she's my sister. We're family. We help each other out."

Ty clenched his lips together to keep from saying more. No sense arguing over what had already happened. Out in the yard Walsh hung off the swing while Addie picked dandelions in a shaft of sunlight. He squeezed Betsy's knee. "They are kind of fun to have around though, aren't they?" As the kids' laughter bounced around the yard, he leaned his shoulder against her hip. "But we get our house back soon."

Betsy smiled and nodded.

"Think you'll miss 'em?"

She shrugged. "A little."

Ty watched her carefully, trying to catch a chink in her armor, but she gave nothing away. She rested her arm on his shoulder, but her eyes remained steady on the girls. Addie had left her plucked dandelions in a pile and now approached Walsh on the swing. She whispered something to Walsh, and they both laughed.

"We keep talking about getting away, but I'm going to call tomorrow. Maybe check into that little place in Perdido Key with the wooden boardwalks and the sunsets over the river."

Betsy looked at him. Raised her eyebrows. "My field trips can't pay for that kind of place."

Ty wrapped his arm around her waist. "Don't worry about that. I have a little money put away for something like this. Something for us."

"You do?"

She seemed so surprised that he wanted to kick himself

for waiting so long before taking her away somewhere.
He should have done it months ago.

"Okay then," she said.

"Yeah?"

Betsy nodded. "I could use a vacation."

NINETEEN

JENNA

On her last night of the retreat, Jenna walked toward the barn to meet Gregory, her mind somersaulting with mixed emotions—hope and dread, nerves and confidence. She readjusted the camera strap that hung across her shoulder, as if the camera were heavier with all the photos it held. She'd taken hundreds during her stay at Halcyon. Not even half of them were worth showing anyone, but some—a few dozen—gave her hope. Maybe she was even a little proud of them.

That morning he'd caught her on her way out of the dining hall and asked her to meet him in the barn after dinner. "We both know you won't show up at workshop, but it's part of my job to make sure you get the most out of your time here. Why don't you meet me in the barn? We can go over your work there."

The lights in the barn were dim, except for the gallery spotlights shining on the photos on the wall. When her eyes adjusted to the light, she saw it—her own photo on the far wall. It was a shot of a tall, thick cypress tree on the bank of a bayou in The Bottoms wrapped in the "arms" of a strangler fig. Also called a love tree, the fig both embraced and strangled its host. A flyer in the dining hall detailing plant life around the preserve noted that the host trees often died, their life snuffed out by the determined fig.

She'd been struck by both the sadness and the determination of the two intertwined trees. At some point, the fig would likely win the battle, absorbing all the available light and water, leaving the cypress to wither and die. But right now, they were balanced, both sporting bright-green leaves and healthy bark. Both determined to thrive.

And now, that moment was housed in a black frame, standing out from the pale wall behind it, only Jenna wasn't the one who'd framed it.

"I didn't hear you come in." Gregory entered the gallery from a room in the back. He dropped his bag on the floor and sat on one of the chairs across from her photo on the wall. "What do you think?"

"You did this?"

"It's one you left hanging to dry. I had an extra frame in a closet . . ." He shrugged. "Just thought you might like to see it."

Snappy comebacks and sarcastic brush-offs skirted through her mind, then leaked away. "Thank you. It's hard to believe I took it, really."

"It's all you. You have a knack for getting just the right angles, but you also see things others might not notice. Like that tree there." He nodded to the picture. "A lot of people, myself included, probably would have walked right by it in search of something less . . . mangled. But you saw a different kind of beauty. Sometimes perspective is more valuable than technical skills. You've got that instinct."

"I'm not so sure." She sat in the chair next to him.

"Trust me. I've been doing this a while." He leaned forward in his chair and propped his elbows on his knees. "Let's see what you brought."

She reached into her bag and pulled out a manila folder. It was the first time she'd used the Epson printer in the main studio, and she'd been excited to see how her photos came out. However, while the Epson printed her photos in perfect, crisp color, she missed the almost spiritual process of developing the black-and-white film in the dusky red light of the darkroom.

He sifted through the stack of photos, pausing to look at one or another, then slipping each one back in the stack. When he got to the end, he flipped them back and started over again from the beginning. As she waited for his reaction, she smoothed the bottom of her shirt, pressing it flat with her hands, then rolling the bottom edge in her fingers.

Her second week at the retreat had been drastically different from the first. She'd walked nearly every path, bridge, and sandy mound in the preserve, some with Gregory at her side but often alone. She stayed out all day, often forgetting to stop and eat, shooting until the dusk swallowed the light. Though she felt out of her element when she had first arrived at the retreat, unsure of her ability to capture anything meaningful from trees, leaves, and darting geckos, she now felt as adept shooting nature scenes as she did people. She felt electric, her creativity burning through her as it hadn't since her time in Wyoming, alone and free.

She was beginning to think she could do this—could find a way to fit her art, her creativity, into her routine life of kids, work, bills, and housework. The task seemed impossible—her life at home was so tight, her free time doled out in such small chunks, she didn't know how to add these new urges into her normal, day-to day world. But her new sense of purpose was hard to ignore.

"Tell me about this." His sudden words jolted her from her thoughts. He flipped through the stack and pulled one out. It was the shot of the canoe she'd rescued by the lake. Ugly and rusted, with a shaft of fuzzy sunlight beaming through the jagged hole. "When did you take it?"

"A few days after you took me to the waterfall and blasted me about my amateur photo skills."

"Blasted? I prefer to think I inspired, but whatever I did, it was worth it if it pulled this out of you. The first images you took were bland. Then—*wham*—you come out with something like this."

Relief flooded through her. She loved the shot too. "I was on my way to dinner when I saw it. I wasn't even thinking about what I was doing."

"That's when the best stuff happens—when we're not overthinking. It's a good way to live, really. Don't overthink, just do. Works in a lot of situations. It's already working for you." She inhaled, the corners of her mouth pulling up into an involuntary smile. "But you still need practice. Let me show you a few things."

He spent the next few minutes dissecting a handful of photos, pointing out where she'd missed her angle or lost perspective. She was glad for the critique—to grow as a photographer, she needed the honest feedback—but it was hard not to hear his words as marks against her hard work. Against her.

"Do you agree?"

He was watching her, waiting for an answer, but she'd missed the question. "I'm sorry. Do I agree with what?"

He reached forward and dropped her photos on the low table in front of them. "All right. What's going on?"

"Nothing. Please, continue." She swallowed back the annoying lump in her throat. "You were talking about how I got the shadows wrong, I think."

He sighed. "Jenna, this is your critique, just like if you'd been in the workshop. If you're an artist, you can't react like this."

"I'm not . . . I'm not reacting in any way. And I'm not an artist."

"Then what are you?"

"I'm a photographer, right? Isn't that what you want me to say?"

He leaned forward, close enough that she could see gold flecks in his brown eyes. She looked down at her hands. "But what is a photographer if not an artist? Are you not creating something beautiful, something that will make the viewer feel, or escape, or dream? Something that challenges the way we see the world, or encourages someone, gives them hope or direction? That's what art does. Isn't that what you're doing?"

"I'm trying to." Her words were clear and as sharp as his, but she still couldn't look in his eyes.

He reached forward and tilted her chin up with one finger, forcing her to look at him. "Don't guess. Know it. You are an artist. Get it through your head now or when you leave this place, you'll go right back home and pick up your life as if this experience were nothing more than a blip on your radar."

He sat back in his chair and gazed at her photo on the wall. "Look, there will always be people who criticize your work. I'm trying to help you, to make you better than you think you can be, better even than you're trying to be. But those people who truly criticize, who belittle—their words don't matter. What matters is that *you* can't be the one to drag yourself down, okay? You have to carry on, regardless of whether anyone—me, another mentor, or some idiot walking down the street—understands or appreciates your art. It is yours alone and your approval of it, your acceptance of it, has to come first."

Outside, the world was alive with nighttime sounds, but inside, other than their breathing, it was silent.

"Do you understand what I'm saying?"

She nodded, buoyed by his intensity and the fire in his eyes. "I get it."

"Good. You are a photographer, Jenna Sawyer. Even more than that, you're an artist. A good one. And you have the potential to be even better."

She waited for more, but he stood and looked at his watch. "I have a mentor meeting at nine, so I need to get back. You're welcome to stay here if you want."

"I need to get back too." She gathered her photos.

"It's been a long day. And I need to call my sister and let her and my girls know I'll be heading back soon."

"So they're staying with your sister?" He flipped the lights off and held the door open for her. Outside, the steamy air was quieter than before, as if the humidity were cotton in her ears.

She nodded. "She and her husband live on a farm in Alabama. Lots of room for kids."

"Bet they're having a blast."

"Oh yes. Betsy sent me a photo today of the girls sitting on top of a cow out in the middle of a field. They had such big smiles." She couldn't admit it, but seeing Addie's and Walsh's carefree, easy smiles had been hard. Did they miss her at all?

Their feet made soft sounds on the leaves covering the path through the trees. Their only light was the moon, full, round, and unobstructed by clouds.

"It's good they're with family. Sounds like you don't have to worry about them."

"I'm not really worried." She gave a small laugh. "Betsy's good at everything. She probably figured out the whole mom thing in about five minutes. Five years in and I'm still trying to get it."

He glanced at her. "Seems like it'd take a while to get the hang of parenting. It's probably not something that comes naturally—giving up your wants and needs for someone else."

They came to the bridge over the bayou, the water hazy with moonlight.

"You know you can stay longer if you want."

She thought she'd heard him wrong. "Excuse me?"

"You can stretch out your retreat. Stay."

She stopped where she was on the bridge. "What are you talking about?" When he realized she'd stopped, he backtracked. "What about those hundreds of people who apply for each session?"

He shrugged. "If you want to stay, we try to make it work. As long as there's space, of course, and in this case, we just found out a writer had to back out of his session. He was planning to stay to the end of the eight weeks, so that spot is wide open. If no one here takes it, Casey will call the first person on the waiting list sometime tomorrow."

"You'd have to know tonight?"

He nodded and looked at his watch again. "We're talking about it at the meeting."

"I can't stay. They're waiting for me."

"Okay." He said it so simply, so without care, it aggravated her.

She exhaled and pushed her hands through her hair. "Why are you just telling me about this now?"

"I didn't find out about the spot until late this afternoon. I figured I'd see what frame of mind you were in before I told you. That's the thing—it's not a blanket offer to the whole group. A mentor has to make the case for one of the current artists. Why he or she should be asked to stay, how it will benefit them, how they've grown, how much further they have to go."

"And you think I'm a good fit?"

"Wouldn't be asking if I didn't. I convinced the others to hold off on offering the spot to anyone until I talked to you."

He turned his face toward the creek as if to give her a moment of privacy while she deliberated. She studied his profile in the moonlight, her mind swimming.

Could she? Was it possible? She'd just found her footing here, and leaving before she really even got started would be disappointing.

He turned back to her. "Keep in mind that if you stay, I'd expect you to work hard. I'll help you put together a solid portfolio. You already have a decent head start, but we need to flesh it out. Show what you can do. And I may have some contacts I can share with you. Help you get your foot in the door at a few places."

She clasped her hands together across her middle to keep them from shaking. "Why are you doing this for me? There must be other artists here who'd jump at the chance to extend their stay. Why me?"

He held up his hands, then let them drop. "Maybe it's because I see a little bit of myself in you. Whether that's a good thing or not is anyone's guess." He took a breath and leaned against the rail of the bridge. "Max couldn't have known it, but he did me a favor when he asked me to keep an eye on you. The way you see things—your perspective—it challenges me to be better. To work harder. Maybe we can help each other." He looked at her. "I think you're a worthy artist. I think you need more time here. I want to give you that chance."

Finally, he pushed off the railing. "Come on. I'll tell them you need the night to decide. Just let me know in the morning."

TWENTY

BETSY

Betsy stood over the kitchen sink Magic Erasing mud off the girls' shoes so they could wear them to church. Whenever Jenna arrived, Betsy was sure it would at least be after the eleven o'clock service let out.

Jenna hadn't given her a firm time, but Sunday was the day she was supposed to return, the day that had glowed red in Betsy's mind for two weeks, since the minute she'd opened the gates she'd thought were shut tight. Having the girls in the house had required a delicate dance of exposure and protection. Life spilled on the rugs and countertops, laughter echoing off the walls, small dirty footprints on her kitchen floor. Some of it had felt natural, like slipping into a perfectly shaped second skin. But other parts had been almost unbearable, and she fought the urge to pull her gates closed again, lock them, and hide the key.

While Betsy scrubbed, Addie and Walsh zoomed around the house like they had wheels for feet. Their excitement was catching. As if something bigger than just Jenna's return was imminent.

"Do you think she bought me something? Something big?" Addie asked on one of her passes through the kitchen.

"Well, I don't know," Betsy said. "What if it's something tiny?" She bent down with her hands on her knees, face-to-face with Addie. "What if it's small enough to hold in your hand?"

Addie's eyes grew wide and she peeled off behind Walsh. "Walsh, what if Mommy brings us a fairy?"

Ty finished the morning milking by ten thirty, which left him only a few minutes to shower before Betsy piled them all into her car—Ty's truck didn't have space for the girls' car seats—and sped down the highway to Elinore United Methodist Church. The parking lot was full of pickups and other sturdy, practical vehicles, most flecked with mud. Betsy parked under a tree at the side of the oyster-shell parking lot so the car wouldn't be so hot after church.

They unloaded the girls and headed for the front doors with Ty carrying Walsh and Addie's small hand firmly locked around Betsy's. Betsy smiled hello to families in the parking lot while Ty shook a few hands and made the usual comments about the weather. Hot, getting hotter. Tropical Depression 5 had just been given a name—Dawn—which added extra pep to their small talk.

As folks poured out of the double doors from the nine-thirty service, Betsy saw Anna Beth standing to the side in a bright-pink pantsuit and struggling to button her son Jackson's collar. He kept batting her hand away as only a thirteen-year-old boy could. When she spotted Betsy, she dropped her arms, gave him a hard stare, and marched toward Betsy.

"That boy." She blew a lock of hair out of her face. "First he wanted to wear shorts to church—shorts! I talked him into long pants, but he refuses to button that top button." She shook her head.

"I'll let you two ladies chat." Ty let go of Betsy's hand and joined Anna Beth's husband, Tom, by the wall, uncomfortable in his Sunday best. Ty still carried Walsh in his arms, as natural as if he were carrying a newborn calf. Addie clung to Betsy, creating a pocket of heat between their hands.

Behind Anna Beth, Jackson yanked on his collar, then noticed Betsy watching him. She smiled.

"It is about 90 percent humidity out here," she said. "It has to get hot under those tight collars."

"It's church!" Anna Beth said. "It's not about comfort—it's about reverence. Oh, there's my new boss." She smiled and waved at Duncan Burgess, the new principal at Elinore Elementary. "Better go make nice."

As Anna Beth worked her way toward Mr. Burgess, Betsy and Addie waited for the rest of the congregation to file out of the church. When the crowd cleared, Ty waved at her and she and Addie joined him at the front doors.

They took bulletins from the ushers and made their way to their regular seats—left side, five rows from the front. The girls began to fidget as soon as they sat down, turning around and staring at people in the row behind them, bouncing up and down on the cushioned pews.

"I'll be right back," Myrtle Davis, who sat at the end

of their row, said. She appeared a moment later with children's coloring sheets and crayons. "You won't make it through the service without these." She winked. Betsy thanked her, embarrassed for not thinking to get them herself.

The organist started and Betsy opened her bulletin. Being in church usually calmed her, took her outside her own head and into another place, somewhere higher than her usual day-to-day frustrations. But today she was antsy. She crossed her legs and her foot bounced up and down, quick and hard. Ty rested his hand on her knee and she stopped. Took a deep breath and tried to concentrate.

During the pastor's prayer, she bowed her head like everyone else, but she kept her eyes open. She always did that. Something about closing her eyes while praying made her feel too loose, like she might float away if she wasn't anchored by the sight of the wooden pew, the red hymnals, Ty's leg next to hers. Instead of Ty's leg, it was Addie's knee and a fistful of crayons, but it helped.

After another hymn, the pastor began the sermon. Next to them, the girls' crayons quietly scratched across the paper. Walsh asked Ty to draw a unicorn and he took on the task with his usual focused attention. He was adding a flowing mane and pointed unicorn horn when Betsy saw a glow from the side pocket of her purse on the floor. She glanced at Ty, then leaned down to check the screen, although she already knew who it was.

She pulled the phone out of her purse, covering the

glowing screen with her hand, then ducked her head and walked quickly down the center aisle. By the time she exited the double doors into the breezeway, she'd missed Jenna's call, of course. She tried to call her right back, but it went straight to voice mail. She typed out a quick text.

Sorry, in church. Call back.

She paced the breezeway while she waited. The only other person outside was a young mother holding a fussy baby. The mother rocked on her feet, gently bouncing the baby in her arms. When Betsy passed her, she heard the woman singing "You Are My Sunshine." She tried not to stare, but the baby's cheeks were so pink, her eyelashes so long. Her dimpled chin so perfect.

She turned so the woman wouldn't think she was crazy and stared at the phone instead, willing it to ring. Instead of ringing, she got a *ding* that meant Jenna had left a message. She walked to the edge of the breezeway, sensing the need for privacy, and held the phone to her ear.

"Hey, Bets." Jenna paused, then sighed. Betsy could almost see her sister, her fingers fiddling with something, her hair a mess of curls, her blue eyes big and round. "I really don't want to leave this in a voice mail, but I'm afraid I might not get cell service again for a while. Something's come up. My mentor here gave me the option of extending my retreat and I . . ." She took a deep breath. "I took it."

Betsy closed her eyes.

"It sounds crazy, I know. It's just that I've only now

had a sort of breakthrough to where I can . . . I don't know, see straight, I guess. I've finally gotten to the place where things are clicking. The first two weeks barely scratched the surface." She paused. Betsy crossed her free arm across her stomach, holding herself tight. "I know this is so last minute and I'm being irresponsible, but, Betsy, I just can't . . . I'm so sorry to ask this of you. I can't leave now, and I don't know how else to explain it." Jenna exhaled and so did Betsy. "I know the girls are having a blast. I hope they're not too much trouble and . . . I hope you can understand this. Please understand. I'll call again as soon as I can. And tell . . . please tell them I love them."

Betsy pulled the phone away from her ear and tried to call back, but no answer. She closed her eyes again and touched the phone to her forehead. Behind her, someone stopped. "Are you okay?"

It was the mother with the baby. Betsy nodded. "Thanks."

"Just checkin'." The woman swayed to keep the baby asleep on her shoulder. "You looked a little faint. Thought I might have to find a chair or something for you."

Betsy took a breath and pulled open the door. From the back of the sanctuary, she could see between other heads and shoulders to where Ty, Addie, and Walsh sat, their heads bowed, all probably still working on their crayon masterpieces. Next to them was the empty space reserved for her. Fingers of emotion squeezed her heart and tears prickled at the corners of her eyes.

She strode back to their pew. When she sat, Ty looked over at her and raised his eyebrows. *Jenna?* he mouthed.

Betsy nodded and turned her gaze to the front of the church where the pastor was wrapping up his sermon. Ty reached across the back of the pew and laid his big warm hand on her shoulder.

TWENTY-ONE

Ty

*Tropical Storm Dawn has made a sharp
curve to the north, heading north/northeast
at 40 mph. It is expected to continue on this
track over the next 2–3 days. Residents of
the central Gulf Coast should take proper
precautions in the event Dawn gains speed.*

The radio spit out Dawn's coordinates as Ty opened
the gate for the remaining forty cows to exit the
barn. When the last one trailed out, swishing her tail as
if waving good-bye, he grabbed the water hose. Aiming
it at the floor of the milking parlor, he turned the faucet
on full blast.

To his right, fifteen curious faces pressed up against
the wide window of the observation room. A group
of YMCA summer campers had come early today to
watch the milking. They were the second field trip this
week, which was probably a good thing. Something

to distract Addie and Walsh from the fact that their mom did not, in fact, show up as she was supposed to with their promised treats and a ride back home to Nashville.

As soon as Betsy sat back down in church on Sunday after receiving the phone call, he knew something was wrong. She filled him in as they made the girls' lunches after church. Ty took a deep breath to keep his anger in check.

"Did you ask her when she's coming back?"

"I couldn't ask her. It was a voice mail."

"Did you try calling her back?"

"Of course I did. She didn't answer. Or it didn't go through. Or something."

Ty laughed low. "Of course she calls you while you're in church. Where else would you be at eleven thirty on a Sunday morning? Leaving a quick message is much easier than explaining yourself." He dragged his hand through his hair.

"I don't think she purposely called while we were in church."

He gave her a look and rolled his eyes.

"You're not getting mad at me, are you? This is not my fault."

Their whispers had grown harsh—not what he intended, but he couldn't help himself. With one call to the Betsy Franklin Rescue Service, Jenna was off the hook. Again.

"I know it's not your fault. I just don't like the way she uses us. Uses you."

"I'm her sister, Ty. I don't have a choice."

"Yes, you do. You do have a choice, though it looks like you're dead set against using it." He stood from his kitchen stool. "Let's go talk to them then." They had to tell the girls something. Well, mainly Addie. Walsh seemed happy as a clam no matter what she was doing, but Addie was sensitive. Aware. Betsy had wanted to make it sound simple, like Jenna's car broke down or she had to make an extra stop before coming back, but Ty pushed for the truth.

"I can't tell them I don't know when she's coming back," Betsy said.

Ty nodded at Addie, whose face was pressed up against the window in the living room, watching the driveway. "Twenty bucks says she'll know you're lying."

Finally, Betsy told them Jenna just needed some more time. It was a version of the truth, at least.

Since their "discussion" in the kitchen, they'd danced around the subject of Jenna. They didn't bring her up, but her presence—the *lack* of it—filled up their house anyway.

"Whatcha think about the weather report?" Carlos wrenched Ty from his thoughts, bringing him back to the barn. "It's headed for the sweet spot."

Ty looked up just in time to see Betsy smile from the window in the observation room, the kids in a swarm all around her. Ty lifted his chin in response, then remembered she hated the "cool guy nod," as she called it, and held up a hand instead. Addie and Walsh were mixed in with the other kids—two innocent, wide-eyed faces in the sea of middle schoolers, all equally as enthralled as the girls.

Ty turned back to Carlos. "Too early for the sweet spot. And she's still just a tropical storm." He directed the stream of water to the remaining hay and sawdust on the floor.

The "sweet spot" was a very nonscientific method Ty used to predict which storms would affect them—either by a direct hit or by putting coastal Alabama on the east side of the eye, pounding them with the worst of the wind and rain. When storms hit a certain path in the Gulf of Mexico, they often seemed to get caught in a current that funneled them north toward the Mississippi-Alabama border. No meteorologist worth his suspenders would put stock in Ty's "sweet spot" method, but he'd been right so many times, he'd lost count.

Carlos grabbed the wide broom and pushed the standing water out of the barn. "Here's hoping you're right. I'm taking Gloria to Panama City next weekend. Donna—"

"Dawn."

"Whatever. She better not mess up my plans."

Ty turned off the faucet, then curled the hose around the hook. "I was supposed to take Betsy somewhere like that soon. A vacation." A bead of sweat dripped from his forehead into his eye as he wound the hose. He swiped his face with the back of his hand.

"And? What's stopping you? I can take care of things here."

Ty nodded to the window. Betsy had directed the kids' attention to the old black-and-white photos lining the walls of the observation room, but Addie and

Walsh remained pressed against the glass. They both grinned when he looked their way.

"Yeah, I've been meaning to ask you about that. Didn't want to pry. How long are they staying?"

Ty chuckled. "The million-dollar question."

Behind the glass, the kids trailed out of the observation room toward the door. Betsy led them over to the side yard where a cow had wandered over to the fence, likely suspecting small hands full of sweet treats. Without even seeing the characteristic diamond-shaped spot on her nose, Ty knew it was Rosie. She was the most affectionate of the whole herd. She pressed her cheek against the wooden posts, and the kids reached through the fence to pet her face and back.

Ty kept four bulls on the farm, and the Grantleys up in Stapleton had a herd of fifteen. When Ty's four hadn't had success with Rosie, they tried several of the bulls from the Grantley farm. Ty had done all he could do for her—all he could stomach. Rosie couldn't seem to get pregnant and the vet had no answers for them. But the girl was maternal and nurturing to everything she saw, whether cow, person, or barn cat. She licked, she nuzzled, she even cleaned other cows' calves.

After a moment, Rosie walked away from the kids' curious hands and fingers to visit another heifer, number 046. Forty-six was easy to spot because she was all white except for the black on her tail and her legs below the knees. A year younger than Rosie, 046 had been successfully impregnated three months ago. From the looks of it, they'd have a Christmas calf. Rosie sidled up to 046 and rubbed her cheek against the other cow's neck.

• • •

That evening after a quick and chaotic dinner with Betsy and the girls, Ty retreated to the barn to put away the extra bags of feed and hay he'd bought that afternoon. Some might think that after being in the barn all day, a farmer would relish closing the door behind him at the end of the workday and leaving it behind. The truth was, nighttime was Ty's favorite time in the barn. While the sky outside grew dark, the barn was lit with warm light. The cows were well fed and content, moths fluttered in the lights, and industrial fans on either end of the barn swirled lazily, taking the edge off the heat. The aroma of the cedar beams and rafters filled the air.

As he pulled out a half-used yellow legal pad to note which supplies he still needed to add to their stock, the screen door slammed, then Addie's and Walsh's voices carried through the dark. He looked up to see Betsy following the girls to the barn.

"I thought y'all would be asleep by now," he said as Walsh ran to him and hugged his leg. He looked up at Betsy and she shrugged.

"They weren't even close to settling down. They begged to come see you, so here we are."

He stood and pried Walsh's arms from around his legs. He patted her on the back, and she ran off to the other side of the barn with Addie. "How are you?" he asked Betsy. He shoved his hands into his pockets. "Sorry I had to come back out here. I wanted to get this stuff put away before we need it." He gestured to the pile of bags behind him.

"You getting ready for Dawn?"

"Well, not her necessarily. She won't be too bad. But there'll be more."

"She's in the sweet spot," Betsy said.

Ty laughed, rubbed a hand over his eye. "That sweet-spot business is ridiculous. You know that, right?"

"No," she said with a smile. "If Farmer Ty says it's real, I believe it."

She looked so beautiful in her black sleeveless top and white shorts. Her long legs had the first hints of a summer tan. Wisps of brown hair brushed her cheeks.

"What is it?" She looked down at her clothes, then back at him.

Why did he all of a sudden feel uncomfortable around his own wife, this woman he'd been married to for eight years, known for a decade? He was fidgety, nervous. Words bounced around in his mouth, but the right ones refused to come out.

"Have you talked to Jenna?" he finally asked, his voice quiet so the girls wouldn't hear.

The smile that played at the corners of her mouth disappeared. She shook her head. "Texts mostly. Nothing substantial."

"Nothing about when she's coming back?"

Betsy shook her head.

"And you're okay with that?"

"What can I do? She's six hours away, at least. I can't sit her down and force her to talk to me."

"Did she tell you any more about this extension? Or what she thinks is going to happen when it's over?"

"I don't know any details. Just that she had a

breakthrough and wasn't ready to pack everything up and leave just yet. They gave her the chance to stay longer and she took it."

Ty sat back down and picked up his legal pad again. Crossed out a few words, wrote them again. Pulled his cap off. "What are we supposed to do?"

"Nothing. We can't kick them out. It's not their fault." She reached up and tucked a loose strand of hair into the knot at the back of her head. When it fell down into her eyes again, she swatted it away.

"That's not what I mean. I know we need to take care of them. I *want* to do that. It's just . . . It's frustrating that she only thinks about herself. Not about how this affects anyone else."

Their whispered conversation stopped when Addie ran back into the barn. "Can I feed one of the cows?"

Ty exhaled and stood. "I think I know of a girl who needs a late-night snack. Come on." He glanced back at Betsy, then led the girls to Rosie's stall along the back wall of the barn. Rosie stood facing out to the barn, as if she'd been expecting guests. Ty dipped a cup into a bag of oats hanging on the wall and handed it to Addie. "Here. Hold this up to her mouth." Addie giggled when Rosie stuck her tongue down into the cup.

Ty tugged on Betsy's arm and they moved a few steps away from the girls. "I know she's your sister and we need to help," he whispered. "There's just got to be a limit to how much we can do."

She took a deep breath and exhaled through puffed cheeks. "Fine. If you want them gone so bad, I'll tell her she has to come back. Now. Tomorrow."

Ty slapped his cap against the side of his leg. "That's not— I don't know what else to say, Bets. I'm not the bad guy here."

"I know," she said, her words clipped, her mouth tense.

He shoved his cap back on his head and pulled it down low. He was done trying to fix this tonight.

What he and Betsy had put back together in the months since they last left the clinic was like an eggshell. A fragment of what they used to have. He wanted his wife back—he wanted it all back—and he wasn't sure they could continue to build it with the girls here. It had been hard enough with just the two of them. Well, the two of them, five farmhands, two hundred cows, and assorted knobby-kneed schoolkids darting around, making a mess of his barn.

Maybe that was the problem. Too much intrusion, not enough privacy. Maybe if things could just settle down for once—be calm and still and easy—they could get each other back.

But he was a smart enough man to know life wasn't like that.

TWENTY-TWO

BETSY

Dawn rolled into Mobile Bay as a Category 1 hurricane, confirming Ty's theory that the Gulf waters weren't yet warm enough to sustain a strong storm. Despite the low rating, however, Dawn arrived at high tide, resulting in downtown Mobile covered in five feet of floodwaters. Thankfully, flooding wasn't an issue in Elinore, twenty-five miles east of Mobile, but the gusty winds and heavy rainfall made for a rough night of sleep.

While the winds blew and rain pounded, Walsh slept and Addie cried. Ty spent the night downstairs, ready for action in case the house or barn sustained damage, and Betsy spent most of the overnight hours in and out of the girls' room consoling Addie.

"When will it stop?" Addie sobbed as a strong gust of wind lashed the side of the house.

"Soon, soon," Betsy murmured. She sat on the edge of the bed, rubbing what she hoped were comforting circles on Addie's back. "Hurricanes blow hard for a few hours, but eventually they just run out of steam. Then morning will come and it'll all be over."

"What about the cows?" Addie sniffed. "Are they okay?"

"They're just fine. Uncle Ty put them out in the back pasture so they're away from trees or anything else that can hurt them."

"I hope so. Oh, I hope Rosie isn't scared." Thoughts of Rosie caused a new gush of tears. Betsy grabbed a tissue from the dresser and wiped Addie's nose. Just a few feet away, Walsh slept in peace, as if all was right with the world.

Did Addie always react like this to bad storms? Granted, this wasn't an average thunderstorm, but Betsy and Ty had encountered much worse. Then again, Addie was only five, and hurricanes didn't make it all the way up to Nashville. Still, Betsy wondered how often Jenna had sat up late at night with one of the girls, knowing she'd have to be at work early the next morning.

Finally, sometime after midnight, Addie lay still, exhausted by her tears and the late hour. When Betsy's own eyes began to droop, she brushed Addie's hair back from her face and stood to leave.

"Could you stay with me?" Addie's voice was quiet but pleading. Betsy paused. The last time Addie had asked her to stay, she'd woken up with both girls tucked in next to her and her heart thumping.

"Please?"

Betsy sighed. "Of course I'll stay." But instead of lying down next to Addie, she sat on the floor next to the bed, one arm raised over her head to hold Addie's hand. She could handle the floor, her arm falling asleep, her hand sandwiched between Addie's small, warm ones. She woke the next morning with a crick in her neck and shoulder, but her heart felt okay.

. . .

Two days later, Betsy stood at the washing machine staring at a pile of small, damp, dirt-streaked clothes. As the wife of a farmer, Betsy had all kinds of stain-removal methods in her arsenal—Tide bleach pen, OxiClean, Fels-Naptha, vinegar and lemon juice, hair spray, salt crystals—but after stomping in puddles and exploring the rain-soaked farm for hours the previous day, the girls' clothes were covered in mud and Betsy was at a loss. How in the world had Jenna kept their clothes so clean? Betsy made a mental note to ask if there was some miracle stain-stick she'd yet to discover.

Behind her, Addie lay sprawled out on the floor coloring while Walsh explored the dark recesses under the couch. Betsy shut the door of the washing machine and turned it on. One more try wouldn't hurt, but they needed new clothes.

"Hey, girls," she called. "How about a trip to Target?"

Addie scrambled off the floor fast as lightning. "Mommy lets us pick something from the dollar bins."

"Oh yeah?"

Addie nodded. "If our hands don't get too grabby in the store."

Betsy smiled. "I think we can make that happen."

The rain had fizzled, so Betsy rolled down the windows in the car to take in the water-cleansed breeze. Dark clouds zipped across a mottled sky. No sunshine yet, but it would come soon, heating the moisture to a steamy wall of humid heat.

"What are those birds, Aunt Betsy?"

Addie pointed out the window to three spindly legged, long-necked birds soaring over Highway 35.

"Those are blue herons. They fly over water looking for fish to eat."

"But there's no water here. It's just a bunch of grass and cows."

"Well, we're not too far from the Gulf. And we have the creek. Remember where you and Uncle Ty threw sticks?"

"Yeah."

"The creek is full of little minnows and fish, so the herons like to stick around. One time I found a mama heron sitting on a big nest down by the creek."

"Did she have eggs?"

Betsy nodded. "She did. Pretty ones."

Betsy had been cutting overgrown brush at the back of their property when she'd spotted a blue heron perched on a pile of sticks and leaves on the other side of the creek. It was nestled in the tree line next to the water, almost camouflaged. The heron's head was turned to the side, but Betsy knew it was staring at her with that one tiny eye. When she took a careful step backward, away from the creek, she stumbled over her pile of brush. She caught herself before falling but the noise spooked the heron and it flew off, revealing eggs in the nest. Five blue ones about the size of a child's fist.

Betsy came back every day after, hoping to see the heron on the nest, but the bird never returned. The eggs remained in the nest until one day, the only thing left was a mess of shells and wispy gray feathers stuck to the leaves. She read somewhere that once a heron has been disturbed while sitting on eggs, she will deem the area unsafe and abandon the nest and the eggs. When that happened, predators—dogs, alligators, hawks— would often get the eggs.

Betsy chose to believe the heron came back for her babies and Betsy just missed seeing her. She imagined five little baby herons poking along behind their mother down the creek, miles away from her meddling eyes.

Just before Betsy pulled onto Highway 59, the main thoroughfare through Baldwin County, her phone rang. Thinking Ty might be curious about where they'd gone, she grabbed it out of her purse.

"Betsy? Hi." Her sister's voice was quiet, a little cautious. "How are things going?"

"Well . . ." Betsy turned and glanced over her shoulder. Addie was airplaning her hand out the open window and Walsh was playing with Addie's stuffed elephant. "The girls are fine. I wish you'd talked to me about all this first though. It's . . . it's a lot." She tried to keep her voice low.

"I know. I'm so sorry to have dropped it on you like that. It's just that I had to give a quick answer or they would have offered the extension to someone else."

"Would that have been a bad thing? Don't you need to get back to work?" *Or see your kids?*

Jenna paused a beat. "Well, technically I'm between jobs right now, so staying here a little longer won't affect my work."

"What do you mean, 'between jobs'?" Betsy's heart picked up speed in her chest.

"They could only hold my job for the two weeks I told them I'd be gone. I talked to my boss yesterday and he said since I couldn't give him a firm answer of when I'd be back, he's going to have to fill the position, which I totally understand."

"Wait—but you . . ." So many questions bounced around in Betsy's mind, she struggled to form words to ask any of them. She took a deep breath. "You don't know when you're coming back?"

"Not . . . specifically. They've left it up to me how long I stay. The whole thing wraps up August 15th, so I guess that'd be the very latest."

"Jenna, this is . . . You can't lose that job. You have insurance with it and they've been so good about giving you time off when you need to take care of the kids. How are you going to find something like that again? And what will you do for money while you're looking?" She hated sounding like the mom, but someone had to ask the right questions.

"I have some money saved up, believe it or not. It won't tide me over for too long, but it's enough to cover rent and bills while I'm here. We'll be fine. I'm very good at being frugal. And about the job, I have manager experience, so I should be able to pick up a job at another coffee shop with no problem. Anyway, I'm hoping I don't have to go back to making coffee. That's kind of the whole point of being here."

Betsy recognized the familiar determination in Jenna's voice, and she bit back the avalanche of words threatening to pour out.

Jenna sighed. "I know it seems like a spontaneous, flaky thing to do, but trust me when I say I've put a lot of thought into this. I've worked hard to take care of my girls, and there's no way I'd leave a steady job if I didn't think what's happening here could put me in the position to make a better life for them. For us."

"You're putting a lot of stock in this place. Are you sure it's going to be able to give you what you want?"

"Am I *sure*? No, I'm not. But I've been given a shot—maybe my only shot—at providing something good, something meaningful for me and the girls. For them to see me pursuing a dream for myself. Shouldn't I take it?"

The haze of anger and frustration that had clouded Betsy's brain since the Sunday-morning phone call cleared for a minute, providing space to breathe and think. On the surface, giving up her job seemed crazy, staying at this artists' retreat all summer seemed crazy, but knowing Jenna and her fierce determination to forge her own path, it made a strange sort of sense.

"Gregory—he's my mentor— he's helping me with contacts and building up my portfolio of work so I can use it as a résumé. Lots of artists leave this place and land jobs because of their time here. It could happen for me too."

Betsy nodded slowly. "So August 15th. That's, what, a little over a month away?"

"It could be less than that, but I don't want to leave until I've squeezed everything out of this place that I can."

"I hope you get what you want. I really do. I . . . can't say I totally agree with all this, but I know you, and I know you put your heart into whatever you're doing. If anyone could squeeze something meaningful and life-changing out of all this, it'd probably be you."

Jenna exhaled. "Thanks."

Betsy glanced in the rearview mirror. Addie was watching her. "Addie wants to talk to you. I'm going to hand the phone over. Check in again soon, okay?" She reached behind her seat and passed the phone into Addie's waiting hands.

Addie wasted no time when she put the phone to her ear. "Mommy? When are you coming home?" After a pause, she gave a small, "Okay." Betsy waited for the tears, the pleas for her mother to come back, but instead, Addie smiled. It was small, but it was there. Then she launched into an explanation of the new hen Linda Daily had brought by for them.

Betsy rested her elbow on the window ledge and ran her hand through her hair. How was it that Jenna was allowed to slide her responsibilities onto Betsy—again, as Ty had reminded her—yet Betsy was the one feeling like she'd done something wrong?

"Her feathers are all different colors and we named her Rainbow Shine. Do you like that name? She's going to lay some eggs soon. Maybe you can meet her when you come back."

· · ·

At Target the girls spotted a red shopping cart the size of a small bus and scrambled up into it. Betsy was used to seeing women pushing these carts through the store, expertly angling them around displays and racks without incident, even with children crawling in, around, and all over the carts. Today, Betsy learned that kind of maneuvering took skills she didn't possess.

She wheeled between racks of kids' clothes, bumping here and there, drawing raised eyebrows and sighs from other shoppers until she finally abandoned the cart behind a wall of Disney princess pajamas. She was pulling Walsh out of the seat when she heard a deep rumble of laughter behind her.

"I don't envy you, having to push that thing through the store," a man said.

Betsy set Walsh down and turned. Mr. Burgess, the new principal, smiled back at her. His gently lined face and kind eyes soothed a bit of the tension in her shoulders. She kept a hand on Walsh while Addie looked through a rack of Little Mermaid bathing suits. She smiled back at him. "That was a first for me, and I don't plan to try it again."

He laughed. "I'm Duncan Burgess." He reached out his hand. "And you're Mrs. Franklin, right?"

"I am, but it's just Betsy."

Walsh pulled out of Betsy's grip and raced to where Addie stood in front of a floor-length mirror trying on sun hats.

"I've been hoping I'd run into you, actually. You do the field trips, right? To your farm?"

Betsy nodded. "Fewer in the summer, but we still have them."

"I think it's a great program and I want to try to send a few more classes this next school year. I'd love your input on how to coordinate the trips with lessons on healthy eating, maybe community support. You can probably give the teachers some pointers for lessons that'll tie in well."

"I can try to help, although your teachers will know more than me. I can adjust the regular talk I give to the kids if they want me to focus more on a certain aspect of the process. Make it more science-based or more health-oriented. Whatever they want."

Mr. Burgess was nodding. "Wonderful. I figured you'd have some good ideas. Once we get a little closer to the start of the year, maybe we can sit down and talk through the details."

Over his shoulder, Betsy spotted Addie and Walsh between the racks. They'd left the mirror and now ventured toward the toy section. "Sorry, I'd better . . ." She gestured toward the girls.

"Right. Go grab 'em. You'll be in here all day if they make it to the toys. They're adorable. Your older one—she's about six?"

"That's a pretty good guess. She'll be six in December."

He held his hands up. "I've been a principal for thirty years. Comes with the job."

"I guess so. Well, they're my nieces."

"Ah, babysitting. I have three grandkids, so I do

quite a bit of that myself. And I suppose being a school principal is a little like babysitting too. For the biggest family you can imagine." He laughed. "I do love children, but I'll tell you what—one of the best things about having kids is seeing the change in your spouse. I loved Carol in a whole new way after we had our first daughter. Children change people. They change everything." He shook his head, lost in memory. "Do you have kids?"

Betsy shifted her bag on her shoulder. "We don't. Not yet."

"Then you understand that particular beauty of babysitting. You get to be around kids all day, then go home at night and enjoy the peace and quiet."

She just smiled.

· · ·

Betsy and Ty met in early fall of her junior year. By Christmas, she was ready for him to meet her parents. She had friends who took every college boyfriend home to meet the parents, but Betsy hadn't dated anyone she wanted to put through the particular agony of dinner around the Sawyers' antique walnut dining table. For the life of her, she didn't know why she'd chosen a farmer as the first boyfriend to bring home. She could imagine her father's glances at Ty's callused hands, so different from his own milky-white hands that floated through the air each night as he conducted symphonies and concertos. She imagined her mom taking in Ty's tan, freckled skin, a clear indicator in her mind of inevitable skin cancer.

But she brought him anyway. Ever since their first date—he'd taken her to church at Auburn United Methodist, then to lunch at Amsterdam Café—she hadn't been able to shake the peculiar sensation that she no longer wanted to do life without him. That she needed him. That his singular strength, solidity, and masculinity was tied to her—knots and tangles that probably began long before she was born.

When she brought up the idea of him coming to her home over Christmas break, he agreed without a second of hesitation. The day after Christmas, he pulled up the driveway to her parents' house in his Chevy truck that rattled a little too loudly for her dad's taste.

"What is that racket?" Her father lowered the newspaper an inch and peered around the edge of the Arts and Culture section.

Jenna, a freshman at Alabama and eager for any kind of excitement, jumped out of her seat and ran to the front door just as their mother walked out of the kitchen drying her hands on a dish towel.

Ty barely had a chance to knock on the door before Jenna flung it open. Betsy imagined the scene from Ty's point of view: Jenna's blonde curls springing out everywhere, clunky black Dr. Martens, white sweater that looked appropriate until she turned around and you saw it was open in the back all the way to her waist. Their dad still in his chair, polishing his glasses with the end of his silk tie. Their mom standing poised in a pristine white apron—pristine because she'd ordered their meal from Highlands instead of attempting to cook something presentable for their first child's boyfriend. Betsy could almost hear her mother's thoughts. *Highlands for this guy?*

Dinner went as she'd expected it to. Food delicious, silences awkward, conversation stilted. But under the table, Ty gripped her hand, his thumb rubbing small circles into her palm. With his hand wrapped around hers, he answered her parents' questions as well as he could. They asked about his parents and his major. His grandfather's farm and how he'd make it profitable again after his grandfather's death two years before. He spoke of the dairy industry as a whole, and his family's farm in particular, with obvious pride.

"I knew I was going to be a dairyman before anyone even asked me what I wanted to be when I grew up." He took a sip of water and sat back in his chair. "It's been in my blood my whole life."

Her dad merely nodded, sipped his wine, and set the glass down. "I imagine it'd be hard for your livelihood to depend on something as fickle as the weather. Unpredictable animals. Crop prices."

Ty nodded. "It's an understandable concern. But honestly, sir, cows are pretty predictable, as far as animals go." He smiled. "Once you have a herd that's reproducing regularly, you milk 'em twice a day. That's the thing about cows—rain or shine, heat or cold, hurricane or drought, you've got milk coming twice a day. When milk means money, it's just a matter of getting that milk ready to sell. And I plan to grow most of our own crops in the fields, so we won't have to buy them. That eliminates the problem of fluctuating crop prices."

Her dad raised his eyebrows. "You seem to have it all

figured out." He turned to her mom. "Maybe I should have been a dairy farmer, honey."

"Not sure you're cut out for such a rustic life, dear," her mother responded.

"I'm not sure anyone in this family is," her dad said.

Betsy folded her napkin into a neat square. "I can decide that."

From the other side of the table, Jenna winked at Betsy and smiled.

Ty cleared his throat. "Obviously there's a bit more involved, but that's the gist of it." They spoke like Ty was dense, but Betsy knew he picked up on their dismissive attitude. It rolled across the table in waves.

That night Betsy and Ty sat in her father's garden, wrapped in a blanket she pulled off the couch in the living room. Dozens of rosebushes, meticulously groomed by Jenna and their father, towered over the bench where they sat. "I'm sorry about my parents. They can be terrible sometimes."

"Not terrible. They've probably just never met anyone like me."

"I've never met anyone like you."

Ty laughed, low and quiet. "Is that a good thing?"

She nodded, aware—almost painfully so—of his leg pressed against hers, the heat from his hand pouring into her shoulder, her neck. Every nerve danced on edge, ready to jump.

"What do you think about my life? The life I'm going to have? Is it something you want?"

"I wouldn't be here if I didn't. *You* wouldn't be here if I didn't."

Ty smiled. "All this? The house, the fancy food, that Mercedes in the driveway?" He looked up at the house—two stories, Tudor-style, historic marker with an old family crest on the bricks by the door. "I can't give you all this. I'll give you everything I can, but there's no way it'll be like this."

"I didn't choose all this." She placed one finger under his chin and turned his face to hers. "But I did choose you."

TWENTY-THREE

JENNA

Jenna squatted on a fallen tree and tried to capture the lacy layer of mint-green fungus covering the bark. Gregory stood a few feet away. "Take it like that and you'll flatten out the texture." He stepped closer and pointed. "See what I mean?"

He'd been by her side instructing her for most of the week since she'd made the decision to extend her stay at Halcyon, sometimes snapping his own shots, other times stopping to give her a quick lesson on lighting, balance, composition. It was as if he'd taken her decision to stay as permission to actually teach her the more technical aspects of photography. His tutorials reminded her of excursions with Max back in Nashville.

Max would chew his lips to keep from giving her unsolicited tips or pointing out where she messed up. Sometimes she'd give in and let him say his piece, but other times she'd ignore his agitation. He was always a gentleman, albeit a grumpy one, never giving advice unless asked. Gregory, on the other hand, didn't care whether she wanted to hear his opinions. He just gave them anyway. That both thrilled and annoyed her.

"I'm trying it anyway," she responded. "Can I experiment or does that break one of your rules?"

Exasperated—both from the stifling heat and from Gregory's insistence on getting everything just right—she sat back on her heels and pushed her hair out of her face. As she did, the tree trunk she was perched atop shifted and sent her to the ground hard.

"Good save on the camera." He chuckled and reached down. She ignored his offer of help and pushed herself up with one hand, holding the camera away from the sand and dirt.

She stood and wiped her hand on her shorts. Though she was satisfied with the shots from the morning, the midday heat was wearing on her. "This isn't working. I think I need to stop and just try again tomorrow. Or at least later when it cools off."

"Cools off? It's Florida in the summer. It doesn't cool off." He looked at his watch. "I have an idea though."

Twenty minutes later, Jenna sat in Gregory's old Jeep Wrangler as he drove them away from Halcyon and toward the beach.

"I can't believe you've been here three weeks and haven't seen the Gulf yet." The top of the Jeep was open and the wind carried his words into the humid afternoon air.

"I almost forgot we were so close. Halcyon makes it feel like there's nowhere else to go."

He nodded. "That's the point. But it is good to get away sometimes." He grinned. "And you need a break."

She leaned her head back against the seat and closed her eyes. As they exited the preserve and crossed into cellular civilization, Jenna's phone began dinging with texts. After a quick look at the screen, she smiled.

Mario: Where are you, girl? No one can run this line like you can. The new manager is an idiot and we NEED you back here. So does your boyfriend ;)

Max: Heard through the grapevine you decided to extend your stay. Halcyon must be treating you well.

Delores: Hi dear. I don't want to bother you, but I noticed you're not back from your trip yet. Just making sure you're okay.

Betsy: Meet Rainbow Shine. And the girls send kisses.

Betsy's text included a photo of the girls staring through the fence of the henhouse at a huge hen with black-and-white polka-dotted feathers. Walsh's hand was up in a wave and Addie gripped Walsh's other hand.

"Everything okay?" Gregory looked over at the phone in her hands.

Jenna scrolled through the texts again, lingering on the photo of the girls. Her desire to touch them—to be with them—was so strong, she had to bite her lips to keep from asking Gregory to turn around and take her back so she could pack her things. "It's fine."

A few minutes later, he pulled off the road next to a long walkway leading to the beach. When their feet touched the sand, they went separate ways. Gregory set up his tripod near the edge of the water, and Jenna headed toward an abandoned lifeguard stand. Even from far off, she could see the splintered and broken boards on the side of the tower. With no houses or condos nearby, the beach was deserted, but she was still surprised no one had come by to repair the damage.

Bits of driftwood, shells, and damp seaweed littered the sand below the tower. It reminded her of an old *I Spy* book she and Betsy had read as kids. They'd both loved studying the pages and picking out a marble or lollipop or domino from the tangle of miniature objects the photographer had painstakingly set up and photographed.

She knelt in the shade below the tower, the cool sand scratching her bare knees, and pulled her camera to her eye to capture the array of marine life stranded dozens of feet away from its home in the calm, blue-green water. Pastel-colored coquina clams, still closed tight, were nestled against sharp splinters of wood and clear blobs of jellyfish. She nudged a piece of seaweed with the back of her hand and uncovered a chunk of green sea glass. She picked it up and ran her fingers across the smooth, tumbled edges. Veins of dark blue threaded through the green. She slid the glass into her bag and lifted her camera again. Time slipped away as she shot the remains of countless high tides and all they'd left behind.

Sometime later, she glanced up at the sound of feet squeaking on the sand behind her. Gregory shaded his eyes from the sun's glare and set his bag and tripod down on a log of driftwood set back against the dunes.

"Looks like you've given up."

Jenna looked around her and smiled. "It seems so." Her camera rested on top of her button-down shirt where she'd peeled it off earlier, leaving her in a gray cotton tank top and shorts. Her legs were stretched out in front of her in the sand and she leaned back on her elbows. She'd done all she could today.

He sat down in the shade a couple feet away. Sand covered his calves and coated his forearms up to his elbows. She sat up and hugged her arms around her knees, absently twisting the purple-and-blue pipe-cleaner bracelet around her wrist. She'd worn it every day, just like she promised Addie.

They were quiet for a moment before he broke the silence. "What's going on in that head of yours?"

She hesitated, but the warm air and gentle breeze invited honesty. "I don't know if staying here was the right decision."

"Okay."

"As soon as I get it in my head that it was the best thing, I start to feel guilty about it. I keep going back and forth. It's just . . . I've worked so hard to show I've changed from who I used to be, but then here I go making yet another impulsive, selfish decision."

"Impulsive, maybe, but selfish? You really think being here is selfish?"

"I don't know. Maybe." A sand crab dashed across the hot sand in front of them. Jenna moved her foot and it darted in the other direction.

"Tell me why you're here. Why did you decide to stay?"

"I'm here for my girls. And for me too. To try to make things better for all three of us."

"And what about that is selfish? You're away from home, away from your children, away from work, all so you can focus on this talent—this *incredible* talent— that you hope can help give your family a leg up. And if it allows you to do something you love, then all the better. That's not selfish. Seems pretty selfless to me."

Jenna wiggled her feet under the sand until it felt cool to her toes. "I don't know. I don't know if Betsy sees it that way."

"You need to decide now—today—to trust that the decision to stay was a good one. It was the best thing because it allows you to keep working toward your goal of pursuing your passion and providing for your family. You have talent and you have drive—that combination can take you a long way in this industry. Connections don't hurt either, and that's where I come in handy." He grinned and she smiled in return.

"When it's all over and done, everyone will understand why you came here. Though I don't particularly care what anyone else thinks about why you came or why you stayed. It matters to me that you believe in yourself. If you do that, your girls will too."

"Who knew you were such a motivational speaker?"

He laughed. "Seriously. I don't think I've ever been so . . ."

"Encouraging? Uplifting?"

"I was going to say sentimental and sappy, but your way sounds better."

"I think you're in the wrong profession."

"Maybe so." He leaned back on his elbows and stretched one leg out in the sand. "I'll let you in on something else about me: I disappointed everyone in my life when I chose photography over a steady, stable job. My dad's a doctor, his dad was a doctor, and they all expected me to follow in line. It hurt them deeply that I didn't. But I couldn't abandon my dream for theirs. It would have been like giving up the best part of me, and I wasn't willing to do that."

"That sounds familiar."

"A retreat like this makes you feel refreshed. Energized. It's easy to expect everyone else to have changed because you have, but reality is still out there churning away. Your time away changes you, but it doesn't change anyone else." He sat up and brushed sand off the backs of his legs. "That's why I just keep going."

She smiled. "You just keep taking the next job? Keep moving forward?" She was kidding, but then she saw that he wasn't.

He reached down to where the sand crab raced back toward them, then disappeared down a tiny hole in the sand. "I've been offered a job in California. UC Berkeley. I'd be the head of the photography department. It's the only full-time job I've considered in twenty years of being on the road."

"Wow. That's big. Are you're taking it?"

He shrugged. "Thinking about it."

"You should take it. Who knows? Maybe you'll enjoy staying in one place for a while."

He stared out at the water as slow waves crept up the shore. "It'd be an incredible deal for me. I'd get an assistant to help with paperwork and some of my classes. I'd still be able to travel some for freelance gigs." He shrugged. "I don't know though. It'd be a big change, to have something regular. To have a boss. That might not go over well."

She imagined what it'd be like to have a job where she could challenge herself, excel, help others find their own creative eye. To work in the field that excited her, that made her feel alive. It was too much to contemplate.

She stood and brushed sand off her shorts and legs. "You'd be an idiot not to take it."

He laughed. "Do you always say exactly what you think?"

She nodded. "About as much as you do."

He stood and picked up his camera bag, then turned toward the Jeep. "We should get back. Tonight's fried chicken. I need to get all the Southern food I can get if I'm going to head west."

"What's the start date?"

"*If* I decide to take it, the job starts the beginning of fall semester. But I'd probably need to get out there a little early to settle in."

She tied the shirt around her waist as they stepped across the hot sand toward the road. She couldn't even think about fall.

When she opened her door and climbed in, she noticed her phone sitting on the seat. She hadn't meant to leave it behind. She scooped it up and checked the screen for any missed messages or calls. One voice mail. As Gregory cranked the engine and pulled away from the beach, Addie's voice trailed out of the phone.

"Mommy! Walsh caught a fish! Uncle Ty took us fishing in the creek behind their house. I didn't catch anything. We threw Walsh's fish back so it could go back to its family . . . What? . . . Aunt Betsy wants to talk to you."

After a moment of muffled voices, Betsy came on the line. "Walsh is quite a good fisherman. She pinched off a piece of hot dog, stuck it on the hook, and dropped the line in the water like she'd been fishing her whole life." She let out a small laugh. "Anyway, hope things are going well. Give us a call when you can."

Jenna dropped her phone back into her bag. She propped her elbows on her knees and leaned her head into her hands, then turned her face to him. "My kids are having a lot of fun. They sound happier than ever."

"That's a good thing, right? You can concentrate on you."

She nodded, then sat back in her seat. The wind whipped through her hair and fluttered her shirt against her skin.

"Ever been to California?" he asked.

TWENTY-FOUR

BETSY

"A unt Betsy?"

Walsh's voice was a whisper at the edge of Betsy's consciousness. She had her laptop open and papers—a calendar, QuickBooks printouts, notes from three dairy association meetings, and a YMCA summer camp flyer—spread all over the heart-pine kitchen table. It was only ten o'clock, but with the girls up before six, the morning had been a long one.

"Aunt Betsy?"

Five minutes ago, when Walsh had called her name multiple times, Betsy had jumped up and walked to where Walsh sat in the window seat only to find that Walsh's big toe itched and could Betsy please scratch it?

Fool me once, Betsy thought with a tight smile. This time she tuned out Walsh's calls and kept her eyes on her laptop. She'd been going back and forth with the director of Forsythe Ranch, a horse farm a couple miles away that hosted children's camps throughout the summer. The director was hoping to find a regular field trip slot for the rest of the summer. A set group coming each week would be a chunk of extra money for the farm.

"Aunt . . . Bet . . . sy."

"Hang on just a sec," Betsy mumbled as she clicked to open the latest e-mail from the director.

"Aunt Betsy, I have to go *potty*!" Walsh's voice rang out, her voice louder with each word. She stood right next to Betsy, her dark hair a messy halo around her head, her face twisted in frustration.

Betsy sighed, then smiled and snapped her laptop shut. "Okay. Let's go." She shuttled Walsh down the hall to the bathroom.

While Walsh sat on the toilet and sang, Betsy perched on the edge of the tub, her chin in her hand. As someone who liked things to be on time and in order, having two kids in the house with no concept of or desire for a schedule was difficult. Plans and routines helped keep Betsy's mind from wandering to painful places, and while she tried valiantly to stick to those routines, the girls were just as eager to mess them up. They didn't do it on purpose, but knowing that didn't make it any easier.

Once Walsh finished her business and Betsy helped her wash her hands, they found Addie on her stomach in the den, rolling a pink bouncy ball to Etta, whose whole body was under the couch. Only the cat's arms stuck out, batting at the ball. Walsh joined in and Betsy crossed through the room toward the kitchen. On the way, she caught a glimpse of Ty outside. With a large bale of hay in his arms, he walked around the side of the barn and disappeared in the back.

Betsy filled a glass with water and took a sip, then grabbed a damp rag and wiped at a sticky spot on the counter. Behind her in the den, Addie and Walsh whispered, their voices growing louder as they disagreed on something, then settled down. Then footsteps crossed the hardwood floor into the kitchen.

"We're playing house," Addie announced. "I'm the big sister and she's the baby sister. You can be the mommy."

"Girls, I need to finish up some work on the computer. I'm sorry. Can you be the mom and let Walsh be the sister?"

"But I'm not big enough. We need someone big."

"I'm sorry. I can't do it right now. You'll have to figure it out on your own."

Addie's lip stuck out, and a swift wave of irritation mixed with Betsy's guilt, creating a stifling blend of unfamiliar emotion.

"Mommy always plays the mommy for us."

"That's because she is your mommy." Betsy's voice was testy as she tossed the damp rag into the sink.

Addie paused for a moment and Betsy braced herself. But then Addie turned to Walsh. "I'll be the fancy lady and you be my puppy."

Walsh promptly dropped to her hands and knees, barked, and crawled off to the den. Addie followed behind holding an imaginary leash.

Just as Betsy sat back down at the computer, she heard the back door open and two sets of feet scurrying outside. She took a deep breath. Maybe she could finish her work now. It was so peaceful, twenty minutes passed before she thought to check on the girls. She glanced toward the backyard, then reluctantly closed her laptop.

Outside, she found Addie sitting on the grass next to the henhouse, making quiet clucking noises to Parsley, a sweet Speckled Sussex hen pecking near the fence.

"Addie? Is Walsh with you?"

Addie kept clucking but shook her head.

"Do you know where she is?"

Another head shake.

Betsy peered around the edge of the henhouse and scanned the backyard. She checked Walsh's usual hiding spot behind a big hydrangea near the porch steps. Nothing.

"Walsh?" she called. "Walsh, come on out!"

After a quick walk through the house in case she'd missed Walsh coming back inside, Betsy's heart started to beat a little faster. Logically, Walsh couldn't have gotten far, but telling herself that didn't slow down her heart. She focused her eyes on the entrance to the barn and the sheds surrounding it. No movements small enough to come from a tiny Walsh.

"Walsh? Walsh!"

Picking up on the panicked decibel of Betsy's voice, Addie crossed the yard and wrapped her arms around Betsy's leg. "Where is she?"

"I don't know," Betsy said, peeling Addie's arms from her legs. "If you'd kept your eye on her—" She stopped herself—had she really expected a five-year-old to babysit her three-year-old sister?—but the damage was done. Addie's chin trembled and her eyes filled.

Betsy knelt in front of her. "I'm sorry. I didn't mean

that. It was not your job to watch your sister. It was my job. But we can find her together, okay?"

When Addie sniffed and nodded, Betsy took her hand and half led, half pulled her toward the barn. Ty rounded the corner just as she made it to the barn door. He smiled but stopped when he saw Betsy's face. "What's wrong?"

"I can't find Walsh."

"What do you mean, you can't find her?"

"I mean, I don't know where she is. I was inside working and I thought they were both out in the yard. When I came out, Addie was with the hens and Walsh was nowhere." She took a breath. "I've looked all around the house. Inside and out."

"Okay, well, she's got to be somewhere. Walker's in the barn. I'll check with him."

Inside, Walker was adjusting dials on the tanks, getting the morning's milk ready for transport. He shook his head when Ty asked if he'd seen Walsh running around. As Betsy passed him on her way to the other side of the barn, she heard him mumble, "Didn't know babysitting was part of my job description."

Back out in the sunshine, she and Ty called for Walsh over and over, looking in every small space they could imagine Walsh might want to inspect. Tears were pricking the backs of her eyes when she saw Carlos strolling toward the barn with Walsh by his side. Betsy exhaled.

"I found someone out in the side pasture," Carlos called. "This little lady was pretending to drive the tractor. Good thing the keys weren't in it. From the looks of her, she'd have figured out a way to drive off with it if given half a chance."

Betsy squatted in front of Walsh, who grinned, her cheeks still smeared with jelly from breakfast. Betsy wanted to ask her what in the world she'd been thinking, but that was just it—Walsh hadn't been thinking. All she knew was she wanted to explore, so she did. She hadn't meant to do anything wrong.

"Please don't leave the backyard unless someone is with you. A *grown-up* someone. Deal?"

"Deal."

Betsy rubbed jelly from the corner of Walsh's mouth, then stood. When Addie and Walsh scampered off toward the backyard, with Addie pulling Walsh's hand and telling her about Parsley the hen, Betsy turned to Ty.

"That could have been bad."

Ty ran his hand over the top of his head and sighed. "Jenna's got her work cut out for her with that one." He squeezed Betsy's hand. "Sorry, but I've got to get back to it. Milk truck's gonna be here any minute."

Betsy nodded and followed the girls toward the house. Back inside, they went right back to their antics, bouncing the pink ball around in the den, oblivious to the panic that had just ripped through Betsy's morning. She was beginning to see why Jenna wanted to get away for a little while.

Just as she sat back down to work, the pink ball bounced into the kitchen, ricocheted off the fridge and Betsy's shoulder, and knocked over her glass of water. Etta followed, looking frantically for the ball, her claws skidding on the hardwood floor. The girls were close behind in a fit of giggles.

Betsy jumped up and mopped the water with a dish towel before it could reach her computer. She picked up the dripping YMCA flyer and dropped it into the trash can, then shut the laptop. *Not gonna happen today.* She gathered her papers, set them on top of the computer, and put the whole stack on the washing machine, the only place she could be sure the girls wouldn't find it. On the way back through the kitchen, she grabbed her phone.

"Hey, you," Anna Beth boomed. "How's it going?"

"Oh, fine, just losing my mind. And Walsh."

Anna Beth laughed.

"You think I'm kidding. I lost her. Carlos found her sitting on the tractor in the pasture. All I wanted was to get a tiny bit of work done this morning, but between trips to the potty and spilled drinks and missing children, I still have a million e-mails to send and phone calls to return. Is it always like this?"

"Pretty much. But that's when you just give up and get out of the house. It's not any calmer over here, but you're welcome to come by. I have wine in the fridge and a glass with your name on it."

Betsy smiled. Anna Beth actually did have a wineglass with Betsy's name on it, a holdover from when Anna Beth hosted a monthly book club at her house. The club was never really about the books though. "Thanks, but some adult company's all I need. We'll be there in ten."

. . .

Anna Beth's house was a hive of activity. Jackson and his friends were upstairs playing video games, their voices careening down the staircase. Lucy and a neighbor were spread out at the kitchen table making beaded bracelets. "Everyone wears them," Lucy explained when Betsy asked. Addie stood still as a statue next to the table, watching the older girls with focused attention.

"If you want, I can make you one too," Lucy said.

Addie nodded. "But you have to make one for Walsh too."

"She watches out for little sister, doesn't she?" Anna Beth said to Betsy. The two of them sat on the couch, their legs propped on the coffee table.

Betsy nodded. "For the most part." Recalling the events of the last hour, she wanted to add that it would have been nice if Addie had been watching out for Walsh this morning, but she bit back the pointless thought. "They fight too—and over such silly things—but Addie takes her big sister job seriously, I think."

"Still no word from Jenna?"

"Oh, there's word, just nothing definite. The retreat shuts down in mid-August, and she's not sure if she'll stay until the end or leave early. They left it up to her to decide. She wants . . . She feels she still has more work to do before she wraps up."

"And you're just hanging on until then."

Betsy shrugged. "We're doing okay."

Anna Beth shook her head and readjusted the pillow behind her back. "I can't imagine. You're taking to it so well. If my sister dropped her kids off at my house, I'd be hot on her trail, tracking her down and yanking her back here to take them home. Granted, her kids are full-blown teenagers and as sullen as the day is long. Nose rings, black clothes, the whole bit. Your two are a bit easier, I'd imagine."

Betsy gave a small laugh, her fingers busy working a knot out of a long plastic necklace. When she loosened the strands, she handed the necklace back to Walsh, who quickly tied it back together. "I don't know. In some ways, it seems kids who did their own thing might be easier."

"Maybe. I guess there are pros and cons for all the ages."

Betsy waited until Walsh scampered back to the kitchen table. "They're just so . . . They *need* so much from me all the time. I feel like I'm constantly running on all cylinders. I'm not used to it. And losing track of Walsh? That was scary. I don't know how Jenna does it."

Anna Beth's eyebrows scrunched together. "Sorry to tell you, but everything about parenting is scary. It's good, but scary too. When you're thrown into parenthood—whether it's planned or unplanned—you just learn to figure things out. And feeling like you're running around all the time? That's part of it, but when it's your own kids, it's a little different. It doesn't make it a total cinch, but I know Lucy's and Jackson's quirks and habits almost better than I know my own. When it happens for you, it won't feel so chaotic." She paused, listening to the thump and roar of the group of boys playing upstairs. "Well, that's a lie. It'll always feel chaotic. But you'll be up to the task. You'll be great."

Betsy lifted a corner of her mouth in a sad smile. "I

think you're the only person who still thinks it'll happen for us."

"If you don't believe it, then it's my job to believe it for you. That's a job I take seriously."

Betsy sighed and smiled, thankful not to have to pretend with Anna Beth.

"I remember those days like they were yesterday," Anna Beth said. "Not being able to get anything done without someone needing something *right now*. The potty, a snack, a Band-Aid, whatever. These days, the requests are just more expensive. This morning Jackson storms into my bedroom and tells me he needs four hundred dollars. Four *hundred* dollars. I asked him what in the world for, and do you know what he said? He said he needed it for a new PlayStation. I mean, the nerve."

Jackson bounded down the stairs then, his buddies just behind him, all of them sounding like a herd of cattle thundering down the hallway. As he pleaded with Anna Beth to drive them up to the gas station for Slurpees and the girls at the kitchen table burst into laughter, Betsy closed her eyes. Just a five-second moment of nothingness. When she opened them, Walsh was digging in Betsy's purse.

"Walsh, what do you need, honey?" She rose from the couch to pull Walsh's curious hands out of her purse.

"My snack," she replied. "I'm hungry."

"Me too," Addie called from the table. "What'd you pack for a snack? And I'm thirsty too."

Betsy swiveled her head toward Anna Beth, one eye squeezed shut. "I forgot snacks."

Anna Beth hopped up off the couch. "Don't worry a thing about it. I have enough snacks to feed the neighborhood."

. . .

After dinner that night, Walsh wanted to see the hens. "Can we go?" she begged, her brown eyes round and hopeful. A cookie crumb clung to her cheek despite a quick swipe with a handful of napkins. Betsy reached down and brushed it off.

"Please?" Addie was already shoving her feet into her shoes.

Betsy thought of her computer on top of the washing machine, where it had sat untouched since earlier in the day. An array of dirty dishes lay on the counter and table.

"I'll take 'em." Ty set his plate and glass in the sink. "Let's go, girls." He opened the back door and waited while they zipped under his arm and down the porch stairs. "You want to come too?" he asked her.

Outside, the light had softened into that perfect twilight hour when everything seemed easier, lighter, like anything was possible. The light crept in the kitchen windows and filled the room with a pink glow.

She shook her head. "You go ahead. I'll finish up in here. Don't keep them out long though. They need baths, then bed."

"They do or you do?"

"Very funny."

As she stood at the sink with her fingers under the

faucet, waiting for the water to heat up, she watched the girls running around, using every bit of energy left in their little bodies. Ty pretended to chase them, then fell down as if asleep.

"Uncle Ty! Wake up!" They crawled all over him, their laughter floating across the yard and through the open back door.

He finally straightened up and unlatched the hen-house door. The girls crept in, hoping, Betsy knew, for little brown-and-white speckled treasures.

All at once, the water flowing from the faucet was scalding. No buildup, just a quick scorching. She slapped the handle, turning it to cold to stop the burning in her fingers. After a moment, she set it to warm and got to work, washing pots and loading the dishwasher.

A few minutes later, Ty led the girls back into the kitchen. They smelled of outside—evening heat, thick grass, fresh straw from the henhouse. A mixture of nature and childhood. Not her childhood, but someone else's.

"Go ahead and show her," Ty whispered to the girls. He patted them on the back, then turned to Betsy. "I'm going to jump in the shower. I'll start their bathwater for you." He headed up the staircase, peeling off his T-shirt as he went.

Addie and Walsh stood in front of Betsy, their hands behind their backs. She dried her hands on a dish towel, then bent down to their level. "You didn't find anything interesting out there, did you?"

They beamed. "We did!" They pulled their arms from behind their backs and presented their treasures. Both of them held a single egg in careful hands.

"Can we save them so they'll turn into chicks?" Addie asked. "We can keep them safe until it's time for them to hatch."

"I'm sure you would keep them very safe, but these eggs won't turn into chicks. They're for eating, not for babies."

Walsh peered at her egg, shook it, and held it up to her ear. "No baby chicks?"

"Nope. No babies. Just food. But that's an important job. Our hens help feed us."

"I guess so," Addie said. "Baby chicks would've been more fun though."

They handed her the eggs before bounding up the steps. Betsy placed them in empty spaces in the egg carton in the fridge.

. . .

Commercials on TV always made bath time with kids look like the highlight of any parent's day. Bubbles and giggles. Sweet smiles. Soapy hairdos. Maybe Betsy just wasn't doing it right. The laughter and bubbles lasted for a few minutes, then things usually devolved into warfare.

"She splashed me!"

"That's *my* cup!"

"*I* had the soap first!"

Tonight Betsy had one hand on Walsh's shoulder and one on Addie's to stop a splashing war when her phone rang behind her, high on a shelf so it wouldn't get wet. "Okay, you two, freeze!"

The girls stared at each other, then dissolved into laughter. Crisis averted for the moment.

She swiped a damp lock of hair from her forehead and grabbed her phone. Jenna.

Not now.

The tension headache that had begun when she realized Walsh was nowhere to be found now throbbed in her temples, dull and persistent. She sat on the closed toilet and shut her eyes for a second. "What's up?"

Addie looked up sharply from the tub where she'd been pouring water back and forth between two cups. Betsy smiled at her.

"Not much," Jenna said. "I drove into town to pick up a few things at the drugstore. I'm on my way back for dinner now."

"And things are okay?" She forced brightness into her voice.

"Yeah, yeah. Things are good. Really good, actually. I'm working hard and sending résumés out left and right."

"Résumés. Wow." Betsy realized then that a part of her hadn't expected Jenna to follow through with her plan to change things up in her life. She thought this would be a good experience for Jenna but that she'd return to Nashville with the girls and pick right back up where she left off. "So you're really doing this?"

"Trying to. Gregory has connections all over the country—and some are with big names in the industry. I just . . . I'm excited, Betsy. I mean, not much has happened yet, but the potential is there. Who knows where this could take me?"

"You? You mean you and the girls."

"Of course. The three of us."

"Because this isn't all about you." Betsy turned away from the girls so they couldn't hear her words. As if they could hear over their own squealing anyway. "This trip of yours involves other people. Four of us, actually."

"I know that. I—"

But Walsh and Addie began to kick their legs like mermaids, drowning out Jenna's voice. Water splashed everywhere—the walls, the floor, Betsy.

"Girls. Please." She grabbed a towel and wiped her arms and the front of the cabinet. "Give it a rest for just a second."

"Oh, they're in the bath?" Jenna asked. "Walsh gets so wired at bath time. You'll have to make sure she's calmed down before you put her to bed."

"Thanks. I'll make a note." She struggled to keep the sarcasm out of her voice.

"I'm sorry. You've probably already figured that out. You've probably figured it all out by now."

"Not really. I'm just winging it here. And I can't . . . Look, I do want to talk to you and hear more about these plans . . ." She lowered her voice to a whisper, although with the girls busy playing yet another loud, splashy game, the whisper was unnecessary. "But this just isn't the best time. It's been a long day and they're wet and riled up. I don't want them to know—"

"It's fine, I get it."

"Unless you want to talk to them. They'd love that," Betsy said as she wiped water off the wall with the damp towel. "I can hand them—"

"You know what? Let's try it another night. Or tomorrow. They're having fun and your phone will get wet . . ."

"Well, if you don't . . . I mean, I can . . ." She exhaled hard, frustrated by feeling like she needed to convince her sister to talk to her own kids. She stuck her head out the door into the hallway. "Ty, could you come in here for a minute?"

Back in the bathroom, Addie's eyes were focused on her.

"So is that it?" Betsy stayed by the door, her back partially turned but her eyes on the girls. "I mean, I'm glad to hear things are going well, but I kind of have my hands full here."

"Is that Mommy?" Addie asked.

"It's . . ." Betsy froze. "What do you want me to say?" she whispered.

Ty tapped on the door to the bathroom. "Whatcha need?" His hair still dripped with water from the shower.

"It's . . ." She pointed to the phone. *Jenna*, she mouthed.

"Betsy, I'll just let you go," Jenna broke in. "I'm sorry for calling at a bad time."

"No, wait—"

"I'll call again soon. I promise."

When the line went quiet, she set her phone on the counter. It hit a puddle of water and slid right to the floor. She pressed her forehead to the wall a moment, then leaned down and turned the phone over. The cracked screen looked like a spiderweb.

Ty knelt next to her and took the phone from her. "What'd she say?"

"Oh, not much, except that she's trying to find a new job and who knows, maybe it'll be across the country. That and I shouldn't be bathing them so close to bedtime." She laughed, even though it wasn't funny.

"Why don't you take a breather? I can . . . I'll do something in here while they play."

"No, I'm fine." Betsy turned back to the bathtub and grabbed a washcloth. "Who wants to get clean first?"

"Was that Mommy on the phone?" Addie asked again.

Betsy nodded. Pumped Aveeno baby wash onto the washcloth. "It sure was. She said she'd call again soon so you can talk to her."

"Why didn't she want to talk to us now?"

"I don't know, honey. I guess she was busy." Betsy squeezed the washcloth to get it soapy, then rubbed it on Addie's arms, the back of her neck.

"Wait!" Addie screeched. "Mommy always washes our hair first. Then she does the soap. Not soap first!"

"We'll just do it like this tonight."

"No! This isn't how she does it."

"Well, Mommy isn't here right now, is she?"

She caught the decibel, the hard edge to her voice a second too late. Addie dropped the cup she'd been holding and Walsh's bottom lip quivered.

Behind her, Ty cleared his throat. "Why don't you take a second, babe," he said, one hand on her shoulder. "I can take over here."

"I'm sorry, I—"

"I got it. You need a break," he whispered.

She dropped the washcloth into the water. On her way out the door, Ty grabbed her hand and gave it a squeeze. She pulled away and left the steamy bathroom. Down the stairs, one foot in front of the other, she finally made it out the back door into the yard. The air around her wasn't exactly refreshing—the night was warm and still, without even the slightest breeze rustling the leaves—but the openness felt like coming up from a pool of water after being under for too long. She inhaled deeply, big gulps of air that helped relieve the suffocating helplessness she'd felt in the bathroom.

All she wanted was to not hurt. Before Jenna showed up with the girls, she'd been so close to getting past it all. She reached up and pulled her hair down from the knot at the back of her head. She ran her hands through her waves, untangling snarls with her fingers, and smoothed it back into a bun.

From the bottom porch step, she surveyed the land that stretched beyond the backyard. The barn was dark, its edges sharp against the navy sky. Faint lowing from the cows, sleepy within their stalls, trickled across the grass.

The fence that separated the backyard from the pasture beyond had stood strong for nearly a century. Ty, and his grandfather before him, had mended it from time to time, replacing rotted or cracked wood when necessary, but on the whole, it was the same fence Ty's great-grandfather had built in the 1920s. It was the same with the house and parts of the barn.

When Betsy thought of the longevity of those wood

boards, the bricks and mortar and rafters that held their physical life in place here, she felt so small. A farmer's wife. Just one woman in a line of them, their joys and sadness, hopes and hurts mixing together and settling within the cracks and folds. Ty's grandmother had suffered two late-stage miscarriages before giving birth to Ty's father—her only child. His great-grandmother had lost her first husband to tuberculosis. Betsy's hurts and losses were nothing in comparison. Insignificant pains in the face of such tragedies.

And yet her hurt remained. Maybe it always would. Her one constant dream for herself—that of giving and nurturing life, of spending herself for the sake of her own—had yet to be realized. According to Dr. Fields, future prospects didn't look hopeful, but a tiny ember of hope deep in her heart refused to die away.

Upstairs, Addie's and Walsh's voices seeped out through the window Betsy had left open a crack. A moment later, Ty's voice—growling like a bear—drowned them out, sending shrieks and laughter into the dark night.

Betsy stood, one foot on the ground, one on the porch step, caught between two worlds. One of old hurts and pain that she desperately longed to escape and one of laughter and lightness, promise and new dreams. She yearned for that one with an impatient heart.

. . .

The girls were wrapped in fluffy white towels, their wet hair clinging to their cheeks and shoulders. Ty was stooped over next to Walsh, holding her footed pajamas up next to her, visibly confused about which end to start from.

"I'll take over," she said from the doorway. Both girls looked up and Ty exhaled, dropping the pajamas on the bed.

"Thank the Lord. I'm out of my league here. I'll be downstairs if you need me."

"Thanks," she said as he passed by. "I needed that."

"I know. You okay?" He paused and leaned against the wall just outside the doorway.

She shrugged. "Better." She offered a small smile.

"Aunt Betsy, I need you!" Walsh called.

Betsy took a deep breath and ran her hand across her forehead. Ty leaned over and gave her a soft kiss. "You're a good woman, Betsy Franklin."

He headed downstairs and she paused before entering the girls' room. Jenna's words ran through her head. *Connections all over the country. Potential. Who knows where this will take me?*

She knocked softly and sat on the bed. The girls were on the floor, their towels drooping as they worked to get dressed.

"Can you help me?" Walsh fumbled with the feet of her pajamas. Betsy leaned over and gathered the material so Walsh could fit her feet inside. Once her legs were in place, Walsh grabbed the pajamas and pulled them up. "I can do it myself." She pulled the zipper over her pale belly and up to her neck.

Next to her, Addie yanked her shirt over her head, then jabbed her fist around trying to find the armhole, her face pink and determined. "There," she said when her hand slipped through.

After brushing their hair, Betsy folded back the sheets on the bed and helped the girls climb in. When they settled, she looked at them, right in their eyes. "I owe you both an apology."

Walsh held a Beatrix Potter book in her hands, flipping the pages back and forth, but Addie stared back at Betsy. "For what?"

"I lost my temper earlier in the bathroom and I'm sorry."

"I'm sorry too." Addie lowered her eyes and fiddled with the edge of the knitted blanket.

"What are you sorry for?" Betsy asked. "You didn't do anything wrong."

"I'm sorry about the soap."

Betsy smiled and cupped her hand on Addie's cheek. "The soap doesn't matter at all. Next time I'll wash you however you want, in whatever order you want. Deal?"

Addie grinned. "Deal."

"Will you read us this book?" Walsh held out *The Tale of Jemima Puddle-Duck*.

"Sure." Betsy leaned back against the pillows and opened the book. Before she could read a word, the girls rearranged themselves, the weight of their heads resting against her chest, their legs warm next to hers. Finally, they settled and were still. "We're ready," Addie said.

As their breath came and went, their chests rising and falling, something in Betsy shifted, like tectonic plates bumping and sliding into each other, forever changing the landscape above. Instead of moving them off her, instead of pushing away both the pleasure and the pain, Betsy let herself relax. Rested. Pretended, for one selfish moment, that they were hers.

TWENTY-FIVE

TY

A few days later, in the stillness of a hot afternoon, Addie and Walsh appeared in the barn. By now, Ty knew the girls' schedule well enough to know they should have been napping. Instead, Walsh tromped around the barn, saying lil to the cows and trying to feed them anything she found on the floor, while Addie just stood and watched.

Holding Walsh back from feeding a handful of straw to number 051, he glanced up to the house where Betsy stood on the porch steps. He pointed to the girls and held his hands palms up.

Okay? she mouthed, then gave a thumbs-up sign.

Before he could call back that they weren't exactly okay, that the girls would just be a distraction—to both him and the cows—she waved and retreated into the house.

Ty took off his cap, brushed his hand through his hair, and settled it back on his head. "Okay, I guess y'all are with me. Stay where I can see you. Got it?"

The girls nodded.

"And you know if you're out here during milking time, I'm going to put you to work."

Walsh's eyes lit up, but Addie looked unsure. "Work how?" She watched Carlos hook a cow up to the milking machine. "Does that hurt them?"

"Nope. It's very gentle. Almost the same as milking them by hand."

He walked the girls to the end of the line where the last ten cows were waiting for their second milking of the day. He handed Walsh a brush and showed her how to brush along the length of the cow's side and avoid the tail. She got to work, taking her job seriously.

"Where's my brush?" Addie asked.

"You're not brushing. You're milking." Addie's blue eyes grew wide and Ty laughed. "Don't worry, it's not hard." He grabbed two buckets off a set of hooks on the wall, turned one over next to number 073, and set the other one underneath the cow. He patted the overturned bucket and Addie sat down.

He'd chosen this particular cow because her milk supply was low. If it was high, the cow would be too uncomfortable to put up with the slow release of hand milking.

"Watch my hands." He grasped an udder and used his thumb and forefinger to pull down, drawing the milk out. It sprayed into the bucket, startling Addie. She jumped back. "It's okay, that's how it comes out. You try."

"I don't know." She covered her mouth with her hands. "I don't think I can."

"Sure you can. Just try."

She took a deep breath and gingerly pulled on the udder, but nothing happened. Ty rearranged her hand and fingers and she tried again. This time a steady white stream shot into the bucket and Addie gasped. "I did it!"

While Walsh brushed and Addie milked, Ty went along the line and hooked the rest of the cows up to the machines. When he finished, he sat on a bench along the wall just behind Addie and took it all in: the old barn that had been worked by men before him—better men, stronger men. The cows that put food on his table, a roof over his home with Betsy. Carlos and Walker at the other end of the barn, waiting by the door to the pasture, ready to herd the cows out at the right time. And Addie and Walsh, happily absorbed in their own "work."

He couldn't remember a time when he hadn't been aware that he'd be the next Franklin man to work the farm. His grandfather had made it official when Ty was fifteen, but he'd known long before then that his future would be tied to Franklin Dairy. His father had chosen accounting over the family farm and had hoped his only son would make a similar choice. To *not* link his livelihood to cows, milk, and land. But Ty had been determined, going against his father's wishes and instead following his dream down the same path his grandfather had walked. After college Ty returned to the farm, worked the land hard, coaxed it into obedience, tended to the cows until they trusted him. He and Betsy had built a solid life here.

Addie and Walsh's presence reminded him there was only one thing left that they hadn't done. One dream they'd yet to fulfill.

Number 073 had grown tired of Addie's tugging, so Ty stood and patted Addie on the back. "Let's give her a rest, okay?" Addie backed away while Ty hooked the cow up to the machine to finish the job. Walsh was still brushing, so Ty looked around for another brush to give to Addie.

"Uncle Ty?" Addie sat on the bench. "Why do your cows wear earrings?"

"They're not earrings, they're ID tags." He sat next to her and stretched his legs out in front of him. "You know how dogs wear tags on their collars?"

Addie nodded.

"These tags tell us the cow's birthday and who her mother was."

"Does she forget who her mother was?"

"Well, no, I don't guess she does. But when the mothers and babies are separated, the ID tags help us keep them all straight."

Addie swung her legs back and forth, her shoes scraping across the wooden floor. "Why do you separate them?"

"It's just our process. After the moms give birth, they go back out into the pasture and the babies—we call them calves—go into a special pen so they can get stronger. We feed them and take care of them . . ."

He could explain it away, but the truth was, the act of separating calves from their mothers was the one part of dairy farming that still, after all this time, made Ty uncomfortable. Most farms separated calves from their mothers within hours, but he often gave the calves two or three days, allowing them to drink the nutrient-rich colostrum directly from the mother and to soak up as much of her attention as possible before he moved them to another pen. The separation was necessary to get the amount of milk they needed, but whenever a calf was born, he dreaded interrupting those natural routines of early life.

"Are the babies sad?" Addie's eyes filled.

"I think they're just fine," Ty said. After all, the calves were happy as long as they had food coming. Whether from their mom or a bottle didn't matter. It was the mothers who had the hardest time. Some of those cows mourned for their absent babies for days, moaning and stomping in their stalls. Ty swore he could hear those moans in his sleep at night. Others went right back to eating and grazing after giving birth. When Ty moved their calves, those cows hardly noticed.

"I bet the babies are still sad." The tears that had welled up in the corners of her eyes spilled over. "Don't they want their moms?" She leaned her head against Ty's arm.

"Addie," Ty said quietly. "Hey, hey." He pulled his arm around her and held her close. With her face turned in toward him, he felt her hot breath against his shirt. "Shhhh."

"Why isn't Mommy coming back?" she cried, her voice muffled. "Doesn't she want us anymore?"

Across the walkway, Walsh turned at the sound of Addie's cries. She dropped the brush and ran to her sister. "Addie?" She craned her head to see Addie's face, still buried in Ty's side.

Ty closed his eyes and bumped his head against the wall behind him. He'd feared this moment, when his and Betsy's breezy explanations of Jenna's absence would fail them. And it had to happen when he was alone with them, without Betsy's words to soothe the rough edges.

"Your mom is . . ." How did he explain to a five- and three-year-old that at that moment, he didn't know exactly where their mom was or why she wasn't at home. In Nashville. With the two of them.

"Are we going to stay here forever?" Addie looked up at him with wide, wet eyes, her nose red and running. Walsh's little face was both cautious and curious. Alert.

He took a deep breath and blew the air out in a thin stream, thinking fast. "I think you can stay here as long as you need to. Then your mom will be back."

Addie nodded, wiped her nose with the back of her hand. "I like it here. But I miss Mommy."

"I know you do. But you know what? I could use an extra helper around here. You see Mr. Carlos over there?" He pointed in Carlos's direction. Addie nodded. "He's not as good a helper as you are. Would it be okay if I ask for your help from time to time? Just for special projects? You too, Walsh."

Addie nodded again, sniffed. Offered a small smile. Walsh grinned and bobbed her head up and down.

They heard a rustle, then one of the barn cats zipped through, chasing an unseen menace. Addie and Walsh both hopped off the bench and ran, chasing the cat and laughing. Ty exhaled. It was the grace of childhood that allowed kids to change course in a split second. He almost wished he could go back to that place where emotions and concerns only lasted until the next new thing came along. He knew the break was temporary, that the questions would come again the longer Jenna stayed away. He hoped the next time, he and Betsy would have a better idea of what to say to them. What to say to themselves.

With the girls distracted by the cat, he and Carlos finished the last group of cows and sent them out to pasture. Ty shooed the girls from the barn so they could clean up. On their way back to the yard, the girls spied Ty's Gator parked under a shed. He promised them a ride when he finished his work, so that evening, once the barn was clean and the cows were fed, he piled Addie and Walsh on the seat in the back and put it in gear.

"Can you make it go fast?" Walsh asked.

Ty laughed. "It'll go pretty fast, but I think we'll keep it nice and slow."

They puttered around the field for a few minutes until Ty saw Betsy on the back steps of the house. She sat down and stretched her legs out in front of her, then leaned her head back against the screen door.

Something had changed in Betsy this week. Like something tight inside her had loosened. Smiles came easier and she'd been laughing more. The change was nice, even though part of him still felt like he was walking on ice around her, afraid a wrong step would send him sinking into the chill underneath.

Ty took his cap off his head and pushed his hair back from his forehead. They were going slow, but the light breeze was better than the hot, still air he'd worked in all day. He set the hat back on his head and pointed the Gator toward the house. As they approached, Betsy lifted her head and smiled. Ty jumped down and opened the back gate and drove the Gator right up to the steps.

"Your carriage, ma'am."

The girls giggled.

"Come on, Aunt Betsy, before it turns into a pumpkin."

"Where are we going?" she asked.

Ty patted the seat next to him. "We'll find out when we get there."

She climbed onto the seat and sat down. Her dark hair was pulled up at the back of her head with wisps falling around her face, and she wore a white T-shirt and cutoff blue-jean shorts. He laid his hand on her knee. She covered his hand with hers and squeezed, then stretched her arm across the seat behind him.

A few hundred yards from their driveway, a small creek flowed under the highway. Ty pulled under a tree and stepped on the brake, then reached around and lifted the girls out of the back.

"I'll show you what I used to do when I was a kid and spent the night with my grandparents here at the farm," he said to them. Betsy sat on the concrete wall overlooking one side of the creek.

Ty took Addie and Walsh to the other side of the road and reached down and picked up a couple of small sticks. "Watch this." He dropped the sticks into the flowing water, then took the girls' hands and hurried them back across the empty road to where Betsy sat. He leaned over the wall and pointed down. "Wait just a second . . . There they are." His sticks floated downstream.

"Can I do it?"

"Sure."

Back and forth they went, dropping in sticks, flowers, and leaves on one side, then running across to see them reappear on the other side. They had to pause a couple times for cars, but at this time of evening, they had the road mostly to themselves. The sun was low in the sky, but sharp rays sneaked between the pines, turning the girls' faces pink.

Ty sat next to Betsy while the girls searched for more items to throw. He kept one hand on Walsh's back to keep her from launching herself over the wall, and he wrapped his other arm around Betsy's waist. Her fingers nimbly tied clover flowers together into small bunches.

At one point in her search for perfect objects to toss, Addie jumped up and ran to Betsy, stopping in front of her with her hand outstretched. "This is for you." In her hand was a small heart-shaped rock. It was dirty, little clods of dust and dirt crumbling into Betsy's hand, but the lopsided heart shape was there.

Betsy curled her fingers around it. "I love it. Thank you."

Addie nodded and ran back to Walsh. Betsy slipped the rock into her pocket.

When it was time for dinner, Ty loaded the girls

back into the Gator and pulled it up to the side of the road. He waited for an old pickup to rumble past. The man in the driver's seat stuck his arm out the window and waved. Ty tipped his cap and pulled the Gator out onto the road behind him.

"Wow," the girls breathed when they saw the load of watermelons in the back of the truck.

A little down the road, the driver slowed and pulled over to the side. He motioned for Ty to do the same. When they stopped, the old man pushed open his creaky door and lumbered to the bed of his truck. He thumped a few melons, then chose one off the top and carried it back to the Gator.

"For your family." He handed it to Ty.

The man walked back to his truck, then paused. "Sun-warmed, straight outta the ground. Best way to eat 'em. Maybe a little salt sprinkled on top, if that's your thing."

Back at the farm, Ty spread newspaper across the picnic table under the big oak and split the watermelon open. Inside, the deep-red flesh was flecked with seeds, and sweet juice dripped onto the table. Betsy brought out a bowl of cold pasta salad and a pitcher of lemonade on a tray with two tall glasses and two small plastic cups. She bustled around the table, setting everything out, making sure they had everything they needed. Ty took her hand and eased her onto the wooden bench next to him.

"We're good," he said. "Let's eat."

The girls ignored the pasta but ate slice after slice of watermelon.

"Ah well," Betsy said. "Watermelon has vitamins, right?"

Ty smiled. "There's gotta be something good in there."

When their mouths and cheeks were bright red, Ty taught them how to spit the seeds. Addie couldn't quite get the hang of it, but Walsh hit the fence post on her first try. Betsy took Addie over to the swing and pushed her under the thick canopy of dark-green leaves. Addie tipped her head back and let her hair fly behind her as she swung back and forth, higher and higher, all traces of earlier sadness long forgotten. Ty smiled when Betsy's laughter joined Addie's.

Later, as the sky turned orange and the temperature dropped a couple of degrees, the four of them lay back on the grass and watched fireflies. The sky deepened in color and stars began to pop out.

Addie held her arm straight up and pointed. "I see the first star!"

"Actually, that one's a planet," Betsy said.

Ty turned his head to her. "You sure about that?"

She nodded. "It's Venus," she said, her voice quiet.

"I think it's a star," Addie said. "We should all make our wish."

"You're right," Betsy said. "We should."

Ty turned to Addie when he heard her whispering, "Starlight, star bright, first star I see tonight." Her eyes were squeezed tight, her hands clasped in front of her.

Ty smiled and turned to Betsy to tell her to look at Addie, but he stopped. Betsy's eyes were closed as well, her mouth moving with her own silent wishes.

TWENTY-SIX

BETSY

Elinore hosted a Summer Festival every year in late July. At one time, it was a Fourth of July celebration, complete with a potluck picnic on the grass and a fireworks display that tried, but usually failed, to compete with nearby Gulf Shores' fireworks. That tradition ended when the fireworks went haywire six years ago and caught an empty field on fire. Smoke spread throughout the town, scared cows, sent flocks of birds to the sky, and terrorized Elsie Roberts's schnauzer. Elsie, then-president of the Friends of Elinore, had left her windows open that night before leaving for the celebration. She said her schnauzer, Terry, was never the same.

No one was physically hurt during the fireworks mishap, but Elsie ended the fireworks show right then and there. And since the Friends all agreed they couldn't very well host a Fourth of July celebration without fireworks, they moved the party to later in the month and called it the Summer Festival. Same potluck picnic, but without the side of danger.

The day of this year's festival was hot and humid—
not so different from most days, but this day was extra
damp, a clear indicator of wet weather ahead. Betsy
could almost sense Elsie's panic, even though Ms.
Roberts lived three miles away in downtown Elinore.

Knowing the girls would be up later than normal
with the picnic and games afterward, Betsy put them
down for a late nap. Their clothes were covered in dirt
and grass from the morning outside, so she peeled
them off and helped the girls into clean T-shirts and
pajama pants. Walsh was asleep in minutes, and Addie
lay quietly in the dim room with a handful of books.
Betsy tiptoed out, leaving the door open a crack.

While the girls rested, Betsy straightened up, did
a load of wash, then made potato salad for the picnic.
She pulled out her favorite white mixing bowl and
all her ingredients—red potatoes, hard-boiled eggs,
dill pickle relish, mayo, mustard, paprika. The first
year she brought it to the festival—Ty's and her first
summer on the farm—the Friends of Elinore came
over and shook their hands, welcoming them to town.
Elsie said they were welcome at the festival every year
as long as they brought that potato salad. Betsy had
brought it every year since.

She could make the dish with her eyes closed, automatically reaching for the right ingredients, her hands
doing the work on autopilot, but today she concen-
trated on the simple act of stirring. Mixing separate
ingredients together to make something new, something whole.

After a final stir, she covered the salad in plastic

wrap and slid it into the fridge for later. She checked the pitcher to see if there was enough tea left for Ty to have a glass when he came in to get ready.

It had been a month since he had told her he wanted to take her on a trip. When he first mentioned it, she was hesitant, but then she allowed herself to get excited about it. Lazy naps on the beach, as much fried shrimp as they could eat, fruity frozen drinks. Maybe if they pretended things were like they used to be—free, easy, unencumbered—they would be.

But Jenna hadn't come back, Ty never booked the vacation, and now it was as if a distance—not angry, but obvious—had crept between them while they weren't looking. Or maybe they had been looking but hadn't had enough energy to do anything about it. With the longer hours Ty worked to get more Franklin milk on store shelves and prepare the farm for the hurricane season—not to mention the girls' constant needs, wishes, and curiosity—the two of them had been mostly in survival mode.

But that happened, right? After almost nine years, no marriage could keep up the passion and excitement of those first few. That's what the pastor had told them during their premarital counseling sessions as he sat across from them, chin in hand, nodding and squinting.

At the time she scoffed, unable to see her passion for Ty fading in five decades, much less one. And now, approaching the end of that first decade, she still loved Ty with her whole heart. She appreciated his hard work, tried to be a good partner, slept with him, laughed with him. Looking at the big picture of their eight married years, she'd have to say things had been good. She did as well as she could, but at the edges of her mind—the far reaches of her consciousness—something told her it wasn't enough.

As she worked tension out of her head with her fingers, a soft noise came from the second floor. She tiptoed upstairs and peeked into the girls' bedroom through the open inch. Addie and Walsh were sitting up in bed playing with their ponies.

As she watched them, their soft words a balm to her tense spirit, she heard the back door open downstairs. Ty crossed the kitchen floor to the fridge. A glass on the counter, the pitcher of tea, silence. Then his feet were on the stairs.

"I'm here. I just need a few minutes to shower, then we can head out."

Betsy turned to him, but he'd already entered their bedroom and pushed the door closed behind him. She bit her lip, then knocked on the girls' door. They both looked up.

"Is it time to get ready for the festival?" Addie asked.

"Yep. Let's get you dressed."

When they were dressed and ready, she told them to wait there. "Let me check on Uncle Ty and I'll be back in just a few minutes to get you. Okay?"

Across the hall, she opened their bedroom door just as Ty slid the shower curtain open. Steam billowed out of their bathroom. Betsy made the bed and picked up a stack of folded clothes from the bench at the end of the bed. She sat and waited.

A moment later he walked into their room, a white towel wrapped around his waist, his blond hair wet and dripping on his shoulders. He pulled on boxers and a pair of clean blue jeans and sat on the bench next to her. "Are the girls ready?" he asked, his voice end-of-the-day tired.

"They've been ready since last night."

"Did you make the potato salad?"

"Of course." She smiled.

"Good." He rubbed the towel across his head, his face, then tossed it onto the bed. "Wouldn't want to get on Ms. Elsie's bad side." He pulled on his shoes, then sat up and stretched his back. He stood and crossed the room to the chest of drawers and pulled out a collared shirt. His hair made small damp dots on the back of the shirt.

It was just her husband getting dressed after a shower—his cheeks still red from working out in the heat, his muscles stretching and pulling under his shirt, his strength coupled with his visible fatigue. All of it chipped at Betsy's heart and she ached with tenderness. Desire and regret.

She walked to him, reached her arms around him, and pressed her cheek to his back. He froze. She thought he was going to pull away, but then he covered her arms with his own, turned to face her, and pressed his forehead to hers.

"What's all this?" he whispered.

"Aunt Betsy!" Addie called from the other room. "Is it time to go yet?"

Ty closed his eyes. Betsy stood on her tiptoes and kissed his lips softly. "Later," she whispered back.

Ty drove to the picnic with his hand on the gearshift, as he always did. At the beginning of their marriage, as soon as Betsy would slide into her seat next to him, she'd cover his hand with her own, and his fingers would lift and curl over hers. It became habit, their hands finding each other like two puzzle pieces. It had been a while since she'd done that, so she did it now.

It felt good, memory meeting reality. Ty looked over at her and she didn't look away. Without a word he lifted his fingers and curled them around hers. Behind them, the girls chattered and giggled. A warm breeze and the sharp, fresh scent of grassy fields entered the car through the lowered windows, filling the air like a promise.

The community park was abloom with banners, balloons, and tables of food stretching across the grass. The high school jazz band had set up under a small pavilion, and folks were splayed out on blankets and folding chairs. Elsie Roberts hurried around to each group warning of the coming rain and urging them to eat first, talk later. No one listened, this being the only time in the whole year everyone in town came together. When it began to sprinkle a half hour into the picnic, no one cared but Elsie.

Addie and Walsh ran nonstop with dozens of other kids whose combined feet made a giant mud pit on one side of the damp field. After a few minutes of keeping her eyes on the girls, Betsy relaxed, eating and chatting with other farm owners and neighbors. When Walsh crossed the field toward their blanket—crying, tears dripping off her chin—Ty jumped up and ran to her, dodging paper plates and cups on his way.

When he reached her, he knelt low and put his head close to hers. She pointed to her knee and cried fresh tears at the sight of whatever scrape was there, real or imagined. Ty blew on her knee, then whispered something to her that made her laugh.

Linda Daily, sitting next to them, tapped Ty on the shoulder and held out a Band-Aid she'd fished from her purse. Ty smiled his thanks and spread the bandage on Walsh's knee. Walsh responded with a teary smile, then bounded off to rejoin the other kids.

Back at their blanket, Ty sat down and exhaled.

"You're good at that," Betsy said.

"What? Putting on Band-Aids? Same as putting it on me or you."

"Not that. Calming her. Making her feel better."

Ty shrugged. "She's a kid. Just needed a little attention. Someone to tell her she'd be okay."

. . .

It never rained hard, but the steady sprinkle ensured no blanket, plate, or article of clothing stayed dry or clean. By the time the band packed up their horns and drums and Betsy tossed their empty plates and cups, everything was mud streaked, especially Addie and Walsh. Betsy and Ty herded them toward their car.

"Do we have to go?" Addie squirmed in Ty's arms.

"Yep, we do," he said. "You two are splattered head

to toe with mud, and Walsh has potato chips in her hair. It's time to take this party home."

The girls had been wound tight right up until Betsy buckled them into their car seats, but as soon as they were secured, their energy leaked out, leaving wet noodles behind. During the silent drive back home, Betsy glanced behind her. Walsh was already asleep, and Addie's eyes were at half-mast.

The heavy rain they'd been looking for all evening finally began as they pulled down the driveway. Ty carried Walsh inside and Betsy ran with Addie through the downpour. Even in the rain, the cicadas' wild vibrations in the trees sounded electric. Addie stuck her fingers in her ears, but Betsy had always loved the sound. Their loud, scratchy symphony made her feel almost hopeful. It was the sound of summer, familiar and safe.

After cleaning up the girls and settling them into bed, she pushed open the bedroom door expecting to find Ty, but the room was empty and dark. Downstairs, only a single lamp was on, the TV off. Through the back window above the kitchen sink, she saw light in the barn. She took a deep breath and opened the door to the porch, slipped her shoes back on. She held the screened door so it wouldn't slam shut behind her and ran through the rain that fell harder by the second.

That evening, during the picnic, laughter, and conversation, the air between them had been tense. Not unpleasant but taut. Waiting, wondering. As she stood in front of him in line for Solo cups of iced tea and sat next to him on the blanket, their shoulders close but not touching, the space between them felt warm and thick, almost alive. All she wanted to do was reach over and touch his cheek, his neck, his hair. Anything to bring him closer, to erase their separation, to prove they were okay.

The prospect of being alone with him now, though, was unnerving. She'd pushed away so much, for so long, she wasn't sure how to pull closer now. But she had to try.

By the time she got to the barn door, her skin was wet, her hair damp, her clothes soaked with rain. She tried to wipe some of the water off her face and hair, then gave up the effort and looked around in the dim light for a clean towel.

"Hey."

Betsy looked up. Ty stood at the back of the barn, the light from his office glowing out from the open door. In the half-light, he was only curves and angles. Shapes and shadows. Her heart was a knot of wires in her chest, each wire coming alive in succession.

She forgot about the rain on her arms and face and crossed the floor toward him. A moment later she was in front of him and all thoughts of speaking, of explaining herself, escaped into the night. She pulled him close and pressed her lips to his. Expecting to feel his arms around her, his lips moving in response, she was surprised when he gave her a small kiss, then stepped back.

"What's wrong?" she whispered.

He gave a brief smile. "Wrong? Nothing, I just . . . I was working on . . ." He glanced behind him toward his office. "I was kind of in the middle of something. Can we talk later?"

"I . . ." Betsy stammered and no more words came. Heat crept up her cheeks and her heart hammered in her chest.

"Oh, were you wanting . . . ?" He chuckled, but stopped when she put a hand to her forehead. "I'm sorry. It's been a long day and I'm exhausted. I don't think I can . . ." He smiled. "Were you thinking we'd just . . . ?" He gestured toward the open door to his office. "In there?"

"No, I—I just thought . . ." Her whole body, fingertips to toes, tingled.

He waited, eyebrows raised in confusion. The fatigue, the strain, was right there on his face, but at the moment, she didn't care. Anger ripped through her desire, and all thoughts of intimacy, of connection, evaporated. They might as well have been on opposite cliffs staring at each other across the divide.

"Forget it." Without meeting his eyes again, she turned and strode through the barn and out into the rain.

"Betsy, wait," Ty called behind her, but in her embarrassment, she didn't stop. She stomped across the grass and pumped her arms, pushing against the downpour to get away faster.

On the porch, she kicked off her shoes and took the stairs inside two at a time. At the top, she remembered the girls sleeping in the room across from her bedroom and slowed her steps in response. She entered her bedroom and leaned against the counter in the bathroom, calming her racing pulse, trying to slow her hot, angry breaths.

Downstairs, the porch door opened. She closed her eyes and waited. A quick moment later, Ty blew into the room, wiping water off his face and breathing hard.

"Why'd you run? We need to talk about this."

"Talk about what? How I came out there and you completely embarrassed me?"

"I embarrassed you? How?"

"Well, I . . . but you didn't . . ." She was so frustrated, she couldn't even form a sentence.

"Babe, this is not me rejecting you. But you've been all over the place lately. Now you decide you want me and you expect me to just drop everything? I have stuff going on too."

She exhaled hard and covered her face with her hands, then pulled them down again. "I don't get why you're making this so difficult."

"I'm the one making it difficult?" His voice was tinged with a brittleness he rarely, if ever, directed at her. "I'm trying here, Betsy, but I cannot figure you out. I don't even know how to just *be* with you anymore. Lately, it seems like you're happier around the girls than me, like I've done something wrong, but I have no idea what that is."

He inhaled and turned around. Paced a few steps away, then came back and faced her. When he spoke, his voice was low and controlled. "I'm out there working every day, trying to provide for us, fixing broken machines, watching for storms, and now I've taken your sister's kids in—what else can you possibly want from me?"

"You're going to make this about the girls?" But she

knew he was right. Not just about the girls—about all of it. She turned and grabbed a hand towel off the hook by the sink. She pressed it to her face, breathed in and out, then wiped her shoulders and arms.

"Well, I wasn't going to, but sure. Let's talk about them. I love them, you love them—we agree on that. But you should have asked me about keeping them here for the summer. Don't you think I at least deserved a chance to think it through first?"

She tossed the towel down and turned back to him. "I didn't know it would be this long. You know that. It was supposed to just be two weeks. And you think this is easy for me—to spend my days accompanied by two little reminders of what my body can't do? My sister, who didn't even want kids in the first place, can do it perfectly. You think I wanted that thrown in my face all summer?"

She pushed past him into the bedroom. Rain slapped the windows and pounded the roof like a thousand tiny fists. She stood in the center of the room with her back to Ty, her hands clenched, her fingernails digging into her palms.

"I'm sick of wanting," she said. "I want to be able to go through my days like you do, with all the crap from the last two years gone and behind me. I'm tired of wanting something I can't have—wanting it so badly I can't breathe sometimes."

A sharp cry from the girls' room pierced the air and they both stopped, waiting. Betsy pleaded in her mind for the cry to come again so she could escape the suffocation of the room and the storm swirling in her heart and mind, looking for a place to make landfall. But nothing came. Just quiet.

She sat on the bed, tucked her hands under her thighs. Neither of them spoke. The quiet stretched so long she finally looked up at him, but she couldn't read his face.

"That's what all this has been about?" he asked. "Us not having kids?"

Betsy made a sound that was supposed to have been a laugh, but it came out somewhere between a cry and a snort. "All? You say it like it's nothing. Like it's not everything."

Ty knelt on the floor in front of her so their faces were at eye level. "That's the thing, Bets. It can't be everything. I get it. It's disappointing, it hurts, it's not what we imagined for our life." He stopped, looked down, and swallowed hard. "But whatever happens or doesn't happen in our life, I'm here to stay."

He reached up and ran his hand through his wet hair. "When things get rough, we have to deal with it. We talk, we fight, then we make it okay. We make it better. That's what we do. But it has to be both of us together."

In the glow from the lamp on the other side of the room, Betsy could see every tired line around Ty's eyes, each freckle across his nose, the patch of gray hair at his temples. She wanted to believe his words. Wanted to soak in his strength and pain, his joy and sadness, and let them carry her.

He rested his forehead on her knees for a moment, then sat on the bed next to her. "You have no idea how much it kills me not to be able to give you children, to do something to make it happen for you. For us. But I wanted you long before kids were even a thought in my mind, and that hasn't changed." He put his hands on the sides of her face. "It doesn't matter if we have a dozen kids one day or if in forty years it's just me and you, sitting in our rocking chairs out front. You are enough for me."

She breathed in all of him, deep into her lungs. "I'm sorry," she whispered. "I should have asked you about Jenna and the girls. And I should have talked to you about all this before it boiled over."

He shook his head. "You said you were good, and it seemed like things got somewhat back to normal." He stopped, hung his head, and rubbed his forehead. "You know what though? I knew you weren't okay. Deep down, I knew. But it seemed easier, better for you somehow, if I just let it go. Or maybe that's a cop-out too. Maybe it was just easier for me."

"It's better that you did let it go. Before tonight, I probably would have said I was fine. I thought everything *was* good. In my mind, I'd moved on, but having Addie and Walsh here . . ."

"I know."

"But it's been good too, in a way. Hasn't it?" She looked up at him.

He nodded. "We're going to be okay."

She leaned her head on his shoulder and he wrapped his arm around her, kissed her head.

"It's late," he whispered after a moment. "Let's go to bed."

Under the sheets with the lights off, they remained on their own sides of the bed, as if separately digesting their argument, mentally rehashing all that had been said. It felt good to let some things out in the open, but Betsy knew there was more to come. She wanted to turn to him, to curl herself around him, but she didn't. Finally, she turned to her side and closed her eyes. Sometime later, he rolled toward her, the warmth of his body radiating into her back. Then she could sleep.

TWENTY-SEVEN

JENNA

Jenna sat at a corner table and rested her laptop on her knees. Out the window the afternoon sun glimmered on the Gulf waters, just across the street from the coffee shop. Halcyon may not have offered Wi-Fi, but that didn't stop the artists from seeking it out on their own when necessary, and Sunset Coffee was the closest place that offered a steady stream of Internet connectivity.

She tapped her fingers on the smooth cover of her laptop. Since mentioning her old Etsy shop to Gregory that first week in the darkroom, she hadn't been able to quit thinking about it. She'd once had several hundred people following her site—both loyal customers who came to her whenever they had a specific idea in mind for their home or office, and new customers who found her through the site or heard of her through word of mouth. Back then, she'd been an entrepreneur, a shop owner, even if that shop was just online, and enjoyed a decent side income from her prints.

She used to daydream about where her photography could take her. Maybe a celebrity would find her site and order one of her prints, setting off a firestorm of orders. Or maybe a travel magazine would notice her work and give her an assignment to some exotic locale. She'd had so many ideas, so many desires. So much possibility. But it had all changed with the appearance of two pink lines on the plastic stick, the boyfriend who hit the road, the life that had altered so dramatically within such a short span of time.

She hadn't checked her Etsy page in years. A few of her frequent customers had continued to contact her after she stopped posting new inventory, asking for more prints or new arrivals. She'd wanted to say yes, but exhausted and scared and trying to keep life going for herself and her new daughter, she had no spark left to offer to her photography or her customers. Finally, the requests dwindled, then stopped, and she set her camera on a shelf in the closet.

But that was then, and possibilities were again opening themselves up to her. Since she'd been at Halcyon, she had amassed a collection of photos she loved, shots she could hardly believe she'd captured herself. It seemed the longer she was here, the more she saw the unexpected dignity and grace of the world around her. Not the "beauty shots" she attempted when she first arrived, but the grit and strength of life that refused to be snuffed out.

Gregory was just as pleased with her progress— more even, if that was possible. A few days before, he'd contacted editor friends of his and talked up the "new talent" he'd discovered. They'd all been interested and said they'd take a look at her new online portfolio.

"Good things are coming for you," he'd said.

And she believed him. But at the same time, she didn't want to sit around and wait. Etsy was familiar to her, a way to ease back into the art world without diving headfirst. She chewed on a fingernail as she waited for her computer to power up. Would she have any followers left, or had they all moved on to other photographers who regularly posted new product? When she arrived at her page, she scanned until she saw the number next to the little heart. Seventeen.

It doesn't matter. You're starting now.

The first thing she did was change her shop description, noting that she'd been gone for a while but was back and posting a new collection called Ray of Light. She'd thought about it a lot this week, the idea that light can seep in—through cracks and around corners—at the most unexpected times. The idea comforted her. Then she scrolled through Etsy's "Top Tips for Shop Success" and read the new seller rules and follower etiquette, Google analytics and search engine optimization. It was enough to make her head hurt, so once she posted her new collection and added prices, she pressed Save and closed her laptop. A smile crept up her cheeks. Who knew what could happen?

Her cell, practically bursting with phone service, sat in the side pocket of her bag. She pulled it out and walked to the front porch swing. As she sat down and pressed the button, a brisk gust of wind rattled the palm fronds along the edges of the porch. That morning she'd overheard the kitchen staff talking about a storm out in the Gulf. Apparently it didn't have a name yet, and therefore wasn't anything to worry about. She breathed in the scent of salty sea spray and a faint hint of coconut on the breeze.

"Let me guess," Max said when he answered. "You've decided to stay forever." They'd sent some texts back and forth, but this was the first time they'd actually spoken.

"Ha. Not quite. But I am still here."

"Well, go ahead. Tell me all about it."

She recounted the highs of the previous weeks— from her initial awkward shots to The Bottoms, the canoe shot, the darkroom, and even helping some of the new artists get settled when they arrived for their own retreats. When she finished, he laughed. "What is it?"

"I've just never heard you like this. You're almost giddy. It's like a vacation high and a creativity surge all rolled into one big ball of energy. I'm a little jealous, I'm not going to lie."

"What do you have to be jealous about? You have all the time in the world to focus on your photography. It's your passion *and* your career. That's my goal. It's why I stayed."

"I get it. I do. I think you'll get there one day, and this is a great first step. How are your daughters doing with your sister?"

"I think they're doing just fine." The day before, she'd talked to Betsy from that same porch swing. Betsy had been taking a nap when Jenna called. She could hear the fatigue in her sister's voice, even though Betsy denied it. She'd said the girls had been up extra early that morning, asking for chocolate milk and tractor rides.

"That's good," Max said. "How are you doing without them?"

She stretched her legs out on the coffee table in front of the swing. Another strong breeze lifted the hair from around her face and blew a stack of napkins to the ground. Jenna closed her eyes. "I miss them. A lot. But I'm trying to be someone they can be proud of. And I'm doing good things here, Max. You'd be proud too."

"I'm always proud of you, sweetheart. You can't do a thing to change that."

TWENTY-EIGHT

BETSY

Everything Betsy knew about gardening could fit into a teacup, but even she knew late July wasn't an ideal time to plant anything other than maybe some heat-tolerant petunias and hope for the best. Still, she kept finding herself standing in the middle of her long-abandoned garden at odd times, imagining clouds of pink and red, mounds of white and yellow, stalks of green. Soft petals, smooth leaves, a sweet aroma of life and jasmine on the breeze. She had an urge to dig her hands in the dirt, to rip the dead roots and twiggy stalks from the earth and start over.

Unable to sleep once her mind began churning with ideas and the day ahead, she rose early one morning and padded to the kitchen. She was at the kitchen table with a pile of old *Southern Living* magazines and a thick stack of gardening books when Ty shuffled into the kitchen.

"Morning," he mumbled, then kissed her cheek, his face still warm with sleep.

Ever since the night of the festival, they'd been polite with each other. Kind, gentle—casual, even. But there'd been a vein of tension running through all their interactions. They'd yet to go back to the conversation they'd had that night. Conversation, argument, fight—she didn't know what to call it, only that it felt like they'd stuck their toes into untested waters. The morning after, he'd slipped out of bed early, and neither of them had brought up the topic again. Now, almost a week later, she wondered if they should just let it drop altogether.

His eyes scanned the table, taking in the array of books she'd dog-eared and pages she'd ripped out of the magazines: "Flowers for Southern Home Gardens," "Plant These Now to Reap a Fall Harvest," and "Planting in the Dog Days of Summer? It Can Be Done!"

Ty smiled.

"Don't laugh."

"I'm not laughing," he said. "I think it's great. It's about time."

"What do you mean?"

He poured coffee into a mug. "I've seen you poking around out in the garden. I figured it wouldn't be long before you decided to give it another go."

"I don't know what I'm doing, but I can't stop thinking about getting in there and getting my hands dirty."

He smoothed his hand down the back of her head. "Whatever you decide to do with it, it'll be great." He opened the porch door and slid his feet into his boots. "What about peas? Is it the right time to plant those?"

She leaned over and pulled a book toward her.

Southern Vegetables for Every Season. "I don't know, but I'm sure this will tell me."

"I'd love some field peas. Oh, or purple hulls." He closed his eyes and she knew he was imagining the meals his grandmother used to cook. He'd told her about them—piles of field peas, collards, butter beans, fried okra, thick hunks of cornbread. She'd never cooked like that, but maybe some late-season peas would be a good place to start.

. . .

After a field trip from ABC Daycare that afternoon, Betsy buckled the girls into the car and drove up the road to Sweet Peas Nursery. She could have driven farther to a big box garden center, but she preferred the smaller garden shop that only folks in Elinore and the surrounding small towns knew about. Plus, the owner, Marjorie Clarke, was an old friend. She and Marjorie had grown close back when Betsy worked in the garden often. She used to visit Sweet Peas at least once a week to purchase plants or seeds, or sometimes just to chat. Marjorie had lived in Elinore for seventy-five of her eighty-two years. She knew everyone and, in Betsy's estimation, everything about both gardening and life.

Betsy parked in the dirt parking lot and helped the girls out of the car. A tire swing and a small plastic slide were set up in the shade under the low arms of a live oak to the side of the shop. The girls made a beeline for the tree, squealing and yelling.

"Y'all be careful on that swing," Betsy called. "I'll be just inside."

She stepped onto the creaky front porch of the shop. Inside, Marjorie was ringing up a customer while her great-grandson Malik, who was at least a foot taller than the last time Betsy had seen him, slid a pallet of butter daisies into a brown paper sack. While Marjorie finished up, Betsy walked through the shop, trailing her fingers on pots of ivy, small hand-painted birdhouses Marjorie's husband, Moses, made, and delicate wind chimes that clinked together in the blast of air from the window AC unit.

Behind her, Marjorie sent the customer out the door with one of her customary strong-armed hugs that belied her age and small stature and a few last words of wisdom. "Now, don't forget to water those sweet things. They're not fussy, but they might rebel if they get too thirsty. Just like Mo if I don't keep enough sweet tea in the house." She laughed and patted her friend on the back, then turned to face Betsy.

"My dear." She held her arms out. "It has been much too long."

Enveloped in Marjorie's soft arms, Betsy smelled fresh soil and the faint aroma of Bengay. It was a familiar scent she'd missed. "It's good to see you, Marjorie."

"Mm-hmm, it is." Marjorie pulled back and held Betsy by the shoulders, looking her up and down. "You don't look any worse for the wear, although with those two young'uns running around out there, you have some explaining to do. It's been a while, but not that long."

Betsy smiled. "They're my nieces. They've been spending some time with us this summer."

"Well, that's nice. Always good to have family around. Isn't that right, Malik," she called.

The young man popped his head up from behind the counter and slyly hid his iPhone behind his back. "Yes, ma'am."

"Your daddy's out on a delivery, but when he gets back, I imagine he won't want to see you sitting there playing on that phone."

"Yes, ma'am." He sighed and grabbed a spray bottle of Windex and a roll of paper towels. "I'll be in the back if you need me, Nana."

"Good boy." Marjorie rolled her eyes at Betsy. "Those phones, I tell you. Now, I know you didn't come out here just so those girls could play on that old tire swing. What can I do for you?"

"Well, I let my garden go, which is probably obvious since I haven't been here in ages. I know it's not a great time to plant, but I'm ready to get back in there. I was hoping you could help me."

"Honey, it's always a good time to plant. God gave us enough variety that we can always find something to stick in the ground and grow. It may take extra work in this heat, but you're not afraid of a little hard work, are you?"

"No, ma'am."

"I didn't think so. Come on, let's see what we can find."

Marjorie took Betsy's elbow and led her through the shop toward the back door. On the way she gave Betsy's arm a gentle squeeze. "Last time you were in here, you mentioned going to see a doctor."

Betsy smiled. Marjorie wasn't one to beat around the bush. She thought back to the last day she'd visited Sweet Peas. She'd come in for some marigolds to keep rabbits from eating her flowers, but instead she sat in Marjorie's back office and cried. After a year of trying to get pregnant on their own, she'd just called to book an appointment for her and Ty with Dr. Fields.

Marjorie had tried to get her to look at it as a step in the right direction. "He'll get you fixed up in no time. Healthy girl like you, you shouldn't have any trouble at all."

But even then, weeks before they started any kind of real treatment, Betsy had sensed it would be an uphill battle. She just didn't realize her garden would be an accidental casualty.

"Did you end up going to see him?" Marjorie prodded.

"I did. We spent a lot of time in his office over the last two years. Can't say it did any good though. I don't think we'll be going back."

"Mm-hmm," Marjorie murmured. "In my experience, no time spent on a worthwhile goal is ever wasted, even if you don't get what you want right then." She patted Betsy's hand before pushing open the screened door to the greenhouse. "You never know what may happen down the road, my dear."

The walls of the greenhouse were lined with shelves of terra-cotta pots, some empty, some bursting with blooms and herbs. Marjorie had a green thumb like nothing Betsy had ever seen. In even the driest, hottest summers or the coldest winters—cold for south Alabama, anyway—Marjorie coaxed blooms from the ground, pots, even old feeding troughs. She never used commercial fertilizer, just natural, organic fertilizers she mixed herself. She said she used the same recipes handed down from her grandmother and great-grandmother, all plant whisperers just like her.

She led Betsy to a table in the courtyard outside the back door of the greenhouse. "Now, remind me, how sunny is your garden? All day sun, a few hours, dappled shade . . . ?" Marjorie poked around in various pots and containers, checking tags and markers as she spoke.

"It's full sun until about midafternoon. Then it's partly shaded by our big oak tree."

"And you're wanting flowering plants or edibles?"

"Both? I was thinking flowers, but Ty asked for peas. Maybe I could plant some flowers in with some vegetables?"

"Yes, this'll work well." She pulled a few pots out and set them on the ground. Then she crossed the court-yard to a rack of seeds inside the greenhouse. She spun the rack until she found what she was looking for and pulled a handful of packets down. A few minutes later, the ground by Betsy's feet was covered in pallets and pots of various sizes.

"Let me tell you what we've got." Marjorie handed her the seed packets. "Pinkeye purple hulls for your husband. An inch deep, two inches apart. Winter but-ternut squash, some Champion collards. These General Lee cucumbers are good for salads. And carrots—it's a little early, but you could try them. I grabbed the

Thumbelina variety. Figured your little nieces might have fun with those, and they'll be great for roasting and stews in the fall.

"Now for flowers, these mix just fine with veggies and take the heat pretty well." She nudged each pot with the toe of her Nikes. "Lantana, salvia. Your sweet potato vine might get a little leggy in the heat, but you can just pinch it back. Make sure they get enough water. I have hibiscus and mandevilla. You could use either one, but make sure they have something to climb up on—a trellis or porch rail. Even some fishing line strung up tall would work."

Betsy reached down and touched the bright-orange hibiscus petals. "They're beautiful."

Just then, Addie and Walsh came running around the side of the shop. "Aunt Betsy?"

"I'm out here, girls," Betsy called.

"Wow." Walsh peered down to sniff the flowers.

"None of these have much of a scent," Marjorie said. "But go try those big white blooms over there." She pointed to a large gardenia bush planted at the side of the shop. The girls ran over and stuck their faces up to the blooms.

"That bush came from a single cutting of my grandmother's gardenia," she said to Betsy. "I planted it there when Moses and I first married and we started this nursery. I gave it a little plant food here and there, but I mostly left it alone and let it do its own thing. Never could have imagined it'd still be here sixty years later. Just goes to show good things can happen even when you're not looking for them."

Malik helped Betsy load up the plants in the back of her car. When Betsy called the girls to come back to the car, he ran inside and brought out a bowl of lollipops. The girls each chose one—red for Addie, blue for Walsh—and gave him shy thank-yous.

Betsy hugged Marjorie before she climbed in. "Thank you. For the plants and the chat."

"You know you always have a friend here, my dear. As long as I'm still ticking along, you're welcome anytime. Oh, I almost forgot." She reached into her back pocket and pulled out two pairs of kid-size gardening gloves. "Give these to those two sweet girls. And let me know if you have any questions about your seeds. Best to plant them early morning or late evening, when the sun's not too strong. No need to burn them up when they're just getting started. And please tell your husband I said hello."

Betsy smiled. "I'll do that."

. . .

After a bright start, the afternoon grew overcast, and now, in this space between dinner and the girls' baths, thunder rumbled in the distance. Betsy was glad for the reprieve, even a slight one, after a week of relentless heat.

"Okay, girls, are you ready? Everything's gotta go."

"Ready," Addie said, her eyes on the dirt.

"On your mark, get set . . ."

"Go!"

And with that, Addie and Walsh were off, tearing through the abandoned garden wearing their new gardening gloves. Betsy had instructed them to pull out everything but the dirt, and for a few minutes, they took the job seriously. Addie knelt over a patch of daylilies that had long ago dried up and pulled with glee, flinging clods of dirt as she went. But when she dropped the first pile of weeds and plants into the wheelbarrow, she grabbed its handles and pushed it through the yard, her mission forgotten. Walsh yanked fistfuls of weeds before discovering a line of roly-polies in a muddy spot at the back of the garden.

As the girls played and yanked a few weeds here and there, Betsy did the real work. Remnants of her years-ago project—nurturing a garden that would produce both a bounty for their kitchen table and blooms they could sell in bouquets to farm visitors—fell away beneath her fingers, loosened by the roots.

She'd once been determined to carry on the gardening tradition passed on from Ty's grandmother, a woman known for her luscious blooms and vegetables she shared with neighbors. As the newest Franklin woman to live on the farm, Betsy had felt the pressure to be the best farmer's wife she could be, and that meant doing things just as they'd been done before her.

Much to her surprise, she discovered she enjoyed gardening: the immediate satisfaction of pulling weeds, creating a clean space for plants to thrive. Seeing tiny sprouts pop up where the day before there had just been small mounds of soil. Bright green in spring, deeper emerald green in summer. Gardening had been a comforting outlet, a distraction from monthly disappointments.

Yet the pressure remained—an internal drive to

work hard, to bring forth life out of the hard ground, to not fail the women who had come before her. When she resorted to making an appointment with Dr. Fields, the garden became too much life, too much vitality, and she'd walked away.

This time around, she'd work the garden for herself, no one else. Maybe they'd end up with some vegetables later in the year, maybe not. Maybe they'd have flowers, maybe they'd have nothing. Betsy would do what she could to claim her own green thumb, but it wasn't up to her, and this time she was okay with that. It would depend on the generosity of the hard-packed dirt, the summer rain and sun, the survival of these plants in this garden.

For Betsy, it was already a success. Her hands in the dirt, the quiet twilight around her, new life waiting to be sunk down into the ground. Just doing something purposeful—something solely for her—felt good.

As she pulled the last of the old plants from the ground, the porch door slammed. A moment later, Ty called to Addie and Walsh and handed them watermelon Popsicles. While they raced against the heat—trying to lick the Popsicles faster than they melted—Ty joined her by the garden.

She stood, then laughed when her knees popped. "I guess I'm not as young as I used to be."

Ty picked up a pot and inspected the label, then placed it back on the pallet. "A lot has changed since you were last out here."

Betsy stared at the fresh plot of earth, her mind on the past, her heart drifting toward the future.

"You done for the night?" he asked.

She shook her head. "I want to get all this in the ground before I head in. The garden deserves to be full again. And as you can see, Marjorie loaded me down today."

"Do you want any help?"

"I don't think so. It shouldn't take me long."

"I'll take the girls for a spin then. Let you finish up here in peace."

He whistled and pointed to the Gator sitting in its shed by the barn. The girls cheered and ran ahead of him through the gate and out to the field beyond. By the time the engine roared to life a few moments later, Betsy had begun digging the first set of holes—one inch deep, two inches apart, just like Marjorie said—and dropped in the purple hull peas. Collards came next, then carrots and squash.

When she finished the vegetables, Ty was just walking back into the yard with the girls, their cheeks sticky and their hair curling around their faces from the humidity in the air. Fireflies winked in the low limbs of the oak tree and hovered in the grass around their feet. He paused to wait for her, but she waved them on, wanting to finish before dark.

After loosening the lantana and salvia from their pots and settling them into the ground, she sat back on her heels to survey her work. Everything was ready for sunshine and afternoon rain showers. Over time, the blossoms and leaves would fill the empty space next to the split-rail fence Ty's grandfather built around the garden so many years ago. New hope growing next to old dreams.

TWENTY-NINE

Ty

Tropical Storm Ingrid nearing hurricane intensity. Center of the storm located southeast of the Lesser Antilles moving west at 18 mph. Gradual turn to the west-northwest expected in next 24 hours.

Ty considered it a good day if he made it back into the house before dinnertime with Betsy. Prior to this summer, most days were good days, but with the arrival of Addie and Walsh and their five-thirty dinnertime, he couldn't make any promises. Often he was still in the barn—filling his notebooks with notations and checkmarks, cleaning, preparing for the next day—while Betsy fixed the girls' dinner, fed them, started their baths.

This evening, though, he wrapped up in the barn earlier than usual and entered the kitchen while Betsy was still stirring pasta on the stove. The girls were huddled on the den floor with a five-hundred-piece puzzle.

"Planning to keep them busy for a while?" He rested his hand on the small of her back and nodded in the girls' direction.

"I don't even know where they found that. They were running around chasing Etta, and the next thing I knew, puzzle pieces were all over the floor."

"You remember the puzzle though, right?"

Betsy smiled and nodded. "I remember."

When Ty and Betsy had first started dating, he brought a puzzle to her apartment one night. She'd been surprised, but he knew it'd be a way for them to talk, to get to know each other. He also knew it'd give him something else to concentrate on when all he wanted to do was tangle his fingers in her hair and kiss her all night. The puzzle was his attempt to be a gentleman.

"I had good intentions, you have to admit." He stuck a spoon in the sauce simmering on the stove. "Are those capers? Think they'll like it?"

Betsy shrugged. "I hope so. It'd keep me from having to make two dinners."

Ty sat on one of the stools at the counter and stretched his legs out in front of him. He needed to run upstairs and shower, but it felt so good to just sit for a minute.

Betsy tapped the spoon on the edge of the pot and laid it on the spoon rest. "I may have some peas for you in the fall. If everything goes well."

"You have Gran's cast-iron skillet, don't you? We could make cornbread to go with them." His grandmother had made cornbread with almost every meal when Ty was young. And she'd served it on the same kitchen table he and Betsy used now.

Betsy wiped her hands on a dish towel, then sat on a stool next to him. "Maybe after all these years I'll finally turn into the wife who'll cook meat-and-three dinners." She poked him in the chest. "You'd love that, wouldn't you?"

"If I just wanted someone to make me meat-and-three meals, Ollie's is right up the road. I'd be happy there." He grabbed her finger and pulled her closer. "I have you for other reasons."

"Oh, is that right?" She smiled and he relished the lightness on her face.

With her hand still in his, she shifted on her stool and turned toward the den where Addie and Walsh were still sprawled on the floor with puzzle pieces scattered everywhere. "The girls are happy here."

Ty nodded. "They seem to be."

"I think if we could pack Rosie up in a suitcase, Addie would take her everywhere. She's crazy about that cow."

Ty laughed. "I think you're right."

"And the hens, the swing, the creek. This is what childhood is supposed to be like—barefoot and dirty, going to bed exhausted."

"That kind of describes our days too. Except the barefoot part for me."

Betsy smiled. Other than the sauce simmering and the water boiling, the kitchen was silent. "Jenna's looking for jobs, you know. She has it in her head that this place, Halcyon, is going to open all kinds of doors for her."

"And you don't think so?"

"I have no idea. She's just pinning a lot of hopes on this retreat and what it can lead to as far as jobs. She said her mentor has his foot in the door at places all over the country."

"Hmm," Ty murmured. "I guess it wouldn't surprise me if at the end of all this, she decides to shake things up."

A squeal came from the den. "This is it!" Addie yelled, holding up a single puzzle piece. She handed it to Walsh, who dropped it and went back to rolling a small stuffed ball to Etta.

He smiled and turned back to Betsy, but she was looking down, oblivious to Addie's elation, her brow creased in concentration.

"What is it?" he asked.

"We have good schools around here," she said after a moment.

He straightened up in his seat.

"The elementary school. It's good."

"And?" he said slowly.

"Jenna hasn't said when she's coming back. And you said it yourself: she could go on from the retreat to something else."

He willed himself to nod, his mind working to come up with the right words, and quick. "I was thinking more along the lines of her finding a new job—not that she'd stay gone. She has to come back for her kids. She knows that."

"I know. I just . . ." She shrugged. "It's already August. What do we do if school starts and she's not here?"

"Betsy, I . . ." He stopped, pressed his lips together. "I think it's a little early to be thinking about that. The kids have their own school and friends in Nashville. They'll want to get back home."

She gazed in the direction of the girls, but he feared that instead of seeing them, she looked past them, through them, to other possibilities, other dreams. Finally, she turned back to him. "You're right. I know you're right. It was a crazy idea."

"Is it time to eat yet?" Addie yelled from the den.

Betsy swiveled her head to the girls, her face caught somewhere between disappointment and relief. "Yes, it is," she said after the briefest pause. She hopped off the stool and touched Ty's arm. "Iced tea or water?" she asked, her voice casual.

• • •

All through dinner, Ty's mind whirled with their fractured conversation. Betsy didn't seem affected by it. In fact, she seemed lighter somehow, even more animated. She laughed at Walsh's impersonation of Walker falling off an overturned bucket and indulged Addie in a lengthy session of "One Hundred Questions."

An hour later he was about to step in the shower— could already feel the hot water loosening his muscles, washing away the heat and stress of the day—when Betsy's phone vibrated on the dresser. She'd left it there before taking the girls into the hall bathroom to bathe them before bed.

He left the water running and crossed the room to check the screen.

Jenna.

He sighed and ran his hand through his hair. He wanted to just let voice mail pick up, but at the last second he answered. "Hang on," he said in place of a greeting. "Let me get Betsy."

Without waiting for an answer, he took the phone across the hall to the bathroom. He peered in through the half-closed door, just enough to see Betsy with one hand on a wet, wiggling Walsh and the other hand trying to cover a shivering Addie with a towel.

He crossed back into his room and closed the door behind him. "Give her a few minutes to finish up what she's doing." With reluctance he turned the shower off in the bathroom and sat on the bed. "How are things going?"

"They're going really well."

He raised his eyebrows, surprised to hear the confidence in her voice. "That's great, Jenna."

"I can't imagine what you must think of me, staying gone this long. But I'm making some real progress here, so . . ." She paused. "Thank you. For taking care of the girls, for letting me work on . . . well, on me."

"Yeah, well, your sister really loves you." He squeezed his eyes closed and ran his hand over the top of his head. "I do too, of course, but Betsy wanted to do this for you. She's thinking something big is going to come out of your trip down there."

Jenna let out a gentle laugh. "But you think otherwise?"

"I don't know, Jenna. I'm just not sure what's going on. Remind me what you're doing at this art thing."

"I'm trying to build something different for our life. For my life with the girls."

"How so?"

She paused, then sighed. "My job is to make coffee for people who spend as much on their caffeine habit as I do on groceries. I train employees. I clean up messes and defuse hot tempers and give away free drinks when a barista makes a mistake. Day in, day out."

"But—"

"I come home to the girls exhausted, but I haven't done anything all day that I'm proud of or that they can be proud of. I don't want them to see me as someone who's given up her dream just for a paycheck." Her voice rose as she spoke. "Even if nothing comes of this, I want them to know I worked for it. That I tried to follow my calling. Does that make sense?"

Despite his frustration, it did make sense. He followed his heart to the farm instead of accepting the life of relative ease that an accounting job would provide. But he wasn't ready to admit that to Jenna. "There's nothing wrong with steady work. I have the same schedule seven days a week, every week of the year. And you want to talk about exhausted? How hard is it to pour coffee?" He leaned forward and propped his elbows on his knees. "I'm sorry. It's just . . . What you do brings in a paycheck. It pays your bills. Not everyone has that."

"I get that. I do. And I appreciate that steady paycheck. But I want to get to a place where I can try to pay bills with my art. Or at least make it a bigger part of my life. This place is opening my eyes to how I may be able to do that." Through the phone, he heard a door open, then a chorus of loud nighttime noises.

"I thought you didn't get cell reception there."

"I don't. I called from my cabin. I had to charge it to my credit card, but I didn't want to worry about the call dropping." The chains of a porch swing creaked. "Things are changing for me, Ty. My mentor has talked to some magazine editors to see if I can start as a freelancer. And I've opened my Etsy shop back up. I posted a new collection of photos I've taken here and I've already had two orders." Pride filled her voice.

Part of him was glad for her, but his frustration made him keep pushing. "That's great, but what comes next? What happens if another too-good-to-miss opportunity comes on the heels of this one and you just have to take it? Do we keep the girls indefinitely while you keep following your true calling?"

He was being harsh, but he couldn't stop himself. His and Betsy's life had changed with the arrival of the girls. While Betsy was leaning into the unknown, even welcoming it, Ty was getting nervous. And Betsy's comments about school had only increased his tension. Sure, she agreed that it was a crazy idea to think about enrolling them in school, but he knew her ache was still there. The unmet desire.

"No, Ty, that's not it." Jenna exhaled forcefully. "I don't think I'm explaining myself very well."

"Well, while you're figuring it out, don't forget we have two little kids living in our house. *Your* kids."

"I know that, and I know I'm walking a fine line staying away from them for this long."

"I think you may be right on that."

"But they sound happy every time I talk to them. Like they're having the time of their lives. Like they don't mind that I'm still gone, because they're with fun parents now."

"That's ridiculous. You're the parent. We don't know what we're doing. We're just stand-ins until you get back." As he said the words, he thought of all he and Betsy had learned about parenting during their six-week crash course. Then he thought of Betsy in the other room getting the girls ready for bed. "Look, it's late. I don't want this to turn into a fight."

"Do you think I'm a bad mother?" Her voice was quiet. "That I can't take care of my kids? I want to hear it if that's what you think."

"No one's saying that, Jenna. To be honest, Addie and Walsh seem to be happy, well-adjusted kids, and that probably says a lot about your mothering skills. It's up to them to decide what kind of mom you are, but I have to tell you, your sister skills could use a little work."

Jenna was silent. Ty continued.

"You pack up your kids and drop them off with Betsy—the sister who for five years has been unable to have her own children—and expect us to just accept it. To kick back and wait for your little adventure to end so you can blow back in here whenever your time is done and whisk these girls away. Then you get to return to your life with Addie and Walsh while your sister—*my wife*—is left with a silent house."

Ty rubbed his hand across his eyes, pushing hard until colors exploded behind his eyelids. He glanced toward the bathroom—steam still fogged the mirror from the hot water running only minutes ago. He wished he were in there now, scalding water pounding his back, beating the tension out of his shoulders.

"I didn't know," she stammered. "About Betsy. And you. Five years?"

"She'd been off the pill for six months when you called and told her you were pregnant."

"Oh," Jenna breathed. "I had no idea. I just figured y'all were . . . I don't know, waiting. So when she stayed with us last summer, she was talking about some tests . . . I didn't ask for details. I should have asked."

"We'd just done our first IUI. It's where you . . ." He cleared his throat. His anger had leaked out, leaving him drained. And his head was pounding. "Anyway, it didn't work and we found out the day before she left. She'd been hoping . . . We'd both hoped it would turn out differently."

Jenna groaned. "I can't believe she didn't tell me. Why wouldn't she say anything?"

"Would it have made a difference? Would you have skipped the retreat if you'd known?"

"I don't know, I . . ." She exhaled.

Ty scanned the perimeter of their bedroom. Their wedding photo framed on the wall, their clean, folded clothes mingled together on a side chair, a pair of Betsy's sandals on the floor. His eyes rested on a glass jar sitting on her nightstand, next to a glass of water and a paperback she read every night before bed. The jar had a smattering of debris at the bottom. It took only a moment to realize what it was. After Addie found the first heart-shaped rock at the creek and passed it to Betsy, it became a game between the three of them—Betsy and the girls. Whenever they came across anything heart shaped—mostly rocks, but leaves and pieces of bark too—they'd stick it in their pockets. Ty didn't know Betsy had saved them.

"I don't think it was the easiest thing for her to talk about. But knowing Betsy, even if she had told you what was going on, she still would have wanted you to go on this trip. To do what you needed to do. But she's my wife and it's my duty to protect her. I'm sure you plan to come back here at some point, but until then, we have a life, a farm to take care of, and two kids to try to love and entertain while you're gone. Just do me a favor and give us a heads-up before you come back this way."

He waited for Jenna to explode back with as much force as she could muster, but she didn't. "Are the girls still awake? I'd like to talk to them."

He wanted to say no, but she was their mother. "I can check."

Ty crossed the hall and tapped on the door. Addie and Walsh were in bed but still awake. Betsy sat on the edge of the bed talking quietly to them. "Girls? Your mom's on the phone."

Betsy moved to make room for Ty, and he handed the phone to Addie. "Hold it out so you both can hear."

"Mommy?" Addie asked.

"Hi, baby. How are you?"

Sitting so close to Addie on the bed, they could hear

Jenna's voice coming through the phone as clear as if she were sitting right there with them.

"Good."

"What have you been doing?"

Addie shrugged.

"Addie?"

Betsy leaned down and whispered, "Tell her about the henhouse."

"We get to check the hens for eggs every morning. Yesterday I found four all by myself."

"I found two," Walsh added.

"You did? That's so cool. Will you show me the hens when I get there?"

"Are you getting here tomorrow?"

"No, baby, I won't be there tomorrow. But I'll be back soon. I promise."

"But that's what you said last time."

"I know. You just have to trust me, okay? I love you both so much. When I see you, I'll hug you in the tightest hugs you've ever had. How does that sound?"

A smile played on Addie's lips. "Super-duper tight?"

"Super-duper-duper-duper tight. How about that?"

"Good," Walsh said.

"Okay, sweet girls. I'll talk to you soon."

"Okay. I love you, Mommy."

"I love you too."

. . .

Lying in bed, Ty wanted to tell Betsy about the call with Jenna—the longing he heard in her voice, but the determination too. The things that worried him. But when it came to Jenna, he didn't know how to navigate the sore places in Betsy's heart.

Her impossible idea of enrolling the girls in school still weighed heavy on his mind, and he knew he wouldn't sleep with so much unspoken between them. He rolled onto his side and looked at her, her profile sharp in the light coming in through the window. "You awake?" he whispered.

She opened her eyes, her gaze on the ceiling. The quiet moment before she spoke seemed to last an eternity. "You know what I need? New gardening boots. For my birthday."

Ty exhaled and tried to make it sound like a laugh. "Really? That's what you want for your thirtieth birthday?"

She nodded. "The toe in one of mine is busted. I got a boot full of dirt today."

"Boots for your birthday. I can handle that."

He waited for more about the girls, Jenna, school—something—but Betsy turned in silence and reached her arm across him. Ty smelled the lemon scent of her shampoo when she rested her head on his chest and closed her eyes. Instead of bringing it all up again, he closed his own eyes. Finally, he felt the rhythm of her breath deepen.

Boots for your birthday, he thought before sliding into sleep. *You deserve so much more than that.*

THIRTY

JENNA

Jenna's phone rang while she was still several steps away from her cabin. She hurried to open her door, fumbling and dropping her camera bag, though thankfully her camera still hung around her neck. She'd spent the morning shooting one of the artists, a painter who had set up his easel in the bow of a canoe and rowed it to the center of the lake so he could better observe the reflection of the trees' canopy on the water.

Jenna was fascinated by his concentration, his determination to angle the canoe in just the right position to study the reflection and transpose it onto his canvas. She was so enthralled, in fact, that she hadn't realized until now that she'd left her cell sitting on her kitchen counter instead of sticking it in the pocket of her bag before she left her cabin.

Once inside, she grabbed the phone without looking to see who was calling.

"Oh, Jenna dear. It's Delores. It sounds like I caught you at a bad time."

"No, no. It's fine." Jenna flopped down on the small love seat and kicked off her shoes. "I was just hurrying to get to the phone. How are you? It's been a long time."

"It has and I'm better now that I hear you're okay. I started to worry when I didn't see you and the girls back at your house. Are you still at the art retreat?"

"Yes, ma'am. And I'm sorry for not calling to let you know my plans changed."

"It's no worry. I would have called sooner, but I didn't want to be a bother. Now, tell me all about it. What happened to make you stay longer?"

"Well, the first two weeks were hard. I wasn't even sure why I'd come. But things started to pick up for me toward the end, and when my mentor offered me the chance to extend my stay, I took it. All the first two weeks did was tell me I needed to be here longer." She ran her hand through her tangled curls, then grabbed a clip out of her bag and pulled her hair back, away from her face. "It's been great, being able to focus on my work and really push myself to try some new things."

"That's wonderful. The time away must be a good thing. I know you miss your girls though. Are they still with your sister?"

"They are. They're turning into little farm kids. But I do miss them." She shifted in the love seat to lie with her legs hanging over the arm.

"I'm sure they miss you too. This is turning into a long trip. I'm glad things are going well for you there though."

Jenna sighed and closed her eyes. She'd been focused on her work, adding quality shots to her portfolio and soaking up instruction from Gregory, but she hadn't been able to shake the phone conversation with Ty. He was an honest and forthright man and she'd always appreciated that about him, but when the brutal honesty was directed at her, the words stung. She struggled to push his words away, but at the same time, maybe they were the exact ones she needed to hear.

"Hon?"

Delores's voice was so concerned, so gentle, Jenna had to struggle to hold back tears. "You must have some kind of miracle phone powers." She sat up and put her feet on the floor. Forced a small laugh. "I get terrible reception here, but your call came through with no trouble."

"Oh, I don't think it's any kind of miracle. Just good timing. I've been thinking about you and figured one phone call wouldn't disrupt your muses too much."

Jenna smiled. "Is your computer close by? I'll show you a little of what I've been working on."

She gave Delores the address of her Etsy shop, then listened as Delores's fingers tapped on her keyboard.

"I've almost got it . . . there." She paused. "This is your work?"

"Some of it. I have a lot more to add, but I wanted to get my shop back up and running now that I'm shooting again."

"These are beautiful. I'm impressed, though I'm not surprised. Those photos of Addie and Walsh on your living room wall told me you were talented, but I didn't know you had all this in you."

"I didn't either, to be honest. But I'm building my

portfolio to show more of a range of work. I've been researching jobs—event photographers, photo assistants. Just entry-level jobs right now. And I've applied for a few freelance positions. I know I won't get them, but it's good to get my name out there anyway. It's hard to get picked up if no one knows who you are."

"That all sounds wonderful. I'm curious though—now that you know what you can do, will coming back home to Nashville feel like small potatoes?"

Jenna laughed. "I don't know about that, but it definitely would be hard to put the photography on the back burner again and go back to just making coffee. I don't think I could do it. Not now."

"But why would you need to? Women were born to multitask. You're already a mother, a friend, a strong woman—a *talented* woman. You can work your job and raise your kids and do your photography too. It doesn't have to be one or the other."

Jenna stood and paced the small cabin to have something to do, a way to relieve the anxious energy coursing through her limbs. "I don't know." She paused by her camera on the kitchen counter. When she'd first arrived, it had felt as mysterious to her as a book in another language. Now it was familiar, an extension of her own hands and fingers. According to Ty though, that familiarity—that gift—had come at a cost. "I don't know. A better mother would have packed up by now and headed back home to her kids. It's just . . . It feels like if I don't do this now, I won't get another chance."

"I understand the feeling," Delores said, her voice soft. "But you're a fine mother and pursuing your dream is something you *can* do, no matter where you are. Even if you're back home."

Jenna thought of her little house full of blankets and Barbies. Her girls' laughter, their feet pounding the floor. Her camera gathering dust on the shelf. She felt like a different person now—would her life back home be different too?

"You may be right. You're usually right about most things."

Delores laughed. "I wish Willard were around to hear you say that. Now, I have one more question. This is another subject entirely, but I'm curious. Have you spoken with that nice boy from the coffee shop since you've been gone?"

"Sam?" Her smile was involuntary. She thought of how he looked sitting across the table from her in the mornings. Brown hair a touch too long for a corporate job, button-down shirt rolled up to his elbows, charming grin.

"Yes, that's the one. You were seeing him pretty much every day before you left, right? I'd imagine he's pretty disappointed to be missing his dates with you."

"They weren't dates, they were just coffee. We texted a bit soon after I got here, but we haven't talked since the last day I was in the shop. I'm sure he's found someone else to have that cup of coffee with."

"That's too bad. From what you said about him, he sounded . . . sincere."

"That's a good way to describe him."

"Trust me when I say in the long run, sincerity is a good quality to have in a man. Much better than those flashy bozos I see strutting down the street when I go out to get my hair done."

Jenna laughed. "I'm not really in the market for a man, sincere or otherwise, but I'll keep that in mind."

"I've said this to you before, dear, and I'll say it one more time. You're young and smart and you have your whole life ahead of you. Don't make the mistake of thinking there's only one road you can take, only one life you can live. You'll figure out how to make the different parts of your life come together. I have all the faith in the world in you."

THIRTY-ONE

BETSY

Hurricane Ingrid advisory 28. A hurricane warning is in effect for Jamaica and the Cayman Islands. This is a dangerous storm that could reach Category 4 before landfall. Maximum sustained winds are 145 mph. Ingrid is moving west-northwest at 15 mph.

The morning of her birthday, Betsy woke to giggling coming from the door to her bedroom. Then shushing, then more giggling. Outside, a soft rain fell, tapping on the windows. She kept her eyes closed, feigning sleep, until she felt a tap on her shoulder. She cracked one eye open.

"Happy birthday, Aunt Betsy!" Addie and Walsh yelled.

Ty stood behind them, his expression displaying both apology and amusement. "Told you it'd be a good day for you to sleep in." He leaned down and kissed her lightly. "Happy birthday," he whispered.

She smiled and stretched, then sat up against the pillows. "Is this all for me?" She eyed the tray tipping precariously in Addie's hands. Ty reached down and straightened it.

Addie nodded. "Blueberry muffins, orange juice—"

"And chocolate chips!" Walsh added.

"Walsh insisted on those," Ty added.

"Well, why not? Chocolate chips go great with breakfast, in my opinion." Betsy winked at Walsh.

"And coffee." Ty handed her a large steaming mug.

"Thank you," she murmured, her lips already on the edge of the mug. "What time is it?"

He checked his watch. "Seven thirty."

"You need to go, don't you?"

"I do. Carlos and Walker covered the milking for me, but we've got a load of straw bales coming later this morning. I need to get ready for that." It was part of the farming life—weekends were just like regular days. Cows still needed to be milked, fields tended to, barns repaired. None of that stopped just because everyone else took a two-day break. Or because a storm was brewing in the Gulf.

"Go on then. It's fine. The girls and I may move this party downstairs, turn on *Curious George*, and do some more lying around."

Ty smiled. "Whatever you want. It's your day. Little rainy"—he eyed the window—"but not too bad. I was thinking later on, why don't you leave the girls with me for a few hours? You could take off and do something on your own."

Betsy shrugged. "I don't have anything I need to do."

She glanced at Addie and Walsh and lowered her voice. "And what about Ingrid? The news last night sounded pretty bad. Is there anything you need to . . . prepare, just in case?" She didn't want to be too specific with Addie listening, especially not after her fears the night Dawn came through.

He shrugged. "Nothing that can't wait until tomorrow." His voice was light, but it didn't hide the tension on his face. "Look, it's your birthday. Go out and do something you want to do. Get your nails done or something."

"Do you know who you're talking to? When's the last time I had a manicure?"

"I don't know. Don't all women like those?"

She laughed. "Sure. Maybe I'll get my nails done." She held her hand up and studied her fingernails. They were smooth and rounded, despite the week's gardening, but nail polish felt like a foreign concept. "I did read about a master gardener seminar at the library this weekend. I can look it up and see when it is. Maybe I'll learn a few tricks to keep all these new plants alive."

"Perfect. Just bring the girls out when you're ready to leave."

"If you're sure."

He smiled. "Girls, I'll see you a little later on, okay? Thanks for helping me with breakfast."

Walsh reached over and grabbed a chocolate chip from Betsy's plate and turned to Ty. She flung her arms around his leg and squeezed, then reached up and handed him the chocolate chip. "For you."

He popped it in his mouth, grinned at Betsy, and waved good-bye.

. . .

When Betsy and the girls came out later that morning to bring Ty the leftover blueberry muffins, the barn was unusually silent. Instead of the regular music pumping from the barn speakers, brooms and hammers and machines moving and working, the space was still. While the cows grazed in the pasture, a knot of men huddled around the laptop on Ty's desk, the tinny voice of a meteorologist floating from the speaker.

Betsy didn't know how he did it—if it had something to do with his "sweet spot" internal hunch or if it was something else more science based—but Ty had always known which storms to concern himself with and which ones to ignore, regardless of what the weathermen said or how other farmers in the area chose to prepare.

He'd predicted the ferocity of Hurricane Mabel six years ago with startling accuracy, even when the storm was still more than ten days out. He moved the cows to the middle of the back pasture, away from the buildings and tall trees, even when other farmers thought he was overreacting. They preferred to err on the side of hope—a flimsy thing in the face of Mother Nature's fury—but Ty chose to be realistic.

After Mabel blew through, leaving fallen trees, dead animals, and busted houses in her wake, Ty and Betsy found their cows munching wet grass in the pasture, only a few skittish heifers in the whole bunch. Their barn survived with minimal damage thanks to his preparations—a few missing shingles, some loose boards—and they didn't miss a milking. Few doubted his instincts after that.

Seeing Ty hunched over that laptop, his lips a thin, straight line, his hat flung carelessly on the desk, she knew it was serious.

"I don't know about you, Terry, but this reminds me a lot of how Ivan started way out in the Atlantic," the voice from the computer said. "Maybe even Frederick. No one's really talking about it yet, but I'd say—"

When Ty saw her and the girls, he closed the laptop. "I'd say we've heard enough for now, boys."

The guys straightened up and looked around, as if coming out of a dazed sleep. They blinked and rubbed their heads and beards, smiled at her and the girls.

"Hey there, Bets," Carlos said. He bent down to Addie and Walsh. "I'm going to need some help later this afternoon. Think I can count on the two of you?"

The girls nodded with enthusiasm.

"How's Gloria doing these days?" Betsy asked. "I haven't seen her in a while."

"Oh, she's good. She'll be happy to see you—"

Ty cleared his throat and Carlos stopped. "I'll tell her you said hello."

Betsy smiled. "Okay then." She glanced at Ty, but he'd lowered his gaze to his desk, straightening a pencil and a stack of paper.

When the guys dispersed, Ty grabbed his hat and slapped it back on his head. "What's this?" He nodded to the basket under Betsy's arm. "Those were supposed to be for you."

She looked at him another quick moment before handing the basket over. "The girls were concerned that you farmers get hungry during the day and don't have enough food out here to munch on. They said I really should share."

"And we had extras," Addie said. "There's one for you, one for Mr. Carlos, one for Mr. Walker . . ." She called out each man's name like they were special friends.

Ty leaned against his desk. "I'm sure they'll appreciate it. Why don't you run and catch them before they get too busy?" The girls trotted out into the barn with the basket.

"What's going on?" She nodded to the computer.

Ty sighed. "Ingrid. It's looking like she could turn ugly. Already is for some places."

"What's your plan?"

"We're in pretty good shape here. We did a lot of prep at the beginning of the season so no need to cram now. I need to check the shutters on the house, make sure they close tight. And you may want to take a trip to the store in case we lose power like last time. Better to do it now before panic sets in. We still have a few days."

She glanced through the open door. The girls handed Walker a muffin, then ran to the fence for the next delivery. "So it's coming this way?"

He shrugged. "No way to tell for sure. But we're due."

"And you have a feeling."

He nodded, his gaze on the floor. Then he turned to her. "So, time for you to head out?"

"I checked online and that class is at two."

"Great. What else?"

"I . . ." She shrugged.

"Don't worry about us. Walker is working long hours this weekend—I think he's saving for a car. I have extra hands around, so we'll be fine."

"Okay, but what about naptime? It's getting close, and I don't think Walsh should—"

"We'll be fine." Ty placed his hands on her shoulders and turned her around. "Really. They can take a quick nap after they've burned off some energy, then I have their whole afternoon planned. All you have to do is relax. And don't come back before dinner. The girls and I are going to cook you up something special."

"Okay," she said, still unsure.

"Why don't you call Anna Beth? See if she can meet you for a drink."

"In the middle of the afternoon?"

"Why not? It's your birthday."

Betsy kissed him and waved to the girls. On her way back to the house, she walked past her garden. The earth was still freshly turned and deep black where she'd mixed fertilizer in with the soil. The fledgling plants were ready, waiting. She said a little prayer that their shallow roots would soon take hold so if the storm came, they'd be grounded.

· · ·

The gardening seminar lasted an hour and a half. Betsy planned to stay for only a little while, just long enough to ask about aphids on her cucumber plants, but the speaker, a spry woman of about seventy, was so enthusiastic and knowledgeable, Betsy didn't have the heart to duck out early. She took Ty's advice and let herself relax, enjoy the absence of Goldfish crackers and myriad questions, and the company of other adults, even if those adults were all at least three decades older than she was.

During the talk, the woman in the seat next to Betsy leaned over and whispered, "Have you heard the talk about the storm? It's still way out in the water, but it's coming."

Betsy nodded. "Yes, ma'am, I just—"

"It makes me nervous as a June bug. Sylvia's up there talking a blue streak about the beauty of our native azaleas and pitcher plants, and all I can think about is that darn storm coming and ruining everything."

When the seminar was over, Betsy gathered her things and picked her way to the door, dodging tight knots of folks discussing both Sylvia's talk and the meteorologists' gloomy forecasts. Betsy was on her way to the exit when she heard laughter and an animated voice coming from the children's department. She paused, then backtracked and peeked her head in.

In one corner of the room, a young woman in pigtails danced across a small stage, acting out scenes from Goldilocks. A group of moms sat on the floor in front of her with children in their laps. The kids laughed when the woman jumped out of a too-small chair. The moms smiled at each other—knowing smiles, tired smiles. *We're-in-this-together* smiles. Afternoon story time. The camaraderie of parents, members of the mom-club. Betsy felt something twist in her chest.

"Are you looking for anything specific?" A librarian reshelving books paused and looked up at Betsy.

"Oh, uh . . . maybe something about flowers?"

"Sure." She stood and motioned for Betsy to follow her to a shelf across the room. "This is our nonfiction section. Books about flowers and plants are right down here."

Betsy stooped and ran her fingers across the spines. Titles jumped out at her. *A Seed Is Sleepy. Planting a Rainbow. The Curious Garden.* Nothing like her vintage *Henderson's Book of Fanciful Flowers*, but she grabbed a handful anyway. She smiled thinking of Addie and Walsh curled up in bed with these books.

Out in her car Betsy tapped on the steering wheel, trying to decide what to do next. Manicures weren't her thing, but she didn't want to disappoint Ty by coming back too soon, making him think she didn't trust him to take care of the girls on his own for just a few hours. The truth was, this summer had shown her what she always suspected but just hadn't seen in action—he would make an amazing dad. In acting as a stand-in father to Addie and Walsh, he was everything she knew he'd be. Gentle and caring, firm when he needed to be, a good partner, a strong guidepost.

She clenched and unclenched her hands around the wheel. She knew Jenna was trying her best. Her sister was always full of good intentions. With their mom no longer around—not that she was ever very present even when she was alive—Betsy saw Jenna as mostly her responsibility. If that extended to her children, then so be it. But she'd been as accommodating to Jenna as she could. She backed out of her parking place and turned onto the road, trying not to think about where she was going, what she was doing.

The sign for Elinore Elementary School, painted in bright red-and-blue stripes, beckoned from the side of the road. The long red-brick building was shaded by overhanging oaks and Spanish moss, and its U-shape welcomed like outstretched arms. A handful of cars sat in the parking lot. She got out and dashed through the light rain, hurrying so she wouldn't lose her nerve.

Just inside the front door, the secretary sat behind a computer, her phone pressed between her chin and shoulder. She held up a finger to Betsy. "That's right," she said into the phone. "Teachers come back on the 15th and students begin on the 20th . . . Okay, you just let me know. Bye now."

After replacing the phone, the woman looked up at Betsy. "Can I help you?"

"Yes, I'm looking for Mr. Burgess?"

"I'm afraid he's busy at the moment. If you leave your name, I'll let him know—"

"Betsy?"

The woman and Betsy both looked down the hall. Duncan Burgess walked toward them, his hands in his pockets, a smile on his face. "Did I forget a meeting?"

"No, no. I just stopped by on the chance that you might be here."

"Well, you found me. I came in to go through some student files. Just trying to get things squared away before the chaos starts."

Betsy smiled. The woman at the desk cleared her throat. "Mr. Burgess, I've been holding your calls like you asked. I have several messages." She held up a handful of small pink slips of paper.

"Thank you, Mrs. Kline. I'll take those." He held out his hand and Mrs. Kline passed him the messages. "Mrs. Franklin and I will be down in my office if you need anything."

Mrs. Kline cocked an eyebrow in Betsy's direction. "Yes, sir, Mr. Burgess."

Betsy followed him to a small office overlooking the playground at the back of the building. "It's good to see you again." He cleared off a stack of manila envelopes from the chair across from his desk. "Sorry it's such a mess in here. Sit, please." He sat in his desk chair and motioned for her to sit as well.

A coffee mug on his desk held ballpoint pens and one red pencil with an eraser shaped like Mickey Mouse ears. The mug read *World's Best Grandpa*. Betsy shifted in her seat.

"Is there something I can help you with? Or did you come to talk about the field trips? You know, I thought about talking to the kindergarten and first-grade teachers to see if we can link the trips to the farm with a lesson on health—you know, nutrition and where food comes from. That's a little different than they've done it in years past, but I think it would be interesting. What do you think?"

Betsy nodded, her head fuzzy. "Sure, that . . . that sounds great. I do have one other thing I wanted to talk to you about. It's not about the field trips though."

"Okay." He leaned forward and propped his elbows on the desk. "I'm all ears."

She took a deep breath. "Would it be possible for me to enroll a child in the school when she's not technically mine?"

There it was. The urge she couldn't even explain to herself, much less to her husband. She tried the other night in the kitchen, but when she voiced the idea, it didn't sound the same as it had in her mind. Ty thought it was crazy. And it was crazy—the idea of the girls staying, settling—but it kept dancing through her mind at inopportune times. In and out, here and there, but she kept forcing it away. Then it went and burrowed its way into her brain and hung on tight. It didn't make sense, it was impossible, but it was out now.

"By 'not technically yours,' you mean . . . ?"

"It's my niece. The older one. You saw them when we ran into you in Target."

He gave a slow nod. "I remember." He exhaled and sat back in his chair. "Is that . . . Are they going to be staying with you and your husband? Permanently?"

"I'm not sure. Maybe." She kept herself from wincing at the lie. But she'd heard Mrs. Kline. School started in mere weeks. It was likely the same for the girls' school in Nashville, and Betsy still didn't know exactly when Jenna would be back. She shut off the competing voices in her head. "If they do end up staying with us—for the school year—what would I need to do to enroll Addie in kindergarten?"

"Well, timing isn't the big issue. You can enroll a child anytime during the year. The real issue would be showing that you're her legal guardian, and that may take a while. You'd have to fill out paperwork to file for guardianship." He ticked items off on his fingers. "You have to get a letter of consent from the child's parents, interviews with the court, usually a home visit to establish living conditions. It's a lot to tackle, especially before the August 20 start date."

He paused, straightened a notebook on his desk. "I was under the impression that you were just keeping the kids for a little while. Babysitting." He looked up at her. "I guess plans have changed?"

"Something like that," Betsy said, unable to explain further. Her head felt like it was underwater.

"My suggestion would be to talk to your sister. If she agrees the kids should start school here, then get the paperwork started. I'll take care of enrollment."

Betsy rubbed her hands up and down the top of her thighs, then picked up her bag from the floor. "Thank you. I'm not sure about everything, but I'll let you know if we decide something firm."

He nodded. "Okay."

She was halfway down the hall when Mr. Burgess called her. He met her in the hall, glancing behind her toward Mrs. Kline's office, then spoke quietly. "I have to tell you, these things often don't work out well. If you have both parents' consent, then fine. The process should be pretty smooth. But if not, then you have to prove abandonment, and if the parents don't agree, going against their wishes is hard. I've seen families ruined over this."

Betsy swallowed hard. Nodded.

"Just make sure this is really what you want to do."

In the privacy of her car, Betsy threw her bag down on the passenger seat and let out a shaky breath. What had she just done? She hadn't meant to say the words out loud. Not really, anyway. Yet she'd let her guard down for a minute and they'd come. But then Mr. Burgess's last words—abandonment. Ruined families. An intrusive whisper in her mind told her she'd gone too far, but on the other hand, life had to go on for these girls, right? If that meant getting them in school when everyone else started, how could that be a bad thing?

Rainwater dripped off trees onto the windshield and pulled her from her thoughts. The rain had finally let up but the clouds were still thick, making it feel later than it was—only five o'clock. Betsy's stomach rumbled in protest of her skipped lunch. She rolled down her windows on the way home and savored the breeze on her cheeks that almost felt cool—nothing like the usual stifling humidity after a summer rainstorm. She let the wind carry away her thoughts and quiet the noise in her mind.

THIRTY-TWO

BETSY

She saw the lights before she pulled into the driveway—hundreds of tiny white orbs set against the blurred gray sky. A handful of extra trucks lined the edge of the driveway, and stretched between the back door and the oak tree was a huge banner. *Happy Birthday Betsy* spread across the top in big, blocky letters, the rest decorated with Magic Marker polka dots and squiggles.

Betsy let out a laugh, then ran her hands through her hair and checked her reflection in the rearview mirror. "Of course," she murmured. "Of course he did."

She took a moment to gather her bag and books, her stomach fluttery with nerves, then thought better of it and left the books in the car. As she climbed out she took a deep breath and pushed the last hour from her mind.

Friends were scattered throughout the yard. Carlos and Gloria stood by the picnic table loaded with bowls and trays of food; Linda and Roger Daily watched their grandkids on the swing with Anna Beth's Lucy; Anna Beth and Tom and a sullen Jackson, who probably would rather have been anywhere but an adult's birthday party, stood near the cooler. A few friends from church and neighboring farms completed the gathering.

Ty leaned against the fence near her garden wearing a wide smile. He pushed off the fence and made his way toward her. As he passed a metal tub, he stuck his hand in and pulled out a bottle of Blue Moon, uncapping it as he walked.

"Happy birthday, Aunt Betsy!" Addie and Walsh yelled, running across the yard. "We made the sign ourselves!" Addie said. "Uncle Ty helped with the words, but we did all the drawings."

She leaned down and rubbed their backs. "I love it." The girls beamed.

Ty handed her the bottle and kissed her. She wrapped her arms around his neck and pulled him close.

Behind them, Carlos whistled. "Get a room, kids," he called. Gloria slapped at him and let loose with a string of rapid-fire Spanish. "Sorry, sorry," he said.

Betsy laughed. "I can't believe all this."

"Come on," Ty said. "Get yourself a plate. Anna Beth and Tom brought barbecue."

She let Addie pull her toward the food table and point out all the offerings. Mounds of barbecue, macaroni and cheese with bread-crumb topping, potato salad that looked very familiar—"Ty gave me your recipe and asked me to make it," Anna Beth said. "My lips are sealed, I promise"—fluffy biscuits, broccoli salad, and enough desserts to feed double the crowd. A *tres leches* cake courtesy of Gloria, banana pudding, chocolate brownies, and a pecan pie that was missing a few pecans along the edge. Linda and Roger's grandson stood nearby licking his fingers.

Friends milled around in various stages of eating and relaxing. Ty had packed the metal tub full of beer and a few bottles of wine—juice boxes for the kids—and music flowed from the back porch. The combination, plus the early-evening air that still held that bare hint of coolness, was just enough to loosen laughter and hips. Betsy caught a glimpse of Linda doing a little shimmy under the oak tree, her lips moving to the Eagles' "Take It Easy."

"This is too much," Betsy said, adding a scoop of macaroni and cheese to her plate.

"Not enough, I'd say." Ty reached across the table and grabbed one more bite of barbecue.

"I don't mean the food. Everything. It's perfect." She sat on one end of the bench and balanced her plate on her knees. Ty sat next to her and leaned back against the table behind them.

Before he could speak, Roger appeared before them, a plate of banana pudding in one hand, a fork in the other. "Ty, we need to talk about the storm," he said around a bite of pudding.

"Right now?" Ty's arms were stretched out on the edge of the table, a picture of ease. "I hate to talk shop after hours."

"You know as good as I do farmers don't have 'after hours.'"

Ty grinned. "I know, I know. You're right." He sat up

straight and tipped back the bill of his cap so he could see Roger clearly. "What's up?"

"It's already changed directions from the two o'clock report."

Ty's face clouded. "West?"

"North-northwest. Warnings up for Cuba now." He finally swallowed his last bite. "Blasted thing just keeps getting bigger."

"Do they have any idea where it'll make landfall here?" Betsy asked.

Roger shook his head. "Right now, much of the northern Gulf Coast has a target on its back."

Ty's knee bounced up and down, shaking the entire bench.

"Y'all go talk," Betsy said. "I'm fine here with my food."

He shook his head. "No, this is your party. I can check all that later."

"It's fine. Go check it out and I'll see you in a bit."

He set Betsy's drink down on the table behind him, kissed her on the cheek, and stood. "I'll just be a few minutes."

Roger and Ty headed toward a cluster of men on the other side of the yard, one of them holding an iPad. Just a few feet away from them, the kids ran and tumbled in a scrambled version of hide-and-seek. A moment later something bumped her leg. Betsy looked down to see Lucy peeking out from under the picnic table. Lucy held her finger up to her lips.

As Betsy surveyed the crowd and worked on her plate of food, Linda slid onto the bench next to her. "I saw your garden. It's looking good."

"Thanks."

"A few things you could have done different. For example, I never would have planted carrots next to cucumbers. My experience is they mix well in a salad, not in the ground. But it's your garden. Who knows? Maybe it'll work out for you."

Betsy hid her smile. She knew Linda well enough to know the woman would burst if she wasn't allowed to share her opinions. "If it doesn't work, I'll try something else next time."

Linda nodded. "They've got shallow roots, all of them, since you just planted. If this storm comes our way, you may end up having to replant some of them. But that can be done."

"You worried about the storm too?" Betsy asked.

Linda shrugged. "I try not to get too worried until the thing's knocking on our door. I've been around long enough to see 'em change directions at the last minute, and I'm left with a pantry full of canned beans and D batteries doing nothing but taking up space. Roger, on the other hand, probably needs anxiety medication at the start of every hurricane season. It's all I can do to get him to turn off the Weather Channel.

"As far as your garden, sometimes storms can be helpful," she continued. "All that wind and rain shows you which plants are the strongest. Those are the ones you keep, plant more of next season. But the ones that break under the force of the storm—well, you just toss those and pretend they never set foot in your garden in the first place. Eventually you learn to choose strong ones from the get-go. You know how it is around here.

Everything needs to be strong. Plants and people." She patted Betsy's knee, then made her way to the dessert table.

As Betsy watched her go, she imagined the roots beneath her new plants growing and spreading, holding the delicate new blooms and fledgling plants firm in the soil, preparing them for the storms to come.

. . .

When the men finished their huddle, Ty and Carlos took the Gator out into the fields with a pile of kids on the back. Afterward, Ty closed and latched the gate, then grabbed Betsy's hand. It wasn't completely dark yet—a line of bright orange still illuminated the western horizon behind the pines in the distance—but stars had already popped out in the indigo sky.

"Do you hear it?" He nodded toward the music flowing from the porch.

She smiled and nodded. Van Morrison's "Moondance" always reminded them of a particular chilly October night in Auburn. They'd danced under the stars on the outskirts of town, music from his truck pouring into the cool night air. They'd only known each other a few weeks.

Tonight he led her to a spot away from everyone else in the backyard and wrapped his arms around her. She nestled her head under his chin, and his shoulders relaxed. Together, they swayed to the music, neither of them bothered by the side glances and broad smiles of their friends. Betsy had the sense they were alone on

an island of calm, but the words from the principal—
"guardianship, abandonment"—cascaded through her
mind and told her the moment wouldn't last. Real life
was calm and chaos, fights and forgiveness, that delicate dance of marriage.

But for right now, the moment was enough.

"It's a good night," she said.

"It is."

She looked up at him. "I can't believe you kept all
this such a secret."

"Carlos almost blew it this morning. I thought you'd
suspect something was up."

She shook her head. "How'd you keep the girls quiet?"

He laughed. "I didn't tell them. I knew they wouldn't
be able to keep their mouths shut. I waited till you left
this afternoon. Anna Beth and Tom came early to help
set up, and everyone else came a little before five. I'm
glad you stayed away long enough. We cut it close as
it was."

He pulled away and took her hand, spinning her
slowly before reaching for her again. His arms settled
around her hips, his hands on her lower back. Their
friends still mingled under the twinkle lights and stars,
the sky now clear after the day of clouds and rain.
"Where'd you go today? Did you get your nails done?"

She smiled, swatted him on the rear. "I told you I
wasn't going to do that. I'm not that kind of girl."

"I'll tell you a secret." Ty leaned down and put his
mouth close to her ear. "I'm kind of glad you're not," he
whispered. "So you didn't pamper yourself, you didn't
go shopping—what'd you do all afternoon?"

Her stomach clenched with nerves. "I went to that gardening meeting I told you about. At the library. And I stopped in the children's department and got some books for the girls. I think they'll like them."

"That's great."

She took a deep breath. A little voice in her head told her to stop, but she ignored it. "I also stopped by the school."

With her arms around his shoulders, she felt his muscles shift and tighten. "Why?"

"I was just curious. What it would take to enroll the girls there. I mean, if we decided to do it."

He pulled away from her and dropped his arms. "If we decide to do what?" he asked, his voice hard.

"To—I don't know. If Jenna doesn't come back and we—"

"Betsy, they're not puppies. We can't just take them in."

"But isn't that what we're doing?"

"This is temporary. They already have a mom."

She inhaled, sharp and involuntary. "I know that."

"Then why? You can't go around making choices for our life without talking to me about it."

She held her hand up. "I'm not making any choices. I was just getting information."

"But even going to the school . . ." He raked his hand through his hair and released a long, tired breath. "Who'd you talk to? Some secretary who's going to blab to everyone in town that we're taking in your sister's kids?"

"No, the principal. He won't say anything." She reached for his hand, but he didn't move. "I just needed some answers and figured he'd be a good person to talk to."

"You're taking this too far." He shook his head, took one step back, then another.

"Wait a minute. Ty, please."

He shook his head again. "No. I need a minute." He started to walk away, then paused and turned back to her, his hands out at his sides. "I'm never going to be enough for you, am I?" Then he turned and crossed through the grass toward the barn.

Across the yard, Roger stood and circled his hand around his mouth. "Ty?" he called. "You going to check the weather?"

"No," Ty yelled, before softening his voice. "I just need to grab something. I'll be back in a minute."

Betsy reached up and lifted her hair off her neck. She pulled an elastic band from around her wrist and tied her hair back. Ty's words buzzed in her ears. *"Never enough."*

The kids had started to slow down, their jubilant voices a notch quieter, their games less frenzied. Parents began rounding them up, shushing their protests and carrying the ones too tired to walk all the way to the driveway. Betsy said her good-byes and thank-yous on autopilot, apologizing for Ty not being there to offer his thanks. Out in the barn, the lamp in his office lit up a small rectangle of light on the grass. Soon, everyone was gone except Roger, Linda, and Anna Beth and her crew.

Linda and Anna Beth picked up stray forks and plates and tossed them in a trash can next to the picnic table. When Roger dumped his third scraped-clean plate of banana pudding in the trash, he called to Linda, who wiped her hands on a napkin and waved good-bye.

"Tell Ty to give me a buzz tomorrow," he said. "No doubt things will worsen overnight. We'll need to make sure all the farmers in the area are ready, even if they don't think they need to be."

Betsy nodded. "I'll do that, Roger. Thanks."

Anna Beth motioned for Betsy to join her by the table. "Everything okay?" she asked as Betsy sank onto the picnic bench and sighed.

"I think I screwed up."

"What happened?"

"I talked to the principal today."

"Mr. Burgess? About what?"

"About the girls. About possibly enrolling Addie in school."

Anna Beth's eyes grew wide. "What? Why? Did something happen with Jenna? What'd she say?"

"No, nothing happened. It's what *hasn't* happened."

Anna Beth narrowed one eye. "What did Ty say? He didn't look too happy on his way to the barn."

"He's mad I didn't talk to him first. We did talk about it once, but . . . we didn't get very far. And he's right—I should have told him before I went today."

Anna Beth chewed on her bottom lip, a sure sign she needed to say something Betsy wouldn't like.

"I know it sounds nuts, but I'm just planning ahead," Betsy said before Anna Beth could speak. "Ty's doing the same thing—all his preparations for a hurricane that may or may not even come this way."

"Honey, planning for a hurricane and planning to keep your sister's kids are two different things. They're whole different universes."

"But why can't it work? Why does it have to be ridiculous? It's August! School starts in a couple weeks and Jenna's not here. What else am I supposed to do?" Her voice rose like stair steps, carrying across the lawn to where Addie and Walsh sat on the back steps, polishing off the last of the brownies.

"These girls, Betsy, they're . . . they're not your kids."

Betsy stared at the ground as the sting of her friend's quiet words sank in deep. "I have to get them to bed." She stood abruptly. "Thanks for helping Ty with the party." She turned and walked toward the girls on the steps.

"Betsy, wait. Don't be mad at me."

"I'm not mad." Betsy dug the heel of her hand into her eyes. Embarrassed was what she was. She'd shown her hand to the two people closest to her and she'd been turned down. Probably for good reason, but that didn't make her feel any better.

That night Ty stayed outside putting the tables and chairs away in the storage closet while Betsy settled the girls in bed. Expecting him to be back inside any minute, she sat on the bed and waited. From the window, she could see light in the barn.

She curled her fingers over the edge. *Stay up or go to sleep?* She knew it was never good to go to bed angry—or let your husband do so—but tonight it seemed better than the alternative. There was still so much left to say, but what good would it do? Jenna was a mystery, Betsy was planning ahead, and Ty didn't like it. Nothing they could say to each other would change any of that.

Finally, she reached over and turned off her lamp, pulled the sheet up over her legs. The bed felt emptier tonight than other nights when Ty had to work late. Tonight it felt cavernous, a deep and uncharted territory, and she didn't have the tools—or the energy—to examine it. She tried to relax, but Anna Beth's words continued to tumble through her mind. *"They're not your kids."*

THIRTY-THREE

BETSY

*Hurricane advisory 31. Hurricane Ingrid
lashes the Cayman Islands. Interests in
the northern Gulf of Mexico should closely
monitor the progress of this storm.*

The morning Ingrid reached the Cayman Islands, Betsy woke to an empty bed. Ty hadn't rolled over and kissed her cheek as he usually did, waking her just enough to make her smile, before tiptoeing out of the room. This morning, just like the two before it, he left without a kiss, word, or touch.

It had been three days since their fight. Squabble, as Anna Beth would have said. Three days since they'd had a real conversation. Granted, Ingrid, now a dangerous Category 4 hurricane, was taking much of Ty's time. With talk of the destruction she'd flung onto the western edge of Haiti and Jamaica, coupled with his regular farmwork, he was coming in at night long after the girls were asleep. He'd fall onto the bed, still damp from the shower, barely awake enough to mumble good night.

It was still early, at least an hour before the girls would wake up. Thank the Lord they were late sleepers. Downstairs, she poured herself a mug of coffee, then slipped her feet into shoes and crossed the dewy grass to the barn.

"Hey, Betsy," Carlos called. "What's up?"

"I just need to talk to Ty for a minute. Is he out here?"

Carlos pointed toward the pasture. "He'll be another hour at least." Ty's tractor had just emerged from behind a stand of trees. "He's preparing the back pastures in case we need to send the herd out there. Walker and I are handling the milking today."

"Will you tell him I'll have breakfast for him when he's ready? You, too, if you're hungry."

"Thanks. I'll tell him."

Back in the house, she turned on the *Today* show for distraction, then clicked over to the local news for a weather update. The rosy-cheeked weather girl on Channel 9 pointed out the predicted track of Ingrid—continuing through the Caribbean and over the extra-warm waters of the Gulf of Mexico. Landfall, expected somewhere between New Orleans and Pensacola, was estimated at midweek.

Betsy's phone buzzed with a text. She turned off the TV and checked the screen as she headed to the stairs to check on the girls.

Ty: Sorry, can't make breakfast. Busy day. Will see you tonight.

She checked the time. Eight fifteen.

Upstairs, the girls' room was dim and cool, the ceiling fan rustling a pile of coloring pages on the dresser. Addie lay curled in Betsy's grandmother's white knit blanket. Walsh had flung all her covers off and lay stretched out flat, arms overhead. Betsy stroked the girls' arms and faces until they woke.

"How about a trip to the beach today?" she whispered.

With a note left on the counter—as cool and impersonal as Ty's text—Betsy and the girls left with a cooler of food and two bags stuffed full of towels and sunscreen.

. . .

The public beach in Gulf Shores was packed, umbrella to umbrella in some spots. Sand buckets, beach towels, foldout chairs, and Yeti coolers filled every available inch of white sand. It was only a matter of days before the parking lots and high-rise condos emptied out, everyone chased away by the threat of screaming winds and fierce undertow. But today, the sun was still bright.

Betsy took one look at Addie and Walsh, the glee on their faces when they saw the sparkling blue water, and packed them back into the car.

"We're leaving?" they asked, verging on tears.

"Just moving down the beach a ways."

Betsy drove through Orange Beach, past the Flora-Bama, then onto the narrow two-lane road that ran through Perdido Key only a few hundred yards from the Gulf. She pulled off the road onto an oyster-shell parking lot. A long walkway led to the beach, and the crowd was lighter here. It wasn't empty, but tourists were no longer jostled together like pickup sticks.

Betsy and the girls gathered their bags and began the walk past mounds of sand dunes, some topped with waving sea oats, others covered in gnarled shrubs and oaks. The salt-tinged breeze whipped around their faces, sharp and damp, stronger than usual. As they approached the water, the walkway dissolved into sand, sugar white and powder fine.

Addie and Walsh dropped their towels and buckets and darted toward the water. They squealed when the water touched their toes, then backpedaled to dry sand. After a few excited minutes, they settled down, Addie with a bucket and shovel, and Walsh squatting low watching coquina clams burrow into the wet sand after each wave receded.

Betsy flagged down a teenager renting beach chairs and paid for two long padded chairs with a large umbrella between them. With the girls happy in the sand, their pale skin slathered in sunscreen, Betsy sank into the soft chair. It had been a while—a year at least—since she'd been to the beach. Living just twenty miles from the Gulf, it was a shame, regardless of how the farm and field trips took up her time. Knots of tension in her shoulders and neck began to loosen, one knot at a time.

Time passed quickly as the sun made its arc through the sky. When it was overhead, Betsy called to the girls and pulled from the cooler their Ziploc bags of sandwiches, apple slices, and crackers and three bottles of water. Addie and Walsh sat in the shade of the umbrella with their legs crisscrossed, a thin layer of sand covering much of their skin.

Betsy watched the water as she ate. On such a clear day, it was hard to imagine a storm swirling almost directly south of them. The waves were still slow and lazy.

"Why don't you come here every day?" Addie asked around a mouthful of Ritz crackers.

"It's a little far to come every day, but I should come more often," Betsy said.

"I think Uncle Ty would like it," Addie said.

"You do?"

Addie nodded. "Maybe you could come on a date."

"A date? What do you know about a date?"

"It's what you do when you love someone."

"Oh, I see," Betsy said. "Have you ever been on a date?"

Addie nodded. "Mommy takes me on dates sometimes. She picks me up from school and takes me to the park for Mommy-Addie dates. She does it with Walsh sometimes too, but not together. We each get our own dates."

Walsh nodded. "We eat cookies and swing and slide."

"That sounds like fun," Betsy said.

"Yep." Addie chewed thoughtfully for a moment. Betsy watched them. They so rarely talked about Jenna, even when Betsy knew they were thinking of her. It was like a plug kept their words in tight.

After lunch and making drip castles in the wet sand, Walsh climbed up on the chair next to Betsy and laid her head down.

"Are you tired, sweetheart?"

Walsh shook her head no.

"If you want to close your eyes, you can. I'll wake you up if I see a dolphin."

"Okay," Walsh said, her eyes heavy.

Addie joined her not long after. "I'm not tired, I'm just going to rest a little bit." She sat back against Betsy's shins. After a few minutes, Addie dozed next to her sister.

Betsy pulled out her phone to check the time. Half expecting to see a text from Ty, she was disappointed to see only a red banner at the bottom of her phone alerting her to the hurricane watch in effect for the coast. She tucked her phone back into the bag and closed her eyes.

Ty was the proverbial man of few words, but when he spoke, what he said was important. Each word measured and careful. Because she'd been on the receiving end of such sweet, thoughtful words from him, the absence of his words now felt like a knife twist.

While the girls slept, she returned to a conversation she'd had with Ty a few days after their last appointment with Dr. Fields back in January. She'd canceled two field trips, unable to muster the energy necessary to keep the kids' attention. Ty had found her lying in bed at noon, fully clothed, with the lights off. He sat next to her.

"I just need a few minutes." She wiped tears off her cheeks. "I'll be fine."

"I'm worried about you, babe."

"I'm fine. I'll be fine." Why couldn't she be more like

him? Somehow he was able to pick up and continue on, seemingly unfazed by the prognosis the doctor had given them.

"Anything's possible," he'd said. *"You could always try praying."*

"I was thinking," Ty said, taking his cap off and rubbing his head. It was unusually cold this January, and the chill clung to his clothes. Temperatures had dipped into the twenties and thirties for long stretches, downright frigid for south Alabama. "He didn't say it couldn't happen. Or that it would never happen. We'll just keep trying."

"I'm tired of trying. I'm tired of looking at my calendar, counting days. Of having to be so careful and exact. It's exhausting."

"So let's not do it like that. Let's just get back to me and you, minus the calendar. Like it used to be."

Betsy sniffed and wiped her cheeks again, unsure if it was possible to go back to that carefree, casual place they'd been before they decided to start a family. Maybe for him it was. But it wasn't a possibility for her. Not yet.

"There's also adoption," he said.

She looked at him. He held his hat in his hands and smoothed a frayed string at the edge of the brim.

"Do you even know how much that costs? Way more than IVF."

"Not always. I've done a little research." He took a deep breath and let it out slowly. "If you go international, yes, it's expensive, but adoption within the U.S. is less, maybe even more so if you stay within the state. And there's even a program where you can foster a child first, then apply for adoption. That brings the cost down more."

Betsy blinked hard and pushed herself up until she was sitting. "Is that really what you want? To adopt?"

"Betsy, I have what I really want. Do I want children with you? Absolutely. But *you* are who I want. I know you want this more than anything, so I'm trying to figure out a way to make it happen."

She'd known it then, even in her haze of grief and disappointment. Deep down where it mattered, she knew now. He loved her. *Her.* He was reserved, but forthright. Calm, but decisive. When he spoke, she knew she could trust him. They'd chosen each other, above all, and she'd make the same choice again every time.

Three days of silence was long enough. She pulled her phone back out of her bag and tapped out a quick text.

Will be home for dinner. Let's talk tonight. ❤

· · ·

When the sun had lowered in the sky and clouds bloomed from the horizon in the south, Betsy followed the girls to the water's edge to look for shells. The wind had picked up and the tide was higher now, creeping up past the soggy mounds of their sand castles, inching toward beach chairs that had been on dry ground hours ago. As they walked, eyes on the sand, the warm water rippled over their feet.

They came to a stretch where the shore flattened out, revealing a wide strip of damp sand not yet covered by the tide. It was speckled with shells, none of them deemed beautiful or special enough for the stream of shell-hunting vacationers to have picked up earlier in the day. To Addie and Walsh, they were a treasure. Soon their hands and sand pails were full of broken shells in tan, yellow, pink, and blue.

"Look!" Walsh called, her voice high with excitement. "A heart!" She bent down low over a pile of shells and picked up one with a small hole at the bottom. Half the diameter of a pencil eraser, the hole was jagged, making the delicate outline of a heart. "It's for you," she said. "You keep it."

Betsy thought of the Mason jar by her side of the bed where she'd deposited all the heart-shaped items the girls had collected over the course of the summer. The faded yellow shell would fit right in with the others.

"And look at these." Addie peered down at a spread of coquina shells with both halves still attached. "They look like butterflies." She picked up a handful and passed them to Betsy. "These are for you too."

Betsy laughed, her hands full. "I don't know if I can hold any more. You're filling me up with too many pretty things."

As they continued their walk, clouds overtook the sun. Betsy found a tan-and-white spiraled shell half buried in the sand. Wide at the top and twisted to a fine point at the bottom, it fit snug in the palm of her hand. While Betsy rinsed the shell to rid it of sand, Addie ran to her holding something in her hand.

"Look," she said, hushed and reverent. A quarter-size sand dollar, bleached white by the sun, sat in the center of her palm.

"Wow," Betsy breathed. "I can't believe no one picked it up already."

"It was hidden under another shell."

"Well, it must have been there just for you to find. Want me to add it to my bucket?" She held out the pail so Addie could place it inside.

Addie shook her head. "No, this one's for Mommy. I'm going to give it to her when she comes back." She held the sand dollar with one hand cupped under the other one and stared down at it. Her long blonde curls, frizzed at the edges by humidity, flared out around her face, just like Jenna's used to in the heat of the summer. Walsh stood on tiptoes next to her sister, her damp hair clinging to her cheeks.

There was a photo at Betsy's parents' house— probably stuck in a box somewhere—of Betsy and Jenna on a beach trip in elementary school, before boys and cameras and textbooks became priorities. In the photo they both wore swimsuits, Jenna's thin, reedy body nestled up against Betsy's, already a little fuller, curvier than her little sister's. Betsy had flung her arm around Jenna's shoulders. Their heads tilted at the same angle, but in toward each other, their cheeks inches apart.

Closing her eyes, Betsy could feel the warmth of her sister's cheek, smell the fruity scent of her hair, feel the wet sand on their skin.

She opened her eyes when Addie spoke. "Careful,

Walsh. It'll break." Addie lowered her hands so her sister could peek inside, their heads close. "No touching. We're going to give it to Mommy. She's going to love it."

Addie and Walsh were Jenna's, no doubt—they both looked like her in different ways—yet something in Betsy's blood ran in those two girls too, linking all four of them together despite time or distance. But life had already laid down its blueprint, already mapped out the roads and detours, disappointments and accidents that had brought them this far.

Betsy breathed in deeply, then out, like a rushing tide. It was time to get them home.

After shoving their sandy towels, plastic shovels, and buckets into the bags, Betsy picked it all up and they started back toward the boardwalk. They rinsed their feet at a water hose propped up on the railing, then slipped their feet into their flip-flops. Walsh turned around as they walked, waving behind her. Betsy turned, but nothing was there but the water and sand.

Just before they made it back to their car, a Perdido Key State Park worker waved to them. "Hope y'all had a good time!" she called. "You're seeing the calm before the storm." She was coiling a long rope in a loop around her hand and elbow.

Addie held up her bucket. "We found shells!"

"Ooh, that's my favorite thing to do at the beach." She crossed the walkway toward them. Her cheeks were pink. and she'd tucked her gray hair under a bright-yellow baseball cap with *PK* emblazoned in blue letters. *Honey* was embroidered on the pocket of her shirt. "What'd you find?"

Addie pulled out the sand dollar.

"Well, looky there. You found yourself a dollar. Not everyone's that lucky. Whatcha gonna spend it on?"

Her brow wrinkled, Addie looked at Betsy.

Honey laughed. "I'm just kidding with you." She turned to Betsy. "And did Mom find anything good?"

Betsy held out the tan-and-white spiraled shell still clutched in her hand like a talisman. "The girls found most of the good stuff. I just have this."

"Hmm," Honey muttered, stepping forward to take a closer look. "That there's a paper fig. Kind of a funny name for a shell, but see how thin it is?" She ran her finger along the shell's fragile edge. "Most of the time they break apart in the waves. Somehow this one made it through in one piece."

Honey slung the coil of rope up on her shoulder and brushed her hands on the sides of her canvas shorts. "Glad you enjoyed your day." She stared at the water a moment, then turned to her pickup idling in the shell lot a few spaces away from Betsy's. "Couple more days, no telling what the beach will look like. We're planning for the worst, but hoping for the best. It's all we can do." She climbed in the truck and stuck her arm out the window in a wave. Addie and Walsh waved back.

They crossed the white shells to their car. After loading the bags and empty cooler in the trunk, Betsy strapped the girls into their car seats, then laid a towel over their laps so they could spread out their shells on the ride home. Addie still held the fragile sand dollar in her hand, her fingers clamped around it.

"You know, it might be safer if you put it down. It

could break by accident with you holding on to it so tight."

Addie shook her head. "I can take care of it."

"Okay." Betsy tucked a strand of hair behind Addie's ear.

She climbed in and buckled her seat belt, the lowered windows ushering in a gentle breeze and easing the heat in the car. Before she put the car in drive, she turned around to the girls. "I had fun with you today."

Walsh nodded, leaned her head back against the headrest of her car seat. Addie cleared the rest of her shells off the towel and made space for the sand dollar. She placed it in the center, then looked up at Betsy. Betsy nodded once and winked. Addie smiled, her cheeks like two round, pink crab apples.

Betsy set her own shell in the cup holder next to her, then held her arm out the window. As she pulled out onto the road, she stretched her fingers in the wind. Ahead of them, the pink and orange sky beckoned.

THIRTY-FOUR

JENNA

W hat am I supposed to do with no cell service?"
Micah asked. "No one told me it would be this
bad."

Jenna bit her lip to hide her smile. Micah was part
of a group of artists from UT Austin here for the last
week of the retreat. With Gregory gone on a quick trip
to St. Augustine for his Lost Florida project, Jenna was
helping Micah, the lone photographer in the group, get
settled. They'd just finished breakfast and were waiting for the welcome meeting.

"You'll get used to it. It's hard at first, but if you just
accept that you're going to be a little out of touch for
your time here—"

"A little? I'm totally cut off. I can't get any news, no
sports, nothing." He scrolled his thumbs across the surface of his phone, his distress increasing by the second.

She laughed, then reached over and took it from
him. "Trust me. Just leave it alone and focus on what
you came here to do." When Casey stood in the center
of the group to get everyone's attention, Jenna leaned

toward Micah and whispered, "There's a spot by the lake where you can get a little service if you stand in the right place. I'll show it to you in a little bit." He smiled.

Jenna looked around the room as Casey began the meeting. The group was mostly seniors about to embark on their last year of college. Fresh, eager, ready to dive into their work. She was both happy for them and a little jealous. Their only responsibility was to their work and studies, nothing to dictate where they should go from here. The world was open to them. She remembered what that felt like.

After the meeting, she walked Micah around the preserve. He lugged two camera bags, a tripod, and a backpack full of supplies with him. She tried to get him to leave everything but his camera behind, but he refused. When they neared a pond with bright-yellow wildflowers poking their faces above the water, he stopped to set up his tripod.

"This is perfect. I have to get this before the light changes. See how the sunlight plays on the petals?"

She nodded and watched. His equipment was expensive, spotless, probably purchased specifically for this retreat. She thought of her twenty-year-old Canon sitting on the counter in her cabin.

"Just remember," she said as he set up his shot, "your first idea of what's photo worthy isn't always the best. Think of the body of work you want to create while you're here. The feelings, the themes. What do you want to say?" She couldn't believe she was repeating the same lines that had made her cringe when she first heard them from Casey and the others. Back then, she'd thought they were empty clichés, but now she knew they held some truth.

"So you're telling me this isn't photo worthy?" Micah asked.

"I'm not saying that. I just think you might be surprised at the photos you're taking by the end of the session. When Gregory gets back, ask him to take you to a place called The Bottoms."

He shook his head. "Why would we go there? Isn't that the ugly part of the preserve?"

She smiled. "Yeah. It is."

. . .

Gregory called her name as she left the dining hall after grabbing a quick lunch. Her shoulders relaxed when she saw him coming toward her. Halcyon had somehow felt incomplete without him.

"When did you get back?" she asked.

"Late last night. I was supposed to be gone a few more days, but I was ready."

Together they walked out of the dining hall and into the thick, warm air outside.

"I'm glad to be back. It feels different here this summer." As they walked he bumped her with his elbow. "How's the new group?"

"Fresh as little daisies. Eager to take the art world by storm."

He laughed. "They're always that way. Although maybe not you though. When you got here, you were more . . ."

"Surly? Oh wait, that was you."

"No, I was going to say you were tentative. Thoughtful. Maybe a little defiant, but that's better in the long run."

She needed to get back to her cabin and pack some of her prints for shipping, but when Gregory sat in the shade under a sweeping oak tree, she sat next to him. The mess in her cabin could wait.

The other artists filed out of the dining hall, ready to gain as much new ground as possible on their works in progress. Jenna waved at Micah. He held up a single camera bag that hung from his neck. She smiled and gave him a thumbs-up.

"You must be teaching him well," Gregory said.

"I'm not teaching. I'm just trying to help him make good decisions. Like not hauling three bags and a tripod around the preserve every day."

"You're a good assistant then. How about that?"

She shrugged and leaned her head back on the chair. "I'll accept that." A breeze kicked up and rustled the sunlit leaves overhead.

"I'm taking the job in California."

"Good for you." She kept her gaze on the trees, holding her breath tight in her chest. The last few weeks with him had felt different. The push and pull, the conversation, the comfortable silence as they worked. It was both enticing and unsettling. She sensed his gaze on her but she didn't turn her head.

"You could come with me, you know."

She laughed to mask her thudding heart. "Me, in California?"

"Sure. Why not?"

She finally glanced at him and something in her shifted, as if she'd just stepped into a boat bobbing in the water. His voice was casual, his body relaxed, but his gaze was firm and unwavering. She rubbed her forehead. "Gregory, you can't just ask me to come to California with you."

"Why not? I just did." He gave her a half grin.

"It's too big." She shifted in her seat to face him. "I can't just . . . I have kids and a life and . . ."

He sat up and leaned toward her. "I know you do. And we'll figure all that out. Look, you've been trying to decide what to do in your life, right? Halcyon was a gift and you took it and look where you are now. Maybe California is another gift and all you have to do is take it."

"California is a gift for *you*. It's your job. I can't just follow you there. I've followed a guy across the country before, and it didn't turn out too well for me. I can't do it again."

"I'm not asking you to follow me just for the fun of it. It's a job for you too. The dean said I get an assistant— an official, well-paid one—and I get to choose who it is. You'd be helping me with grading and paperwork, but you'd have plenty of time to do your own thing. California's a beautiful place for photography. It could be a fresh start."

She closed her eyes. It couldn't, wouldn't work. When she opened her eyes, he was watching her.

"What do you say?"

"Hey, guys," a voice called from up the path. Jenna

looked over Gregory's shoulder and saw Casey walking toward them, a bright-red envelope in her hand.

"Will you come to my cabin later?" Gregory asked, his voice quiet. "We can talk there."

She nodded and he stood.

"How's it going?" Casey said when she reached them.

Gregory nudged a rock on the ground with the toe of his boot. "Just catching up on what I missed while I was gone."

She nodded toward Jenna. "Your mentee has done a great job with Micah."

He smiled. "I knew she would." He shoved his hands in his pockets. "I need to get going. I have a lot to do tonight. I'll see y'all later." He looked back at Jenna once before turning and walking through the trees.

"Sorry for interrupting," Casey said when Gregory was out of earshot.

"It's fine. I was just telling him about Micah."

"This came for you in the mail." Casey held her hand out. "It looks important."

Jenna took the envelope and turned it over in her hands. She smiled when she recognized Addie's drawings. Addie always drew extra-long eyelashes on her smiley faces and hearts on their cheeks. Betsy had written Jenna's name and the address, and the girls had decorated the rest of the envelope with faces, dots, and flowers.

"From your kids?"

Jenna nodded. She slid her finger under the flap and pulled out a sheet of pink construction paper. She took a deep breath.

"How are they doing with you being gone?"

"I think they're doing okay," Jenna said, her gaze on the drawing.

"That's good." A strong breeze whipped around the lake, carrying the scent of pine needles and salty air. "I wonder if this wind is coming off the storm."

Jenna looked up. "What storm?"

Casey raised her eyebrows. "Ingrid? Big hurricane?"

Jenna shook her head. "I haven't seen any news in a while."

"I can tell. It's a big one, out in the Gulf. The predicted track keeps wobbling, but they're thinking Mississippi. We should stay clear of it, but if it moves east at all, there's a whole list of things we have to do to get ready. Including getting all the artists out of here."

Jenna thought of the girls at the farm. They weren't too far from Mississippi. She reached into her bag on the chair and pulled out her phone. One bar of service.

Casey tucked her hair behind her ears. "I heard about Gregory's job offer in Berkeley."

Jenna nodded, her attention on her phone as she scrolled to Betsy's number. "He's taking it."

"Wow, I hadn't heard. That's—well, good for him."

"That's what I told him."

"What about you?"

Jenna looked up. "What about me?"

Casey shrugged. "I don't know. The two of you seem to work well together. I know there's the assistant position . . ."

Jenna shook her head. "There's no way that would work."

"Yeah, you're probably right. Plus it's scary to uproot your life."

Casey's voice was soft, but Jenna heard something else, as if she was saying two things at once.

"Anyway, I just wanted to make sure you got your mail." She headed back up the path, then turned her head and called back to Jenna, "It's sweet to know your girls miss you so much."

Jenna checked her phone again for that single service bar, but it was gone.

. . .

That evening, when she knocked on Gregory's door, he opened it dressed only in blue jeans.

"Sorry, I just hopped out of the shower. Let me . . ." He ducked into what she assumed was his bedroom. "I figured you weren't coming," he called, his voice muffled. When he came back, he wore a wrinkled plaid shirt with the sleeves rolled up. His hair stuck up in damp spikes, like he'd just run a towel over his head. She remained on the porch, her feet rooted to the hard floor.

"Do you want to come in?" he asked slowly.

She nodded and he held the door open for her. All around the room sat open boxes. On the floor, a chair. Through the bedroom door, she spied an open suitcase on the bed. "You're packing."

"Yeah, I got a call that they want me out there sooner than I thought. This storm is causing a mess at the airports already, so I'm heading out tomorrow. I have to pick up a few things at home before I go."

"What about the artists here now? What about Micah?" The poor kid needed a mentor.

"Casey called another photographer, a guy from Birmingham who's worked here a few sessions. He'll take my place this last week."

"They didn't take long to replace you."

"I think they knew I'd take off eventually. They've probably had a replacement lined up since I got here."

Jenna walked through the cabin—larger than hers, but still simple and rustic—and peered into one of the boxes filled with books.

"Jenna." His voice behind her was close, then she felt his hand on her shoulder.

She moved away from his touch and sat on the couch with her back against the arm. He sat facing her and waited. With the front window open, the room was warm, and she was glad for the ceiling fan sending down a cooling breeze.

"I thought Max was kidding the first time he mentioned this place to me. I laughed when he suggested I apply for it."

"Why'd you laugh?"

"Because it sounded so ridiculous. Managing the time off, figuring out what to do with my kids. And the idea of being on my own for two weeks with my camera . . . I never thought it'd work."

"Yet here you are."

"Here I am. Little longer than I planned to stay though."

He nodded. His jeans had a hole in one knee and he pulled at a fuzzy string. "Are you glad you stayed?"

She hesitated. Everything racing through her mind made it hard to think straight. "I think so. But . . ."

He propped his elbow on the back of the couch. His hand hung down and grazed the top of her knee.

"I don't know how to put these two parts of my life together. I love my children, but I also don't want to give up all this . . . this . . ."

"You. You don't want to give up on yourself."

"I guess that's it. It's like I've rediscovered this fundamental part of my life that's been missing and I don't want to lose it again."

"Then don't lose it. Don't give it up." He took her hands in his and squeezed. "Come to California with me. You can have the creative life you want and nothing will get in the way of it."

"But I have the girls. I can't uproot them too. I can't do that to them."

"You've done it once already. They've been at your sister's for what—going on two months now, right? And you've said it yourself—they're happy there. What if . . . ?" He paused, closed his eyes, then took a breath. "You made the choice to give up a life in the arts when you had your children. And that was a good choice for you at the time. But now you have a chance to make another choice. You can choose not to leave that life behind."

"That's crazy," she murmured. But as she sat next to him, staring at their hands together, she let herself imagine what it could look like—another life, the life she'd once wanted so badly. A new but not unfamiliar sensation pulsed from their hands, up her arms, through her body.

He shook his head. "It's not that crazy." He looked down a moment, then back at her. "I've worked with a bunch of photographers over the years. Most of them were good. A couple were really good. But you're different. You have the skills—you know composition and balance and lighting. You've learned patience and waiting for the right shot. But you also have an eye most people don't have. You're able to see worth and goodness where others just see something broken and ugly."

He chuckled and his vulnerability surprised her. "I don't usually have trouble moving on, but I don't want to leave you behind. We can make a life in California, however you want that to look. Travel, work, art." He leaned in close, brought his face close to hers. "Come with me," he whispered.

When he brought his lips to hers, she didn't pull away. For a minute—just a little slip of time—she let herself get lost in his hands and his touch, the scent of his skin, the way his muscles moved under her fingers. It was easy, natural, and she remembered what it used to be like. What she used to be like.

Don't do this again, Jenna. The voice in her head was insistent. Then Gregory's words came back. *"A life in California. However you want."*

"No. Stop." This time she spoke the words out loud.

She put her hands on his shoulders and forced herself to sit back. When she did, she heard the crinkle of paper in the front pocket of her bag and remembered Addie and Walsh's drawing she'd tucked inside. She'd memorized every scribble and line on the pink sheet of construction paper. It was the three of them—their family—sitting around a table. Addie had drawn their hands linked with so many fingers wrapped together, it was hard to tell where one hand stopped and another one began. All three of them had hearts for eyes. "Hearts are for love, and we love each other," Addie always said. At the top of the paper, Addie had written, in her large, exaggerated print, *When are you coming home?*

Jenna squeezed her hands together and imagined holding their hands, their fingers pressed against hers. She breathed in deep and for a moment forgot Gregory was sitting there in front of her.

She had plenty of jagged places inside her, but Addie and Walsh were smooth. Soft, tumbled edges, like sea glass. They were her light. She'd made a choice for them once because she had to—she chose them over the life she thought she'd live. But she was in control of her own life now. If she wanted to go to California with Gregory, she could do it. Maybe that's all she needed— just to know she *could* make that choice if she wanted to. She didn't doubt that she'd made the right decision all those years ago—to love her babies, to put down her camera and take on motherhood and all its beauty and limitations. And she'd do it again. But this time, she'd keep her camera with her.

All of a sudden, going home sounded like the simplest thing in the world. Her girls. Home. Nothing else mattered. Not California, not Gregory, not even her own fears. With the decision made, extricating herself from this temporary life was just a matter of leaving. She was good at that—leaving one place when her time there ran out—but this time was different. Instead of leaving, she was returning.

Gregory still looked at her, studying her.

"I can't do this." Jenna stood, pulling her bag onto her shoulder.

"I'm sorry, I shouldn't have—"

"No, it's not you. It's just . . . I have to go home."

"At least let me walk you back." He rose to stand next to her.

"It's okay." She moved to the door and opened it. "I know my way."

She left him standing on the porch, moths fluttering around the bare bulb hanging over the door.

"Jenna?"

"I'm sorry," she called, her feet quick on the trail back through the trees. "I just have to go."

And then she ran. Heat lightning flashed in the distance but she kept running. Finally the glow of her porch light appeared through the trees. Instead of going straight to her cabin though, she stopped at the spot by the lake where she usually could find a whisper of cell service. Her phone screen lit up the dark, attracting two moths that danced in the light. She brushed them away and held up her phone. When the one service bar appeared at the top of her screen, she typed out a text to Betsy. Just a few words to explain, then she'd call tomorrow.

I'm finished here. Will be there tomorrow. I miss you and the girls so much.

In the cabin she flung her bag onto the tiny kitchen table and pulled the girls' drawing out, scanning it with her eyes, taking in the hearts and hands. The love they poured onto the page. She'd been gone for almost two months, yet there they were, still thinking of the three of them together. Upstairs in her bedroom, she tucked the note under her pillow, and she imagined seeing them, holding them. She'd never wanted anything more.

THIRTY-FIVE

BETSY

Back at the farm, the girls ran inside and emptied their buckets on the kitchen table, sand and bits of shell going everywhere. They talked over each other, telling Betsy everything about each shell as if she hadn't been there all day with them.

"Where's Uncle Ty?" Addie asked. "We have to show him all this."

Betsy dumped the pile of wet towels in the laundry room, then noticed the remains of Ty's dinner—or maybe a late lunch—in the sink. The TV was on in the living room, tuned to the Weather Channel. Ty didn't usually trust "the big boys," as he called them, much preferring the local meteorologists. She peered out the window toward the barn. All the lights were blazing, Carlos's and Roger's trucks parked in the grassy lot by the barn.

When she opened the fridge to find some dinner, she saw his note pinned to the door with a smiling cow magnet.

Working on the back fence. I'll be in as soon as I can. Please wait up.

"I think he's still going to be a while," Betsy said.

While she pulled together a quick meal for the girls, they organized their shells into piles—big ones and small ones, pale and bright, smooth and bumpy. They instructed her to leave the piles on the table so Ty could see them when he came in. "Don't even move them an inch," Addie directed. "They might break."

"You got it," Betsy said. "But you'll have to help me move them tomorrow. We'll need our table back."

"Yeah, before the storm comes for sure. I'll need to put them somewhere really safe then."

Betsy nodded, surprised. She didn't know the tension brought on by the approaching Ingrid had trickled down to Addie and Walsh. What else had they picked up on when the adults around them thought they didn't understand?

After dinner and a quick bath, she put the girls to bed. Fatigue from the full day in the sun hit her as she closed their bedroom door behind her. A shower perked her up enough to head back downstairs and grab the laundry basket full of the girls' clean clothes. She paused by the kitchen window, straining her eyes to see whether the guys' trucks were still parked in the dark driveway. It was hard to tell, but she assumed they were still hard at work preparing the fences and property. Regardless of where on the coast Ingrid made landfall, they were all in for high winds and heavy rain at the very least.

On her way out of the kitchen, she spied a bottle

of wine left over from her birthday party. She wasn't afraid to choose a bottle of wine for its label, and this one featured a shoreline, a setting sun, and a set of footprints in the sand. She smiled, poured herself a glass, and took it upstairs with the laundry basket.

She'd just set the basket down on the floor when her phone lying on the dresser buzzed with a text. Thinking it'd be Ty giving her an update on when he'd be finished, she grabbed it and opened up her messages. She froze, wineglass halfway to her lips. Jenna.

Just a few words and her world shifted beneath her like sand.

. . .

Half an hour later, the porch door opened downstairs. She heard Ty drop his boots by the back door, then climb the stairs. He pushed open the bedroom door and stopped in the doorway, taking in the small stacks of folded clothes, the girls' duffel bag on the floor, partially filled.

Confusion crossed his face. "What are you doing?"

"Jenna's coming back," she said quietly.

He exhaled and pushed the door closed behind him. Crossing the room toward her, he put his hand on her shoulder and squeezed. "Are you okay?"

She set down a stack of shirts and turned to face him. "I'm good."

He stared hard, not speaking.

"Really. I'm good. It's okay, it's time." Then with no request made or permission given, the tears came. She covered her face with her hands and he wrapped his arms around her.

"I'm sorry for going behind your back and talking to the school. I went too far." With her face buried in his chest, her voice came out muffled, but she knew he heard because his arms around her tightened. "My head has been turned around for so long, and I know I haven't treated you very well. I'm the one who pulled away, not you. You've been standing in the same place, waiting for me to come back. And I've missed you so much."

Fresh tears fell as he ran his hand down her hair, rested his cheek against hers. "I've missed you too," he whispered.

She pulled back and looked in his face. "You are such a good man. You're more than enough for me, more than I could ever deserve."

He shrugged. "Well, you have me. Can't do much about that." A corner of his mouth pulled up and she brushed her thumb over that little half smile. "I'm sorry too. Not for being mad, but I overreacted. It was childish of me not to come back and talk to you about it after the party. I just . . . I didn't have the words. I didn't know what to say."

"I know. I don't blame you. Not about anything. Let's just . . . Can we start over? Start from right here, tonight?"

When she kissed him, his response was immediate. His lips on her face, his hands on her back, his body melding to hers was all she knew. Together, the two of them were more than enough.

Afterward, they lay next to each other, still and quiet, her cheek against the soft place just below his shoulder, their legs intertwined. Outside the window, a barn owl hooted somewhere in the darkness. After a moment, a second call answered it. Back and forth the calls went, a mysterious language she would never understand. She found Ty's hand on his chest and covered it with hers. He lifted his fingers and curled them around hers, wrapping her hand tight.

THIRTY-SIX

JENNA

Halcyon was whisper quiet the next morning as Jenna loaded her suitcase, binder of prints, and camera bag into her car. Even the cicadas and tree frogs were silent. Down at the lake, streaks of dark purple in the sky reflected on the calm water.

On her way out of the preserve, she made two stops. At the main studio she tucked two envelopes in the edge of the doorway. One held her cabin key and a note to Casey apologizing for her quick departure. The other envelope contained a note for Micah. She smiled as she thought of the words she'd written to him, basically repeating the instructions Gregory had given her when they'd first met: *Find your creative eye. Keep your skin thick.*

Her last stop was Gregory's cabin. She knew it was a risk to come—he could already be awake. Could be on the front porch waiting. But he wasn't. His cabin was dark, the curtains inside pulled tight against the strong morning sun that would soon hit them.

She set her last envelope on the chair by the door.

In it, she'd tried as best she could to capture her feelings on paper. Her gratitude. Her appreciation. What twisted and turned in her heart. Despite her rambling words—she was never very good with those—somehow she felt he'd understand.

It was 6:30 a.m. when she pulled down the preserve's long, winding driveway through the trees. Moss and vines hanging from tree branches looked ghostly in the glow of her headlights. As she turned north and headed for the interstate—no slow two-lane highways this time— the barest tinges of fuchsia and violet swept the sky.

It was too early to call Betsy, but Full Cup would already be open.

"It's a beautiful day at Full Cup Coffee. How may I help you this lovely Tennessee morning?"

Jenna smiled. Mario answered the phone with a different jingle every day. "It's Jenna."

He whooped. "Girl, it's about time. Please tell me you're coming back."

"I will if there's a job for me."

"Hallelujah. The imbecile they hired to replace you threw his apron down yesterday and quit. It was that Rich woman. You're the only one who knows how to handle her."

"What about Melissa? She was doing well before I left."

"Oh no, she quit too. Couldn't handle the pressure. Things fall apart when you're not here. Oh, and your boyfriend still comes in every day. He's a sad little puppy."

"He's not my—"

"Yeah, yeah. So when are you coming back?"

"I have a stop to make on the way, then I'm coming home."

THIRTY-SEVEN

Ty

Hurricane advisory 33. Winds from Hurricane Ingrid continue to increase. A gradual turn to the north is expected today. Ingrid is expected to make landfall within 24 hours as a dangerous hurricane with winds of at least 150 mph.

Ty awoke to news that the world had changed. Well, not the whole world, just their little corner of it. While they were sleeping, Hurricane Ingrid had charged ahead like a freight train toward the northern Gulf Coast.

When he reached the barn at four forty-five, his radio was already on, tuned to the local weather. For all of the previous day, the cone of uncertainty had shifted between the Louisiana-Mississippi coast and the Mississippi-Alabama coast. Now it appeared it was zeroing on extreme western Alabama, putting Elinore squarely on the stronger east side of the storm. Basically the worst place to be.

Carlos sat in Ty's office, his hat in his hands. Ty leaned against the desk and sucked in a mouthful of hot coffee. As it scalded the back of his throat, eliminating any remnants of sleep, the phone in his pants pocket buzzed. He pulled it out and checked the screen.

"Mornin', Roger."

"Just making sure you'd heard the news. It's headed this way."

"Sounds like it. But we've suspected it for a while."

"Yeah, well, this is the one we hoped wouldn't come."

When he finished with Roger, assuring him he'd take all the necessary precautions, he turned to Carlos.

"Well?" Carlos said.

Ty shrugged. "We get to work. Cows have to be milked, hurricane or no hurricane. We'll adjust the last milking time to make it as late as we can, then put the herd in the open pasture. Glad we got those fences fixed already. We'll move the tractors and equipment out there too." He rapped his knuckles on the desk. "We need to check water pumps and the ID tags on the cows."

"Pray," Carlos said.

Ty nodded. "Already a step ahead of you." He nudged Carlos's foot with his boot. "Go ahead and refill your coffee. It's gonna be a long one."

While Carlos and Walker double-checked the generators and fuel supply, Ty walked through the field, taking stock of the herd. He didn't know if it was some acute sense of smell or hearing, but the cows always seemed to know when bad weather was coming. They'd skitter around, startling easily and generally acting like nervous old women. Today was no exception.

He ran his hands down their backs and murmured soft words to them the way his grandfather had taught him all those years ago. He scratched their ears while he made sure their ID tags were in place and legible. Nevertheless, they remained nervous and jumpy, not calming at his touch as they usually did.

The sky was cloudy from stem to stern, no differentiation in any direction, so the casual bystander with no knowledge of hurricanes might think it was just another cloudy day with impending rain. But Ty sensed the coming storm as his cows did—tasted it, smelled it. He could almost feel it, like his skin was extra sensitive to the barometric pressure and electricity in the air. A strong wind already whipped through the trees.

By noon he was tired. The humidity made the air feel heavy, pressing on his shoulders, weighing him down. He worried for his herd, but more than that, he worried for the three girls waiting up in the house. And the fourth—Jenna—who was on her way.

After receiving the news last night that Jenna's return was imminent, Ty wasn't sure what Betsy's state of mind would be this morning. Last night she'd fallen into what appeared to be a peaceful sleep. She got up once during the night to check on one of the girls who was having a bad dream, and when she crawled back into bed, she wrapped her arm around Ty's middle, a band of warmth seeping down deep. He'd slid out of bed at four thirty, kissed her on the forehead, and tiptoed out of the bedroom.

Early afternoon he made the trek across the windswept yard to the house for a quick bite to eat. He was surprised to find Betsy alone in the house making peanut butter sandwiches. The girls were upstairs playing.

"She's not here yet?"

Betsy shook her head. "She just texted from Pensacola though, so she won't be long. Says the roads are packed." She gestured to the sandwiches on paper plates in front of her. "Want one?"

"Sure. Thanks." He washed his hands at the sink, then opened the fridge for something cold to drink.

"Everything going okay out there?"

"As well as it can. Ingrid's wobbled a little farther east. Now they're saying somewhere near Bayou La Batre."

Betsy set down her peanut butter–covered knife and faced him, her hip pressed up against the counter. "That's bad for us."

He took a long swig of lemonade. "It could be. Then again, it could keep moving east. They have all these predictions, but I'd rather watch the storm and see what it's doing. Once it hit the Gulf, it's been pretty steady north-northeast. If it stays that way, it could skirt past us and hit Florida." He set his glass down and rubbed his eyes. A few dozen miles could make a big difference in destruction to this town or another one. "I'd rather it not be us, but . . ."

"I know." Betsy picked up the knife again and spread jelly on the other slices. "You don't want it to hit anyone."

"That'd be my preference, yes. It's gonna be bad somewhere."

They ate lunch in bursts, interrupted by phone calls and texts from friends and neighbors checking on each other. Before heading back to the barn, Ty found the girls in the den playing with Etta.

"You know what?" he asked.

Addie glanced at him as she rubbed the cat's back. "What?"

"I think you two are my favorite little people in the whole world."

Addie grinned but Walsh jumped up to her feet. "I'm not little. I'm strong." She held her arms up in a muscleman pose.

He kissed them both on top of their heads.

A band of light rain and rumbling thunder was moving through as he descended the back steps. "Let me know when she gets here," he called back to Betsy, who stood on the porch with one arm holding the screen door open.

She nodded, then glanced up at the rolling sky. With her hair loose around her shoulders and her hand on her hip, she reminded him of a woman carved onto the bow of a ship charging through open waters. Solid, firm, sure. A fixed point.

THIRTY-EIGHT

BETSY

*Hurricane advisory 36. Hurricane Ingrid
continues northward toward the Gulf
Coast. A warning is in effect from Grand
Isle, Louisiana, to Apalachicola, Florida.
Conditions will deteriorate rapidly
within the next 24 hours. Fluctuations in
intensity are possible prior to landfall.*

Two months ago, Betsy had sat on her front steps unsure of what the arrival of her sister would bring. She'd been nervous, waffling between her desire to love and her fear of withholding love at the same time.

Today was different. Today she knew what Jenna's arrival would mean.

Anna Beth had come over that morning to sit with the girls for a bit while Betsy helped Ty secure a tarp over the henhouse.

"If I ever meet your sister, I'm going to give her a

good talking-to," Anna Beth said on her way out the door.

"Oh yeah?" Betsy smiled. "And what would you say?"

"Just a good woman-to-woman talk. I could say things you can't because she's not my blood. Anyway, you rarely say what you mean and I always do."

Betsy laughed. "You're right about that. But I'm trying."

Anna Beth hugged Betsy and kissed her cheek. "I know you are."

She walked toward her car in the driveway with a plan to head home and bake cookies. "It's what I do when these storms come in. I bake till the power goes off, then I eat. It keeps me calm. And fifteen pounds over my goal, but calories consumed during acts of God don't count. I'll bring some by if we're all still here after this thing blows over." She pulled open her car door and a strong gust of wind blew it closed again. "I still can't believe your sister is driving here today of all days. She has some timing."

. . .

The air was always the same in the hours before a hurricane hit—strange and swirly, the sky a creepy combination of yellow and gray, the clouds zipping past each other in their constant counter-clockwise motion. Bands of wind and rain kicked up, then tapered off, driving up the dense humidity.

Ingrid was still hours away, but late that after-noon, the farm was like a beehive. Carlos and Walker and a few of the other guys helped Ty move vehicles and equipment out of the barn and sheds and to the open fields. Betsy knew they were waiting until the last possible moment to milk the herd before the other men headed out in high winds to their own homes.

Just as a clap of thunder sent the girls running through the drizzle to the cover of the porch, the gravel at the end of the driveway crunched and Jenna's car finally appeared around the curve. Behind Betsy, the girls gasped and darted back down the steps.

"Hold on." Betsy put a hand on their shoulders. "Wait until the car stops."

Jenna opened her car door and stood, then eased it closed behind her. The soft raindrops made dark spots on her blue tank top. Betsy scanned her little sister top to bottom, trying to detect something—a hint of doubt, a whisper of uncertainty. Any second thoughts. But Jenna seemed resolute. Stable. Sure. She gave Betsy a small smile, then turned to the girls, her eyes damp and bright.

Betsy's heart brimmed with emotion—a desire to both hug her sister and chastise her. Love her and punish her. But then Walsh flew down the steps with Addie close behind. Jenna bent down and held her arms out. The girls wrapped themselves around her, arms and legs like the sweet potato vine that grew up and over the garden fence.

Jenna laughed and kissed their cheeks, their foreheads, their noses. The girls talked nonstop, over and around each other so their words formed an unintelligible noise. While Jenna tried to take it all in, Betsy turned and walked to the end of the porch. She turned her eyes to the sky as if studying the clouds, but really she wanted to give them—their little three-person family—a moment of privacy. Or maybe it was she who needed the privacy.

After a moment, Jenna straightened. "Let me talk to Aunt Betsy for a minute, then I want y'all to show me everything."

Jenna approached Betsy, a flicker of hesitation in her eyes. When she reached the top step, Betsy hugged her. It felt better than she expected, both of them letting their shoulders relax and drop.

"You have impeccable timing, you know, driving here the day of a hurricane." Betsy sat on the swing at the end of the porch, and Jenna sat next to her. The girls climbed onto Jenna's lap and she pulled them close. The fast-moving rain band had already passed, though the winds were still strong and steady.

"I thought I'd get here hours ago, but so many people were on the roads. I knew the storm was out there, but Halcyon is pretty cut off. No TV, no newspapers. Terrible phone service, as you know. I just didn't know it was so big or so close." She pushed her curls out of her eyes. "Florida was okay, but the closer I got to Alabama, the crazier things got. I stopped to fill up and the first place had already run out of gas. I had to sit in line at the next station for twenty minutes."

"I'm not surprised. The thing keeps moving around, so everyone from New Orleans to Florida is on edge. They're thinking Mississippi now, but lots of folks have left already, just in case. You were probably the only person driving toward the storm."

Jenna nodded and readjusted Walsh on her lap.

"Highway Patrol stopped me as I was exiting I-10 to come here. They asked me where I was going and why, then strongly suggested I reconsider my destination. I promised them I would."

Betsy gave a small laugh. "And they just let you go?"

"I told them I had two little girls waiting for me." She turned to Betsy. "And my sister. I told them I understood the risks, but I was willing to take the chance."

. . .

The next few hours were chaotic. Ty finished the last milking and blew in the back door as the winds intensified. "The cows are in the pasture and the men have all headed home. Nothing to do now but wait."

Betsy helped Ty close and latch the shutters on the sides and back of the house while the girls flitted from one toy to the next, one lap to the next. Having woken up early and skipped their afternoon naps, they were keyed up on hyper energy and lack of sleep.

Jenna waffled between the weather reports on TV and trying to play every game the girls came up with—I Spy, hide-and-go-seek, and hopscotch. They brought her coloring books, crayons, and puzzles. It was as if they were trying to fit two months' worth of playing into one frantic afternoon. Betsy and Ty stayed glued to the TV and the front windows as the rain bands lengthened and strengthened.

When the third NWS bulletin flashed at the bottom of the screen, issuing a piercing alarm and stern words, Ty stood and motioned for Betsy to follow him to the stairwell. He put his head close to hers. "Either we're all sleeping on the floor, or we'll have to bring mattresses downstairs. I don't feel comfortable with us spending the night upstairs. Not with these old trees in the wind."

Jenna took the girls upstairs to get ready for bed, and Ty and Betsy pulled a mattress and a few sleeping bags into the living room. They tucked the mattress against the wall below the stairwell, and Betsy piled it with blankets and pillows, hoping to make it look like a fun way for the kids to sleep and not a safety precaution.

As she tossed down the last pillow, Ty came up behind her. "How are you?" His hand was warm on her back.

"I'm good, I think. The flashlights are ready and we have plenty of extra batteries. We have candles too, if we need them." She ticked the items off on her fingers. "While you were in the barn, I did as much as I could for the garden. And we'll just have to hope for the best with the hens. I wish I'd been able to—"

Ty put his hands on her shoulders and turned her to face him. "Bets, we've done all we can. I meant how are *you*?" His words were slow, deliberate.

She took a shaky breath and let it out. "I'll be fine. I just want to get past tonight, then we'll be able to see a little clearer. This all makes me nervous." She waved her hands around, as if to encompass the storm, the house, and the people in it.

He kissed her forehead as hard rain pelted the windows. "I know. I'm anxious to see what tomorrow will bring." He pulled her close and rested his chin on her head. "And whatever it is, you and I will be okay."

She turned her face up to him. "I know."

. . .

Through the evening hours, Betsy watched Jenna. She saw how gentle she was with Addie and Walsh, how she laughed with ease, touched them often. Her body was relaxed, her tough, defensive exterior gone. Then again, maybe it had been gone for a while. Betsy had expected Jenna to be the same girl she'd been years ago, the last time they'd spent any substantial time together, but maybe she'd changed over time without Betsy realizing it. Or maybe the summer had changed her.

In fits and starts around the activity in the house, Jenna told Betsy about Halcyon—her cabin, the lake, some of her photos. Betsy told Jenna about the girls' explorations of the farm, their obsession with Rosie, their rides on the Gator. But Betsy knew they were both leaving out parts—likely the most important parts—of the last seven weeks.

The unsaid words and misunderstandings sat between them like a living, breathing thing. She had no doubt some of it would remain unspoken, settling quietly into each woman's heart, but she feared if they didn't find a way to put at least some of those thoughts and feelings into words—and do it now, tonight— something would slip between the cracks and they'd lose their chance.

When the girls were hungry, Jenna asked if she could make them some dinner. "Just sandwiches or something easy."

"I can do it." Betsy pulled open the fridge door.

"No, let me. Please."

Betsy backed away. The girls climbed up on the stools and watched as Jenna pulled out bread, turkey, apple slices, and carrot sticks.

Occasionally Jenna's phone rang or buzzed with a text. She'd check the screen but then go back to whatever she was doing, undisturbed by whomever was trying to get in touch. When the girls finally began to tire, exhausted from their excitement over the storm and their mom's return, Jenna settled them on the mattress near the stairs. She kissed their faces and whispered in their ears until they were calm and still.

Despite the increasing strength of the storm outside, Jenna seemed at peace.

Ty was still awake at eleven o'clock, pacing through the house and watching the red spiral symbol on the weather map moving steadily onward. Outside, the winds had begun to howl, whipping through the trees and sending small limbs and branches to the ground. At one point, Betsy heard a meteorologist say that while the storm's track continued to wobble, it seemed to be tilting farther to the east, causing them to readjust their landfall predictions.

About this time, Ty's eyes closed, then jerked awake. Betsy laid a hand on the side of his face. "Why don't you go ahead and lie down? I'll wake you up if we need you."

"You know I can't sleep on nights like this."

"At least get some rest then. You need it for whatever tomorrow brings."

He swung his legs up on the couch. "Are you going to try to sleep?"

She turned and looked back at Jenna, who sat on a stool in the kitchen, a mug of tea in her hands, her gaze on Addie and Walsh across the room. "Maybe later. I'll keep an eye on things for now."

The windows that looked out over the porch were the only ones not covered by shutters. Betsy stood next to them, peering into the dark to try to make sense of the swirling chaos outside. Bright staccato bursts of lightning illuminated the blue plastic tarp over the henhouse, one corner of it flapping in the wind. She could only hope the hens were tucked in their nests inside the main structure of the house. If the rest of the tarp held, it was possible they'd make it out just fine. She didn't even want to think about the cows, their livelihood, huddled together in the back pasture. But the herd had made it through hurricanes before.

The red spiral on the TV weather map was still offshore, but judging by the relentless winds pushing against the house and making it creak and moan, Ingrid seemed to be just next door. And angry. But there was nothing any of them could do now. They were safe inside while the storm raged and cast its ominous gray-green light over the farm.

Despite the rushing noise from the wind, the girls slept. Ty remained awake on the couch for a while, but he finally nodded off, his head slumped sideways on the couch cushion. When the power went off, only Betsy and Jenna noticed.

THIRTY-NINE

JENNA

With the house dark, the pounding wind outside sounded even louder than before, louder than any storms Jenna had been through in Nashville. Betsy gathered a few candles from the counter and set them in the middle of the table along with a box of matches. With the scrape of the match and the accompanying glow of burning candles, Jenna sensed the barriers between them slipping away.

Betsy pulled a bottle of wine from the cabinet and poured two glasses. "I figure we may need this." She passed one to Jenna, then sat on the stool across the counter.

Jenna pulled her glass toward her and ran her fingers up and down the stem. It was cool under her touch. She glanced up as Betsy took her first sip and closed her eyes a moment. Sadness, regret, and affection bumped around in her heart as she watched her sister. It was the same as the night she'd overheard Betsy and their parents discussing Jenna's trip to Seattle. Back then, she didn't have words to express how she felt—words to explain her jumbled emotions. Tonight, so many years later, she still wasn't sure if she had the words, but she knew she had to try.

"I have something for you." Jenna reached into her bag and pulled out a thin silver picture frame she'd bought at a shop near Sunset Coffee. Inside the frame was a five-by-seven photo of two cypress trees twined together. Like the purple-and-blue pipe-cleaner bracelet Addie had given her, the two trees were wrapped around each other, each the same size and thickness. The trees had essentially become one, neither able to survive on its own without the support of the other.

"Jenna, this is gorgeous." Betsy ran her fingers over the glass. "You took this?"

Jenna nodded. "I missed your birthday. I wanted to get you something special, but . . ."

"This is special. It's perfect. Thank you."

Outside, something heavy hit the porch roof. They paused, waiting to hear if the noise would rouse the girls, but they slept undisturbed.

"Are you glad you went to Halcyon?" Betsy sipped her wine and watched Jenna from across the top of her glass.

Jenna nodded slowly. "I am. If I hadn't gone, I'd still be thinking the best of me had already come and gone."

"And now?"

"Now . . . now I see what I'm capable of. This will sound crazy, but I'm kind of proud of myself." She bit back a smile. "I know it was hard on y'all to have the girls here for so long, but I think that extra time there is what helped me settle into myself. It showed me who I am. That I'm more than just a girl who got knocked up—twice—and works at a coffee shop."

"Is that how you saw yourself?"

Jenna smiled. "Well, with no evidence to the contrary . . ."

"Jenna, I've always known you were capable of so much more."

"Even though Mom never did?"

"I think she . . ." Betsy sighed, propped her elbow on the counter, and rested her chin in her hand. "I don't know what she wanted."

"I know what she didn't want. She hated that I took photography and art theory instead of marketing and statistics like you. She made it clear you were the one who made good life decisions, I was the cut-rate, disappointing second child."

Jenna hated the sound of her voice, the words coming out of her mouth, but it was now or never. She wanted these thoughts and feelings out and gone, to clear the air between her and her sister so they could move past it. She wanted them safe and close, like they used to be.

Betsy pulled the rubber band from the messy knot at the back of her head and raked her fingers through her hair. "You've got it all wrong." She twisted her hair back up.

"What do you mean?"

"After you moved to Wyoming, she used to call me

to see if I'd talked to you, if I'd checked on you, how you were doing. I think she knew she'd handled you wrong but was too proud to just call you up and fix it. She cried a lot."

"Mom cried?"

Betsy nodded. "I could hear it through the phone. She was heartbroken, both over the fact that you left and that she played such a part in your leaving."

"I don't . . . I can't . . ." Betsy could have been talking about a different woman altogether, not their cool, distant, scientific mother. Why did Jenna never see this side of her?

"It's true. You were special to her."

"But you did everything right. You had all the grades and accolades and the nice boyfriend who always brought you home ten minutes before curfew. That was you, not me."

"You think I was the golden child, but it wasn't always that way." Betsy laughed. "That job I was supposed to have after graduation? With Prescott Branding? The summer internships, the informational interviews . . ."

"Sure. You were practically on their payroll before you even graduated high school."

"Right. I gave it up for Ty."

"You . . . what? I thought that was your dream job."

Betsy nodded. "It was my dream—when I was willing to choose a career based on what would please Mom and Dad and impress their friends. I realized one day the path was laid out in front of me and all I had to do was follow it, so that's what I did. I chose the right major, scheduled the right classes, made good grades, worked at Prescott every summer. It would have been a fine job, but my heart was never in it. And when I met Ty, giving it up was an easy choice."

"Wow," Jenna breathed. "What did Mom and Dad say? And how did I never know any of this? I just assumed the job didn't pan out or was filled in-house."

Betsy shrugged. "You were off on your next big adventure. I didn't think you cared that much about what was going on back at home."

"That's not true." But it was, wasn't it? She'd been so focused on doing what *she* wanted, on flaunting their parents' expectations, but she did it at the expense of knowing what was going on in her sister's life.

"Anyway, they were livid, as you can imagine. Good little Betsy daring to rock the boat. And to marry a farmer, of all things." She gave a half smile. "You know what though? That one moment—telling them I wanted a life with Ty more than the job in Birmingham—it was liberating. I remember thinking, This must be what it feels like for Jenna. To forget the rules and follow your heart instead."

She paused and slowly twirled her wineglass. "I think I've always been a little envious of your ability to do exactly what you want without feeling the pressure to do the right thing. I wish I'd done that more."

Jenna propped her chin in her hand. "And here I've been, most of my life, jealous of how perfect you seemed. Of how Mom and Dad adored you."

"There was no adoring going on for a while. I even thought Mom might skip the wedding, but Dad talked her down."

Jenna shook her head. "I feel like I'm seeing a whole side of our family I never knew. I guess that's what I get for trekking across the country and leaving everything—and everyone—behind."

Betsy leaned toward Jenna and tapped her finger on the counter. "But you see, all my rule following, all my doing the right things—it was the only way I knew to get her attention. Of course, I didn't realize it at the time, and even if I had, I never would have admitted it, just like you probably wouldn't admit that all that sneaking out and coming in late and moving to a commune in Wyoming was just to get her attention, to try to make her *see* you. We were both doing the same thing, just in a different way. You rebelled; I tried to be perfect."

"Until you weren't."

Betsy nodded. "Until I wasn't. And that one little break from the rules felt so good."

A sharp crack of thunder exploded outside, causing them both to jump. The candle between them flickered, making the shadows on the wall of the kitchen jump and shake. Lightning flashed, illuminating the emotion swimming across Betsy's face.

Jenna opened her mouth to speak, to try to make sense of it all, but another deep rumble of thunder rolled across the sky and Walsh cried out, her voice a scared whimper. In an instant, Jenna was out of her seat, crossing the room to the mattress. "Shhh." She smoothed Walsh's hair away from her forehead. "You're okay." Her daughter's eyes never opened, but when she shifted and resettled on her side, Jenna could tell the fear was gone. Walsh's face was calm.

The back door was open and she followed the brush of cool air coming through the doorway. Rain fell in a soft cascade, a stark contrast to the pummeling deluge of the last few hours. Betsy was sitting on the porch in the dark, and she turned when Jenna's foot bumped something. "Your eyes will adjust after a minute." She patted the seat next to her and Jenna sat down.

"Is it over?" Jenna asked

Betsy shook her head. "This is the eye. It gets strangely calm before the other side of the storm hits. But that side's usually not as strong as the first push. Everything okay inside?"

"They're fine. And Ty's asleep too."

"Good. He'll have a lot of work to do tomorrow. He'll need his rest." She rubbed a hand across her eyes. "We probably do too."

In the distance a siren blared, and a couple of cars zoomed down the highway. "That's a good sign. At least the road is still open."

Through the gauze of clouds covering the moon, it was impossible to tell the extent of the damage. Jenna could see big branches in the yard and a wide piece of what looked like metal sheeting pushed against the side of the henhouse, but that was just what was close to the house. Who knew what lay beyond? "It doesn't look too bad right here. Think everything else is okay?"

"It's hard to tell. At least the trees stayed off the house. Ty was worried about that."

Jenna stretched her legs out on the ottoman and leaned her head on the pillow behind her. The air smelled like rain and damp earth. And a little salt.

"So what's next for you and the girls when you get back home?"

"Well, I talked to my boss on the way here. The guy they hired to replace me just quit and they need a shift manager. I told them I could start as soon as they put me back on the schedule." She glanced at Betsy. "I asked for a raise too."

"You what?"

"I know. I ditch my job for two months, then have the nerve to ask for a raise. But I was feeling bold. And he said yes."

Betsy chuckled.

"I think it was strategic on his part, to keep me from leaving again. But I don't care why he agreed to it, just that he did."

"Good for you."

Jenna nodded. "But I'm going to look for something else part time too. Maybe in an art gallery or a photo studio. Something I can fit in while the girls are in school. I can start there and see what happens."

Betsy smiled. "That'd be great. It sounds like things are mostly going back to normal." She paused. "Is that what you wanted?"

Betsy wanted to ask more, Jenna could tell. And she understood it—when she'd left for Halcyon, she'd been almost breathless in her desire for change. Now here she was, appearing to go right back to life as it was before.

"At first, I wanted everything to be different—me and everything around me. I wanted something to shake me up and spit me out in the life I once thought

I'd be living." She hesitated, but the time for hiding truths was over. "And I had a chance to do it. To leave and start over somewhere else."

Betsy looked at her. "What do you mean, start over?"

"Gregory got a job in California and asked me to come as his assistant." She swallowed hard. "I considered it, but it didn't take long to realize the best part of me, the only part I don't want to change, is what I have with Addie and Walsh. They're the only good things I've ever done and I don't want to let them down. Everything I do is for them. So, to answer your question, I think some things will go back to the way they were before, but I'm not the same person I was when I left Nashville. So maybe it's something in between."

They were silent for a moment.

"I see the change in you. I saw it when you got out of the car this afternoon. When you arrived here in June, you seemed conflicted. Nervous. You made me nervous."

"I was. But I'm not anymore."

"I'm not either. And I'm not worried about the three of you. You're a good mother. If I've learned anything this summer, it's that. Well, that and I had no idea what it took to keep two kids alive."

Jenna smiled. "I think you did just fine. The girls seemed great every time I talked to them."

"I just didn't tell you everything. I lost Walsh. I almost caused the girls to choke on whole grapes because I didn't know you had to cut them up. I had no idea what to do when they refused to go to bed. I realized how much you do on your own. How challenging it must be for you."

Jenna shook her head and laughed. "You lost Walsh?"

"She was out in the pasture trying to drive the tractor. And I thought she was in the yard playing with Addie. She's a sneaky little thing."

"Yes, she is."

"My point is you think you've done a poor job with these kids, but you haven't. You've established routines for them. Order and structure. They're happy and kind and compassionate. They're *good*. And so are you."

Jenna squeezed her eyes closed, her sister's words like a comfort, a cure, and a release all at once.

Overhead, a lone cicada chirped in the dark tree branches as the rain fell harder. Jenna stood and followed Betsy back into the house, then closed the door softly behind them. While they were outside, Ty had moved to the floor next to the girls' mattress. He had one hand on the mattress holding Walsh's hand, the other hand under his head as a pillow.

Betsy grabbed the sleeping bags and pillows from the end of the couch and Jenna spread a blanket on the floor on the other side of the girls' mattress. They unrolled the bags and set their pillows side by side. Jenna lay on her stomach, her chin on her hands. Betsy did the same and they peered at each other in the dark.

"We need chocolate pudding," Jenna whispered. Betsy laughed softly. When Addie stirred, Betsy leaned up and pulled her blanket a little higher. Jenna's heart ached for her sister. Betsy had always been her rock. An oasis—a safe place to find rest. She'd make the best kind of mother.

"Betsy," Jenna whispered. "I didn't know about you

and Ty. About the doctors. Ty told me on the phone a few weeks ago."

Betsy lay her head down on her arms, her face to Jenna.

"I just . . . I'm really sorry. I probably shouldn't have asked you to keep the girls. I shouldn't have just expected you to take that on for me."

Betsy shook her head. "It's okay. This time with them has been good for me. For me and Ty."

"You're an amazing woman, you know that, right? When I grow up, I want to be just like you." Jenna scooted over and laid her head on Betsy's pillow.

"You're crazy, you know that, right?" Betsy laid her head next to Jenna's, their faces close together.

Jenna smiled. "I do know that."

FORTY

BETSY

*Hurricane advisory 39. Ingrid is moving north/
northeast across northwest Florida as it weakens
to a tropical storm. All watches and warnings
west of the MS/AL border have been canceled.
Storm is moving at 14 mph with gradual
decrease in wind speed expected during the next
24 hours. Skies are clearing behind the storm.*

When Betsy's eyes opened, she wasn't sure what had woken her up. A voice? A knocking? Her alarm clock? She sat up when she heard a rustle and a groan. On the other side of the girls' mattress, Ty sat up too, rubbing his eyes and rolling kinks out of his neck.

Addie was still asleep on the mattress near Ty, one leg flopped over the edge. Next to Betsy, Jenna lay on her side curled around Walsh, who must have crawled in her mother's sleeping bag during the night. Her head fit right underneath Jenna's chin.

Betsy and Ty looked at each other over the mattress. At this early hour, before trucks began rumbling down the highway and the whine of chain saws filled the air, everything was quiet. The only sounds were Walsh's light snoring and the whir of the ceiling fan in the den. At least the power had come back on while they slept.

"I'll make coffee," she whispered.

While they waited for the coffee to brew, the heady scent curling through the kitchen like incense, Ty wrapped his arms around Betsy and she leaned into him, inhaling deep. With the shutters closed, it was impossible to tell what damage Ingrid had left for them to discover. After a moment, he pulled away. "It's not going to get any better the longer we wait. Might as well go check the damage."

Ty opened the back door and they descended the steps with trepidation. Betsy counted at least four trees down, a kayak that didn't belong to them lying on its side in the driveway, and strips of roof shingles dotting the yard. Though tree limbs and branches covered the grass like carpet, the big oak in the center of the yard appeared to have survived the onslaught with minimal harm. Only the swing was missing, its ropes frayed at the ends where the wood had ripped away in the wind.

From where they stood in the yard, the barn looked structurally okay, but she knew Ty would inspect every inch of it when he got there. "I need to get out to the pasture." He turned to her. "Tell Jenna she can't leave yet. Not until we find out what the roads are like."

"I already thought of that. I'll tell her."

"I'll be back in when I can, but it may be a while. What are you going to do?"

She raised her eyebrows. "Well, I'm not going to sit around drinking coffee while you work."

"Okay, I . . . I just figured you might want to take it easy today . . ."

She smiled. He was fumbling, trying to say the right things and avoid the wrong ones, the hidden emotional mines that might set her off.

"Put me to work, Boss. I'm ready."

"You got it." He held his hand out to her and together they headed toward the barn to assess the damage, their boots making wet squelches as they stepped through the debris.

• • •

The next day Betsy followed Jenna's little blue car up Highway 59 toward the interstate. They'd said their good-byes at the farm, each trying to get in as many hugs and last words as possible. Betsy had fished two heart-shaped rocks out of her Mason jar full of bittersweet summer memories. She painted them gold and, once dry, pressed them into the girls' hands. "You can use them to start your own collection when you get back home."

Addie smiled, her eyes round and damp. "Then we'll pick out the best ones and send them back to you."

"That sounds perfect."

There was so much more to say to these girls, so much she wanted to thank them for, but they were young, happy to be with their mom, happy to be going home. There was no need to burden them with a grown woman's heart, even if it did feel whole for the first time in years.

Ty hugged Jenna, then bent down low to the girls, his voice steady and quiet. A tear slipped down Betsy's cheek. She flicked it away with her finger, then reached out to hug her sister. "You know I'm going to follow you out of here, right?"

"You don't have to do that. We'll be fine."

"I know you will, but I just want to make sure. My mind's made up."

Jenna smiled. "Thank you. For this, for them." She nodded toward the girls who were climbing into the back of the car. "For everything."

Jenna's car stopped at the light to turn onto I-10. Betsy sat behind in her own car. When the light turned green, Jenna beeped the horn and three arms stuck out of the windows and waved wildly. Betsy waved, then made a U-turn and headed back home.

Out in the barn Ty was in the middle of the morning milking. The day before, he'd found 216 of his cows in the pasture where he'd left them before the storm. Two were missing and he'd yet to find them. It would take the herd some time to calm down and settle back into routine, but considering all they'd been through, they were doing fine.

"It's later than I'd like to be doing this—definitely later than they'd like—but they're happy now," Ty said. "We should be back on the regular schedule tomorrow."

He stood and kissed her head, pulled her in close, as

if he thought by holding on tight to her, he'd keep her from coming apart. That was the thing though—she didn't feel like she was coming apart. Instead, it felt like bits of her were returning, strands and wisps settling back into place after a long time away. Still, she let herself melt into his arms. He felt rock-solid.

FORTY-ONE

JENNA

A few weeks later, Jenna sat in her car outside the Nashville Gallery of Arts trying to get up the nerve to open the door. She'd applied for the job—as photography assistant—on a whim just days after returning from Halcyon, not thinking she had a chance but feeling just brave enough to try.

"Good for you," Delores had said. Once Jenna had returned to Nashville, she and Delores had picked right back up with their nightly visits after the girls went to sleep. Delores clinked her wineglass to Jenna's. "I'm proud of you, dear."

Jenna had been proud too. And a little giddy, which only intensified when she received an e-mail the next week asking her to come in for an interview. But now, staring at the sleek glass building, she was wracked with nerves. What had she been thinking? Jenna Sawyer—no college degree, only one summer of intensive photography instruction under her belt, and applying for a job like this?

She smoothed her hair from her face and pulled her shoulders back. *Do it, Jenna. Get out of the car.* Before she could second-guess herself, she pushed open the car door, grabbed her bag, and entered the cool, temperature-regulated air of the lobby.

"Thank you for agreeing to come in so early for your interview," the museum director said as he led her down the hall to a large, airy office in the back. "We're hanging a new installation later this morning, and this was the only time all day I could guarantee a few quiet minutes."

He sat and gestured for her to sit in the chair across from his desk. "Halcyon Art Retreat?" he mused as he scanned her résumé over the top of his glasses.

"Yes, sir. It's in central Florida, near the coast."

"Oh yes, I'm well aware of it. A few of our artists on display here have spent time at Halcyon. And I see you worked with Gregory Galloway." He tapped his pen on the desk and looked up at her. "A lot of people would love a chance to spend the summer under his mentorship. I bet you learned a lot."

She took a deep breath and nodded. "I did. Much more than I expected to. It was . . . life-changing."

The director raised his eyebrows. "I see."

Half an hour later, she walked out of the gallery into the morning sunshine with a grin on her face. The interview had gone well. Very well. And who would have thought Gregory would have played a part in it?

On a whim, she swung by Full Cup on her way home. She was off today, but she hadn't yet had a chance to catch up with Mario and a few other baristas she used to work alongside. Her shifts started at ten now, and by that time, business was in full swing and there was no time for chatting.

She found a space out front and checked the time before she hopped out to pay the parking meter. Nine fifteen. As she approached the glass door, she saw Mario standing at the counter handing a whipped cream–topped drink to a lady with white hair and cowboy boots. A barista she didn't recognize was ringing up a customer. Another one stood in the back on tiptoes pulling a syrup bottle off the top shelf. Jenna pushed open the door, prepared to go straight to the counter to talk to her friends, but almost involuntarily, her eyes searched the room.

Or maybe not involuntarily. If she was honest, she'd have to admit he was the person she most hoped to see.

After a quick scan, she determined she'd missed him. Maybe he grabbed his coffee to-go now. Or maybe he didn't even come here anymore.

Just as she was waving to Mario, a group of ladies in the back stood to leave. As they made their way to the front of the store, tossing leftover bits of pastry and lipstick-stained napkins in the trash, she saw him. His back was to the door and his thumbs were busy typing out a message on his phone. Other than his phone and a sheaf of papers, his table was empty.

Mario cleared his throat. Jenna held up her hand and mouthed, *Sorry.* He rolled his eyes, and Jenna made her way to the back of the store.

She hesitated before speaking. His back was still turned—she could leave now and he would never even know she'd been there. But even from behind, he felt good. Safe. A little like home.

"Sam?"

He turned. A slow smile stretched across his face.

"Can I buy you a cup of coffee?"

FORTY-TWO

BETSY

In the weeks after the storm, Betsy had mostly ignored her garden. There was so much else to do around the farm—clearing debris and hauling trash, finding the two missing cows and the owner of the rogue kayak. Helping neighbors whose homes or property hadn't fared as well as theirs had. A tree had fallen clear across the garden during the height of the storm, crippling the split-rail fence on three sides and coating her carefully planted rows in splintered bark and wet leaves. With everything else going on, it seemed easier to just leave it and come back to it later.

But today when she passed the garden on her way back up to the house, the rich, dark soil called to her. What she thought would just be a quick walk down the rows to see what, if anything, had survived had turned into a half hour on her hands and knees in the dirt collecting handfuls of sticks and acorns and tossing them away from the garden.

She'd just paused in the shade of the oak tree when

she heard the screen door open, then slam shut. She smiled. Ty was coming to check on her. When he reached her, he handed her a glass of ice water. "Remember what the doctor said. Don't try to do too much."

"I know." She took a long sip of water. "He said to keep my stress level low. Gardening is about as low stress as it gets. And you're going to have to stop worrying about me. It's not like this is the first time we've done this."

"I know, I know." He reached over and brushed dirt off her cheek. "I want you to rest if you need it."

"I will. You have my word. Now let me get back in there and fix my garden."

"Yes, ma'am."

She still couldn't believe she'd had the nerve to go back to see Dr. Fields again. Or that Ty had been the one to suggest it.

"A lot has happened since we were there last," he'd said. "We're stronger now. Maybe we give it one more shot."

She'd been hesitant to go back to that waiting room of muted colors and hushed voices, the blood draws, the urine specimens, everyone's cautious optimism. But Ty had a feeling, so they tried one more IUI. It was as strange and awkward as it had been the other three times they'd done it, but this time they laughed as they left the office, their hearts not heavy as before. Ty took her out to an early dinner at LuLu's and they celebrated with shrimp po'boys and dancing to a bluegrass band.

They wouldn't know the results for at least another week, but unlike last time when she chewed through her fingernails while waiting on the call, this time she felt calm. Whatever happened, she knew they'd be okay.

She was walking down the last row of the garden when sunlight filtered through the high clouds and something caught her eye. Approaching carefully, she saw a bright-green shoot pushing up from the earth. It was next to the trunk of the fallen tree they'd yet to clear away—a few more inches and the bud would have been flattened. As it happened though, it stood proud and tall, unscathed by the storm, having pushed itself through the mangled vines and splintered wood of her garden.

She knew what it was. She and the girls had planted the autumn crocus bulb a few weeks before the storm. Addie had set the bulb down in the shallow hole and Walsh covered it with a layer of dirt.

The bud looked so vulnerable—a lone spot of life in the wreckage. She was tempted to protect it, to pluck it out of the ground and bring it inside the house where nothing could harm it. She imagined the green stem and delicate purple bloom perched in a milk glass vase in the center of her kitchen table, reminding her daily of life, precious and sweet.

But when her fingers closed around the shoot, she paused. Having weathered and survived the storm's fury, the stalk felt strong and healthy beneath her fingertips. It had already proved itself. She pulled her hand away. It would do just fine on its own.

That night after dinner, she and Ty sat on the swing together on the back porch. Fireflies blinked in the darkness and cicadas scratched out their nightly concert. As they rocked back and forth, Betsy thought of the hurricane that had flung itself so mercilessly at the Gulf Coast. Weeks before landfall, the storm had begun as a puff of air, a gentle breeze that floated across Africa, picking up dust and dirt and red Saharan heat. It coasted to the ocean where it spread out over the water like milk from an overturned bucket.

The warm water of the Atlantic agitated that formerly gentle breeze, particles mixing and mingling, until it became a cauldron. A tempest. An angry, steaming force to be feared. It unleashed its fury at the point of landfall, then moved inland, leaving a trail of damage and upheaval in its wake.

Yet it also left behind unexpected beauty and bursts of new life. A tiny green shoot pushing through the garden soil. Hope shining like a beacon in the dark places.

ACKNOWLEDGMENTS

I understand now, more than ever, how it takes a village—an enthusiastic, generous, and savvy village—to launch a book into the world.

Thank you to the entire Thomas Nelson family, especially Amanda Bostic, Allison Carter, Paul Fisher, Kristen Golden, Jodi Hughes, Kristen Ingebretson, Karli Jackson, and Becky Monds. Thank you to Allison and Kristen G. for answering my million questions and helping me navigate this new world of publicity, marketing, and general author business! Thank you to Karli for your incredibly wise and insightful reading and careful editing of *Hurricane Season* and to Jodi for jumping into *Hurricane Season* in Karli's absence and taking care of me. Thank you to Kristen I. for another gorgeous cover. Thank you to Julee Schwarzburg for another round of careful and fun edits. Thank you to the entire sales team who works so hard to get my books into the hands of bookstores around the country. Thank you also to my sharp and savvy agent, Karen Solem, who is always quick with encouragement and can tamp down my anxiety with just a few calm words.

Thank you to my friends in Alabama Writers

Connect: Doug Bullock, Michael Calvert, Nancy Dorman-Hickson, Anna Gresham, Chuck Measel, Denise Trimm, and Jennifer Walker-Journey. Thank you for throwing the yellow flag when necessary. You all helped me dig deeper than I thought I could, and *Hurricane Season* is much stronger for it. I'll bring the wine next time.

Thank you to friends who read this story in the early stages and gave helpful feedback: Anna Gresham, Ella Olson, Sara Beth Cobb. A huge thank-you to Will Gilmer of Gilmer Dairy Farm in Lamar County, Alabama, and Kerra Middleton and Robert Middleton of Middleton Farms in Moss Point, Mississippi, for answering my questions about cows, storms, and dairy farming. You all provided such helpful feedback, and if I got anything wrong, it's on me, not you!

Thank you to all the book bloggers, book communities, and book reviewers who helped spread word about *The Hideaway* to new readers. You're a tremendous help to authors, especially new ones like me, and I was honored time and time again by the welcoming embrace you all gave me! Thank you especially to Kristy Barrett, Barbara Bos, Jen Cannon, Dena Charlton, Danielle Feliciano, Kellye Garrett and the 17 Scribes community, Holly Hamblin, Lisa Munley, Jenny O'Regan, Laura Rash, Kristen Swanson, and Jessi Tarbet. Thank you also to bookstores and librarians all over the country who put *The Hideaway* on your shelves. I hope you and your readers enjoy *Hurricane Season* just as much.

Thank you to Eric Holsomback for answering a pile of questions about cameras and darkroom procedures.

Thank you to Laura McLeod and my mom, Kaye Koffler, for being my south Alabama publicists! Thank you to Anna Gresham for the brainstorming, laughter, and conversation that continues to be a lifeline. So glad you Facebook stalked me.

Thank you to my sweet little family: Matt, Kate, and Sela. Thank you for putting up with papers and Post-its spread all over the house, for letting me escape when necessary to figure out the characters and other worlds in my head, and for sharing in my excitement and joy over this crazy book-writing thing. I love you and am so thankful for you. Thank you to the rest of my wildly supportive, funny, and loving family: Randy and Kaye Koffler, Joe and Charlotte Denton, Jake and Leigh Koffler, William and Connie Seale, and assorted Kofflers, Rolls, Handwergers, Cranes, and Kirbys. Thank you to everyone who read *The Hideaway* and took time to tell me you enjoyed it, and thank you for telling other friends about it!

Thank you to writer Dani Shapiro for the enormous encouragement and wisdom found in her book *Still Writing*. Her essays about the struggles and joys of writing helped pull me through the "I can't do this" sections of *Hurricane Season*.

Even though I've been breathing in books like air for as long as I can remember, this is a "job" I never imagined I'd actually be doing. Thank you, Lord, for the opportunity, and I pray I can continue to write stories that entertain as well as allow readers to feel a sense of connection and of being heard.

DISCUSSION QUESTIONS

1. At the start of the book, Jenna loved her children but she also longed for a way to pursue her creative impulses. Did you understand her feeling of not knowing how to balance motherhood obligations with the need/desire to pursue her art and live a creative life? Or was it frustrating to see her making choices you wouldn't make?

2. Betsy longed to have children, but when it looked like pregnancy wouldn't happen for her, she closed the door on that dream. Do you have any experience with having to mentally move on from something you desired that wasn't totally in your control to achieve?

3. As much as he could, Ty tried to understand Betsy's feelings and choices. Do you agree with how he handled her dealings with Jenna and her decision to talk to the principal about school? Should he have responded or handled the situations in a different way?

4. Is there one character you connect with more than the others? Maybe because of his or her actions, inaction, hesitations, or desires?

5. If a woman takes time off from work or family obligations to pursue something she enjoys, do you think our society's reaction to that mother's choice is different from a man wanting the same thing? Would a man receive comments like "You're a parent—you really should be home with your children"? Would it be easier for a man to pursue his passions and hobbies because he doesn't have mom guilt? Or do you think parents across the board battle guilt and pressure when trying to balance family obligations with personal desires?

6. It's often difficult for people who experience no trouble having children to understand the internal feelings of those whose path includes infertility. What was your reaction to how Betsy handled her feelings of failure and inadequacy? If you feel comfortable sharing, have you or has someone you know ever dealt with infertility?

7. Toward the end of the book, Jenna had the option to continue pursuing her art by moving to California and taking the job as Gregory's assistant at Berkeley. Do you think she could have made that option work? What about her children? Ultimately, she decided all she needed was to feel she had a choice in the matter but that she didn't need to take the job and go to California to feel fulfilled—she could do that at home with her children in the life they'd made for themselves. How did you react to her choices at the end?

8. What was your reaction to Gregory? Did you understand the connection between him and Jenna? Did you see him as trying to get her to make bad or selfish choices or as honestly trying to help her pursue the creative life she desired?

9. Over the course of the few months before Jenna left Nashville, Sam Oliver became a constant in her life by showing up every day (except Friday) to have coffee with her. What do you think he represented to her? What do you think he saw in her that kept him coming back? Was he just a distraction for Jenna or do you think they could have developed a deeper connection once she returned to Nashville?

10. Jenna's two friends were Max and Delores, both much older and wiser than she was. Why do you think she developed such important relationships with these two people? How did they affect her throughout the book?

Don't miss Lauren Denton's
USA Today bestselling debut!

When her grandmother's will wrenches Sara back home, she learns more about Margaret Van Buren in the wake of her death than she ever knew in life.

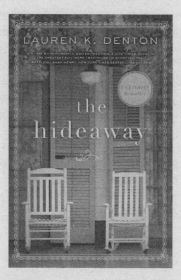

"A story both powerful and enchanting: a don't-miss novel in the greatest southern traditions of storytelling."

—Patti Callahan Henry, *New York Times* bestselling author

Available in print, e-book, and audio

COMING MARCH 2019!

Written in Lauren Denton's signature Southern
style, *Glory Road* tells the story of three generations
of women navigating the uncertain pathways of
their hearts during a summer that promises to bring
change—whether they're ready for it or not.

Available in print, e-book, and audio

ABOUT THE AUTHOR

Born and raised in Mobile, Alabama, Lauren K. Denton now lives with her husband and two daughters in Homewood, just outside Birmingham. In addition to her fiction, she writes a monthly newspaper column about life, faith, and how funny (and hard) it is to be a parent. On any given day, she'd rather be at the beach with her family and a stack of books. *The Hideaway* was her highly acclaimed and *USA Today* bestselling debut novel.

. . .

LaurenKDenton.com
Facebook: LaurenKDentonAuthor
Twitter: @LaurenKDenton
Pinterest: Lauren K. Denton, Author
Instagram: LaurenKDentonBooks